Simon Scarrow has been passionate about writing since an early age. After a childhood spent travelling the world, he pursued his great love of history as a teacher before becoming a full-time writer. His Roman soldier heroes Cato and Macro first appeared in 2000 in *Under The Eagle*, and have subsequently fought their way through many best-selling novels, including *The Blood of Rome*, *Day of the Caesars* and *The Gladiator*.

Simon Scarrow is also the author of the *Wellington and Napoleon* quartet, chronicling the lives of the Duke of Wellington and Napoleon Bonaparte, and of *Sword & Scimitar*, the epic tale of the 1565 Siege of Malta, as well as *Hearts Of Stone*, set in Greece during the Second World War. He is the co-author with T. J. Andrews of Roman era bestsellers *Pirata*, *Invader* and *Arena*, and the co-author with Lee Francis of the contemporary thriller *Playing With Death*.

To find out more about Simon Scarrow and his novels, visit www.simonscarrow.co.uk and like his page on Facebook: /OfficialSimonScarrow

Praise for SIMON SCARROW's novels

'Ferocious and compelling'
Daily Express

'A new book in Simon Scarrow's series about
the Roman army is always a joy'
The Times

'I really don't need this kind of competition . . .
It's a great read'
Bernard Cornwell

'Scarrow's [n   ]   '

'A rip-roaring read'
Mail on Sunday

By Simon Scarrow

The *Eagles of the Empire* Series
The Britannia Campaign
Under the Eagle (AD 42–43, Britannia)
The Eagle's Conquest (AD 43, Britannia)
When the Eagle Hunts (AD 44, Britannia)
The Eagle and the Wolves (AD 44, Britannia)
The Eagle's Prey (AD 44, Britannia)

Rome and the Eastern Provinces
The Eagle's Prophecy (AD 45, Rome)
The Eagle in the Sand (AD 46, Judaea)
Centurion (AD 46, Syria)

The Mediterranean
The Gladiator (AD 48–49, Crete)
The Legion (AD 49, Egypt)
Praetorian (AD 51, Rome)

The Return to Britannia
The Blood Crows (AD 51, Britannia)
Brothers in Blood (AD 51, Britannia)
Britannia (AD 52, Britannia)

Hispania
Invictus (AD 54, Hispania)

The Return to Rome
Day of the Caesars (AD 54, Rome)

The Eastern Campaign
The Blood of Rome (AD 55, Armenia)
Traitors of Rome (AD 56, Syria)
The Emperor's Exile (AD 57, Sardinia)

The *Wellington and Napoleon* Quartet
Young Bloods
The Generals
Fire and Sword
The Fields of Death

Sword and Scimitar
(Great Siege of Malta)

Hearts of Stone
(Second World War)

Blackout

The *Gladiator* Series
Gladiator: Fight for Freedom
Gladiator: Street Fighter
Gladiator: Son of Spartacus
Gladiator: Vengeance

Writing with T. J. Andrews
Arena (AD 41, Rome)
Invader (AD 44, Britannia)
Pirata (AD 25, Adriatic)

Writing with Lee Francis
Playing With Death

SIMON SCARROW

EAGLES · OF · THE · EMPIRE

THE EMPEROR'S EXILE

HEADLINE

First published in Great Britain in 2020
by HEADLINE PUBLISHING GROUP

First published in paperback in 2021
by HEADLINE PUBLISHING GROUP

1

Cataloguing in Publication Data is available from the British Library

ISBN 978 1 4722 5845 8

Map by Tim Peters

Typeset in Bembo by Avon DataSet Ltd, Arden Court, Alcester, Warwickshire

Printed and bound in Great Britain by Clays Ltd, Elcograf S.p.A.

MIX
Paper from
responsible sources
FSC® C104740

HEADLINE PUBLISHING GROUP
An Hachette UK Company
Carmelite House
50 Victoria Embankment
London EC4Y 0DZ

www.headline.co.uk
www.hachette.co.uk

To my son, Nick, in the year of his 21st birthday
and graduation.
Congratulations, respect and love.

ROMAN PROVINCE OF SARDINIA AD 57

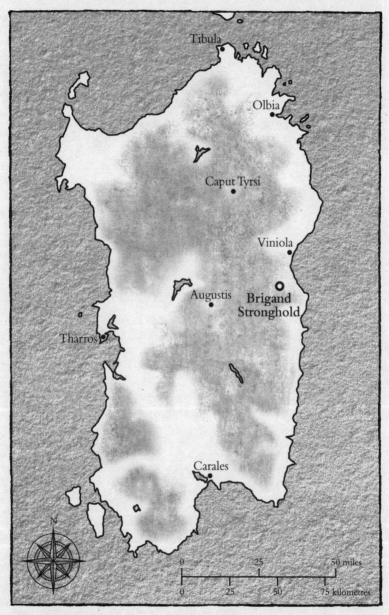

Tibula

Olbia

Caput Tyrsi

Viniola

Augustis

Brigand Stronghold

Tharros

Carales

N

| 0 | 25 | 50 miles |

| 0 | 25 | 50 | 75 kilometres |

CAST LIST

Praetorians

Prefect Quintus Licinius Cato: a young officer, much put upon

Centurion Lucius Cornelius Macro: a veteran coming up to retirement

Centurions: Ignatius, Plancinus, Porcino, Metellus, officers of the Second Cohort of the Praetorian Guard, all good men and true

Optios: Pelius, Cornelius, of the Second Cohort, bound for promotion (and a troubled province)

Cato's Household

Apollonius: an intelligence operative, and intelligent with it

Petronella: wife of Macro, looking forward to his eventual retirement

Lucius: son of Cato, looking forward to growing up and becoming Macro

Croton: major-domo of Cato's household

Pollenus: a slave, formerly owned by Senator Seneca and therefore viewed with justifiable suspicion

Cassius: a ferocious-looking mongrel with a heart of gold

Imperial Palace

Emperor Nero: vain playboy ruler of the Roman world

Senator Seneca: Nero's patient mentor

Prefect Burrus: Nero's impatient adviser

Province of Sardinia

Governor Borus Pomponius Scurra: an indolent aristocrat promoted far beyond his meagre abilities

Decianus Catus: adviser to Scurra; a man who knows how to pull strings

Decurion Locullus: a soldier on Scurra's staff

Claudia Acte: Nero's exiled mistress, and none too pleased about it

Centurion Massimilianus: senior centurion of the Sixth Gallic cohort

Optio Micus: a courageous young officer of the Sixth Gallic cohort

Pinotus: magistrate of the town of Augustis

Lupis: a former hunter turned auxiliary soldier

Calgarno: a young brigand who has bitten off more than he can chew

Barcano: a mule-team owner who values his business above his life

Vespillo: a mule driver who values his life above his employer's business

Benicus: a brigand leader, who values other people's property above his ethics

Milopus: a shepherd who knows more than is good for him

Others

Olearius Rhianarius Probitas: owner of a no-frills shipping company

Prefects: Vestinus, Bastillus and Tadius, cohort commanders of the Sardinian garrison

CHAPTER ONE

Rome, summer AD 57

There was a fine view of the city from the garden of the Pride of Latium. The inn was atop a small rise just off the Via Ostiensis, the road that led from the port of Ostia to Rome, some fifteen miles away. A light breeze rustled through the boughs of a tall poplar tree growing a short distance from the inn. The tables and benches in the garden were sheltered from the stifling glare of the mid-afternoon sun by an arrangement of trellises over which vines had been trained. The Pride of Latium was well positioned to take advantage of the passing trade. There were merchants and cart drivers travelling along the route that carried goods to the capital from across the breadth of the Empire, officials and tourists coming and going from the recently completed port complex at Ostia. There were travellers leaving Rome to voyage across the ocean, or, in the case of the small group seated at the table with the best view of Rome, returning to the capital after a period of service on the eastern frontier.

There were five of them: two men, a woman, a young boy and a large, wild-looking dog. They were being watched closely by the owner of the inn as he wiped ants off his counter with an old rag. He was shrewd enough to recognise soldiers when he saw them, in or out of uniform. Even though the men were

1

dressed in light linen tunics rather than the heavy wool of the legions, they carried themselves with the assurance of veterans, and they bore the scars of men who had seen plenty of action. The oldest of the party was shorter than average but powerfully built. His cropped dark hair was streaked with grey and his heavy features were lined and scarred. But there were creases about his eyes and each side of his mouth and a ready smile that indicated good humour, as well as the marks of hard-won experience. He had fifty years under his belt, the innkeeper estimated, and must surely have reached the end of his career. The other man, sitting beside the boy, was also dark-haired but well over a decade younger, perhaps aged thirty or so. It was hard to be certain as there was a thoughtfulness to his expression and a controlled grace to his movements that revealed a maturity beyond his years. He was as tall as his comrade was short and as slender as the older man was bulky and muscular.

They were as mismatched a pair as any two men the innkeeper had seen, but they were clearly tough cases, and he was grateful they were only on their first jar of wine and sober. He hoped they would remain that way. Soldiers in their cups could be cheery and maudlin one moment, and angry and violent the next, on the merest of presumed slights. Fortunately, the woman and the boy were likely to be a moderating influence. She was sitting next to the older man and shifted closer to him as he wrapped a hairy arm around her. Her long dark hair was tied back in a simple ponytail and revealed a wide face with dark eyes and sensuous lips. She had a full figure and an easy manner and matched the men in drinking the wine cup for cup. The boy was five or so, with dark curly hair, and had the same thin features as the younger man, whom the innkeeper assumed was his father. There was a sly mischief about the child's expression, and as the adults talked, he reached a small

2

hand towards the woman's cup until she swatted it gently away without even looking, as women will when they have developed the uncanny sixth sense that comes with raising children.

The innkeeper smiled as he tossed the rag into a bucket of murky water and made his way over to their table, keeping his distance from the dog.

'Will you be having anything to eat, my friends?'

They glanced up at him and the older man replied. 'What do you have?'

'There's a beef stew. Pork cuts – hot or cold. There's roasted chicken, goat's cheese, fresh-baked bread and seasonal fruit. Take your pick and I'll have my girl prepare you the best roadside meal you'll ever eat on the Ostian Way.'

'The best food over a whole fifteen miles?' The older man chuckled and continued in a wry tone. 'Wouldn't be much of a challenge to put that to the test.'

'Leave off, Macro,' the younger man intervened as he turned to address the innkeeper. 'We need a quick meal. We'll take the cold cuts of pork and chicken with a basket of bread. Do you have olive oil and garum?'

'Yes, for a bit extra.'

'Don't like garum,' the boy muttered. 'Horrible stuff.'

The older man smiled at him. 'You don't have to eat it, Lucius. I'll have your ration, lad.'

'What's the price?'

The innkeeper did a quick mental calculation based on the cost of the raw ingredients, but mostly based on the quality of the men's clothing and the likelihood of them carrying their savings from their previous posting. In his experience, such men returning home tended to be willing to spend over the odds without creating a fuss. He scratched the side of his head and cleared his throat. 'I can do you some good scoff for three

3

sestertii a head. Garum, oil and another jar of wine included.'

'Three sestertii!' the woman gasped in derision. 'Three? You are joking, mate. If we paid five for the lot we'd still be paying over the odds.'

'Now look here . . .' The innkeeper arranged his features into an indignant expression and took a half-step back. But she cut him off before he could go any further, thrusting a finger at him and looking down its length as if she was taking aim with an arrow.

'No! *You* look here, you gouging weasel. I've bought food in the markets of Rome since I could walk. I've also been to country markets and those in the streets of Tarsus the last two years. Nowhere have I seen anyone try it on like you are doing right now.'

'But . . . but prices have increased since you were away,' he blustered. 'There's been a famine in Sardinia, and a plague, and it's driving up costs.'

'Pull the other one,' she shot back.

The younger man could not help laughing. He took her hand and gave it an affectionate squeeze. 'Easy there, Petronella. You're scaring the man. This is my treat.' He looked at the innkeeper. 'Let's split the difference, for the sake of peace and amity, eh?'

'Ten, then,' the innkeeper replied swiftly. 'Can't do it for any less.'

'Ten?' The man sighed. 'Let's call it eight, or I'll set Petronella loose on you again.'

The innkeeper glanced at her warily and sucked in a breath between his stained teeth before he nodded. 'Eight, then. But no wine.'

'With wine,' the other man insisted firmly, all trace of humour gone from his voice as he stared hard with dark eyes.

4

The innkeeper puffed out his cheeks, then turned and scurried back to the door behind the counter that led to the kitchen, shouting instructions at his serving girl.

'That's my lass,' said Macro. 'Fierce as a lioness. I have the scratches to prove it.'

'You shouldn't have paid eight, Master Cato.' Petronella frowned. 'It's too much.'

Cato shook his head, mildly amused that she still deferred to him as her master on occasion. He had freed her over a year ago, after Macro's affection for her had been made clear. And now they were married and the veteran centurion was determined to apply for his discharge so that the two of them could settle into peaceful retirement. In truth, peace might be a little bit more difficult to achieve than Macro assumed, since they were shortly bound for Britannia, where he was to take up his half of the business owned by himself and his mother. Cato knew her well enough to be sure she would match Petronella's fierce personality claw for claw. If he was any judge of either woman's character, then Macro was going to have his hands full. The centurion would soon be wishing he was back serving with the legions facing somewhat less fearsome conflict. Still, that was his choice and there was nothing Cato could, or would, do about it now that his friend had made his decision. He would miss having Macro around – would miss him greatly – but he must find his own way ahead. Perhaps their paths would cross again in the future if Cato was assigned to the army in Britannia.

He put thoughts of the distant future out of his mind and clicked his tongue at Petronella. 'Let's have no more of you calling me master. I am no more your master than your husband will ever be.'

Macro grinned and slid his hand down to slap her rump

gently. 'I've broken in far more challenging recruits than her in my day. By the gods, Cato, you were one of the biggest drips I'd ever clapped eyes on that night you pitched up at the Second Legion's fortress.'

'And look at him now,' Petronella cut in. 'A tribune of the Praetorian Guard. While you've never got beyond centurion.'

'Each to his own, my love. I like being a centurion. It's what I am best at.'

'What you *were* best at,' she said deliberately. 'Those days are over. And you'd better not have any notions of treating me like some bloody recruit or I'll give you what for.' She bunched her fist and held her knuckles under Macro's nose for a moment before relaxing.

Lucius nudged Cato. 'I like it when Petronella gets angry, Father,' he whispered. 'She's scary.'

Macro roared with laughter. 'Aye, lad! You don't know the half of it. The love of my life is as tough as old boots.' He shot her an anxious look. 'But far lovelier.'

Petronella rolled her eyes and gave him a shove. 'Oh, give over.'

Macro's expression became earnest. He raised a hand to turn her face towards him and kissed her gently on the lips. She pressed back and reached round his broad back to draw him into her. Their lips remained locked together for a moment longer before they parted, and Macro shook his head in wonder. 'By all that's sacred, you are the woman for me. My girl. My Petronella.'

'My love . . .' she replied as they stared fondly at each other.

Cato coughed. 'Want me to see if I can get a decent rate for a room for the pair of you?'

★ ★ ★

The food arrived shortly afterwards, carried on a large tray by a thickset serving girl dripping with perspiration from working over the fire in the kitchen. She set the tray down and unloaded cuts of pork and two roast chickens heaped on a wooden platter, a wicker basket containing several small round loaves, two stoppered samianware jugs of oil and garum and another of wine. The portion sizes were more generous than Cato was expecting, and in his present good mood he felt generous enough to tip her a sestertius. She glanced at the coin in her palm wide-eyed, then looked nervously over her shoulder, but the innkeeper was at another table where two more customers had sat down. She tucked the coin into the pocket in the front of her stained stola and hurried back to the kitchen.

'Ah, this is the life!' said Macro as he tore off a chicken leg, closed his teeth over the seared skin and began to chew. 'A fine sunny day. The best of company. Good food, passable wine and the prospect of a comfortable bed at the end of it. Be good to get a hot bath and a change of clothing.'

'I'm sure there'll be something at the house,' Cato responded as he tossed a scrap of meat to the dog, who snapped it up and then nudged his hand for more. He smiled. 'Sorry, Cassius, that's the lot.'

They had left their baggage in Ostia, where one of Cato's men had been charged with bringing it to Rome. They were bound for the large property Cato owned on the Viminal Hill, one of the city's wealthier neighbourhoods. His promotion to commander of an auxiliary cohort some years earlier had brought with it elevation to the ranks of the equites, the social class one step beneath that of senator. He was also a man of some substance, largely thanks to being granted the property and fortune of his former father-in-law, who had plotted against the emperor. The traitors would have succeeded in assassinating

Nero had it not been for Cato's intervention. All of Senator Sempronius's estate had been handed to him as a reward.

Such were the changing fortunes of Rome's nobility under the Caesars, Cato reflected. He was conscious that what the emperor could give, he could just as easily take away. Now that he had a son to raise, he was determined to keep his nose clean and his good fortune intact. Not that it was going to be easy, given the poor start to the conflict with Parthia over the previous two years. An attempt to replace the ruler of Armenia with a Roman sympathiser had led to disaster, and the revolt of a minor frontier kingdom had threatened to spread before it had been crushed. Cato had played a part in both campaigns and now feared he would pay the price once he had submitted his report to the imperial palace.

A chorus of laughter drew his attention to the innkeeper and his other customers just as the former turned to shout an order to the serving girl. Then he crossed over to Cato and his companions and affected a cheery smile.

'Tell me the food's as good as I told you it was, eh?'

'It is satisfactory,' Petronella responded, and made a show of inspecting one of the loaves. 'The bread could have been fresher.'

'It was baked first thing today.'

'It may have been baked first thing. But not today.'

The innkeeper gritted his teeth before he continued. 'But the rest is good? More than satisfactory, I take it? What do you say, sonny?' He ruffled Lucius's curls. The youngster, jaws working hard on a bit of gristle, shook off his hand and raised his eyes.

Cato swallowed and intervened. 'It'll do nicely.'

Despite Petronella's justifiable protestations, he was keen not to annoy the innkeeper unduly. Such men were useful purveyors of gossip and information that they garnered from passing trade, and there was much he was keen to know about the situation in Rome before they entered the city. He hurriedly swallowed the chunk of oil-soaked bread in his mouth and cleared his throat.

'We've been on the eastern frontier for a few years.'

'Ah!' The innkeeper nodded. 'Fighting those Parthian bastards, eh? How's the war going?'

'War?' Cato exchanged a look with Macro. 'It hasn't really begun.'

'No? Last time I was in Rome, the bulletins posted in the forum spoke of a series of frontier clashes. Said we'd given them a good kicking.'

'Well, you can't believe everything you read in the bulletins,' said Macro. 'The date given is true enough. As for the rest . . .' He shrugged.

The innkeeper frowned. 'Are you saying the bulletins are false?'

'Fake bulletins? Not necessarily. But I wouldn't bet my life savings on it.'

'Be that as it may,' Cato resumed, 'we've been out of touch with life in the capital. Anything new we should be aware of?'

'Over the last few years? How much time have you got?'

'Enough to eat this meal and then we're back on the road. So keep it short.'

The innkeeper scratched his cheek as he collected his thoughts. 'The big news is that Pallas looks like he's on his way out.'

'Pallas?' Macro raised an eyebrow. Pallas was one of the imperial freedman Nero had inherited from Claudius and was the emperor's chief adviser. It was a post for which the requisite

9

skills included spying, back-stabbing, greed and ambition, all of which he had honed to the sharpest degree. Only it seemed that he had been caught out, or had met his match in one of his rivals. 'What's happened?'

'He's been charged with conspiracy to overthrow the emperor. The trial's due to start in a month or so. Should be a good show; he's being defended by Senator Seneca. I'd be sure to go and watch the sport if I wasn't so busy here.'

Macro shifted his gaze to his friend. 'Bloody hell, that's a turn-up for the scrolls. I thought Pallas had his snout squarely in the trough. What with how tightly he'd stitched things up with Agrippina,' he concluded in a cautious tone.

Cato nodded as he reflected on the power shift in the capital. Pallas had allied himself with Agrippina and her son Nero in the last years of the previous emperor. His relationship with the new emperor's mother was not merely political. Cato and Macro had uncovered the secret some years earlier and wisely kept their mouths shut. Not that tongues weren't wagging around the dinner tables of the aristocrats, nor amongst the gossips who gathered round the public fountains in the slums. But rumours were one thing; knowing the truth was a far more dangerous situation. Now it seemed that Pallas's prospects were on the wane. Possibly fatally. And not just him, perhaps.

'Is anyone else on trial with him?'

'Not that I know of. He might have been acting alone. More likely the emperor has got his eyes on his fortune. You don't get to be that rich without making enemies. People you've done down on the way up. Or people who simply resent your success and wealth. You know how it goes amongst the quality in Rome. Always ready to stick the knife in . . . so they say.' He glanced at Cato with a flicker of anxiety. 'What did you say your business was in Rome again?'

'We've been recalled. That is to say, my cohort of the Praetorian Guard.'

'Your cohort?' The innkeeper smiled weakly as he realised he had been treading on dangerous ground in offering his opinion of the emperor's motives.

'I'm the tribune in command. Macro here is my senior centurion. We took the first ship bound for Ostia. The rest of the men are on transports a few days behind us, so you may be in luck when they pass this way.'

'I didn't mean any criticism of my betters, sir. It's just the talk on the street. I meant no offence.'

'Easy there. Your views on Nero are safe enough with us. But what of Agrippina? Do you know if she had anything to do with charging Pallas with conspiracy? When we left for the eastern frontier, the two of them were the emperor's closest advisers.'

'Not any more, sir. Like I said, Pallas is on trial, and she's fallen from favour. The emperor has kicked her out of the imperial palace and stripped her of her official bodyguards.'

'That was Nero's doing?' Macro queried. 'Last time I saw the two of them together, she had him wrapped round her little finger. Looks like the boy has grown some balls finally and is running the show. Good for him.'

'Maybe,' Cato mused. From his experience of the new emperor, he doubted Nero had taken such an initiative by himself. More likely his hand was being guided by another faction within the palace. 'So who's advising the emperor these days?'

Even though he was somewhat reassured that his words would not be used against him, the innkeeper lowered his voice. 'Some say the real power is now in the hands of Burrus, the commander of the Praetorian Guard. Him and Seneca.'

11

Cato digested this bit of gossip and then arched an eyebrow. 'And what do others say?'

'They say Nero is a slave to his mistress, Claudia Acte.'

'Claudia Acte? Never heard of her.'

'I'm not surprised, sir. Not if you've been away for a few years. She's only been seen in his company over the last few months. At the theatre, the races and so on. I saw her myself last time I was in Rome. Nice-looking, but the word is she's a freedwoman, and the well-to-do don't like that.'

'I can imagine.' Cato knew how touchy the more traditionally inclined senators were about social distinctions. They regarded the accident of birth that granted them huge privileges as some kind of gods-given right to treat all other people as innately inferior. The affected air of superiority of the worst of them grated on his nerves. Even if they thought their shit smelled better than that of the great unwashed, it didn't. Moreover, the same shit tended to occupy a greater proportion of their heads than whatever residual matter passed for brains. The idea of an emperor showing off his low-born woman to the world and rubbing their noses in it would send the more sensitive of the senators into a conspiratorial frenzy. Nero was playing for high stakes, even if he was unaware of it.

'I'll leave you to finish your meal then, sir.' The innkeeper nodded to Cato and his companions and made his way to his stool at the end of the counter.

Macro took a quick swig of wine from his cup, then burped and smiled. 'Sounds like things have finally changed for the better in Rome. With luck, that snake Pallas is heading for the Underworld and won't be causing us any more trouble. That's worth drinking to.' He refilled his cup and topped up Cato's. But his friend left it on the table as he stared down thoughtfully.

'What is it, Cato? Found some way to see a downside to the situation? Just for once, why not celebrate some good news?'

Cato sighed and picked up his cup. 'Fair enough. But tell me, brother, from our previous experience, how often does bad news follow on from good?'

'Ah, piss off with the pessimism and enjoy the wine, why don't you?'

Petronella nudged him with her elbow. 'Language! You want young Lucius speaking like that?'

Macro glanced at the boy and winked. Lucius grinned.

'Let's hope I'm wrong, then,' said Cato. He raised his cup. 'To Rome, to home, and to a peaceful life. We've earned it.'

CHAPTER TWO

There was always an uncomfortable aspect to returning home after the passage of some years, Cato mused as they entered the capital and made their way through its crowded streets. Even though his senses were overwhelmed by the familiar sights, sounds and scents of the city, there was something about it that seemed strange and unsettling. That feeling that things had moved on and he was a stranger to the place where he had been born and raised. It felt vaguely diminished, too. Rome had once been the entire world to him, vast and all-encompassing. It had seemed impossible to believe that its avenues, temples, theatres and palaces could be surpassed in their magnificence, or the range of entertainments on offer bettered, or the sophistication of its libraries and scholars matched by any others in the Empire or beyond. Yet since Cato had left the city, he had seen for himself the wealth of Parthia, and the Great Library in Alexandria, whose galleries sprawled in the shadow of the towering Pharos lighthouse, far taller and more impressive than any building in Rome. But then, he reasoned, all places, as with all experiences, seemed less impressive when you revisited them. Experience constantly recalibrated the perception of memory so that the recollection of his initial wonder now felt like a slightly shameful naivety.

Even so, there was a comfort in being immersed in the familiar. A jaded sense of belonging, he decided, was better than being rootless. Despite the stench of the drains and the refuse in the street, there was the warm aroma of baking bread, woodsmoke and the heady scent of spices from the markets. Remembered streets and thoroughfares fell into place as they traced their route beside the imperial palace, across the Forum and up the slope of the Viminal Hill, passing through the crowded and crumbling apartment blocks in the slum at the foot of the hill. Taking Lucius's hand to make sure they were not separated in the narrow, busy street, Cato looked down and saw the excited gleam in his son's eyes as he cast his gaze at the people bustling around him.

'Of course. When we left Rome, you were probably too young to remember much about it.'

'I remember, Father,' Lucius replied defiantly. 'I'm six years old. I'm not a baby.'

Cato laughed. 'I never said you were. You're growing up fast, my boy. Too fast,' he added ruefully.

'Too fast?'

'You'll know what I mean when you become a father.'

'I don't want to be a father. I want to be a soldier.'

Cato's expression hardened as memories, gut-wrenching as well as glorious, flitted through his thoughts. 'There'll be time for that another day, if it's really what you wish for.'

'I do. Uncle Macro says I'll be a fine soldier. Just like you. I'll even command my own cohort, too.' He reached out his spare hand and tugged Macro's tunic. 'That's what you said, isn't it, Uncle Macro?'

'Right you are, my lad.' Macro nodded as he held Cassius's leash firmly. Excited by the rich array of scents and noises all around him, the dog was straining to explore in every direction.

'Soldiering's in your blood. It'll make a man out of you.'

Cato felt his heart sink at the prospect. Unlike his friend, he did not see warfare as an opportunity to seek glory. It was a necessary evil at best. The last recourse when every attempt at finding peaceful resolutions of disputes between Rome and other empires and kingdoms had failed. And to restore order in the event of rebellion or other civil conflict. He knew that Macro had little sympathy for his views on the matter and so the two of them rarely addressed the question head on. Which was why Cato felt irritated by Macro's encouragement of his son. He knew his friend well enough to understand that this was not an attempt to use Lucius as a proxy in their differing views; just innocent encouragement. That made it all the more difficult to counter without making it look as if he was over-reacting. Distraction would be a better strategy.

'We must find you a tutor once we get settled, Lucius.'

The boy scowled. 'Don't want one. I want to play with Uncle Macro and Petronella instead.'

Cato sighed. 'You know perfectly well that they will be leaving Rome soon. You'll need someone to look after you and start your education once Petronella is no longer around.'

She shot him a dark look. 'I've taught him his letters and numbers, master. And some reading.'

'Of course. I apologise . . . Thank you. It's not going to be easy to replace you.'

Mollified, she nodded. 'I'll see if I can find someone you can trust. I'll ask round the other households on the Viminal. There's bound to be someone who can take my place.'

'My love,' Macro smiled, 'no one can take your place. Why, you're practically a second mother to the lad.'

'I don't want her to go,' Lucius muttered, lowering his gaze. 'Can't they stay?'

'We've talked about this, son,' Cato replied. 'They have their own life to lead.'

'Can't you order them to stay, Father?'

'Order them?' Macro roared with laughter. 'I'd like to see anyone order Petronella to do something. I'd pay good money to watch them being pulverised.'

They turned into the street where Cato's house sat. There were small shops on either side, leased from the owners of the large properties that lay behind them. At the near end of the street were a few apartment blocks, which gave way to the houses of their wealthier neighbours. The entrances to the larger properties lay between the shops and presented large studded doors to the street. As they reached Cato's home, halfway along, he saw that the ironmonger and the baker who rented their premises from him were still in business on either side of the modest run of steps that rose from the street to the front door. He paused briefly to admire the neatly maintained timbers and bronze studs and then climbed the steps and rapped the knocker sharply.

An instant later, the narrow shutter snapped back and a pair of eyes inspected him briefly through the grille before a muffled voice demanded, 'What is your business?'

'Open the door,' Cato ordered impatiently.

'Who are you?'

'Tribune Quintus Licinius Cato; now open up.'

The eyes narrowed before the doorman responded, 'A moment.'

The shutter rattled back into place and Cato turned to the others. 'Must be a new doorman. Else I have changed more than I thought since we were last in Rome.'

The shutter slid open again and an older man appeared at the grille. One glance was enough; the bolts on the far side were drawn back and the door swung open to reveal Croton, the steward of the household. He bowed quickly and smiled readily as he stepped to the side to allow Cato and the others to enter. 'Master, it does my heart good to see you all return. We had no idea you were coming home.'

'We only landed at Ostia yesterday. We've been on the road since first light.'

Croton swiftly got over his surprise as he closed the door and shut out the noises from the street. In the quiet entrance hall the only sound was the light tinkle from the fountain in the atrium beyond.

'I'll have the sleeping chambers and living spaces prepared at once, master. And you'll be needing food after your journey.'

'Food can wait,' Cato interrupted. 'What we want is a bath and fresh clothes. Have the bathhouse fire lit and then see to the other matters.'

Croton looked them over and cocked an eyebrow. 'And your baggage, sir?'

'Coming upriver from Ostia. Should reach the house tomorrow. It'll be in the charge of a man called Apollonius. He'll be staying in the house with us, so have a room ready for him too.'

'More's the pity,' Macro muttered. He had little affection for the spy who had acted as Cato's guide during his recent mission to Parthia and had agreed to serve with the tribune when the Praetorian cohort returned to Rome. Not that there were many men left on the unit's strength, he mused. No more than a hundred and fifty out of the original six hundred or so had survived the battles of the last two years. Even though their standard had won several decorations for valour, it would be some time before the cohort was built up to its former fighting strength and was ready for battle again. Not that Macro would be involved in that. He felt a moment of regret and longing for the career and the brothers in arms that he would be leaving behind when he departed for Britannia. Cato most of all.

Macro had been there when Cato had first arrived at the Second Legion's fortress on the Rhine, skinny, drenched and shivering. He had grudgingly become the young man's mentor, only to realise the promise that Cato showed once he had got over his nerves and become a good soldier. Since then, Cato had served beneath Macro, then as his equal in rank, eventually being promoted above him. Over the last fifteen years they had been all but inseparable as they served on the Empire's frontiers. Soon they would part company, and given the distance involved, it was likely they would never see each other again. That was a hard truth to bear.

It was of little comfort to know that Apollonius would be at Cato's side in any campaigns to come. Macro had not trusted the spy from the outset. Apollonius had been assigned by General Corbulo to guide Cato in his mission to Parthia. He was thin, the skin of his shaven head clinging to his skull so closely that he looked like some spirit of the departed. His deep-set eyes darted about and his keen intelligence missed nothing. Irritatingly, the same keen intelligence mocked those with lesser erudition and swiftness of thought. If ever the phrase 'too clever by half' was deserved, then surely Apollonius was first in line. Not that the Greek freedman was without redeeming features, Macro conceded. There were few other men who matched his skill with a blade, and he was a fine fighter to have at your side. By the same token, you'd never willingly turn your back on him. There was something about him that made Macro innately suspicious, and he had lived long enough and had sufficient hard-won experience to trust in such instincts.

As Croton led the way to the living quarters, Macro fell into step alongside his friend and spoke in a low voice. 'I'm not sure I'd be so willing to have Apollonius around if I were in your place, brother. He's cut from the same cloth as the likes of Pallas and Narcissus and all those other back-stabbing Greek freedmen.'

Cato smiled thinly. Like many Romans, Macro was inclined to look down on the Greeks as being a race predisposed towards fancy intellectualism and scheming. It was a lazy perception that did little more than flatter the Roman belief in their own plain speaking and superior integrity. In all their years together, Cato had not managed to shift his friend's position, and there was little point in any fresh attempt at this late stage.

'Apollonius proved his worth in Parthia. I would not be alive now if it was not for him.'

'He was out to save his own skin. That he saved yours as well was an afterthought.'

'That's one way of looking at it . . . Anyway, my mind is made up. I'm signing him onto the cohort to take charge of the headquarters staff. We'll see what happens then. But I think you are wrong about him.'

'We'll see. I'd hate to be the one to say I told you so.'

Cato glanced at him and smiled. 'No, you wouldn't.'

They passed through the atrium with its small pool open to the skies and then continued along a passage to the living quarters overlooking the walled garden at the rear of the property. Senator Sempronius had taken pride in his neat designs of hedges and flower beds, and Cato smiled as he saw that Croton and his small staff had tended them well during his absence.

'It's good to be home,' he mused. 'It really is. Perhaps I'll be able to enjoy raising Lucius while I tend to my duties at the Praetorian camp.'

'You'll have plenty of time on your hands,' said Macro. 'Just leave the spit and polish to the centurions and enjoy dressing up for the imperial ceremonies.' He looked at Cato thoughtfully. 'Though I dare say you'll be hankering to return to active duty within a year.'

Cato shook his head. 'I don't think so. I've had enough of that for a while. I want to have some peace and spend time with Lucius.'

He turned and rested his hand on his son's shoulder. 'How about that, my boy? There's plenty to keep the both of us happy. Theatre, books, hunting in the country. The arena, chariot races.'

'Chariot races!' Lucius's expression lit up. 'Let's do that! I want to see the chariots.'

'All right then,' Cato responded. 'We'll go as soon as we can. All four of us. But right now, let's get bathed and into some clean clothes!'

'Do I have to have a bath, Father?'

'Of course you do,' Petronella clucked as she took his hand. 'Come along, Master Lucius. You and me can help Croton start the bathhouse fire.'

As the pair headed across the garden, Cato and Macro stared after them.

'She's going to miss the boy,' said Macro. 'We both will.' He felt a melancholic mood closing in around them and wrinkled his nose in distaste. A change of subject was needed, he decided. He slapped his friend on the back. 'Wine! There has to be some good wine in the house. We'll track a jar down and sit and drink by the fountain while we wait. Come, brother. Let's get hunting!'

CHAPTER THREE

The following day, at noon, Cato was sitting on a bench outside the office of Prefect Burrus, the commander of the Praetorian Guard. He had been greeted briefly and submitted his report before being ordered to wait outside while Burrus perused the document. It was not going to make for good reading, he thought. His cohort had been sent east to act as the personal bodyguard of General Corbulo. As such, there had been no expectation that they would be involved in any fighting; they would return to Rome intact when they were recalled. But due to the lack of troops available to Corbulo, Cato and his men had been tasked with spearheading a mission to install a Roman candidate on the throne of Armenia. The strategic importance of the minor kingdom was such that it had been contested territory for over a hundred years, swaying between Roman and Parthian control. This time the Romans were defeated and the king they had attempted to impose on the Armenians had been captured and executed before Cato and his men were sent back to Corbulo in humiliation.

Corbulo had made as little of it as possible, rightly fearing that such a setback might lead to his replacement as commander of the eastern armies. He had refused to let Cato and his men return to Rome, and then disregarded a message ordering the cohort to rejoin the rest of the guard in their camp outside the walls of the capital. Anything to delay the emperor and his advisers grasping the true scale of Rome's humiliation. It had been a challenge to describe the short campaign without casting a shadow on the reputation of Corbulo and Cato himself, even though he had done the best he could with the meagre forces at his disposal. Nor was Burrus going to be pleased by the subsequent uprising of the town of Thapsis, in the mountains close to Corbulo's headquarters at Tarsus. The Roman soldiers had had to endure a bitter winter and a mutiny, which had been put down with considerable difficulty and loss of life. None of which was going to endear Corbulo and those who served him to the emperor. The only aspect of the report that might gratify Nero and his advisers was the intelligence Cato had gathered on the terrain and political situation inside Parthia while conducting an embassy to the Parthians on Corbulo's orders.

Rising from the bench and stretching his shoulders, Cato adjusted the medal harness that hung over his polished breast-plate. He had turned out in his best uniform to present himself at headquarters, and now carefully arranged his wine-red cloak so that it hung from his shoulders in neat folds. The clerk sitting at the desk to one side of the door leading into Burrus's office looked up, and they exchanged a glance before the man cleared his throat.

'Would you like me to bring you some refreshments, sir? It's a warm day.'

It was indeed. Unseasonally hot even for July. Perspiration was already pricking out beneath the fringe of Cato's hair and down his spine. He shook his head. 'I'm fine, thank you.'

The clerk lowered his head and continued working through the figures on his waxed tablets as Cato crossed to the window and looked over the courtyard of the headquarters building. He had a clear view across the tiled roof of the colonnaded rooms surrounding an open space large enough to parade a thousand men. Beyond lay the barrack blocks, the wall of the camp and then the sprawl of temples, palaces, forums, tenement blocks packed with the poorest inhabitants of the city and the larger homes of the wealthy. The vast bulk of the imperial palace complex that covered the Palatine Hill dominated the skyline. The sounds of the city were muted to a faint hubbub as they carried over the walls of the camp, and closer to him he could hear a centurion bawling insults at his men as he inspected them. Down in the courtyard, clerks and officers paced from office to office along the colonnades; only the sentries on duty stood in the glare of the sun, their foreshortened shadows clearly delineated against the paving slabs. Every one of them was immaculately dressed and equipped, and Cato was struck by the calm sense of order and decorum, a world far from his recent experiences of bloodshed, hunger, mud and filth, biting cold and ever-present danger on the frontier beyond which stretched the lands of Parthia, Rome's most formidable enemy.

His thoughts turned back to the man reading his report in the next room. How would Burrus react to the words Cato had carefully chosen to describe conditions on the eastern frontier? Would he accept that Corbulo was dealing with the difficulties confronting him as best he could and that Cato's role in events had been without blame? Or would he seek to censure a cohort commander who had returned to Rome with less than a third of his men fit for duty? What happened next was critical to Cato's future career. There would be a chance to defend his performance once Burrus summoned him; it was vital that the prefect was convinced to support his version of events when the report was passed on to the emperor and his advisers at the palace. He was aware that Burrus had held him in high regard following the part he had played in putting down a plot to unseat Nero in the early days of his reign and place the previous emperor's natural son on the throne instead. The plot had failed; the usurper, Britannicus, and the rest of the ringleaders were dead. But Cato knew that gratitude was a fleeting quality in the fervid world of Roman politics. Burrus might have followers he wanted to promote in Cato's place.

There was a click from the door as the handle turned and it opened to reveal Burrus. He was a stocky man with oiled dark hair arranged carefully to conceal as much of his premature balding as possible. He wore a silk tunic embroidered with silver threads that made up a pattern of oak leaves running up the sleeves and around the collar. Knee-high closed-toe boots of red leather graced his feet. As they had already exchanged terse greetings, he did not speak but gestured to Cato to join him inside his office before turning and disappearing from view.

Hurrying over to the door, Cato stepped through and closed it behind him. The room beyond took up the entire width of the end of the administration block and was lined with benches and stools for when the prefect needed to brief his officers. There was an open space in front of the walnut desk behind which Burrus settled onto a cushioned seat, his back to the two open windows on the far wall. The report, written on a scroll, weighted by a pot of ink and a dagger, lay before him. He did not invite Cato to be seated, and folded his hands together as he stared fixedly at his subordinate. There was a tense silence before he cleared his throat.

'I have to say, I find it hard to square what is written here with the rather more upbeat reports that Corbulo has been sending from Tarsus. That said, it is closer in spirit to the intelligence fed back to us from the imperial spies serving with the general. They confirm what you say about our would-be king of Armenia. It seems that Rhadamistus is – was – a dangerous hothead. It's possible that he might have caused us more problems if he had succeeded in retaking the throne, so his loss might be the lesser setback. But we shall never know.'

'No, sir.'

'Which brings us on to your conduct of the mission. You seem reluctant to take Corbulo to task for supplying you with insufficient men to carry out the job.'

Burrus paused long enough to indicate that he required a reply. It was tempting to agree with him that a few thousand men was rather fewer than Cato thought necessary to guarantee success, but he was not prepared to undermine Corbulo. The general was a good soldier and it was hardly his fault that the forces placed at his disposal were inadequate to defend the eastern frontier, let alone invade and conquer Parthia. He deserved Cato's loyalty.

'The general assigned as many men to my command as he thought prudent, sir.'

'Prudent?' Burrus smiled coldly. 'But what would your estimate of prudence be?'

'Sir?'

'How many men did you think were necessary to secure Rhadamistus's throne?'

Cato nodded towards his report. 'As you will have read, we had enough men to take his capital and make him king.'

'Only for your joint forces to be beaten by rebels in battle barely a month later. It was a good thing the enemy spared what was left of your column as a peace offering to Rome so that we might accept their neutrality.' Burrus sighed. 'Believe me, Tribune, I understand how limited Corbulo's resources are. But the situation was not so dire that he had to send you and your Praetorians on a do-or-die mission. You have lost over three hundred of the emperor's finest. That will not please Nero, I can assure you. Especially as you were only supposed to be acting as bodyguards and giving Corbulo some weight to his authority. It was not intended that you should be sent into battle.'

'That is the purpose of soldiers, sir,' Cato ventured.

'Do not presume to lecture me, Tribune!' Burrus snapped. 'Ordinary soldiers, yes. But Praetorians are held back as a weapon of last resort. They may be the best soldiers in the army, but that is precisely why they are not to be frittered away in sideshows like Armenia, or putting down uprisings in obscure hill towns that hardly any civilised person has ever heard of. I never even knew that Thapsis existed until I wished it didn't. Corbulo exceeded his authority in deploying your cohort as he did. That I can do nothing about; it is up to Nero to deal with the general as he sees fit. However, you also had your orders. You should have protested when Corbulo said he was sending you to Armenia. As your commanding officer, that is a matter I *can* do something about.'

He unfolded his hands and laid the palms on the report as he leaned forward to address Cato in a formal tone.

'Tribune Cato, it is my decision that you be relieved of your command pending a full investigation into your conduct while serving on the eastern frontier.'

There it was, Cato thought bitterly. The reward for his long years of service to Rome. It should come as no surprise, he told himself, yet Burrus's words wounded him painfully.

'Your senior centurion, Macro, is to assume command as of now,' Burrus continued.

'I should tell you that Centurion Macro intends to apply for his immediate discharge, sir. I have countersigned his request. He will be submitting it to you in the next few days.'

'That's too bad,' Burrus growled. 'Well, in that case, Macro takes command while his request is processed and I find a replacement for you. In the meantime, you are not to leave Rome without my permission. Do you have anything to say in response to my decision?'

Cato's mind reeled with all the things he *could* say. Chief among them was his bitter indignation that he should be treated so unjustly after doing what he had always done: serving the best interests of Rome as well as he could with the orders he was given by his superiors. But he would not give the prefect the satisfaction of seeing his anger and resentment. Besides, he needed time to think and plan a defence of his actions to submit to the investigation. Assuming he was given the chance to present his side of the story.

He took a calming breath. 'Not at present, sir.'

Burrus regarded him closely, then nodded. 'I see. Then our business here is finished. Your rank of tribune is forfeit immediately and I want you to quit the Praetorian camp forthwith. You are not permitted to set foot inside it without my express permission. If there are any personal effects remaining in the cohort's barracks, you may arrange for them to be delivered to your house. You will be informed of the progress of the investigation and any further action that may be taken against you. Do you understand?'

'Yes, sir,' Cato replied through gritted teeth.

'Very well, you are dismissed.' Burrus made a curt gesture with his hand towards the door and looked down as he removed the makeshift weights from the scroll, refusing to meet Cato's gaze a moment longer.

28

Clenching his jaw, Cato turned and strode away, anger seething in his heart and burning through his veins as the shame of his treatment struck home with a pain almost as real as any wound he had endured during his fifteen years of service to Rome.

'Relieved of your command?' Macro's eyes widened in disbelief. 'Are you pulling my leg?'

Cato eased himself onto the marble bench beside his friend and stared at the myriad ripples criss-crossing the surface of the pond as the water from the fountain spattered down. He took a deep breath and sighed bitterly. 'I'm afraid it's true, Macro. The prefect's orders are that you are to take over command until a tribune is appointed to replace me. I doubt that will take long, given the number of aristocrats thrusting themselves forward for a post in the Praetorian Guard.' He gave Macro a sidelong look. 'I'm sorry to be the cause of the delay in your discharge, brother.'

'Fuck sorry,' Macro replied. 'What in Hades does Burrus think he's doing? Did he give his reasons?'

Cato nodded. 'More or less. It's as I feared. The emperor's advisers have learned that things aren't going as well for Corbulo as he has made out. They want to make an example of someone so that Corbulo gets the message: deliver a success or face the consequences.' He stooped to pick up a pebble and threw it at a lily pad at the foot of the fountain. 'My position isn't helped by the losses the cohort has suffered. And when they march into camp, the thinned-out ranks are going to cause eyebrows to rise. The rumour will go round that I'm just another thruster, determined to rise through the ranks no matter how many of my men it costs.'

'That's bullshit. Some might mutter, but when they know the full story, they'll understand.'

'How long will that take, I wonder? You know how it is, brother. A lie travels far faster than the truth and does more damage when it hits its target. When, or if, the true story of what happened on the eastern frontier is known, it'll be far too late. My replacement will be firmly in place and I'll have spent years stuck in Rome waiting for a new command. And given the shadow of doubt hanging over me, I may never be allowed to rejoin the army. My soldiering days could be over.'

'Pfft!' Macro sniffed. 'With your record, no one's going to let your talent go to waste.'

Cato shrugged. 'I hope you're right. But given the nature of people who make decisions in Rome, politics trumps reason every time . . . You'd better report to Burrus as soon as you can. He'll probably want to question you on the contents of my report and see if there are any discrepancies he can use.'

'Use? Use for what?'

'There's going to be an investigation of my handling of the cohort. The prefect will be gathering evidence as swiftly as possible. He wants to be seen acting quickly and sternly with an officer who loses so many of Nero's finest troops.'

'Then you must fight your corner, sir. I'll do whatever I can to help. Same goes for the other centurions and the men. We'll speak up for you. I'll put Burrus straight.'

'Just tell him the truth, Macro. And keep it brief. I don't want you getting caught up in this by saying anything that could be used against you later on. I know you'll be heading for Britannia soon, but as we both know, if you make an enemy in Rome, there is no limit to their reach. They'll hunt you down wherever you are. Same goes for the rest of the lads. You'd better let them know when they catch up with us.'

'They already have. The ships reached Ostia yesterday, late afternoon. Apollonius saw them come in as he was setting off with the baggage. He fetched up here after you set off for the Praetorian camp.'

Cato glanced round. 'Where is he?'

'Bathhouse.' Macro jerked a thumb over his shoulder. 'He's been in there ever since. Typical bloody Greek, lazing around the moment he has any excuse to.'

'He has his uses.' Cato stood up and forced a smile as he held out his hand. 'I suppose I should congratulate you on your promotion, however briefly you are in command of the cohort. Acting Tribune Macro. It has a nice ring to it, don't you think?'

'No, I fucking don't,' Macro growled, refusing to take Cato's hand. 'It ain't right. The situation is more bollocksed up than a randy bull on heat. You should fight this, sir. I'll back you all the way.'

'I know you will. But for now, do your job while we wait for the investigation to take its course. It'll be something to take your discharge having reached the rank of tribune, eh?'

'I was perfectly happy as a centurion.'

'I know. But that's life in the army for you. You rarely know what the fates are going to throw your way. One thing's for sure, though. If you don't get your arse in gear and report to Burrus, there may be an acting senior centurion position going begging as well.'

Cato made for the bathhouse at the bottom of the garden. One of the slaves, a burly man stripped down to a loincloth, was busy feeding split logs into the furnace, sweat glistening across his broad back. Smoke curled from the chimney at the end of the building. It was a modest structure compared to some of those Cato had seen in the wealthiest homes in the capital, but it provided warm and hot rooms, a steam bath and a small plunge pool arranged around the changing vestibule, where a handful of training weights rested on a rack. He paused beside the slave, and the man hurriedly straightened and bowed his head as soon as he became aware of his master's presence.

'I don't recognise you,' said Cato. 'Who are you?'

'Pollenus, master.'

'How long have you been a member of the household?'

'Seven months, master. Croton bought me from the slave market when the previous groundsman died. I tend to the garden and the bathhouse.' There was a distinct accent to the man's voice. Not one Cato recognised, but he had certainly not been raised in Rome or its environs.

Cato nodded. 'How do you know I am your master?'

'I was in the garden when you returned yesterday. Croton pointed you out, master.'

'I see. A belated welcome, then, Pollenus. Do your duty and serve me loyally and we'll do right by each other.'

'Yes, master. I will,' Pollenus replied flatly, and Cato wondered if he heard a trace of resentment in the man's voice, or whether perhaps he was imagining it.

'Who owned you previously?'

'Senator Seneca, master.'

'Seneca? Why did he sell you?'

'We disagreed about the felling of some trees in his garden, master.'

'You disagreed?' Cato arched an eyebrow. 'You dared to disagree with the senator?'

'Yes, master. And I was beaten for it before I was taken away to be sold.'

'Then I trust you have learned your lesson. Being a slave is like being a soldier. Both must obey orders. If you want to remain here, you will not show me the same defiance as you showed Seneca. If you choose to repeat the offence, you'll go back to the slave market. Do your duty here well and you will be looked after and treated fairly. Do I make myself clear, Pollenus?'

'Yes, master.'

'Good. Carry on.'

Cato entered the vestibule and saw Apollonius's clothes neatly folded on a stool, beside his boots. He unfastened the clasp of his cloak and laid the folds on a small wooden bench, then removed his armour and undressed. Pollenus was still in his thoughts. Though he was a tolerant master to the handful of slaves he owned, he expected the same from them as he did from the men under his command. He paused and smiled as he corrected himself: the men he *used* to command. He resolved to have a word with Croton about the new slave. If Pollenus had settled into the household and was causing no trouble, then all was well. Otherwise he would be put on notice and if there were any problems with his behaviour he would be sold. In any case, despite what the slave claimed was the reason for his departure from his previous household, the fact that he was linked to Seneca justified treating him with suspicion for the present.

Once he was naked, Cato picked up one of the linen gowns and a towel from the shelves in the vestibule and made his way into the warm room. It was empty, so he moved on to the hot room, easing aside the leather curtain in the arch that divided the two. Apollonius was sitting on a bench opposite, dimly visible in the light admitted by a small glass window. His sinewy body was glistening with perspiration and he looked up as he lifted a hand slightly in greeting.

'Back from the camp so soon?'

Cato sat on the bench opposite and briefly related what had happened. Apollonius clicked his tongue.

'That's tough. And hardly a fair reward for your service.'

'Quite,' Cato agreed with feeling. 'It seems I might not be able to offer you a position in my cohort after all. I'm sorry about that.'

The freedman thought a moment. 'It is a pity. But all is not lost. The investigation might find in your favour.'

'That's possible.'

Apollonius scrutinised Cato's expression. 'But not likely, you're thinking.'

'I was not one of Burrus's appointments. I was given my command thanks to the influence of Narcissus.'

'And he's long gone,' Apollonius mused. 'So you have no patron at the palace to guard your interests. Tricky.'

'To put it mildly.'

'Is there no one you can appeal to in the Senate to support your cause?'

There was one senator Cato trusted, and who he believed might offer him some help. Vespasian had been the commander of the Second Legion when Cato had joined up. Their paths had crossed several times since then, and Vespasian had been impressed by his performance. However, the senator wielded little influence at present, and Cato found the idea of approaching his former commander more than his pride would bear.

'No. I'm on my own. I'll deal with this by myself.'

Apollonius sighed. 'It's your funeral. But if there's anything I can do to help, I'd be happy to.'

'If it comes to that . . . But I thank you.'

There was a brief silence as Cato began to feel the perspiration pricking out and forming beads on his skin before starting to trickle downwards. 'Given my situation, you might want to attach yourself to someone else. I'd understand if you chose to do that.'

'There's no call for that just yet.'

Cato regarded the agent closely for a moment. He had come to appreciate Apollonius's sharp intelligence and educated understanding of the world. Moreover, there were few men he had met who were as adept with weapons as the freedman. Even though they had served together on Corbulo's embassy to Parthia, and fought side by side, Cato was concerned that he had only the most basic understanding of the other man's character and motivations. He felt the urge to know more, and the change in circumstances emboldened him to transgress the bounds of social propriety.

'Tell me, Apollonius, why did you leave Corbulo's service to join me?'

'It was a simple enough judgement. Corbulo is already yesterday's man. I need a patron with a future. I thought you had potential. I still do.'

'Corbulo is yesterday's man?' Cato shook his head. 'He's been given an important command. He is gathering a large army to invade Parthia. If he succeeds, he'll be given a triumph and will be the darling of the mob and the Senate. I'd say he's a long way from deserving that kind of dismissal of his power and influence.'

'You think so?' Apollonius reached up and mopped the sweat from his brow. 'Perhaps I should explain my thinking. You're right, Corbulo has a powerful army at his back. That will be his undoing, whether he claims a victory over the Parthians or whether he is humiliated by them. If he is successful, I'd be willing to bet that every ambitious senator in the capital is going to be envious. Worse still, if he becomes the darling of the mob, you can be sure Nero will want to clip his wings as soon as possible, or else put paid to any danger he poses with some accusation of conspiracy. If he fails, Nero will need a scapegoat. Either way, Corbulo is doomed. It's just a question of time before he is brought low. I calculated that it was better for me to transfer my allegiance to a patron whose career was still on the rise, but not dangerously so. I doubt anyone at the palace will see you as a threat for the foreseeable future. You fitted my requirements perfectly. So here I am, at your service.'

Cato gave a dry laugh. 'You don't seem to have much faith in my ambition. And that was hardly the most inspiring declaration of loyalty offered by a client.'

'Maybe not. But I think you'll find it is one of the most honest and accurate you are likely to hear.'

'There is that.' Cato laughed again. 'But as I said, I think you may find you have attached yourself to a patron whose fortunes are unlikely to rise any further as things stand.'

'Don't sell yourself short, sir.'

It was a rare thing for Apollonius to address him as a superior, and it pleased Cato.

'Given what I know of you and your resourcefulness,' the agent went on, 'I am confident that you will survive the investigation and your fortunes will continue to prosper. So I am content to remain in your service.'

'Assuming I am happy to keep you in my service.'

Apollonius's expression formed into a knowing grin. 'We both know you'd be a fool to dismiss me.'

That was true, Cato conceded. Especially now that Macro would soon obtain his discharge. Apollonius would be a good man to have at his side in a fight, and was shrewd enough to be a useful adviser. The only mark against him was his ruthless streak. He seemed to be motivated entirely by selfish concerns. Cato found that unnerving, used as he was to the unqualified bond of loyalty and honesty that had existed between himself and Macro for the last fifteen years. It would take a while before he adjusted to his new companion. It would take rather longer before he trusted him. But trust was a luxury he might not be able to afford. As things stood, he needed every ally he could get.

CHAPTER FOUR

The Second Cohort marched back into the camp the following morning, led by Centurion Ignatius at the head of the colour party. The men were as neatly turned out as they could be in clothing and kit that showed the signs of two hard campaigns. They still managed to keep in step and were belting out a marching song as they passed through the arch under the gatehouse. The Praetorians on sentry duty, and others lounging in the shade outside their barracks, looked on with eager curiosity. While a sense of excitement always attended soldiers returning from war, the mood was muted as the onlookers saw how few had survived. There would be plenty of tales to tell in the drinking holes around the camp that night.

Macro was waiting for them on the steps of the tribune's office at the end of the Second Cohort's barracks. He was dressed in his best tunic and cloak and his medals gleamed brightly on the harness he wore over his scale vest. The sun glinted off his helmet and greaves as he idly tapped his vine cane against the side of his heel. Ignatius marched the column along the front of the building, then gave the order to halt. He paused for a beat before calling the men to face right and come to attention. The sound of nailed boots scraping on flagstones and then stamping down echoed off the surrounding walls.

Macro cast his gaze over them fondly. These were men he had come to know well, and he was proud of them. Though he would never openly admit it, they had proved themselves to be every bit as good as his former comrades of the Second Legion. He felt a stab of deep regret in his breast at the prospect of leaving them behind when he took his discharge and left for Britannia with Petronella. For now, he was their new commander and he would discharge that duty to the best of his ability. He drew a deep breath and eased his shoulders back as he addressed the men.

'Brothers! Rome bids us welcome after our service to the Empire on the eastern frontier. The Second Cohort has done itself proud and we have served under our standard with courage and honour. While our comrades in the other cohorts have been sitting on their arses back here in the capital, we have been showing the enemy how real Romans fight. When you go off duty later today, you will walk a little taller and with the swagger of soldiers who have earned their pay. Make sure you let our friends in the other cohorts know it. If they give you any lip about your appearance when you marched back into camp, you have my permission to give them a good kicking!'

There were some laughs and grins from the men and officers in the ranks, and Macro beamed back at them. 'Go easy on them, though, lads. It's been a while since they've had to deal with anything more dangerous than a few disorderly drunks and irate whores.'

He allowed them to enjoy the moment before his expression became serious. He gestured towards the entrance to the barracks. 'When we return to our quarters, your thoughts are bound to turn back to those of our brothers who are no longer with us. For many of you, this is the first time you have returned from campaign. Even though you know this barracks like the back of your hand, it will feel different now. There will be plenty of empty bunks in the section rooms. There will be less of the banter you were once used to. You will find your-selves looking back to happier times and missing the faces of the fallen. They were your comrades and friends and it is natural that you will miss them now that you have returned to the normal routine of garrison duties. You will have time to reflect on the last two years, and time to mourn our dead brothers. Some of you will take the loss well. Others will find the dark-ness of grief catching you unawares. There is no shame in that. I've served long enough to know that no two soldiers are truly alike and that we all deal with what life throws at us in our own way.

'Proud Praetorians we are, and rightly are we proud. But we are also mortal men with hearts and minds as well as the discipline and muscle of the emperor's finest soldiers. Our limbs ache, our flesh bleeds and our hearts must carry the burden of our losses. But there are others we must think of. Some of you will know the families of the dead men. To you I say, be the bearers of kindness to those who will never again see their sons who left them behind to do their duty and die for Rome. They will want to know about their fate. Use kind words and offer compassion. They will need it . . .'

He paused to let his words settle in their minds. Then he cleared his throat.

'There is one further matter that I must relate with a heavy heart. Some of you will be wondering why Tribune Cato is not here to greet you. It is with sadness that I have to tell you that he has been removed from his post and that I will be your acting commander until a new tribune is appointed.'

Some of the men began to mutter angrily. A voice cried out

away to Macro's right. 'What's the meaning of this? What's the tribune supposed to have done?'

'Silence there!' Macro roared. 'You are Praetorians, not a fucking shower of gossiping goatherds! The next man who speaks out of turn will feel my vine cane across his bloody shoulders quicker than boiled asparagus!'

He glared at the men, daring any to defy him. Then he sighed heavily and continued.

'Second Cohort! There will be a full inspection at dawn tomorrow. So have your kit cleaned, see the quartermaster for anything that needs replacing, and get bathed, shaved and spruced up. I want the Second to be the smartest cohort in the camp come tomorrow. I'll have the balls off any man who lets me down. Second Cohort! Dismissed!'

As the men stood to and began to break ranks, Macro noted that some of them were muttering as they hefted their packs and shuffled towards the barracks block. It seemed that they were no happier with the removal of the tribune than Macro was. Centurion Ignatius watched his men pass into the building, then turned and approached Macro.

'So, what's the story with Tribune Cato?'

Macro glanced round to make sure they would not be overheard before he answered. 'Someone at the palace isn't happy with the way Corbulo is handling things and needs to make an example. The official line is that Cato was careless with his men's lives.'

'Fuck that. It's thanks to the tribune that any of us returned from Armenia at all.'

'I know it. You know it. The men know it. But some fuckwit adviser of Nero doesn't give the tiniest shit about the truth. They want to punish our boy as a way of putting pressure on Corbulo to get a quick victory over Parthia. Let the general

41

know what's in store for him if he comes back to Rome without a triumph the emperor can dangle in front of the mob. That outweighs the fact that the tribune did the best job he could with the punishing missions Corbulo dished out to us.'

'What's going to happen to him?'

Macro tucked his vine cane under his arm and unfastened his helmet strap. 'There's going to be some kind of investigation. They might bring formal charges against him.'

'What kind of charges?'

Macro eased his helmet off and wiped the perspiration from his brow. 'I don't know yet. They might accuse him of exceeding his orders.'

'How so?'

'We were sent east to act as Corbulo's bodyguard. We were there for decorative purposes and weren't supposed to go into action.'

'But it was the general who sent us into Armenia.'

'No doubt they'll say Cato's orders from Burrus had precedence over those of Corbulo, and the tribune should have refused to obey the general.'

'Bollocks to that. What's the point in being appointed general if you can't give orders to the men serving under you?'

Macro smiled wryly. 'Quite . . . Then there's the matter of our casualties. They'll try and hold that against him too. They'll say it's down to incompetence.'

Ignatius ground his teeth. 'I'd like to see any of the bastards do better than the tribune.'

'You'd be waiting a long time for that. Look here, Ignatius, they may want to speak to some of the officers and men. If that happens, we need to make sure we back up the tribune's side of the story. Normally I don't hold with getting the men involved

42

in matters above their station, but this ain't right and we owe it to Cato to do what we can to protect him.'

'Right.'

'Meanwhile, I'll try and have a word with Burrus. He might not like it, but it's not as if I have anything to lose by challenging him.'

Ignatius looked straight at him. 'You're still going for the discharge then?'

'Why wouldn't I? If this is how the Praetorian Guard treats one of its finest, I don't want any part of it.'

'Fair enough. But me and the rest of the centurions have some years to go yet.'

Macro got the point at once. 'Just tell the truth. There should be no need to go any further than that if you're asked to testify. If the truth carries any weight, Cato will be back in command of the cohort as soon as this bloody circus is over.' He paused and held up his vine cane, tapping the gnarled head against the other centurion's shoulder. 'You've done good by the tribune. I'll recommend that you take over as senior centurion once I get my discharge.'

Ignatius was moved and struggled to find the words to express his thanks. 'I, er . . .'

'You've earned it, brother. The best man for the job, in my humble opinion. Bar me, of course.'

'It won't be easy to fill your boots, sir.'

'Ah, dry up, you soppy cunt,' Macro growled. 'Before you make me fucking cry.'

They shared a brief chuckle.

'Right, let's get the men settled in, then go and have a drink down the officers' mess. I'm parched. My throat's drier than the arse crack of a camel.'

★ ★ ★

Macro returned to Cato's house at dusk, and was hanging up his cloak in the alcove by the door when he sensed a presence behind him and winced in anticipation.

'What kept you?' Petronella asked testily. She leaned forward and sniffed. 'Wine . . .'

'I had a quick drink with the other centurions after the cohort reached the camp. We had some business to talk over.'

'A drink? Smells like more than one to me.'

'It could well have been,' Macro said, frowning slightly as if he was trying to remember precisely. 'No, I think it was just the one.'

'Cup? Or jar?' Petronella responded with contempt, then turned and paced off towards their sleeping quarters.

'Where's Cato?' Macro called after her.

'In his study. He asked to see you when you returned. That was some hours ago, mind.' She turned a corner and disappeared.

Macro exhaled with relief. He had got off lightly, and he looked up and whispered a quick prayer of thanks to Bacchus for not making him appear as drunk as he felt.

Once he had taken off his armour and wore only his tunic and boots, he went to find his friend. Cato was sitting on a bench outside his study, looking over the garden as the shadows gathered. Cassius was curled up asleep underneath the bench. Cato nursed a silver goblet in both hands, and forced a slight smile as Macro strode towards him.

'You started without me, then?'

Cato narrowed his eyes and wrinkled his nose. 'The other way round, I think.'

'I may have had one or two drinks up at the camp.'

'No doubt. How are the lads?'

'Glad to be back in Rome. But they didn't take the news

44

about you too well. I had a word with the other centurions. They'll back you to a man if they're called to testify at any hearing.'

'It may not come to that. I've been ordered to attend an audience with the emperor in two days' time, after the games. I'll know my fate then. But if it comes to a hearing, or a trial, then I'd be grateful if they spoke up for me.'

'Of course they will. They said as much. I'd have expected no less, mind you. There's not a man in the cohort who doesn't know how much we owe you.'

Cato felt touched by the words but found it hard to accept them at face value. 'Every officer and man did his bit, Macro. I was lucky to have good men at my side, that's all.'

'That's all?' Macro repeated, and gave a quick laugh. 'Seriously, lad, you need to learn to accept praise when it is fairly given. I'm not trying to butter you up. Why would I? In a month's time, I'll no longer be in the army, so I have nothing to gain from flattery. You know me well enough to know I would never bullshit you. So what I say about you is true, and it's true for every man in the bloody cohort.'

'You exaggerate . . .'

Macro stared at him and then frowned. The warmth of the wine in his veins and the slight euphoria in his heart emboldened him. 'I think it's time I told you something. I'll say it now, because I won't have the chance to soon, and I don't want to wait until I've had another drink before I do. If you see what I mean.'

'Frankly, I haven't got a clue what you're talking about.'

'Ah, fuck off with your modesty. Give it a rest. And keep your mouth shut until I'm finished.'

Macro took a deep breath as he arranged his thoughts, while Cato tried to hide his amusement at his friend's maudlin mood.

'Cato, sir, you are without doubt the finest officer I have ever known, let alone served under. One of the best in any legion there ever was, and I should know. I've served half my life in the army. I've seen it all. Seen them bloody thrusters from wealthy backgrounds come in and treat the rankers like dirt, even though they barely know one end of a sword from the other. But you, you're different. You were right from the start. You learned the trade the hard way and earned every promotion you got. You've the heart for it as well as the head. Sharp as a needle, you are, and brave as a lion. And you look after the men, and don't think they don't know it. By rights you should be a bloody general now. If you were, I dare say the Empire would be a far more secure place and good people wouldn't have to worry so much about hairy-arsed barbarians crossing the frontier at night to beat their brains in and run off with their women . . .'

Cassius whined and then growled in his sleep as his paws twitched.

'Have you finished?' Cato demanded. 'You're upsetting my dog.'

'Quiet, you!' Macro stabbed a finger at him. 'I'm sick and bloody tired of seeing you not being given the full reward for your achievements. I'm tired of seeing second-raters taking the credit for your successes. It ain't right. Why, if I was emperor, I'd give you command of all the legions, just like that.' He tried to snap his fingers, but the middle one flopped soundlessly against the ball of his thumb. He glared at his hand and tried again without success. 'Anyway, you deserve no less.'

'If that's what you think,' Cato nodded politely, 'it might be a good idea if we all got an early night. I've arranged for us to go to the races tomorrow. Best we have a proper night's sleep

46

so we can get there early enough to find good seats. Lucius is very excited about it.'

'Damn the races!' Macro grabbed his friend's forearm. 'I'm telling you why you should take some bloody pride in what you've achieved. For the gods' sake accept it. Take what I said as true. I should have told you before . . . I'm proud of you, lad. I know you're my commander and—'

'Not any more.'

Macro raised a finger to his lips and scowled. 'Let me finish. You're my commander . . . my brother in arms . . . my friend. But you've also been like a son to me. That's how I felt. And you turned out as well as any father could hope. You'll see what I mean when Lucius grows up. He's a lucky little bastard to have you to look up to and respect. I never had that. My father was a nobody.'

'Then he was better than mine,' Cato replied. 'My father was born a slave.'

Macro shook his head. 'We are what we are, Cato, my lad. Whether we're born into luxury or the slums of the Subura, into aristocracy or slavery, we make our own way in the world and deal with whatever the fates throw at us. What matters is what's in *here*.' He slapped his chest and stared at Cato wide-eyed, swaying slightly. 'You understand what I'm saying?'

Cato stared back at him and smiled gently. 'I understand you, though some might struggle to right now. And thanks for your kind words. I've always depended on you, brother. If I ever get another command, it's going to be tough to do the job on my own. So there's no more that needs to be said. We'd better get you to bed before Petronella gives up on you.'

'Ah, my woman.' Macro grinned. 'She'll be up for a bit of wrestling tonight, I'll warrant. I'll need just one more drink before I dare to face her.'

47

He reached for the jug but Cato snatched it up. 'No. You've had enough. Go to her, Macro. Before she comes hunting for you. That's my advice.'

Macro looked fondly at the jug before he nodded. 'All right then . . .'

He rose unsteadily and turned in the direction of the rooms that had been made up for him and his wife, walking into the gloom with a cheery wave. Cato watched him go, amused for a moment, before his heart was piqued by the knowledge that a significant stretch of his life was coming to an end. There would be, he hoped, new challenges, new prospects for him. But there would be no Macro there to share them.

'Goodbye, my friend,' he said softly, and turned to gaze over his garden once again.

CHAPTER FIVE

The rising sun was still hidden by the mass of the Viminal Hill as Cato and his small party made their way across the Forum towards the Great Circus. Ahead of them, the lofty heights of the imperial palace atop the Palatine Hill were bathed in the rosy glow of the sun's rays. Cato glanced up at the structure, scanning the colonnades and balconies as if he might catch sight of the emperor or members of his family and entourage, but the only figures in sight were Nero's household bodyguards, tall Germanic tribesmen with long blond hair, their armour and spears gleaming. They were chosen because they were mercenaries and could not speak Latin, and were therefore less likely to be drawn into any conspiracies hatched against the emperor. They also had a reputation for being ferocious warriors who showed no mercy.

Cato recalled the first skirmish he had taken part in on the Rhine frontier; the cohort he had served in was lured into a trap, and when he had seen the barbarian tribesmen charging towards him with crazed expressions on their faces as they roared their battle cries, that was when he had first known true terror. The Germans were big, wild-looking men who appeared frightening enough under peaceful circumstances. Small wonder, then, that they had been chosen to protect Augustus, and every emperor since then. Cato shuddered at the thought of encountering them in the palace on the morrow.

He had no doubt that he had done his duty to the best of his ability and yet he was realistic enough to know that that would count for nothing in the world of high politics, where men of his rank were played and discarded with no more regard than if they were gaming pieces. There was no telling what fate they would decide for him. He might face trumped-up criminal charges, banishment, even death. Or Nero might reinstate him on a whim. The randomness of it all was what truly concerned him. If the peril facing him was known, he could prepare for it. But this situation? He could be ambushed from any quarter.

He held Lucius's hand firmly as they jostled through a small crowd of shoppers in the Forum who had come to the market early to take advantage of the freshest produce on the stalls. Petronella walked on the other side of the boy, a picnic basket in her spare hand, while Macro surged ahead and did his best to clear the way for them. They passed along the thoroughfare to the side of the palace, where the foul odours that wafted up from the city's main sewer tended to hang in the air for days at a time between falls of rain or blustery winds. Lucius's features wrinkled in disgust, while Petronella released his hand and covered her nose and mouth. All four of them increased their pace until they emerged into the large open square that stretched between the end of the Great Circus and the warehouses of the Boarium market. A large crowd had gathered outside the entrances where the chariot drivers and their teams entered the Circus, hoping to catch a view of their heroes before the races began. There was a roar of excitement as a figure in a blue tunic appeared at one of the arches above the entrance gates. Cato and the others paused to watch as the man, light-skinned and fair-haired, opened his arms to greet his fans and smiled at their adulation.

Cato felt his son tug his hand and looked down.

'Why are they shouting?'

'You'll see.' He scooped the boy up so that he sat on his shoulders, and held his ankles. 'See the man up there, Lucius?'

'Yes.'

'He's one of the chariot drivers.'

'He must be famous. Everyone is cheering.'

'All the drivers are famous. Just like all the champion gladiators.'

'Are we going to cheer for him?'

'No, we are bloody not!' said Macro. 'Blues? Never. Bunch of cheating bastards who try and rig every race that's run. It's the red team for us, lad. The pride of the Subura.'

'Reds?' Lucius looked at Macro, who nodded vigorously and cupped a hand to his mouth.

'Up the Reds!' he bellowed.

'Up the Reds!' Lucius echoed, his shrill voice cutting across the throng. Those at the rear of the crowd turned and glared.

'I think that will do for now, Lucius,' said Cato. 'Save your breath for later.'

Petronella dug her elbow into Macro's side. 'And you can pipe down and all. No starting any fights before we even get inside, eh?'

'No, my love,' Macro answered in a chastened tone, then winked at Lucius the moment Petronella had turned away.

They picked their way through the vendors selling cushions, strips of coloured cloth, and snacks, and climbed the stairs of the spectators' entrance. The seats higher up the stands, assigned to the commoners, were already filling up, and the stadium rang with the hubbub of thousands of voices, pierced every so

51

often by a cry of greeting or chorus of laughter. There was still plenty of space in the second tier of seating, reserved for those, like Cato, who belonged to the equestrian class of society. He presented the gold ring on his left hand to the attendant at the barrier and they were ushered through.

The best seats were those on either side of the imperial box, closest to the racetrack and near the area Cato and his small group were making for. Those seats were reserved for the senators and their families, though none of them had arrived yet. Instead, their slaves had been sent ahead to reserve their positions and prepare cushions and other comforts for their masters. Another team of slaves was in the emperor's box, making ready for the arrival of Nero and his entourage later in the morning. Some were arranging garlands, while others prepared small braziers to heat the jars of scented water that would sweeten the air about Nero and his guests.

'Over there.' Macro pointed to a stretch of empty benches close to the barrier, overlooking the sand. 'We'll have a good view of the line-up at the start, and the finish of each race.'

'And we'll be able to see the emperor,' Petronella added excitedly. Like many of her social status, she had a fascination with the members of the imperial household, and their affairs, that was curiously ineluctable.

They took their places, with Lucius resting his hands and chin on the rail as he stared towards the row of arches at the end of the stadium where the teams could be seen preparing the chariots and checking the reins and traces before the horses were put in harness. A handful of attendants were raking the sand, while others carried baskets of bandages on stretchers to the injury treatment posts on the island that ran down the middle of the track. The sun rose and filled the stadium with light and warmth. The banks of seating stretched some six

52

hundred paces from their position to the curved benches at the far end of the arena. The scale of the structure alone and the shimmering mass of tens of thousands of spectators were enough to guarantee the excitement and anticipation that Cato saw in his son's eyes as he gazed at his surroundings in wonder.

Macro ruffled the boy's curls. 'Never seen anything like it, eh, lad?'

Lucius shook his head. 'It's like everyone in the whole Empire is here.'

'Not quite,' Macro smiled.

The first of the senatorial parties arrived, the men dressed in togas that revealed the broad red stripe on the shoulder of their tunics, dutifully doing their best to look dignified as they made their way to their seating area, pausing to wave to groups of their clients in the commoners' seating. As the last of them took their places, accompanied by their wives and children, there was a sudden blaring of trumpets and all eyes turned towards the imperial box, the hubbub dying down. Cato could see the squad of German bodyguards, who had already taken up their positions around the box. As the sound of the trumpets faded away, other figures emerged and took their places, and then there was a brief stillness. A fresh chorus of notes split the quiet and a bearded youth sprang into view and thrust his arms out towards the spectators. They cheered and roared their approval in response, and a chant began, quickly taken up until the sound filled the stands. 'Ne-ro! Ne-ro! Ne-ro!'

'Ne-ro!' Lucius climbed onto the bench and punched his little fist in the air as he cried out the emperor's name. Petronella joined in, followed by Macro and Cato, albeit with less obvious enthusiasm.

The emperor encouraged the acclaim, even blowing kisses

53

to the crowd in a breach of the usual imperial decorum. Macro glanced at Cato and the latter shrugged. If Nero chose to be something of a showman, then who was he to quibble with the individual who ruled over the world's greatest empire?

'What's he up to now?' asked Macro as the emperor undid the clasp of his cloak and let it drop behind him. As a slave hurried forward to sweep it up, Nero strode to the top of the flight of steps that led down to the sand and descended onto the track. A moment later, he sauntered out, waving to the crowd as he made for the nearest of the twelve gates, which had been closed in preparation for the races. At his approach, it snapped back on its springs to reveal two attendants leading out four white horses harnessed to a purple chariot decorated with brilliant gold-painted wreaths.

Cato laughed in disbelief. 'I think our emperor fancies himself as a charioteer.'

'He can't be serious . . .' Macro looked on, scandalised. It was one thing to play to the crowd, quite another to descend to the role of a common entertainer.

The attendants brought the team of horses to a stop and calmed them as Nero paused to pat one on the cheek before making his way round and stepping up into the flimsy body of the racing chariot. He took up the reins in one hand while raising the other to salute the crowd. Behind him the crews of the next four gates readied the release gear and stood by, waiting for the signal. Trumpets sounded again, this time from the spine in the centre of the track, and as the starting official climbed onto his podium, the crowd fell quiet and leaned forward in excitement.

Nero took up the reins in both hands and braced his feet apart as he stared at the seven gilded dolphins above the podium. The official grasped a lever, paused, and then heaved it down.

Above him the first of the dolphins tilted forward, as if diving into the sea. The four gates sprang back and charioteers of the red, blue, green and white teams, wearing tunics in their team's colours, snapped their reins as they urged their horses into action. Wheels spun, sand and grit spurted into the air and the chariots surged towards that of Nero. The emperor flicked his reins and his team of horses trotted forward, breaking into an easy canter at a second command from their driver. He gradually increased the pace into a steady gallop that was comfortably within the pace the horses were capable of. Behind him the other charioteers reined in enough to remain behind the leader as the crowd bellowed encouragement.

Macro tilted his head towards Cato's ear to make sure he would be heard above the din. 'Any idea what odds are being offered for the emperor to win? Can't imagine any bookie taking bets on this farce.'

Even so, the crowd continued to cheer as Nero approached the far end of the stadium and slowed down to a trot to make the turn, forcing the following charioteers to do the same. Briefly the racing teams were out of sight as they continued down the far side of the spine, then Nero appeared again, still leading the field, and carefully rounded the near end of the spine as the second dolphin dipped to signal the start of the next lap.

'The emperor's still ahead!' Lucius clapped his hands together.

'I know,' Cato replied, deadpan. 'How amazing . . .'

'Do you think he will win, Daddy?'

'I would be astonished if someone of his experience and background managed to lose such a race.'

As the race continued, the crowd began to tire of the turgid spectacle. The cheers that greeted Nero as he crossed the winning line were perfunctory at best and motivated by relief that the display was over, rather than any lingering appreciation of the fact that the emperor could actually drive a chariot. The other teams trundled to a halt and the charioteers bowed their heads in defeat to the imperial champion, then a group of officials scurried from the spine, their leader carrying the winner's wreath on a large red cushion. Nero snatched it up and presented it to the crowd before placing it on his own head and striding back towards the steps leading up to the imperial box, to continuing relieved applause. Meanwhile, the chariot teams, with a replacement driver taking Nero's place, made their way back to the large central arch of the main block as the four starting gates were reset for the next race.

Cato looked down at his son. 'I bet you never thought you would be lucky enough to see an emperor do something like that.'

Lucius grinned and shook his head vigorously. 'He can do anything, can't he?'

'I suspect that is what most people tell him, yes.'

There was a sudden change in the tone of the noise from the crowd around the imperial box, and Cato craned his neck to look over the heads of those seated in the Praetorians' area. The emperor was seated on a large cushioned chair at the front of the box. Another chair, only slightly smaller, had been set up beside him, and a young woman with short blond hair in a shimmering purple stola had sat down beside him.

'Who is that?' asked Petronella. 'His wife?'

'Claudia Octavia?' Cato squinted and then shook his head. She was not the woman he had seen with Nero at the imperial palace on a few occasions some years earlier. 'I don't think so.'

There was now a rising chorus of jeers, and Cato saw that some in the senators' parties had turned to look up at the box

56

and were muttering to each other, discreetly pointing at the woman and sneering.

'Unless I miss my guess, I'd say that's Claudia Acte, his mistress.'

'I thought he was supposed to be keeping her in the background,' said Macro.

'Quite . . . It seems he wants to bring her out into the open and some don't like it.'

Even as he spoke, the first of the senators had risen to his feet and gestured impatiently to his wife; now they made off, chins tilted up as if they were walking past an open sewer. Others began to follow their example as the jeers and lewd cries from the crowd around the imperial box rose in volume. Nero sat quite still, staring ahead with a smile on his face, waving occasionally to sections of the crowd. Claudia Acte's lips compressed into a tight line, and she looked at her feet. Nearby, Burrus quickly appraised the situation before pacing over to one of his tribunes and whispering something. A moment later, the officer hurried down to the sand, raced across to the official on the podium rising above the spine and shouted some orders. Preparations for the next race went ahead quickly, and with none of the usual preamble. The first of the reset dolphins went nose-down, the gates swung open and four chariots burst across the sand, faster than those that had emerged for the previous event, converging as they strove to take the lead into the first straight. The crowd's attention snapped towards the action on the racetrack and the jeers gave way to cheers, with coloured strips of cloth swept from side to side in a wild frenzy.

But not everyone's attention was so fickle. A steady stream of senators and those with them continued to file away. Nero, seemingly unperturbed, took his mistress's hand and leaned over to kiss her from time to time.

Macro scratched his chin. 'Looks like some of the quality aren't too keen on Nero's choice of companion.'

'Same goes for the mob.' Cato nodded in the direction of the crowd behind and either side of the imperial box.

'I'm not surprised,' said Petronella. 'Humiliating his wife so publicly is a scandal.' She frowned darkly. 'Why, if her poor old father could have seen this, he'd never have adopted Nero as his heir. It's worse than a scandal; it's an outrage.'

Lucius looked at each of them in turn with a puzzled expression. 'Daddy, what's a scandal?' he asked.

'Oh, it's just a game rich people can't help playing.'

'A game? How do you play it?'

'Let me see . . . You invent some rules and tell people that they are really important, and that everyone has to obey them, and then you don't.'

Lucius thought about this and shook his head. 'Doesn't sound like much fun to me.'

'It's more fun than you might think, lad,' Macro muttered. 'Trust me.'

'Don't you listen to him!' Petronella interrupted sharply. She turned and hissed at Macro. 'Stop putting ideas into his head. Lucius is a good boy.'

'Of course he is. But when he becomes a man, that's another story.'

'Oh, and you'd rather he ends up like you, I suppose?'

Macro looked hurt. 'What do you mean by that?'

'I know what you soldiers are like.'

'And yet you married me.'

'That can be fixed easily enough.' Petronella crossed her arms and turned her attention to Lucius. 'If you get the chance, try not to grow up like your uncle Macro.'

'But I want to be *just* like Uncle Macro.'

The centurion beamed and his wife raised her hands in frustration and turned away.

A loud gasp filled the stadium as the leading charioteer, a chunky man with a shock of blond hair and dressed in a blue tunic, lost control as he came round the spine, his nearside wheel rising off the sand. He tried to adjust his balance, but too late to kill the momentum. The light frame tipped over on its side in a spray of grit, spilling the charioteer onto the ground. His nearside horse was pulled into its companion and the team veered off, dragging the chariot and the man after it. As the spectators leaped to their feet, the charioteer snatched out his dagger and tried to cut himself free of the reins fastened to his leather waistband. The straps parted and he rolled clear just as the other three chariots swerved round the spine and pounded past him.

Cato felt a surge of relief at the man's escape, but noted the look of disappointment on the faces of some in the crowd, who were clearly here for the blood as well as the competition. By the time his attention turned back to the imperial box, he could see that Claudia Acte was on her feet and waving a finger at Nero. Then, before he could react, she turned on her heel, hurried to the back of the box and disappeared from view. Nero looked around helplessly, but all the others in the imperial box were staring fixedly at the racetrack and affecting not to notice the altercation that had taken place. Cato felt pity touch his soul at the thought of the loneliness of the youth's position. Too young to be burdened by learning or experience. Too powerful to be seen to ask for help to make up for the lack of the former qualities. After a moment, Nero stood up, glanced round the stadium and hurried off in pursuit of his mistress. Few in the crowd paid any attention and the cheering rose in a fresh crescendo as the remaining chariots battled to take the lead.

★ ★ ★

The Reds won the first race and the lithe, bearded charioteer collected his wreath before driving his team back to the starting gates. The noise from the crowd subsided and Cato stood up to stretch his back, casually looking over towards the Praetorian seating. He recognised some faces from the Second Cohort and one man waved at him as their gazes met. Before he could check himself, Cato waved back. Some of those around the Praetorian looked up to see what had drawn his attention, and one of them cupped his hands to his mouth and called out, 'Cato! Cato! Cato!'

One by one his friends joined in, punching the air with their fists, followed by more men from the cohort and then Praetorians from other units, turning towards Cato and echoing his name.

'Sounds like word's got round that you've been given a raw deal,' Macro mused as the nearest section of the crowd took up the chant, catching the enthusiasm of the Praetorians and delighting in being part of it.

'Cato! Cato! CATO!'

The object of the veneration saw the commander of the Praetorian Guard look round at his men and frown. He sat down quickly, his pulse quickening.

'Cato!' Macro shouted happily. 'Cato!'

'Stop it!' Cato snarled as he hunched down and lowered his head.

Macro froze, mouth agape. Then he shook his head. 'What's up? Why not enjoy your moment in the sun? Can't do you any harm to be the darling of the mob.'

'Can't it?' Cato glared at him. 'How do you think Burrus is going to react tomorrow when I have to face him and the others? You think he's going to be happy to have my name rubbed in his face like this? Fuck . . .'

Macro got the point and stared ahead. Even with Cato trying to stay out of sight as much as possible, the chant continued to spread until the stadium echoed to his name. Every time it resounded it was like a blow to his ears, and he prayed to the gods that it would end. At length the trumpets sounded for the next race, and the crowd's attention turned to the gates as the starting official reached for the lever.

Cato looked at his boots as the crowd let out a roar and the din of the shouts of the competing supporters crashed together in a deafening cacophony. Any hope that he might present himself to his superiors the following day as a humble officer merely doing his duty had been stripped away. Burrus would punish him for this unwanted, and unsought, acclaim, just as surely as there had been no doubt about the result of the first race of the day.

The rising storm of voices that had chorused his name shortly before now seemed to mock him from every side.

CHAPTER SIX

By the time Cato reached the anteroom to the imperial audience chamber, there were already scores of petitioners there, along with others, like him, who had been commanded to present themselves to the emperor and his advisers. Some sat anxiously on the benches lining the walls, wondering why they were there and fearful of the outcome. Others were filled with indignation over some injustice done to them and were only too pleased to set out their case to whoever they could pin down in the crowded space.

'It's an outrage,' grumbled a thin, swarthy man standing next to Cato. Cato pretended not to hear, and the man stepped in front of him and shook his head. 'Keeping me waiting here while my ships sit idle in port.'

'Oh?' Cato smiled sympathetically, then instantly wished he had not as the man leaned closer.

'That's right. Sitting idle while there's cargoes of grain and oil gathering dust in the warehouses at Carales.' The shipowner frowned. 'It's costing me a fortune, I can tell you.'

'What's happened, then?'

The man's eyes widened briefly. 'How can you not know?'

'I've only just returned to Rome from the east.'

'Ah, my apologies.' He looked Cato up and down, taking in

his uniform and the medals fixed to his harness before quickly calculating that a senior army officer was an acquaintance well worth having. He thrust out his hand. 'Rhianarius is the name, shipowner.'

'So I guessed.'

'I provide low-cost freighting and passenger services to Sardinia and Corsica. Nothing fancy, you understand, just a reliable service at the cheapest rates you can find. If you ever need passage from Ostia to the islands, look me up.'

'I'll be sure to do that,' Cato nodded, wondering what Rhianarius did in order to make good his boast on prices. 'So why are you here? What's the problem?'

'It's these stories of a plague in the southern region of Sardinia. There's even a rumour that the procurator at Ostia is going to quarantine ships arriving from Carales and forbid anyone to sail there. It's nonsense, of course, er . . . Sorry, I didn't catch your name,' he prompted.

'Quintus Licinius Cato, tribune of the Praetorian Guard. Or at least I was.'

'Tribune, eh? Well, I'm glad to meet you, sir. Olearius Rhianarius Probitas is my full name.'

'I'm sure. What's the story on the plague you mentioned?'

'First I heard was just over a month ago. Reports from sailors and passengers arriving at Ostia. Apparently a sickness had broken out amongst the slaves on one of the large estates in the south of the island. It spread to other estates nearby before it reached the towns. Carales has been hit hard, they say, but I've spoken to the captains of ships arriving from other ports and they claim that the whole thing's been exaggerated. It's nothing more than the seasonal sweating sickness that does the rounds of the marshy areas in the region. That's my guess. And that's why I'm here.' He took out a scroll and waved it under Cato's nose. 'A petition from the shipowners of Ostia to protest against any quarantine, before it does any damage to our trade.' He tucked the scroll away. 'How about you?'

Cato was not prepared to reveal the reason for his presence – the shame and pain of being relieved of his command was still too fresh a wound to his pride – but nor was he about to lie to the man. 'I'm here to report on the situation on the eastern frontier.'

'Tribune Cato?' Rhianarius frowned briefly and then snapped his fingers. '*The* Cato? The one the crowd was cheering at the races yesterday. That Cato?'

'Well, I . . .'

The shipowner smiled broadly and pumped Cato's hand. 'I heard about your heroics from a crowd of Praetorians at an inn after the races were over. You're quite the hero, it seems. Everyone was talking about you.'

'I don't know about that.' Cato felt awkward at the prospect of being thought of as a hero by the mob. It was a prospect that might not do him any favours if the emperor and his advisers were aware of his unwanted fame. He backed away from Rhianarius. 'Look here, I'm terribly sorry, but I've just spotted one of my comrades I expected to meet before my audience. I have to go.'

'Oh? All right, then. But don't forget my name. Make sure you ask for me if you need to take a ship at Ostia.'

'I'll do that.'

As Cato eased his way through the crowd to the far side of the room, he heard Rhianarius's voice behind him. 'You'll never guess who that was . . .'

He made for the corner by the door to the audience chamber and bowed his head in order to remain as inconspicuous as possible while he waited to be summoned. Each time an imperial clerk emerged, faces turned hopefully and there was a lull in the conversation. Then a name was announced and they returned to their business as one of their number hurried through the crowd to present himself to the clerk.

The hours of the morning dragged on. Shortly before noon, the clerk came out again and looked at the list of names on his waxed slate.

'Tribune Quintus Licinius Cato!'

Cato straightened up. 'Here.'

'If you'd follow me, sir.' The clerk bowed his head slightly in deference to Cato's equestrian rank. 'A word of warning. The emperor has chosen to be addressed as Imperial Majesty, thereafter simply Majesty, rather than the usual "sire".' He waved Cato through the entrance into the presence of Nero and his advisers.

Cato had been in the audience chamber on several occasions, but was immediately struck by the changes to the decor since the days of the previous emperor, Claudius. Instead of plain ochre, the columns on either side of the chamber were now painted a brilliant turquoise and gilded with depictions of vines and leaves that glittered in the shafts of sunlight streaming from the openings high above. The chamber was some thirty paces long and fifteen wide, and a low dais rose from the floor at the far end. Nero was seated on a purple cushion atop his gilded throne, the imperial wreath on his brow. He wore an elaborately embroidered tunic, longer than was tasteful for a man, and red knee-length boots. The instant impression was that of some crass actor parading before his fans rather than the ruler of a great empire. Burrus and Seneca stood to the right of the dais, along with two scribes. Several more men in togas stood to the left. Cato recognised some of them as senators. A squad of German bodyguards were arranged around the sides of the chamber, with two more standing behind the throne.

'Tribune Quintus Licinius Cato, Imperial Majesty!' the clerk announced.

Nero gestured to Cato to approach. 'What's this about? And let's make it quick. I am tired of all this work. I need a rest. We'll make this appointment the last one today.'

The clerk glanced down at the long list of names on his tablet. 'Imperial Majesty, there are still thirty petitioners to deal with.'

Nero winced and grasped his brow between thumb and forefinger. 'Am I to be forever a slave to everyone else's needs before my own? Is that the burden of office? Is that to be my fate? To be condemned to thrust aside my poetry, my music, my art for the sake of the petty squabbles of the plebs? Oh, I grow so weary of duty.'

Before the clerk could respond, Burrus spoke up. 'You heard his Imperial Majesty. There will be no more appointments today. Send them away. Tell them to come back tomorrow.'

'Yes, Prefect,' the clerk replied, bowing as he backed to the door, which one of the German guards opened for him, closing it behind him with a decisive thud.

Cato strode forward, stopped a pace from the foot of the dais and saluted. He had chosen to wear his military apparel in order to solicit some sympathy for his cause, as nearly every emperor since Augustus had been keenly aware of the need to favour their soldiers, the men of the Praetorian Guard most of all.

Nero glanced at him briefly, with a bored expression. 'I remember you. You were the officer that dealt with Britannicus's plot against me after I claimed the throne.'

'Yes, Imperial Majesty.' Cato's hopes rose. Perhaps the

emperor's gratitude would be helpful with respect to his present predicament.

'What do you want from me, soldier?'

'Want?' Cato was taken by surprise. 'Imperial Majesty, I was sent for.'

'You were? Why?'

Burrus stepped up hurriedly. 'Majesty, this is the officer who was in command of the cohort you sent to protect General Corbulo two years back.'

'I did?'

'Yes, Majesty. He returned to Rome a few days ago with less than a third of his men, after having disobeyed your orders to keep his cohort out of battle.'

Nero shifted his grey eyes to Cato. 'Is this true?'

'I was acting under Corbulo's orders, Majesty,' Cato replied. 'I did my best to minimise casualties. However, the Second Cohort was obliged to fight for its survival on occasion. I was fortunate to return to Rome with as many men as I did, Majesty.'

Nero's expression lit up eagerly. 'You and your men fought in many battles?'

'A few, Majesty.'

'Against desperate odds?'

'We were usually fighting at a disadvantage, yes.'

'Tell me, are those Parthian fiends as dangerous an enemy as we are told they are?'

Cato could sense Burrus bridling, but he realised that Nero's excitement could be turned to his advantage. 'They are indeed the most dangerous enemy I have fought, Majesty. But my men and I were inspired by our devotion to you and to Rome and would have died rather than disappoint your faith in our loyalty.'

'Really?' Nero smiled. 'Did you hear that, Seneca? My soldiers are inspired by me.'

'Why would they not be, Majesty? Every Roman is inspired by you and gives thanks to the gods for placing you on the throne to rule over us and grace us with your tremendous intelligence and flawless good taste.'

Cato forced himself not to smile at this grotesque flattery. He looked at Nero, waiting for the young man's expression to register amusement at Seneca's grovelling praise. Instead Nero nodded sombrely, as if taking the senator's words at face value.

'True. Rome is indeed blessed to have me as emperor. As my legions are blessed to have me as their supreme leader. If only I had not been cursed with the sensitivity of an artist, I would surely have fought the Parthians at your side, Tribune Cato, and no doubt led you to victory, thereby sparing many of your comrades a glorious death at the hands of the most ferocious of our enemies. You are not to blame for not having me there to command you and the men of your cohort. Rest assured I shall not hold you culpable on that count.'

He smiled benignly and Cato bowed his head in gratitude. 'I thank you for your forbearance, Majesty.'

'There is still the matter of the tribune's failure to obey orders, Majesty,' Burrus chipped in. 'Such insubordination should not go unpunished. After all, it was your orders he was disobeying, Majesty. He defied your will. He is also guilty of courting the support of the mob at the Great Circus yesterday.'

'I heard about that.' Nero's smile faded. 'It is a serious matter. My predecessors would have executed a man for lesser offences . . .'

Cato felt an icy tingle down his spine, but managed to keep his expression fixed as Nero regarded him closely.

'But I am not like those despots,' the emperor continued.

'When I came to power, one of the first things I did was to free political prisoners, was it not, my dear Seneca?'

'Yes, Majesty.' The senator nodded. 'You also pledged to put an end to all political persecution and fortune-chasing by informants. You proclaimed that a golden age had begun from Rome.'

'Yes, I suppose . . .' Nero looked disappointed at the reminder. A frown formed on his brow. 'You claim to be a loyal soldier, Tribune Cato, but as Prefect Burrus has pointed out, you disobeyed my orders. Had I not given the pledge to be a just and merciful emperor, your life would now be forfeit. Therefore, the very least you deserve is to be removed from command of the Second Cohort. That, I think, is sufficient for now. Let this be a warning to you, former tribune Cato. If you should ever disappoint me again, I will not be so lenient next time.' He let out a theatrical sigh. 'I am exhausted. After our long discussions last night, and these frivolous appointments this morning, my head is pounding. I must rest. The session is over, gentlemen. Burrus, come with me. We need to discuss the matter of appointing a new commander of the Second Cohort.'

The prefect bowed deeply. 'Yes, Majesty.'

Nero stood up, strode to the edge of the dais and hopped down nimbly before making his way to the door at the rear of the chamber that led to his private quarters. Burrus hurried after him, followed by the German bodyguards. The others in the room bowed their heads until the emperor had left the room, then the senators fell to talking quietly as the clerks packed up their writing materials.

Cato stood apart, his heart heavy with a grave sense of injustice over his treatment. He had saved the emperor's life twice now, and rendered him good service. And yet he was being punished for no better reason than that it might serve as a warning to those who displeased Nero. Still, his fate could have been worse, he told himself. He had been stripped of his command, but he was alive, and Lucius had been spared the misery of being an orphan. There had been no mention of confiscating his property, so at least he would have a roof over his head and could live in comfortable obscurity. Perhaps it was as well that it had happened now, he considered. With Macro retiring, much of the appeal of continuing a military career had disappeared. He had already reached as high a rank as he was ever likely to attain. The only official promotion left open to him was the post of Prefect of Aegyptus, the sole provincial command available to men of equestrian rank. But that seemed a remote possibility now.

Seneca made his farewells to the other advisers as they trooped out of the chamber, then turned to Cato with an apologetic expression. 'You have my sympathy, Tribune.'

'If you'll pardon me for saying so, sympathy is of little use to me.'

'No?' Seneca's lips wrinkled in distaste. 'You may find that you may soon be grateful for any sympathy you can elicit. To be without powerful friends in Rome may be more dangerous than you yet suppose. If I were you, young man, I would adopt a more measured attitude. It would only take a word in Nero's ear from me to bring his full wrath down upon you. Another word might do much to repair your fortunes . . .'

Cato smiled cynically. 'If I become your client, I suppose?'

'Why not? I look after those who accept me as their patron. Ask anyone in Rome. They will confirm what I say.'

'I'm sure they will. But I have had enough of being forced to act as the dogsbody of imperial advisers. You are not the first to try and suborn me. There was Pallas before you, and before *him*, Narcissus. They both had their moment in the sun, but Narcissus is dead, and Pallas has lost his place at the emperor's side – and from what I hear, he will be on trial for his life soon.'

Seneca wafted a hand dismissively. 'He is not in any mortal danger. Not with me defending him.'

'You seem very confident in your ability.'

'My confidence is well founded. I happen to be rather more intelligent than any advocate the Senate chooses to prosecute Pallas. Besides, once I let the prosecutor and the presiding magistrate know that the emperor is minded to be lenient . . .'

'And is Nero so minded?'

'He is, if I choose to make him so. You saw how he is. The innocent boy is inclined to take every scrap of praise at face value, no matter how obvious the hyperbole. I note that you grasped that very quickly and turned it to your advantage readily enough. Other men would not have done. It amuses me that so many people think it is beneath them to flatter the emperor. Where does their stiff-necked pride get them? A smug little niche on the fringes of power. If you want to influence him, you must treat Nero like that cithara he is so keen on. The strings must be plucked in the correct order to create music to soothe his thinking and steer it in the desired direction.'

'And can you play him that easily?'

Seneca clicked his tongue. 'I never said it was easy. As with any instrument, the skill of the player is the result of a combination of innate ability and much practice. Which is why I have rather more influence over him than Burrus, who has all the finesse of a boxer playing the flute with his hands bound up for a fight. It is why I have managed to resolve the rather delicate matter of the emperor's unfortunate obsession with that little flirt Claudia Acte.'

'Nero's mistress? I saw her storm out of the imperial box.'

'And well she might. There is not a senator in Rome who is not scandalised by the way the emperor has courted her. Until last night, Nero was attempting to convince the Senate that she was of high birth and therefore suitable material for him to marry. The truth is that she is as common as muck. I know. I'm the one who found her on the streets and had her scrubbed clean and dressed in finery. I knew she was just the kind of girl to infatuate Nero.'

'Another string of the cithara for you to pluck?'

'Quite so. She was only supposed to be there for the plucking in secret, but Nero insisted on treating her like a princess and having her accompany him in public. That will never do.'

'You said the matter was resolved.'

'It is. Or rather, it will be once she is escorted from Rome. Nero will forget her soon enough once a fresh bauble of the flesh is dangled in front of him.' Seneca paused to appraise Cato in silence for a moment. 'That's where you come in.'

'What do you mean?'

'Nero showered the woman with gifts. One of which is a couple of large estates in Sardinia. That is where she is being sent into exile. She won't be too pleased, as you can imagine. But it is vital that she is escorted there and that she remains on the island and makes no attempt to return to Rome. The governor of Sardinia has already been informed of the island's newest resident.'

Cato felt a weary sense of anticipation. 'You want me to babysit her?'

Seneca looked amused. 'She is no child, Cato. She is one of the more intelligent women I have met, as well as one of the most ambitious, which is why she is too dangerous to be permitted to remain at Nero's side.'

'Then it must be tempting to ensure her removal is permanent,' Cato responded drily. 'I'm sure it could be arranged.'

'How very euphemistic of you. I am sure you could master the imperial cithara given the chance.' Seneca regarded him warily and then smiled thinly. 'One day it may well become imperative that she is, ah, removed, as you say.'

Cato felt his guts tighten in revulsion. 'I am a soldier. Don't mistake me for an assassin.'

'You certainly have a soldier's prickly pride. I am not asking you to be an assassin, merely a guard. Amongst other duties.'

'Other duties?'

Seneca chewed his lip delicately as he collected his thoughts. 'What do you know about the situation in Sardinia? Not much, I should imagine, as you have only recently returned from the east.'

'I know that there has been a famine for the last two years, and that has hiked the price of grain in Rome. I know that some of the tribes of the hinterland have been raiding estates and settlements. To make matters worse, I know that a plague has broken out in the south of the island.'

Seneca tilted his head back and laughed briefly. 'I knew that you were the right man for the job the moment I heard you were back in Rome.'

'What job?'

'Rome needs a resourceful soldier to take command of the garrison on the island and put an end to the depredations of the tribes who dare to challenge the authority of Rome by disrupting the supply of grain and oil. The current governor, Borus Pomponius Scurra, is an indolent wastrel, to be frank. He is not up to the job of dealing with the brigands. He's not even capable of running the province competently. Since your services are no longer required by the Praetorian Guard, you are available for the task.'

'Why me? There are plenty of other officers here who could do the job.'

'That's true. But you are not any other officer. You have singular talents and it would be best if those were put to good use rather than be permitted to go to waste while you sit and stew in your resentment from the comfort of your house on the Viminal. Besides, it might be best for you to be absent from Rome for a while. Out of Nero's sight.'

Cato thought through the task that Seneca had outlined. It was neatly done, as if the imperial adviser had planned it all out well before Cato had presented himself for the emperor's judgement. Not only would he serve as the gaoler of Nero's troublesome mistress, but he would be required to put down the tribesmen and ensure the smooth flow of grain and oil as well. There was no glory to be had in such a mission. It might be true that there were plenty of other officers in Rome who could be handed the task, but few of them would be willing to accept so thankless a command, with little prospect of advancing their careers. If that was true of them, it was equally true for Cato.

He shook his head. 'I'm sorry to disappoint you, but I must decline your offer. I'll take my chances and remain in Rome while I wait for a better opportunity to turn up.'

'Offer?' Seneca's brow creased. 'I think you misunderstand me. I have chosen you for the job. You. No one else. You will do it.'

'And if I choose not to?'

'You can refuse. But if you do, and you reject my offer to be your patron, then I will be in no position to protect you from Nero's anger . . .'

The threat was clear. 'In the event that someone has a word in the emperor's ear to provoke such anger, you mean.'

'It's uncanny,' said Seneca. 'It's almost as if you can read my mind. You might as well make the most of it, Cato. It's a new command after all. I appreciate that it might be something of a comedown after holding the rank of tribune in the Praetorian Guard, but it is the best opportunity you are likely to get to continue serving in the military. Knowing what I do about you, I'd say the army is your life. You are the kind of man who would find civilian life unfulfilling. Maybe not immediately. After all, you have a son to raise and I am sure that would consume much of your time and attention. But give it a few months, or perhaps as long as a year, and you'd be willing to give your right arm for the chance to get back in the field.' He scrutinised Cato's expression. 'Am I wrong?'

'I am sure I could adapt, but then again, I am not going to be given the chance to find out, am I?'

'No. I'm afraid not. You'll need to make preparations. If you haven't unpacked your baggage yet, I might have saved you the trouble.' Seneca smiled at his remark. 'I'll let you go now. You'll have a few days before Claudia Acte is ready to travel. I'll inform you of the departure date as soon as I can.'

'You're too kind,' Cato replied sourly.

Seneca gave a deep sigh. 'You're no fool. You understand life at the imperial court. When a man reaches a certain rank or position in life, he falls into the purview of the emperor. Nero can make or break our fortunes on a whim. A wise man does what he can to make the most of the opportunities and avoid the pitfalls. Today could easily have been your last. As it is, you are alive, and you retain your home and wealth. Moreover, there is still a chance for you to make a name for yourself in Sardinia. Carry out your task well and one day you will look back on this moment as a minor setback.'

Cato considered what he had been told about Sardinia, its internal conflicts and the plague that was spreading across the island. Then there was the small matter of escorting the emperor's mistress to her estate and making sure that she remained there. He cleared his throat. 'I accept, on one condition.'

Seneca smiled faintly. 'And what would that be?'

'I get to take my cohort with me.'

'It's no longer your cohort.'

'Reinstate me.'

Seneca shook his head. 'Out of the question.'

'Then at least let me ask for volunteers.'

'No. I know what you soldiers are like with your simple code of loyalty. If you ask for volunteers, I dare say the entire cohort will step forward. You can imagine how Burrus and Nero will take that gesture. You can forget it.'

'Let me have ten men,' Cato countered. 'If you want my mission to be a success, I must have a cadre of good men I can rely on.'

Seneca thought it over. 'Five men. No more than five.'

Cato felt some small relief over the concession, but there was still the larger unanswered question that weighed on him. 'And what happens to me if I should fail?'

Seneca regarded him coldly. 'You will not fail.'

CHAPTER SEVEN

'Sardinia?' Apollonius plucked an apple from the fruit bowl in the middle of the table and took a bite, crunching on the crisp white flesh. 'Never been there. Should be interesting. It's a shame you'll miss out on it, Macro.'

The centurion did not respond, but turned his gaze towards his wife, who was playing with Lucius by the pond in the middle of Cato's garden. The warm morning had given way to a stifling afternoon, and the streets had been quiet as Cato made his way home from the palace. He had ordered Croton to set up an awning in the garden so that he could sit in the shade while taking advantage of any light breeze that passed over the city. The three men were lying on couches around the table, where a jug of watered wine brought up from the cellar stood. While Macro filled the silver goblets, Cato's thoughts were focused on the task Seneca had forced him to accept, and he could not enjoy the comfort and peace of his surroundings.

Macro coughed and lowered his voice so that Petronella would not overhear him. 'If you need me to stay in uniform for a little longer, just say the word, lad.'

Cato looked at his friend and felt a surge of bittersweet affection for him. In truth, there was nothing he would like better than to have Macro continue to serve alongside him. But it would be an act of unconscionable selfishness to exploit his friend's offer. Petronella would never forgive either of them if Macro went to Sardinia. And, gods forbid, if anything happened to him, Cato would never forgive himself.

'I can't ask that of you. I won't. But I thank you for the offer, brother, with all my heart. You have served Rome for long enough. You've shed blood for the Empire and you have been loyal to your comrades and to me. The time has come for you to put aside your sword and enjoy your life with Petronella.'

'She'll understand,' Macro protested. 'She knows what it means to me.'

Apollonius laughed and shook his head. 'I fear you have no idea how a woman's mind works.'

Macro scowled at him. 'I know my wife.'

'Maybe, but if you choose to go to Sardinia, you're showing her no respect. Women want love, sure, but they want respect more. If you abandon her to go on campaign, you will incur such wrath as the Furies could only dream of.'

'And you're an expert on women?' Macro sneered.

'I'm an expert on human nature.' Apollonius smiled. 'Otherwise I would not have survived as long as I have in my line of work.'

'I'll take advice from a spy when I want it, not before.'

Apollonius's eyebrows lifted briefly. 'Your funeral, friend.'

'Enough, you two,' Cato interrupted firmly. 'Macro, enjoy your retirement. You've earned it a thousand times over.'

'But—'

'The matter is settled. I am not taking you with me.'

Macro could not help starting with surprise, freezing for a beat and then easing himself back with a betrayed expression. He swallowed bitterly. 'As you wish, sir.'

There was an awkward silence before Apollonius swung his legs over the side of the couch and held out his arms.

'This heat is unbearable. I'm going for a dip in the bathhouse pool. Anyone care to join me? No? Very well, alone then.'

He walked away quickly, leaning down to the pond to splash Lucius and Petronella as he passed by. Lucius laughed with surprise while Petronella shot the agent a scowl. Apollonius quickened his pace and disappeared from view between the hedges either side of the path leading to the bottom of the garden.

'You're taking him with you,' said Macro.

'He's good in a fight and he's just as skilful at knifing a man in the back as sticking a sword into his chest. I have a feeling that kind of talent is going to be useful to me in Sardinia.'

'As long as it's not *your* back.'

'Why would it be? Apollonius has no reason to betray me.'

'I wonder. Why do you think he has attached himself to you? He was Corbulo's creature before. You shouldn't trust him. For all you know, he could be in someone else's pay. Someone who wants to destroy you.'

'And who would that be?' Cato asked wearily. 'Most of our enemies are dead, like Narcissus, or have been removed from positions of influence, like Pallas.'

'What about Vitellius?'

Cato recalled the scheming aristocrat they had crossed swords with years before.

'There's always Vitellius,' he conceded. 'But he's keeping to himself for now.'

'Biding his time, no doubt. But we both know his type. He will never forget, nor will he forgive.'

'And if he comes looking for trouble, he'll find me ready, with my sword in my hand,' Cato responded defiantly.

'That's not going to do you much good if Apollonius's knife is between your shoulder blades, my lad,' Macro said with a resigned shrug. 'Look, I see I can't stop you taking him. But be careful. Keep an eye on him at all times. And if you have any doubts about him, stick him with a blade double quick. That's what I'd do.'

'Thanks for the advice.' Cato could not help smiling at his friend's fatherly anxiety. 'I'll watch him closely. I promise.'

He reached for the jug and topped up their goblets before settling back to watch Lucius and Petronella, who had kicked off their sandals and were now splashing their feet, sending up spouts of glittering water in the sunlight while Cassius pounced from side to side and barked at them.

'What are your plans for the boy?' asked Macro. 'Are you going to take him with you?'

'No. There's a plague in Sardinia, so Lucius remains here in Rome. I'll find a tutor for him.'

'Isn't he a bit young for that?'

'Possibly, but it will keep his mind occupied so that he doesn't miss me. Or you and Petronella, for that matter.'

'We'll miss *him*. Petronella particularly.'

'It's not going to be easy for any of us,' Cato mused. 'We're as good as family, the four of us. And the dog.'

'The mutt you can keep,' Macro sniffed. 'I don't know what you see in that mongrel. He's no good at hunting, is as likely to lick a thief as bite him, and he's a waste of rations.'

'Which is why I am leaving him here in Rome. I imagine you held similar views about *me* when I turned up with the other recruits to the Second Legion. But Cassius turned out well, just like I did.'

'Don't polish your tits too much, lad. You've done well enough as an officer, but the gods only know what would happen if you turned up for kit inspection on my parade ground.'

'Ah, bollocks to that. Perfection's never good enough for any of you veteran centurions.'

'True enough.' Macro took a sip of his wine. 'Things were tougher when I joined up. But these days? Just a steady stream of clods and mother-coddled cry-babies we have to try and turn into men. Breaks my fucking heart, so it does. Just as well I'm getting discharged so I won't have to witness that sorry display.'

Cato had heard the grumpy refrain before on many occasions, but this time Macro was finally quitting the army, and all that would remain of his long years of service were the memories. The campaigns they had shared and the men they had known, good and bad, most of whom had died or been left behind as Cato and Macro had been transferred to other units. He raised his goblet. 'To our absent brothers.'

Macro pursed his lips briefly as he recalled their faces in swift succession. 'Absent brothers.'

The next morning, Macro and Cato entered the Praetorian camp and made their way to the barracks of the Second Cohort. Cato wore a simple tunic, as he did not want to draw attention to himself and risk someone reporting his presence to Burrus. Even though Seneca had agreed that he could take five men from the cohort with him, there was no guarantee that he had informed the commander of the Praetorian Guard yet. In Cato's judgement, the senator was the kind of man who would promise something one day without any desire to honour it the next.

When they reached the tribune's quarters at the end of the barracks, Macro stood to one side to let his friend enter first. Cato smiled and shook his head.

'After you, brother. It's your cohort now.'

'Only for the next few days.' Macro clicked his tongue. 'Tribune Macro, commander of the Second Praetorian Cohort. It does have a ring to it. If only my dad could see me now. Always said I'd never make much of myself. Ah well.'

He led the way inside and they made for the office. Macro sent one of the clerks to round up the centurions and optios.

'Let's hope they're in a volunteering mood,' he said as he pulled a spare bench in from the clerks' room and shoved it against the wall. Bunching his fists in the small of his back, he arched his spine with a groan.

'You all right?' asked Cato.

His friend eased forward and loosened his shoulders. 'The usual twinges and aches I've been getting for a while in my back and my knees. All those bloody years trudging around with a laden marching yoke on my shoulder are to blame. Still, I may be growing old and slowing down, but I can wield a sword better than most men half my age, and use my fists better than almost anyone else outside an arena.'

Cato regarded his friend briefly. While Macro's hair was grey at the temples and the once dark locks were now streaked with silver and noticeably thinning, his arms and legs were thickly muscled and he was clearly still a force to be reckoned with. 'Let's hope there's not much call for it when you settle in Londinium.'

'I'm sure I'll keep myself busy throwing out the drunks and making sure none of the local gangs think they can muscle in on our business.' He spoke with a gleam in his eye. 'I'm good for a while yet.'

The sound of footsteps echoed along the corridor and a moment later the first of the officers entered and greeted Cato with salutes and ready smiles.

'Good to see you, Ignatius. You too, Porcino. How was the voyage back from Tarsus?'

Ignatius, a thickset veteran, sucked his teeth. 'A cargo tub is not the most comfortable of billets, sir. Spent most of the time puking my guts up over the side.'

Cato nodded sympathetically. He himself suffered from appalling seasickness in the lightest of swells. He looked to the other man. Porcino was in his mid twenties. He had lost a lot of his ponderous bulk over the last two campaigns and was now lean and fit-looking. He sat down on the bench next to Ignatius.

'What's this about, sir? Are you being put back in command of the Second Cohort?'

'You got a problem with the current management?' Macro demanded, then winked.

'No,' Cato responded directly. 'My service with the Praetorian Guard is over.'

'The lads will be sorry to hear that. They're hoping Burrus will come to his senses and reinstate you.'

'I'm sorry to disappoint them, but it's out of our hands.'

The other centurions and their optios arrived and crowded into the modest office, exchanging greetings with Cato before sitting down. Macro closed the door behind them and took his place at Cato's shoulder as his friend ordered his thoughts.

'The good news is that there won't be any formal investigation into my handling of the cohort. The emperor decided it was enough to strip me of my command. I can live with that, given the alternative of not living at all. Still, it pains me to be forced to leave you all. We've been through some hard marches and tough battles together. Now that's over for most of the men, and it's back to the soft life in Rome. Cheap wine, easy women who like a nice uniform, plenty of coin from the emperor, and chariot races and gladiator bouts to keep them entertained. They – you – have earned those rewards.'

'And you too, sir,' said Metellus, the most recently promoted of the centurions. His courage and quick wits had caught Cato's attention while he had been serving as an optio.

'It seems that my reward is to be sent to Sardinia to take command of the garrison there and bring the tribesmen of the interior to heel. From what I've already learned about the island, the terrain is going to make it a tough job. Made tougher still by the famine that has hit the locals. And if that wasn't bad enough, they are now dealing with some pestilence that has broken out in the south of the island.' He paused and smiled ruefully. 'As you can see, it's a considerable challenge, and a thankless one. If order breaks down in Sardinia, the grain and oil the island supplies to Rome will dry up and there will be hunger in the capital. From what I have been told, our soldiers there are thinly stretched and of dubious quality. I am going to need the help of good men if I am to have any chance of success. I have been given permission to take five men from the Second Cohort with me. Since the imperial adviser in question failed to specify the rank of those men, I have come here to put it to you first. I need a cadre of good soldiers to kick the garrison into shape, and there are none better than the centurions and optios of the Second Praetorian Cohort. Apollonius has already agreed to accompany me. I need five more. Centurion Macro is excluded due to his imminent discharge.'

Macro shifted uneasily but said nothing.

'I'm asking for volunteers. I know you've all been looking forward to the pleasures offered by the capital, and I'll understand if any, maybe even all of you decide not to come with me. I'll bear no grudge against any man who chooses to remain in Rome. The gods know you have nothing to prove to anyone.

You've won your laurels on the eastern frontier, but I fear that Nero may be in no mood to hand out awards and bonus payments. That's the way it goes, brothers . . .'

Cato had intended to say more, playing on the need for sacrifice in the name of Rome, the bond of loyalty that existed between them, and the opportunity to do real soldiering rather than acting as mere props for whatever spectacle Nero decided to put on to impress his subjects. Now that he was facing the officers of the cohort, however, he felt that it would be demeaning to deploy any such rhetoric in an attempt to persuade them to march with him.

'That's all I have to say,' he concluded. 'I don't want your answer now. Think it over carefully and let Centurion . . . Tribune Macro know your decision by the end of the day. I'll await your response at my home on the Viminal. I bid you good day, gentlemen.'

Before he could move towards the door, Macro barked an order.

'Commanding officer present!'

At once the centurions and optios rose and stood to attention facing Cato, shoulders back, chests out and eyes front. He felt his throat constrict as he struggled to contain his pride in their bond and his gratitude for the respect accorded to him by his former subordinates.

'You honour me, brothers. I hope to see you all again some day. For those who join me in Sardinia, I offer my thanks. For those who remain in Rome I wish you the best of fortune for the rest of your career. Farewell.'

He saluted and marched between them towards the door. Stepping into the corridor, he closed it behind him and heard Macro order, 'At ease!'

He turned away and made his way out of the barrack block.

As he continued to the main gate and passed through it, he was acutely conscious that he might never again set foot within the walls of the Praetorian camp.

When Macro returned to the house that evening, Cato and Apollonius were waiting for him on the couches in the garden. Macro undid the clasp of his military cloak as he approached and tossed it onto the spare couch before sitting down heavily and mopping his brow. Cato had seen the hint of an amused expression on his friend's face and said nothing, refusing to take the bait. Letting out a theatrical sigh, Macro swung his boots up and leaned back against the large bolster at the end of the couch.

'Aren't you going to ask me, then?'

'All right, you win. Did anyone volunteer?'

'It would be more to the point to ask if anyone didn't,' Macro chuckled. 'After you left, the feeling in the room was that you had been given a poor deal. Some harsh words were said about Burrus and the emperor.'

'How very indiscreet,' said Apollonius. 'Such words have a way of biting back when they become more widely known.'

Macro turned on him with a sour expression. 'There were only soldiers in the room at the time, not dirty informers or spies.'

'There may come a time when one of the former becomes one of the latter . . . Speaking from experience.'

'We've known traitors before, it's true. But the Praetorian lads are good men,' Macro protested. 'Anyway, they all volunteered. Centurions and optios alike.'

Cato shook his head in wonder. 'You're joking . . .'

'Never about a matter such as this. Face it, lad, the men would follow you almost anywhere. Your battles are their battles, both here in Rome and out there against barbarians and rebels alike.'

It was a humbling prospect to have inspired such loyalty, but then an inner voice rose up inside Cato warning him not to trust the sentiment. Only a fool followed blindly, no matter how accomplished the leader. The officers were reacting irrationally and they'd change their minds soon enough.

'Of course,' Macro continued, 'I reminded them that only five of them could go. Ignatius is the best man to replace me as senior centurion of the cohort. The men will need someone they know and respect, so I told him he's remaining. Same goes for Nicolis. He's not yet recovered full use of the arm that was injured at Thapsis. He'll be better off handling ceremonial duties until he recovers. He wasn't happy about it, but he won't be much good chasing tribesmen across hills and through forests with only one arm. Out of the rest, I picked those I thought would be the best men for the job.' He reached into his tunic and took out a waxed tablet, leaning over to hand it to Cato. 'Here's the list.'

Cato took the tablet and opened it. *We, the undersigned, give notice of our intention to volunteer for service under Quintus Licinius Cato in the province of Sardinia. We do this freely and in accordance with the permission granted by Senator Lucus Annaeus Seneca. Centurions: Plancinus, Porcino, Metellus. Optios: Pelius, Cornelius.*

He knew them all – good soldiers and the best companions he could have hoped for to take with him to Sardinia. He felt his throat tighten with raw emotion as he closed the waxed tablet and set it down. 'I don't know what to say, brother.'

'Then let me help you out. Say, how would you like a nice jug of wine, Macro?'

They shared a laugh and Apollonius joined in before he nodded and rose to stride off towards the kitchen.

Cato thought a moment and clicked his tongue. 'Burrus is not going to be happy about being deprived of some of the best of the cohort's officers.'

'That's Seneca's problem. He agreed you could take five of the men. If he didn't specify rank, then that's his fault.'

'Maybe, but I think it might be best not to tell either of them until the last moment.'

'You're right.' Macro suddenly laughed and slapped his thigh. 'By the gods, I hope I'm there to see their faces when they find out!'

CHAPTER EIGHT

A new commander of the Second Cohort was appointed five days later; the son of a moneylender who happened to hold the debts of Prefect Burrus. The young officer in question had only just completed his year as a junior tribune before seeking to move on to a junior magistrate's position or landing a plum posting in the Praetorian Guard.

'Ah well,' Cato sighed as Macro related the news. 'Fortune favours those with large fortunes. Thus it ever was and ever will be. When does he take command?'

'He already has,' Macro replied as he sat on the edge of the fountain, unfastened his boot laces and eased his feet out, wriggling his toes in the water. 'Burrus swore him in this morning. My temporary rank has come to an end and I relinquished my commission on the spot. I'm not going to take orders from some chinless youth who barely knows his arse from his elbow. I quit there and then, picked up my discharge plaque and outstanding pay from headquarters and left it all behind without once turning back.'

There was regret in his tone and Cato cleared his throat as he sat down on the opposite side of the fountain. 'I'm sorry it had to end this way, brother.'

'It always had to end one way or another. Doesn't bother me.'

'If you say so.'

Macro was still as he stared at his friend. 'I mean it. I've had my time and it's over and I'm starting a new life with my woman. I'm looking forward, not over my shoulder.'

'That sounds like a healthy plan. I trust you'll stick with it.'

Macro looked round. 'Where's Petronella?'

'She's taken the dog and gone to the Forum to buy some new clothes to wear in Britannia. I told her she needs to prepare for the cold and damp.'

'And how,' Macro added with feeling. 'And Lucius?'

'He's with his tutor. First day of lessons.'

'How's he finding it?'

'Hating every moment. At least that's what he said when he stopped for a latrine break. He said his tutor is even stricter than Petronella.'

'Bollocks to that,' Macro laughed. 'I've seen her stare down thirty-year veterans and reduce them to quivering piles of shit. She'd have that tutor for breakfast.'

'No doubt. But he seems competent enough. Seneca recommended him to me when I reported to the palace to collect my orders.'

'Seneca? You trust his recommendation?'

'On matters of education and taste, yes. Beyond that, I'd trust him no further than I could shit a stone.'

'Fair enough. Does the good senator know about your volunteers yet?'

'I've told him I have the men I need, and that seemed to satisfy him. With luck, the first he'll know about it is when Ignatius presents his recommendations for replacement officers to Burrus after we've left for Ostia. By then, it'll be too late. I calculate that Burrus is smart enough to accept the list of promotions rather than make a fuss in front of the emperor and reveal that he and Seneca have made fools of themselves.'

Macro tilted his head slightly. 'I hope you've calculated accurately, lad. If you're wrong, you'll end up in the shit. And even if you're right, the same shit may be waiting for when you get back from Sardinia. You'll have made some powerful enemies.'

'Maybe. But Pallas and Agrippina's influence over Nero lasted less than three years, and Burrus and Seneca may go the same way. I sense the emperor is not a man of fixed ambition or direction. He'll tire of his present advisers soon enough, and any enemies I may make today will soon be impotent.'

'Let's pray you're right . . .'

They sat a while longer as the sun disappeared behind a cloud drifting across the cerulean sky and casting a shadow over the garden.

'How are your preparations going for the journey to Britannia?'

'Almost sorted,' said Macro. 'I've loaded the cart with my clothes and kit. Some presents for Petronella to give my mother to butter her up. I've withdrawn my savings from the banker in the Forum, and the military treasury office has given me my discharge bonus certificate. I'm to be paid fifty thousand sestertii once I reach London, plus a plot of land outside the veterans' colony at Camulodunum. Throw in the savings from my campaign spoils and what pay I haven't pissed away over the years, and we'll live well.'

'Have you decided on a route?'

'Ship to Massilia, overland to Gesoriacum, then sail to Britannia and land in Londinium. Should be there well before the autumn storms make the crossing difficult.' Macro grimaced. 'And then I get to introduce the love of my life to my mother. What could possibly go wrong there?'

'I'm sure they'll get on like a house on fire.'

Macro smiled bleakly. 'I'm hoping for a less incendiary relationship, lad. I'm going to have to live with both of them and I ain't looking forward to being a peacekeeper. That's never been my job.'

'Just don't get between them if you value your hide.'

There was a brief silence before Cato cleared his throat. 'When are you leaving?'

'We've got nearly all we need for the journey. I've talked it through with Petronella and she agrees that there's no reason for any delay. So it's tomorrow.'

'That soon?'

'Why put it off? It'll only make it harder to go.'

'Fair enough,' Cato conceded as he looked down at Macro's disturbed reflection on the surface of the pond. There was much he wanted to say, and thought he owed it to Macro to say, but he could not trust himself to control his feelings. That infuriated him. How could he let his emotions have such sway over him? It was shameful that a man of his experience and rank should allow himself to be ambushed by sentiment.

'It's all right, Cato lad. I understand . . . There's nothing that needs to be said between us.'

'What words could convey the adventures we have lived through?'

'True,' Macro reflected. 'If some cunt wrote it all down, who would ever believe it?'

The pre-dawn chill made Cato shiver as he rose from his bed and pulled his cloak tightly about him. There was a sliver of moon visible through the opening in the roof above the colonnaded walkway. Further along he saw the glimmer of a lamp from the room shared by Macro and Petronella and could just make out their muted conversation. There was an unmistakable sadness to the tone of their voices, and Cato turned away and paced quietly in the direction of Lucius's sleeping chamber. The door was slightly ajar, as the boy was convinced there was some dark creature living under his bed, something that necessitated a quick escape from the room should he wake up in the night and need to relieve himself. Cato eased the door open and stepped into the dark interior. His foot landed on one of Lucius's wooden bricks with a sharp, stabbing agony that made him gasp and then clench his teeth together to stop himself crying out and alarming the boy.

'The times I've told him to put those bloody things away,' he muttered as he limped to the bed against the far wall. As he leaned over it, he heard the softest sighs of breathing and felt a surge of boundless affection for his child. He took in Lucius's form, lying on his side, the two middle fingers of his right hand nestled in his mouth as he slept. The sounds of movement and voices elsewhere in the house interrupted the reverie and Cato gently shook his son's shoulder.

'Lucius . . . Lucius . . . wake up.'

The boy mumbled incoherently as he stirred and then tried to turn onto his other side, but his father lifted him up and swung his legs over the side of the bed, and he sat hunched over as he rubbed his face blearily.

'Why did you wake me up?'

'Uncle Macro and Petronella are leaving. We need to say goodbye to them. Get dressed.'

Lucius did as he was told while Cato picked up the sandals that had been cleaned and left outside his door. Yawning widely as he emerged, the boy joined his father and took his hand. The light in Macro's room had been extinguished and only the loom of the stars and the crescent moon lit their way as they went downstairs. Picking their way out into the garden, they made for the yard beyond the bathhouse, where there was a small stable and some storerooms either side of the gate that opened onto the street beyond. A four-wheeled cart stood before the gate, and Croton and the stable boy were harnessing a team of four mules to it by the light of a torch flickering in an iron bracket mounted on the wall. The bed of the vehicle was packed with bags and chests, and Macro was pulling a leather cover over it as Cato and his son approached.

'Ah, there you are!' Petronella cried out as she hurried over and bent to kiss Lucius on the head. 'It feels like the middle of the night, doesn't it, my lamb?'

Cato raised his eyebrows slightly at the term of endearment, which was novel to Petronella. Lucius nodded heavily and yawned again, but his eyes were wide open as he took in the details around him.

'You are going. For ever?'

'I don't know,' Petronella answered. 'We'll be living far from here, but who knows? Maybe you'll come to Britannia when you're grown up. Or we'll come to visit Rome.'

'When?'

'I can't say yet. But one day, eh?'

Macro tied the cover down and inspected his handiwork and the harnesses of the mule team before he joined them. 'We're ready. The stable lad's coming with us as far as Ostia. He'll drive the cart back from there. Thanks for letting us use it.'

'My pleasure.'

There was an awkward silence before Cato placed his hand on Lucius's shoulder. 'We'll come with you to the city wall.'

'You don't have to do that.'

'We want to.'

Macro shrugged. 'As you wish.'

He turned to Croton and called out, 'Open the gate.'

The slave and the stable boy lifted the locking bar and swung the gates inwards on squeaky iron hinges. Then the stable boy picked up his crop, took hold of the lead mule's bridle and looked round for Macro to give the order.

'Let's be off.'

The mules clopped forward and the wheels of the cart ground across the cobbles, the others following a short distance behind, from where Macro could keep a close eye on the rear of the vehicle. The petty thieves of the capital were sharp-sighted and swift enough to snatch spoils faster than a sparrow at a picnic. But the dark streets were still quiet, even as the first squibs of dawn eased their way into the night sky. No one spoke until they reached the junction at the end of the street and turned onto the main thoroughfare that ran down from the Viminal Hill into the centre of Rome. There were more carts and wagons on the move, their drivers keen to get through the city before dawn broke and wheeled traffic was no longer permitted.

From their elevated vantage point they could see that the Forum and the low-lying areas closest to the Tiber were wreathed in a thick mist above which the imperial palace and the Temple of Jupiter seemed to float. Lesser structures broke through the surface of the mist like the remnants of sea wrecks, and the mood was oppressively sombre.

'It's cold,' said Lucius.

'You'll soon warm up,' Macro replied. 'A bit of marching does the job. Ain't that right, Cato? Come on, Lucius, chin up, shoulders back and stride out, just like I taught you.'

The appeal to his nascent military aspirations was all the encouragement the boy needed, and he let go of his father's hand and trotted a few paces ahead, settling into a march, head held high, as he imagined himself at the front of a column of soldiers like Macro and his father.

'He's a fine boy,' Macro said just loudly enough for Lucius to think he was overhearing a remark not directed at him. 'He'll do you proud one day.'

'I'm sure he will.' Cato smiled back. 'I'm certain of it.'

As the stable boy led the small procession down into the Forum, the mist closed around them, cold and clammy, muffling the noises from the mule and cart. Buildings lost form and became obscured masses of shadow looming up on either side, and the handful of people abroad drifted past or across their path like ghosts. Lucius dropped back, glancing anxiously from side to side. They passed between the Palatine and Capitoline hills, and the familiar odour of the great sewer closed in around them until they reached the curved end of the racetrack and began to climb the Aventine Hill, emerging from the mist. Lucius started to relax and marched ahead again as they entered a slum area of crumbling apartment blocks packed closely together. The sounds of people stirring – babies wailing, cries of early-morning passion, the clatter of pots – crowded in from all sides as the light strengthened overhead and clearly delineated the lines of roof tiles against the sky.

Ahead lay the Ostian Gate, guarded by a section from the local urban cohort, soldiers in name only. Macro's expression wrinkled in distaste as he saw them leaning against the stonework either side of the arches, their spears propped up beside them. The optio in command stepped forward and raised his arm.

'Halt!'

The stable boy reined in the mules and the cart ground to a halt. Cato and Macro made their way round it, leaving Petronella and Lucius to watch the back of the vehicle.

'What's your business?' the optio demanded.

'What business is it of yours to question mine?' Macro growled.

'No need for the surly attitude, friend.' The optio spat to one side. 'What's in the cart? Goods?'

'Personal baggage.'

'There's a lot of it . . .'

'I own a lot of personal baggage. What of it?'

'There's a toll for carts and wagons passing through the city gates. Double if they are carrying goods. So that'll be two sestertii, friend.' The optio held out his hand.

'When did this toll come in?' Cato asked.

'Got the orders yesterday. Maybe you missed the announcement? I'd encourage your friend here to stop being difficult and pay up.'

Cato regarded the optio for a moment. He was a thin man, well into his forties, with thinning hair and half his teeth missing. His uniform tunic was frayed and stained and there was rust on the hilt of his sword. There was an opportunistic cockiness in his demeanour that instantly made Cato suspect he was lying about the toll. It was common enough for members of the urban cohorts to top up their pay by demanding bribes or threats. As long as they weren't too egregious about it, most of the inhabitants of the city endured it rather than cause trouble they might regret. Cato was conscious that his son might observe what was going on and that this was an opportunity to teach him a lesson about authority and the abuse of it.

He addressed the man clearly. 'What is your name?'

The optio's jaw tensed. 'What's it to you?'

'My name is Quintus Licinius Cato. I am a member of the equestrian order and a former tribune of the Praetorian Guard. My friend here is a former centurion of the Guard. Neither of us has heard of this toll you speak of. Let me make something clear to you. If we pay and I later discover that no toll has been authorised, I will report the matter to my friends in the Praetorian camp and we will come and find you and exact a toll of our own. One sestertius for every heartbeat you delay us . . .'

The optio stepped aside and waved his arm towards the gate, calling, 'Let them pass!'

Cato nodded to the stable boy, and the cart rolled forward, the sound of hooves and wheels on cobbles echoing harshly off the stonework on either side and overhead as it went through the arch. Outside the city wall lay a sprawl of simple huts and shelters where some of Rome's teeming masses had spilled out. No more than a hundred paces away there was a rise, and Cato ordered the boy to stop there so that they could make their final farewells.

Lucius hugged Macro and Petronella in turn, and she lifted him off the ground and kissed him on the cheek, tears glinting in her eyes.

'You're crying,' said Lucius. 'I'm sad. But I'm not crying, see?'

'That's because you are a brave little soldier.' She forced a smile, kissed him again and lowered him to the ground. 'Be good for your father.'

'I will.'

She turned to Cato and stared at him, struggling to find the words to express her gratitude to her former master for setting her free to marry Macro. In the end she threw her arms round him and buried her face in his shoulder.

'You've been good to me, master. Thank you. I shall never forget.'

Cato could not help chuckling as he eased her back. 'Petronella, it is I who should be thanking you for raising my

Lucius. You've been as good as a mother to him.' A shadow passed across his mind as he recalled his dead wife. Julia Sempronia had been the daughter of a senator. Beautiful and intelligent, she had turned her mind towards plotting against the previous emperor and had died of an illness while Cato was campaigning in Britannia. Her treachery towards Emperor Claudius had been matched by a more personal betrayal of her husband, and the knowledge of her affair with another plotter still scarred him. 'Better than a mother,' he corrected himself. 'For that I will always be grateful.'

Petronella shook her head with embarrassment and retreated, and Cato turned to Macro, his heart burning with painful regret at their parting. Macro stared back, his eyes twinkling.

'Lad, when I first clapped eyes on you, I thought you were the biggest waste of space ever to have joined the Second Legion. You proved me wrong. You've been the best of soldiers, the bravest of fighters and the most loyal of friends. It's going to be a hard parting. I'll try not to worry about you now that you won't have a proper soldier at your side to keep you out of trouble.'

Cato laughed. 'I'll have to manage by myself then.'

Macro regarded him sternly and nodded. 'You'll manage.'

He placed his hands on Cato's shoulders and impulsively drew him close and held him tight.

'Take care, my lad,' he said tenderly.

'And you, brother,' Cato replied, patting his friend's back.

They drew apart and Macro turned to take Petronella's hand while Cato hoisted Lucius onto his shoulders and stood on a weathered block of stone beside the road. The cart rumbled forward again just as the first rays of sun stretched over the hills to the east and flooded across the landscape, bathing it in a warm, rosy hue. The shadows of the stable boy, the mules, the cart and Macro and Petronella stretched across the uneven ground to their right as they headed down the road towards Ostia. A short distance ahead the road dipped down to pass between some trees, and the cart and those with it slipped out of sight until only a faint swirl of dust marked their passage, and then they were gone.

'Will we see them again?' asked Lucius.

'I don't know, son.' Cato turned away to face the city gates. 'I don't know. All we can do is hope that one day we will.'

CHAPTER NINE

'She's waiting for you inside.' Apollonius indicated the praetor's quarters opposite the entrance to the courtyard around which the port officials had their stores and offices. There were hundreds of clerks, merchants and sea captains milling around while they waited for port charges and import tariffs to be calculated and paid, and export licences checked. Apollonius had come to find his commander as soon as Claudia Acte and her modest retinue had arrived in Ostia. Cato had been busy supervising the loading of his baggage onto the cargo ship Seneca's staff had chartered for the crossing to Sardinia. *Persephone* was to sail to Olbia with imperial dispatches before turning south and making for the province's capital of Carales.

Cato was not in the best of moods, having had to field the protests of Rhianarius before Apollonius turned up. The shipowner had spotted him from the quay and demanded to know why Cato had not contracted one of his vessels. The answer was simple enough, Cato responded. When he had reached Ostia, the port's procurator had advised him not to choose Rhianarius's shipping company as there had been a few complaints. Cato started describing them. The shipowner had beaten a hurried retreat before any other potential customers overheard Cato's harangue.

The Praetorian volunteers had turned up shortly before and boarded at once. Cato had promoted Pelius and Cornelius to the rank of centurion, as he would need reliable officers when he reached Sardinia. They were dressed in civilian tunics and cloaks and carried their uniforms, armour and kit in large bags loaded across a small team of rented mules. It was likely that their absence from the Praetorian camp had already been noticed, but by the time Burrus or Seneca learned the truth about the volunteers, it would be too late. If all went well, they would reach Sardinia unchallenged, and if the emperor's advisers attempted to recall the men, Cato was sure he could avoid or delay the need for any response long enough to complete his mission.

He shifted his gaze to the columned entrance and the five covered wagons parked end to end nearby, guarded by several of the emperor's German bodyguards. 'If that's what I think it is, there won't be room on the ship for all her personal baggage and other effects.'

'I'd like to see you tell her that.'

Cato glanced at Apollonius as they strode across the courtyard and weaved through the crowd. 'Have you met her then?'

'Briefly, while I was waiting outside the praetor's office. I told her I was there to escort her to the ship. She cut me off and told me to be silent while she dealt with the praetor.'

'What's the problem?'

'Apparently she felt he had dishonoured her by not having the streets cleared in advance of her retinue. He said he had received no instructions from Rome concerning the protocol for receiving her.' Apollonius laughed. 'Her response to that might be described as magnificent hubris. She is a head shorter than the praetor and somehow still managed to look down at him while she berated him for not treating her according to her station.'

'Her station?' Cato cocked an eyebrow. 'From what I understand, she was born a slave and taken into Seneca's household as a plaything the moment she was old enough for anyone to admire her looks. Even if she was later given her freedom and became the emperor's mistress, that still doesn't cut it on the social status front.'

'I know. She's quite a character. And she behaves as if those German brutes are there to protect her rather than make sure she doesn't slip away. Our Claudia seems to believe that she, rather than Agrippina, is the empress. From what I heard in Rome, she's been badgering Nero to marry her for the past year. All the fine gifts he showered her with weren't enough. She wanted to sit beside him on her own throne. But she overreached herself when she persuaded Nero to ask the Senate to declare that she was of noble birth. I saw for myself how that played out when the senators and the mob turned on her at the races the other day. She wasn't best pleased. Nor were Nero and his advisers. Hence the decision to pack her off to Sardinia and keep her out of sight.'

'Do you think it will be a permanent exile?' asked Cato.

'Nero's a young man. I'd lay good money on him having moved on to a new mistress within the month.'

'So we're going to be stuck with her.'

They entered the praetor's headquarters and Apollonius led Cato upstairs and onto the balustraded walkway that overlooked the courtyard. In the middle was a wide balcony with tall doors leading into the praetor's office. As they entered, Cato looked round and saw that the room was large, airy and well lit. A harassed-looking man in a linen tunic was trying to concentrate on the waxed tablets spread out on his desk. A woman was sitting on a couch against one of the side walls. In front of her was a low table on which rested a finely patterned glass jug and a platter of small pastries, none of which seemed to have been touched.

The woman turned her gaze towards Cato and his companion. Her eyes were dark as ebony and her skin was pale, almost white. Her hair was fine and blond and unstyled, unlike almost every other woman of note in Rome. It had been cut even shorter than when he had seen her in the imperial box at the chariot races, so that it looked boyish. Her face was full, with a snub nose and fine lips. She wore a plain blue stola of a shimmering material; silk most likely, thought Cato. Her arms were slender, as were what he could see of her legs. Her sandals were also blue, with an emerald on the top of each. The stola was sheer enough to reveal a full bust but no obvious curve of the waist above her hips. His overall impression was that while she was undeniably pretty, she did not strike him as the kind of beauty an emperor would consider defying the Senate and people of Rome to marry. Not that Nero had the backbone to see it through.

Claudia Acte glanced at Cato before addressing Apollonius. 'Is he the one you were talking about?' Her accent was neutral, but there was no hiding the hard twang of those raised in the Subura district.

Apollonius forced himself to keep a straight face as he responded in a deferential tone. 'My lady, this is Prefect Quintus Licinius Cato, newly appointed commander of the garrison in Sardinia.'

Cato frowned. 'I can speak for myself, thank you.'

Apollonius glanced sidelong at him and the corners of his mouth lifted in the faintest of smiles as he whispered, 'She's all yours . . .'

Claudia pointed at Cato. 'Then you're the man in charge of the boat taking me to Sardinia. I'll thank you to make sure my baggage is safely loaded. I can assure you that if any of my possessions are damaged by your oafs, I'll hold you responsible.'

Cato felt indignation flaring up inside his chest. He opened his mouth to respond, but she continued before he could get a word out.

'Another thing. I want you to make sure we have some decent wagons to carry me and my belongings when we reach the island. Those that brought me here were little better than broken-down farm carts. I felt every rut we passed over. So you'll find me something decent, and arrange for cushions for me to sit on, is that clear?'

Cato swallowed and took control of his temper. 'Madam, I am a soldier, not a shipping clerk, and I—'

'I don't care what you are. Just do as I say, and do it now.'

He glared back and she raised her eyebrows.

'Well? What are you waiting for? Stop standing there like the town idiot and get on with it.'

He glanced at Apollonius, who was looking at his boots, hiding a smile. The praetor risked a brief raise of his head; he caught Cato's gaze and rolled his eyes.

Cato sucked in a breath and responded as calmly as possible. 'I will see to your baggage personally. Meanwhile, my friend Apollonius will attend to your every wish until I send word that we are ready to sail. Will that be satisfactory?'

Apollonius looked up abruptly. 'What?'

'Now if you will forgive me?' Cato bowed his head politely.

'Very well, you are dismissed. But don't take too long. I don't know how much longer I can bear the privations of this place . . .'

Cato strode out of the room. He heard Apollonius beg her indulgence then hurry after him. They walked along the balcony without uttering a word until they had reached a safe distance, then Cato stopped and turned to his companion. Both men were silent for a beat before breaking into spontaneous laughter.

'Good gods . . .' Cato spluttered as he struggled to recover. 'I never thought I'd ever feel sorry for Nero. But this?'

'I know. A suspicious man might think he secretly paid the mob and the senators to undermine her.'

It was a startling possibility, Cato reflected. It would mean that she had a hold over her lover that he dared not challenge openly. From his observations of Nero it was clear that he was a fickle and weak-willed individual, but to be so suborned by a woman that he promised one thing to her face while plotting to do the opposite behind her back . . . That smacked of cowardice of the lowest kind, if that was his game. To have such a man running the Empire was unnerving.

'She must have some redeeming qualities,' Cato suggested.

'Oh, I'm sure she does.' Apollonius nodded. 'What she may lack aesthetically she might make up for in technique. Such women can play a man like a flute, if you see what I mean.'

Cato shook off the distasteful image his companion had conjured up. 'Well, we're stuck with her and her charming German friends for as long as it takes to escort them to her estate. You keep her occupied while I see to her baggage.'

'Occupied?' Apollonius winced. 'I'm sure the praetor can do that job just as well.'

At that moment the praetor emerged onto the balcony. Glancing round with a stricken expression, he caught sight of them and hurried over. 'For pity's sake,' he hissed, 'get her out of here! Whatever it takes, just do it.'

'How much is it worth?' asked Apollonius.

The praetor examined his face to ensure the offer was genuine. 'Fifty sestertii.'

'Denarii,' Apollonius countered.

Cato did a quick mental calculation: over two months' pay for a legionary.

'Twenty denarii, then.'

'You there!'

The three men turned to see Claudia standing on the threshold of the balcony.

'Why are you standing gossiping instead of carrying out my instructions?'

'Twenty-five denarii,' the praetor hissed.

'Done.' Apollonius winked at Cato. 'I'll lead her a merry chase through Ostia. By the time we reach the ship, she'll be too tired to cause us much trouble.'

'Good. I'll see you later.'

Cato watched as the praetor led the way back to his office like a cowed dog, then he made his way downstairs to deal with Claudia Acte's baggage.

Apollonius was as good as his word, and the emperor's discarded mistress and her retinue boarded the ship late in the afternoon. As Cato watched her picking her way down the narrow gangway, he could not help wishing that she might tumble into the sea. Just before she reached the deck, she began to lean too far to one side, but her hand was caught by one of the German bodyguards and she was delivered deftly to the ship without further trouble.

Her arrival had drawn the attention of crew and passengers alike. Cato was standing towards the stern with the men who had volunteered to come with him.

'So that's the emperor's squeeze.' Centurion Porcino ran his gaze over her. 'Nice. Just my type.'

'That's what you say now . . .' Cato responded quietly.

He made his way forward to greet her with a quick bow of

his head. 'Welcome aboard, my lady. Your baggage has been placed in the hold.'

'Good. I am tired.' She looked round the ship with more disapproval than interest as the last of the Germans came across the gangway and stepped onto the deck with a heavy thud. 'Where is my cabin?'

Cato winced. 'There are no cabins on this ship. We all sleep on deck.'

Behind her he saw the captain give him a meaningful look; Cato nodded discreetly and the captain gave the order to slide the gangway back onto the quay and slip the mooring ropes. As the lengths of rope were coiled fore and aft, several of the crewmen unshipped the sweeps, the long oars used to man-oeuvre the ship into clear water before her sail was raised.

Claudia folded her arms. 'I will *not* sleep on deck.'

It was too late for her to attempt to return ashore, and now that she was confined on the ship for the duration of the voyage, Cato was no longer inclined to pretend obeisance.

'Suit yourself, my lady.'

Her jaw sagged in shock as he turned to rejoin his officers.

'Wait, you!' she called after him. 'I said wait!'

Cato stopped and gritted his teeth, aware that Porcino and the others were watching him with amused expressions, waiting to see how he reacted. He turned slowly back towards her, took her arm and steered her towards the bow of the vessel, away from the others. The ship's boy was sitting at the stem, legs dangling over the side, and Cato jerked his thumb towards the stern. 'Hop it, youngster.'

Claudia tried to pull herself free. 'What do you think you are doing? You'll pay for this outrage.'

Cato tightened his grip and gave her a savage shake. 'Enough!'

Her eyes widened in shock, and there was fear there too, he noted. But she recovered quickly and raised her free hand, pointing it at his face, the tip of her fingernail inches from his nose. 'Wait until Nero hears of this. He'll have you scourged.'

'I sincerely doubt it,' Cato sniffed. 'Let's stop pretending you are some fine lady with all the snooty airs and graces of the aristocracy. You are the cast-off mistress of the emperor and now no more than the freedwoman you were before you were thrust into Nero's eager little arms by Senator Seneca.'

'How dare you?' she spat back. 'I am a woman of means with many powerful friends. You defy me at your peril, soldier. I have but to click my fingers and command my bodyguards to tear you apart and the deed is done.'

Cato gave a loud bark of laughter. 'Your means are merely the baubles the emperor chose to shower on you. That has come to an end. Count yourself lucky that Nero has not taken back all he gave you. Those you call friends have abandoned you, like they do all those who have risen from the mob and whose moment in the sun has passed. Your association with them is only a source of embarrassment to them now. As for your bodyguards, they are not yours to command. They are not even guards; they are your gaolers, no doubt under orders to make sure you don't slip away and return to Rome to beg Nero to take you back. Even so, how do you think you are going to command them? They were chosen for their position because they have no Latin, apart from the decurion in charge. Do you speak their tongue? No? I thought not. Fat chance of you ordering them to do your bidding. I imagine that's the very opposite of the orders they were given before leaving Rome. As for me, I am no soldier. I hold the rank of prefect and my authority extends to every man of the garrison of Sardinia. While you are in my charge, you will do as I say and you will not cause me any trouble.' He stared at her and saw her gaze fall away. 'If you do, I will bind and gag you for the duration of the voyage and the journey to your estate.'

He paused and let his words sink in before he resumed. 'I hope that is all perfectly clear to you, Claudia Acte. Well?'

He felt her tremble within his grip. She nodded meekly and he released her.

'Good. Now keep a civil tongue in your head and I am sure we will get on agreeably. I find that the most comfortable place to sleep on deck is by the mast. I'll have one of my men make something up for you.'

He left her there and returned to his companions at the far end of the ship as the sailors working the sweeps manoeuvred the vessel into the relatively open water shielded from the sea by the breakwater constructed during Emperor Claudius's reign. As soon as he was certain of a clear passage out of the harbour, the captain gave orders to ship the oars, raise the sail and sheet it home. With the taut expanse of patched leather filling like a fat belly, the ship heeled gently. Those unfamiliar with the motion lurched nervously and grabbed the side of the vessel to steady themselves. Cato bit down on his nausea, widened his stance to maintain a good balance and looked forward to where Claudia clasped a shroud with her white hands, clinging on with an alarmed expression.

'She looks positively stricken,' Apollonius commented. 'What did you say to her?'

'I asked her to behave nicely so that we could all get on more easily.'

'I'm not sure I believe such cordiality would produce useful results.'

'What I said was enough, I hope.'

The ship steered towards the gap between the arms of the

mole. As it encountered the swell of the sea, the bows rose gracefully, then eased down with a small burst of spray. Ahead, the late-afternoon sun burnished the waves with hundreds of glittering jewels of dazzling amber and white, and the woman standing at the bow seemed haloed by honeyed light. It was the kind of image that love-struck poets wrote of, thought Cato. Then her face contorted suddenly and she bent her head over the side, her body lurching in a painful retch. Those sailors nearest her hurriedly took a few paces further downwind. So much for poetry, Cato mused.

He turned his gaze towards the horizon, and soon his appreciation of the natural beauty of the open sea gave way to thoughts of the challenges facing him when they reached the island at the end of the short voyage. In truth, he was more anxious than he cared to admit. Without the reassuring presence of Macro at his side, he felt exposed and fearful that he might be found wanting. So far he had enjoyed much success in his army career. Certainly more than he had thought possible in the early days. But his run of luck could not last for ever.

The freshening breeze quickly swept away the cloying odour of Ostia, and the passengers and crew filled their lungs with the salty tang of sea air.

Apollonius lifted his chin and closed his eyes with a blissful expression on his face. 'If the weather holds, we'll have a fine voyage. Just what's needed to blow the cobwebs away!'

'Enjoy it, then,' Cato said gruffly. 'It may be our last chance for a while.'

CHAPTER TEN

Two days later, as dusk settled over the island, the ship approached Olbia under sail. A column of smoke rose from a signal tower on the headland, and was answered by more smoke from further inland. As they sailed cautiously through the narrow channel at the entrance to the harbour, the lookout sitting on the spar astride the mast called down to the deck. 'Boat approaching!'

Some of those closest to the bows lined the rail to watch, while Cato stepped up onto the small steering platform at the stern and shaded his eyes as he squinted into the sunlight. He could make out the quay and its warehouses and the town beyond, and there, halfway between the shore and the ship, he caught sight of a small craft with a triangular sail tacking towards them.

'Bit late for a pilot to guide us in,' mused Apollonius. 'And too late in the day for a fishing boat to be setting out . . . They're definitely coming our way. What can that be about, I wonder?'

Cato gave a non-committal grunt and continued to observe the boat. When it was no more than a hundred paces away, it tacked across the ship's bow and then gybed so that it was running off the starboard beam on a parallel course to the vessel.

Close to, he could see that three men were on board. A sailor stood at the tiller and another worked the sheets; the third man, wearing a dull red military cloak, cupped his hands to his mouth and called across the light swell. 'What vessel is that?'

The captain moved to the side and shouted his reply. '*Persephone*. From Ostia.'

'From Ostia?' the man repeated.

'Aye!'

'Have you landed anywhere on Sardinia since leaving Ostia?'

'No. Who in Hades are you?' the captain demanded.

'Decurion Locullus. I'm coming aboard. Stand by.'

As the small craft edged towards the ponderous cargo ship, the sailors aboard *Persephone* hung a rope boarding ladder over the side. The decurion reached out for the closest rung and grasped it tightly as he jumped across the narrow gap, then climbed up and over the side, thudding onto the deck. He waved the boat off, and Cato and Apollonius went forward to join the captain as he greeted their visitor.

'What's the meaning of this?' the captain demanded. 'I don't take kindly to people boarding my ship without me knowing why.'

Locullus glanced around those on deck, seemingly looking for someone, before his gaze returned to the captain. 'Are any of your crew or passengers showing signs of sickness?'

'Sickness?' The captain frowned. 'What kind of sickness?'

'Fever, coughing, body aches or spasms.'

'No. Nothing like that.'

'Anything else, then? Any sickness of any kind at all?'

The captain gestured to Claudia Acte and the German bodyguards, one of whom was retching over the side, his huge frame convulsing as he moaned miserably. 'Just some of those landsmen who can't cope with the sea. That's all.'

As Cato stepped up beside the captain, he saw the look of relief that flitted across the decurion's face.

'What's going on here?' he demanded.

'Who are you?'

'Prefect Quintus Licinius Cato. I'm here to take up command of the garrison units of Sardinia. Has the governor sent you to meet us?'

Locullus hurriedly saluted. 'My apologies, sir, but I haven't heard about any new appointment. My orders are to escort Claudia Acte to Tibula. Her ship was expected to call here before making for Carales. That has changed now.'

'I take it that has something to do with the pestilence in the south of the island.'

'Aye, sir, and it's spreading quickly. Governor Scurra has abandoned his palace in Carales and shifted the seat of government to Tibula.'

Cato recalled the map of the island he had studied before leaving Rome. He had paid a scribe to make him a copy, which was carefully folded up in his baggage. 'That's at the northern tip of the island, isn't it?'

'About as far north as you can get, sir.'

He exchanged a glance with Apollonius before he lowered his voice and continued. 'Is the situation as bad as that?'

'It's hard to say, sir,' the decurion replied cautiously. 'We had only just begun to see the first cases of the sickness before the governor decided to take ship to Tibula a month ago. Since then we've had reports that over a hundred have died in Carales alone. There have been more deaths in towns and villages as far north as Sarcapos. The governor has given orders for ships entering the island's ports to be inspected for signs of sickness, and forbidden to land if there are any.'

'Sounds serious,' Apollonius commented. 'Have you

114

quarantined any ships at Olbia so far?'

'None, sir. But it's probably only a matter of time.'

The captain sighed irritably. 'But I've got a cargo to unload at Carales, along with these gentlemen and other passengers.'

'We won't be making for Carales,' Cato responded. 'You can land the dispatches and cargo destined for Olbia and then take us to Tibula instead.'

'Now just a moment. I ain't contracted to sail to Tibula. *Persephone*'s bound for Carales.'

'Not any more. Not unless you want to risk the pestilence coming aboard your ship and striking down you and your crew.'

The captain considered this for a moment. 'If we keep clear of those who are sick, I can unload the cargo and load what I need for the return leg.'

Cato shook his head. 'I'm ordering you to take us to Tibula. If you want to risk sailing from there to Carales, that's up to you.'

The seaman folded his brawny arms. 'I'm the captain. My ship. My orders.'

'And I'm the garrison commander. Moreover, I have more men on this vessel than you do. I suggest you do as I tell you,' Cato concluded firmly.

The captain looked around the deck at his sailors, who had been watching the exchange, then at Cato's Praetorians and the German bodyguards. He weighed up the situation and gave a reluctant nod. 'As you request, Prefect. We'll sail for Tibula at first light.'

They exchanged a nod before the captain paced towards the stern and joined the helmsman to oversee the approach to Olbia.

'He's not a happy man,' Apollonius observed with an amused expression.

'He'll be unhappier still if he continues to Carales and exposes himself to the sickness. But that's his lookout.' Cato glanced to where Claudia was sitting on a coiled rope, resting her chin in her hands as she stared over the starboard beam at the low-lying landscape creeping by. He braced himself. 'I guess I'd better inform my lady that we won't be landing at Carales.'

'You could always leave her onboard for the final leg,' Apollonius suggested with relish.

'Sure, and if anything happens to her, I'll let you explain that to Nero,' Cato replied.

Claudia looked round as he approached, the German guards moving aside to let him by. 'Who is that man who came aboard?'

'One of the governor's officers.' Cato sat on the side rail and took hold of one of the stays before he continued. 'I'm afraid I have some bad news for you. We won't be sailing for Carales.'

'Oh?' Her dark eyes narrowed. 'Why not?'

'It's not safe. The south of the island has been hit by sickness. The governor has moved to Tibula, so that's where we are headed now. I dare say the governor will be happy to accommodate you until it is safe for you to be taken to one of your estates.'

'That's one way of describing a prison.'

Cato took in her hunched shoulders and air of despondency. She had been almost silent since he had pierced her haughty veneer two days earlier. 'There are worse places to be imprisoned.'

'And you would know?'

'Yes.'

'Easy for you to say,' she sniffed. 'A high-and-mighty prefect, born with a silver spoon in your mouth and raised with every

116

comfort that an aristocratic household can afford. I know your type well enough. What would you know of prisons and hardship?'

Cato regarded her for a moment and felt a stab of pity. 'Claudia, my father was an imperial freedman. I was born a slave, as you were.'

She sat up and looked him over, as if seeing him for the first time. 'You were a slave once? I don't believe it.'

'Why would I lie about such a thing? I am proud of all that I have achieved, but I have never forgotten where I came from. Any more than you have, despite your closeness to the emperor.'

She gave a bitter laugh. 'Close enough for him to fuck, but no closer than that as it turned out. And now it is likely I will live out the rest of my life as an exile.'

'I can't help that. I am just saying that you shouldn't feel sorry for yourself. There are countless people in Rome, free-born as well as slaves and former slaves, who would give almost anything to change places with you right now.'

Claudia folded her hands together and pursed her lips. 'Perhaps you are right.'

'I usually am.' Cato smiled at her. 'I have been told by some that it's an annoying characteristic.'

'I am sure it could be.' She smiled back.

He eased himself off the side rail. 'I need to let the commander of your escort know the change of plan . . . You'll be fine.'

He turned to where the optio in command of the Germans was dozing, a wineskin in his lap.

'Prefect?'

He glanced back and saw her nod to him.

'Thank you for being honest with me about your past.'

CHAPTER ELEVEN

The ship landed at Tibula a day later. Leaving his men with orders to remain aboard *Persephone* to forestall any temptation for the captain to put to sea in his absence, Cato went ashore with Locullus and they made their way through the streets to a large colonnaded structure built above the harbour. It was surrounded by a wall high enough to keep people out but not to withstand any attack. Beyond rose the boughs of the poplars, cedars and pines in the gardens that ran down from the terraces at the back of the palace. If this was an occasional residence of the governor, Cato could only guess at the opulence of the accommodation in Carales.

As they approached the auxiliary-sentries at the gate, he took in the easy ambience of the other people in the street. News of the sickness had surely reached the town, but there was little evidence of concern as yet. It was a fine, warm evening, and families were sitting on the steps of their houses chatting with neighbours and passers-by. Cato felt a chill of foreboding.

Locullus exchanged a salute with the duty optio at the palace gate and the two men went inside. A paved path shaded by cedars led to the entrance of the building, and swifts darted between the trees as they snatched insects from the air. Locullus escorted Cato through to the wide terrace that extended across the rear of the palace. A large awning had been erected at one end beneath which several scribes bent over their work at tables either side of a large desk. The chair behind it was empty, but a short distance beyond, a corpulent man with a shock of fine blond hair, whom Cato took to be the governor, was reclining on a couch overlooking the harbour as he talked to a thin, balding adviser with an intense gaze that made him look slightly deranged. The latter stared coldly at Locullus as the decurion approached with Cato at his shoulder.

'Yes?'

'Beg to report, the ship entering the harbour is from Ostia.' That the comment was directed at the adviser rather than the governor was not missed by Cato.

'Who is this?'

Cato cleared his throat and made his reply to the governor. 'I am Prefect Quintus Licinius Cato, appointed commander of all military forces on the island.'

The adviser frowned. 'I assume you have proof of your appointment.'

Scurra turned to look at Cato with puffy, watery eyes. 'Well?'

Cato reached into his sidebag and took out a leather tube. He eased the cap off, extracting the scroll detailing the scope of his authority and sealed with the imperial ring. This he handed to the governor, who unrolled it and read through the document as his adviser leaned over his shoulder to see the contents for himself. Scurra handed the scroll back. 'It seems to be in order.'

'We should check all the same,' said the adviser. 'It is highly unusual for a governor's authority to be superseded in this fashion. Shall I draft a letter asking for confirmation, sir?' The tone of his voice belied the interrogative import of his words, and Cato could not help wondering who was really in charge.

Scurra shrugged. 'All right then. As you, ah, ah, ah, think best. Now then, Prefect, it's a pleasure to meet you.' He stood up with some effort and faced Cato. 'No need to introduce myself. Everyone in Rome knows me.' He grinned. 'Life and soul of any party. As you probably know, eh?'

'I'm sorry, sir, but I have been away from the capital for a while. I don't recall having the pleasure of meeting you before now.'

'Oh?' Scurra frowned with disappointment. 'But I, ah, ah, I'm sure you know me by reputation at least.'

Cato shook his head.

'No?' The governor looked positively pained and slumped back onto his couch. 'No matter. I imagine you've been sent here to sort out those troublemakers hiding in the interior.' He clenched his chubby hands into fists and play-acted a few punches. 'Knock some sense into the scoundrels! Send 'em packing.'

'Well, yes. Quite. If you could brief me on the situation as soon as possible, I'd appreciate it.'

'Of course. Good idea. Decianus Catus here can deal with that. He's my top adviser and major-domo rolled into one. Isn't that right?'

Decianus forced a smile that did not go any further than his lips, and bowed his head. 'As you command, Excellency. I can do that after we conclude the business we were discussing before we were interrupted.'

Scurra shook his head. 'No, I've done enough work for the day. Bored now. We'll pick it up again in the morning, eh? You take the prefect off and get it done in your office or somewhere. There's a good fellow.' He waved them away with one hand while he caught the eye of a slave and beckoned with the other. 'Fetch me some more wine!'

His adviser snapped his waxed slate shut and strode towards the nearest arch leading into the building. 'This way. You will not be needed, Decurion.'

Locullus stiffened at the curt dismissal and turned to march off along the terrace, the stiffness of his posture eloquent expression of his resentment.

Even though Cato had set foot on the island less than an hour before, he was already having grave doubts about those tasked with ruling the place and maintaining order. There were plenty of senators who made fine governors, dedicated to the task entrusted to them. Scurra was not one of them. He belonged to a lesser breed of aristocrat who used family prestige and wealth to secure appointments to lucrative positions of power. The kind of men who cut deals with tax farmers to squeeze as much revenue out of a province as possible before their time in office came to an end. They cared nothing for those they ruled over, only for themselves.

Decianus did not stride so much as strut as he led the way through the arch into a large chamber where two long tables were piled with waxed tablets and scrolls. There was a clear space at one end with some chairs close by. He tossed the slate he was carrying onto the table and pulled up a chair for himself before nodding to Cato. 'Sit down, Prefect.'

His peremptory manner infuriated Cato. It was not that he placed much store in the difference between their social rank. He judged men by their deeds, not their lineage. What rankled was the adviser's arrogance and his unwillingness to conceal it. He paused a beat to calm himself, and considered refusing to sit. Only that would make him look like a man standing before a seated superior. Round one to Decianus, he conceded sourly, dragging a chair over and sinking onto it.

'What are your orders exactly?' asked Decianus.

'They're straightforward enough. The emperor and his advisers are concerned by reports that have reached Rome about the failure to contain some of the tribes of the interior of the island. They are understood to be raiding farming estates and even some of the towns on the coast. Nero wants to put a stop to that and has ordered me to pacify the island. To which end I have been granted full control over the garrison.'

'I see. And what makes you think we haven't got the situation in hand already?'

'Well, have you?'

Decianus's lips twitched irritably. 'We were dealing with it, and would have had the brigands under control if it wasn't for this pestilence causing the governor to uproot himself from the provincial capital and drag us all to the opposite end of the island.'

'I'm sure,' Cato responded flatly. 'But now that I am here, you can concentrate on dealing with the sickness and let me attend to the enemy.'

The freedman weighed the suggestion up. 'By all means, once we have confirmation from Rome that you are who you say you are and have the authority you claim you were given.'

'You saw the document for yourself. You saw the imperial seal. Let's not waste time referring the matter back to Rome. Meanwhile, if you attempt to deny my authority, or undermine it, then I will deal with you first, the bandits second.' Cato held up the leather case. 'I dare say the commanders of the garrison cohorts on the island will be willing to accept this, so let's not play games. After all, we are supposed to be on the same side, aren't we?' He smiled sweetly. 'First thing. What caused this outbreak of brigandage?'

'There has always been some trouble on the island as long as it has been a Roman province. Most of the time it's not much of a problem; cattle raiding and so on. The garrison sends patrols out to try and track the perpetrators down, but they know the interior of the island better than anyone else and can disappear into the forests and hills and hide there until our soldiers abandon the hunt.'

'Aren't there any local guides who can lead you to their settlements?'

'None of the people of the coastal tribes know the brigands' territory well enough to help us.'

'What about offering a reward for someone from the tribes supporting these brigands?'

Decianus sneered. 'Don't you think that's been tried? Just about every other barbarian race we have encountered would be willing to sell their people out if the reward is high enough. But not this lot. They're different.'

Cato leaned closer. 'Different?'

'First off, they are utterly loyal to their chiefs and hostile to outsiders. And that's how they still see Romans, let alone the other tribes, even two hundred years after we took over the island. They'd sooner kill their firstborn than betray any of their own to us. Even when the tribes turn on each other, or when they're playing out some ongoing feud. The other islanders refer to them as "the ancient ones".'

'How so?'

'They were here long before Rome took the island from the Carthaginians. They date further back than any written history; I don't suppose even they know how long their people have been here. Though they have left plenty of traces across the island. I'd guess they were once a rich and powerful people, but you'd never know that from the small number of them that remain. You'll see their carvings on rocks, and from time to time the strange figures they cast in silver and sometimes gold.

They're primitive items, childish to our eyes maybe. But they make interesting additions to the collections of the wealthy back in Rome. The most obvious signs of the power they once had are the towers and forts they left behind. Hundreds of them remain throughout the island. They look like they might once have served a military purpose, but they could be some kind of temple. Most were abandoned long ago and little but ruins remain. But our patrols report that some of them are still used as strongholds.'

'What are these tribesmen like, these "ancient ones"?'

'You'll see for yourself when you encounter them. They look more animal than human. They wear the fleeces of sheep and other beasts and have strange headgear with horns, and masks with twisted features that look like . . . like demons.'

'Demons,' Cato repeated with a chuckle. 'And have you come across any of these demons yourself?'

'Not a living example. There was one who was washed up on the banks of a river near Carales. His body was brought to the governor's palace. Aside from the strange clothing, his skin was almost covered with tattoos.' A look of contempt formed on Decianus's face. 'Bloody barbarian animals . . . They should have been wiped out centuries ago when we took the island from Carthage.'

'Why weren't they?'

'Like I said, they never caused enough trouble. As long as Sardinia produced enough trade and taxes to keep Rome happy, the Senate, and then the emperors, saw no reason to divert the necessary troops to the island to put an end to the problem.'

Cato reflected on this briefly. It was the same in many of the provinces. Small bands of brigands eked out a precarious existence where Rome's forces were too thinly spread. As long as they remained more of a nuisance than a threat to Roman control, there was little desire to waste resources destroying them. Occasionally, such brigands made the mistake of being too ambitious to be ignored.

'Do you know who is leading them?' Cato asked.

'Not exactly. Only rumours, as you'd expect given how remote they are. There's talk of a man who calls himself King of the Mountains. They say he has united most of the brigands, and the tribes that support them. That has made it almost impossible for our patrols to operate in the inland areas he controls. And that's how things will remain until this man overreaches himself, or Rome eventually decides to deal with him.'

'Well, they have now. That's why I am here.'

Decianus gave a contemptuous laugh. 'Do you imagine you are the first man given the task? There have been attempts in the past, but they've all failed due to the lack of sufficient soldiers to do the job. Let me ask you something. How many men have been assigned to your command over and above the cohorts already stationed here?'

Cato leaned back. 'I have brought a cadre of good men to improve the training and morale of the garrison units. They'll make a difference.'

'Really? How many men exactly?'

'Six in all.'

'Six . . . Good luck with that.'

Cato felt his temper rising again and struggled to resist the urge to put the freedman in his place. 'What is the strength of the island's garrison?'

The other man concentrated briefly. 'Three cohorts of auxiliaries. The Fourth Illyrian under Prefect Tadius at Tibula, Vestinus's Sixth Gallic at Tharros, and Bastillus's Eighth

Hispanic at Carales. The Tharros cohort has a cavalry contingent. Then there's the naval squadron at Olbia. Two biremes and a handful of liburnians, which are supposed to cover the trade routes either side of Sardinia and Corsica. Including the marines and sailors I'd say there are no more than two thousand men in all. Two thousand and seven, now that you have arrived.'

Cato ignored the jibe. 'What condition are they in?'

'All the cohorts are under strength and they have been stationed here for long enough that hardly any of them have any campaign experience. Many of them are spread amongst the outposts that surround the interior. They've done a decent enough job of patrolling the roads and keeping the bandits at bay, until recently.'

'What has changed?'

'Two years of failed crops and the hunger that goes with it. The bandits and the tribes they come from suffered the consequences along with everyone else. So they took action and started attacking the farming estates, taking what they wanted from the granaries and storehouses, and looting the villas. When one of their stragglers was captured by a patrol, Scurra decided to make an example of him and he was crucified on a rock overlooking Bosa. After that, the bandits began killing people. Romans mostly. Tax collectors were the obvious target.'

'When aren't they?'

'True, but then they targeted the estate stewards and any owners who were living in their villas. Their friends in Rome and those with property in Sardinia demanded action. Especially when the bandits burned their buildings to the ground and released the slaves. Some of those have joined the brigand bands.'

'Dare I ask if taxes have been raised since the famine began?'

Decianus regarded him with sour cynicism. 'Of course.

126

How else were we supposed to make up the shortfall in revenue?'

'And it did not occur to the governor to make up the difference from his own resources rather than give the tribesmen one more reason to become brigands?'

'You know how it goes, Prefect. Scurra's term of office comes to an end in eight months' time. He's done well out of the contracts he sold to tax farmers. He'll return to his estate near Capua and live in comfort, and the troubles here will become the problem of the next governor.'

'What about you?'

'I'll find a new master to serve. The next governor, or some other Roman aristocrat with sufficient avarice to appreciate my services.'

Cato scrutinised him. 'You're not too fond of Scurra, then?'

'He pays well and is smart enough to understand that I am indispensable to him. In return I am a loyal servant. The arrangement suits us both.'

'I see . . . So Scurra has done nothing to soften the blow of the famine. He's made the situation worse by allowing the tax farmers to make even more demands on the people of the province. I have barely enough men to maintain order, let alone crush the brigands, and now there's the pestilence to complicate matters. How did that start?'

'Who knows? It might have been caused by the bad air in the marshes outside Carales. It might have come in one of the ships that landed there. It's possible that it may be some kind of judgement from the gods. Scurra paid for a bull to be sacrificed to Phoebus to protect us from any further sickness.'

'We can see how well that worked.'

'Be careful, Prefect. Such impiety is often punished by the gods.'

Cato shrugged. 'I'll take my chances. What measures did Scurra take to deal with the pestilence?'

'Besides the sacrifice? Not much,' Decianus admitted. 'What can a man do but look out for himself? Scurra's personal physician advised that we should all take a regular potion made up of vinegar, mustard and the urine of a young boy.'

Cato gave a dry laugh. 'That's a new one! How did it work out?'

'I'm still here, aren't I? Maybe you should try it.'

There was no point in arguing about that, Cato conceded, though he was more than a little sceptical about the efficacy of the potion Decianus had described.

'Thank you, but I'll give that a miss for now. Is there anything else I should know about?'

Decianus stroked his jaw and his thin lips lifted in mild amusement. 'I think that's enough to contend with as it is, Prefect. What are your plans for dealing with the brigands?'

Cato considered the question in the light of the information he had been given. 'I'll set up my headquarters at Tharros and manage the campaign from there, since I don't want Scurra, or you, breathing down my neck. I'll summon the garrison commanders and then make my plans for dealing with the brigands.'

'What makes you think you'll succeed where others have failed? Have you considered relinquishing your appointment, returning to Rome and leaving this all to me and Scurra to deal with?'

'Believe me, I wish I had the luxury of such a choice.'

The freedman's eyes fixed on him intently. 'You were forced into this?'

Cato saw the potential danger at once and cursed himself for revealing information that Decianus might be able to use against him. A report sent back to Rome detailing any setbacks that could be attributed to Cato would find a sympathetic ear from the likes of Burrus. He cleared his throat and quickly redirected the conversation. 'Those grumbling estate owners you mentioned. There happens to be one of them on the ship that brought me here from Ostia.'

'Indeed? And who might that be?'

'Claudia Acte.'

'The emperor's mistress? I knew Nero had granted her some property on the island, but why would she leave Rome to visit her estates?'

'Your information is out of date, Decianus. She is no longer Nero's mistress. In fact she has been sent into exile to live out her days on the finest of her properties. Near Biora, I believe.'

'I know the villa. I handled the documents transferring it from the imperial holdings into her name. It's a pity . . .'

'What is?'

'The brigands attacked her estate shortly before we left Carales. Torched the place. There's nothing left but ruins.'

'They burned my estate down?' Claudia's hazel eyes stared at him intently as she sat in the shade of an awning that had been rigged over the stern of the ship. Tibula was falling astern as *Persephone* surged across the sea on a westerly course, driven on by a strong breeze that filled her sail in a taut bulge.

'I'm afraid so,' Cato confirmed.

'Is there nothing left of it?'

'Not according to the governor's adviser.'

'Then where am I supposed to go? What's to become of me?'

'Do you have any other property on the island?'

She considered this for a moment and shook her head. 'Nothing suitable. A modest villa near Tharros, that's all.'

'Then you can live there until the brigands are put in their place. Once they've been dealt with, your estate can be rebuilt and you can live out your exile in comfort.'

She regarded him with disdain. 'Are you saying I should live in something little better than a common barn until those Sardinian dogs are brought to heel? Me?'

Cato felt a familiar irritation at the woman's arrogance. His patience was wearing thin thanks to the mounting frustrations of his assignment.

'I doubt it will come down to living in a barn.' He was in no mood to indulge her. 'Be satisfied you have any place at all to call your home.'

He turned and marched away along the deck, more anxious than ever to see the voyage come to an end so that he could be rid of the infernal woman. He even felt a small measure of pity for Nero. No wonder the emperor had been persuaded to turn his mistress into an exile.

CHAPTER TWELVE

The fort of the Sixth Gallic Cohort had been built on rising ground originally a quarter of a mile from the port at Tharros, but like so many long-established settlements, buildings had spilled outside the town walls and spread almost as far as the fort. There was a thin strip of bare ground before the ditch and rampart, and the closest civilian houses were within arrowshot of the walls and turrets. Only two sentries were visible as Cato and his party approached on foot. The gates were wide open and unmanned.

'What the fuck are they playing at?' Centurion Plancinus demanded. 'An enemy could walk right by those dozy bastards and they wouldn't blink.'

'They need a kick up the arse,' Metellus growled.

Apollonius nodded. 'Just as well you fellows are here to deliver it. It should make for some entertainment. A quality that appears to be rather lacking in the province, from what I've seen so far.'

It was true, Cato thought. Even Tharros, the largest of the towns, boasted only the most modest of arenas, and no theatre. There was a market and a number of small taverns surrounding it, but the place had none of the bustle and edge of the streets of Rome. Even the handful of temples and bathhouses seemed neglected and underused. The large houses in the town and the villas that could be seen in the countryside nearby revealed that some enjoyed the island's wealth, but it was likely that many of the fine homes were the property of absentee owners in Rome whose concern for the island extended no further than the profits derived from it.

In contrast to the quiet town, the port itself was busy. Most of the ships plied their trade between the island and the coast of Hispania, while others worked the routes from the coast of Africa and Gaul. Large warehouses lined the quay. Until recently, many of them had been filled with Sardinian grain and oil ready to be exported, but due to the famine and brigandage, there was little stock left, and what remained was under guard to prevent the locals from stealing it.

Persephone had moored at noon, and Cato had immediately led his party ashore to take charge of the garrison. Now they marched across the causeway and under the arch of the gate-house unchallenged. Tufts of grass were growing along the foot of the gates' timbers, proof that they had not been closed for many months. Inside the fort, the barracks and stables appeared to be well maintained, but there was little sign of activity. They could hear snatches of conversation from within and caught sight of men through open doors as they strode past, but none emerged to challenge them. The nearer of the two sentries on the wall paused to watch them for a moment and then continued his beat.

Plancinus glanced from side to side. 'I could take this fort single-handed,' he muttered.

Cato was too furious to respond, his lips pressed tightly together as the party continued in the direction of the cohort's headquarters at the heart of the fort. Ahead of them two men in unbelted tunics emerged from between the long barrack blocks and stopped and stared at the approaching officers.

'You there!' Plancinus bellowed, thrusting his vine cane in their direction. 'Stand to attention!'

The auxiliaries shuffled their boots together and stood erect, shoulders back, chests out. They continued to stare at Cato and the others.

'Eyes front, damn you!' Plancinus bellowed. He trotted up to them and jerked his chin forward so that no more than a hand's breadth separated their faces. 'What the bloody hell do you call this state of undress? Where are your belts? Your swords?'

As the taller of the two started to stammer some excuse, the centurion snatched a breath and shouted, 'What's that I smell? Wine? Wine! You stink of it. Are you drunk, soldier?'

'N-no, sir. Leastways, we've had a drink and—'

'Shut your mouth! I don't want to have to breathe the air of whatever brothel you've crawled out of! Do you understand? Nod, you bastards. I swear if one of you opens his hole again, I will ram my vine cane so far down your throat you'll be shitting splinters for a month!'

Both men nodded quickly.

'Good. Now get back to your section room and get kitted up. Next time I see you, I want you to be at the gates, and they are to be closed securely. If there is any filth on your tunic, if your helmets are not gleaming, if there is rust on your swords, then by all the gods, I'll feed your bollocks to the first dog that trots past the gate. Got it?'

They nodded again.

'Good. Now fuck off.'

As the two men ran back the way they had come, Plancinus turned and rejoined Cato and the others, a wicked grin on his face. 'Start as we mean to go on, eh, sir?'

133

'Indeed. From the look of things, we're going to have some way to go before this cohort is ready for what's coming.'

They continued, passing a large wagon outside an empty workshop, beyond which was the headquarters building. A single auxiliary stood at the entrance, leaning on the shaft of his javelin as he half dozed in the bright sunshine. As he turned towards the crunch of boots on gravel, he blinked and then stood stiffly.

Cato spared him a brief nod as he strode through the arch into the courtyard, where grass and weeds were growing in the gaps between the flagstones. Apollonius noticed his angry expression and smiled. 'Quite the horticulturalists, aren't they?'

'I will have them on their hands and knees picking out every last blade of grass and strand of weed before the day is out,' Cato responded sourly. 'It's a long time since I saw such a shambles.'

'Looks like there might be some entertainment to be had here after all.'

'For you maybe. Not for me, nor my officers, and certainly not for this shower of layabouts who pretend to be soldiers.'

There were a handful of men sleeping in the shade of the colonnade running around the courtyard, and Cato turned to Plancinus and gave him a nod before entering the headquarters building. After the bright sunlight outside, the interior was gloomy, and he paused beyond the threshold as his eyes adjusted. Behind him, Plancinus began to bawl at the sleeping men, alerting those within to turn towards the officers standing at the entrance. Cato could make out two clerks rising from their stools. A third slumbered on, head resting on folded arms as he snored. A quick prod from one of his companions caused him to stir with a grumble. Then he saw the crested helmets and hurriedly stood up.

'Where's the commander of the cohort?' Cato demanded.

The men glanced at each other before one of them cleared his throat and spoke. 'Centurion Massimilianus is in his quarters, sir.'

'I don't want Massimilianus; I want to speak to Prefect Vestinus.'

'The prefect's not here, sir.'

'Well, go and find him and bring him to me.'

'Sir, he's in Carales.'

Cato sighed impatiently. 'What is he doing there?'

'That's where he spends most of his time, sir. He only comes back to Tharros every other month.'

'I see. Then go and fetch Massimilianus. Tell him his new commander wishes to speak to him. At once.'

'Yes, sir.' The clerk saluted and hurried past the officers and out into the sunlight.

Cato dismissed the rest of the clerks and then turned to Apollonius and the others. 'Gentlemen, it seems the task before us is more challenging than I thought. We need this cohort to be ready for campaigning in the interior as swiftly as possible. While I introduce myself to Massimilianus, I want you centurions to pay a visit to each barrack block. Turn them over. Make as much noise as you can, and get the men formed up on the parade ground outside the fort. Then we'll see what kind of material we're working with.' He smiled at them. 'Off you go. Have fun, and let them be in no doubt that they're going to have to start earning their pay from now on. Officers and men alike. Go.'

As Plancinus and the others turned and marched out of the building, Apollonius turned to Cato. 'What about me? What role do you intend me to play in your plans?'

'Back in Rome, you told me that I had a promising career

135

ahead of me. I'm not so sure. But if you're right, you're going to have to earn your place at my side, just like the men of this cohort. There will be no free rides for anyone. Including you.'

'I didn't imagine I would be given special treatment, Prefect Cato,' Apollonius responded in a frosty tone.

Cato felt a moment's satisfaction that he had found a chink in the man's armour. The smooth, unflappable persona Apollonius presented to the world masked a fierce pride and sense of integrity, it seemed. Unless, of course, he was playing another role . . .

'I will have cause to deploy some of your special talents when we take the struggle to the brigands. I will be in need of a man who can move through enemy territory unnoticed and report back on their location and numbers. A man who can kill without raising the alarm. Moreover, I need you to find men you can train to develop the same skills. Can you do that?'

Apollonius stared at him in silence and then nodded. 'I've not trained other men before, but I can do it.'

'Good.'

'But I will need a free hand. You must let me pick the men and train them as I see fit.'

'Very well.'

'And if any of those men come to harm, I will not be held accountable. My skills are hard won. I didn't come by them easily or painlessly. Nor will those men I choose. Some will fall along the way. Fall hard. You understand?'

'I understand. It's time we brought you into our fold and gave you an army rank. And the pay that goes with it.'

'The pay I will take, but not the rank. Never the rank. I have no desire to be part of the army. I lack the necessary appetite for formal discipline and the willingness to take orders from others.'

'You have taken orders from me in the past. I will need you to do the same again.'

'I chose to obey your orders because they were practicable. If you had ordered me to do something foolhardy, I would have refused. No man is my master, even if they make the mistake of thinking they are.'

'I see.' Cato met his stare unflinchingly. 'There will almost certainly be a time when I give you an order that places your life in danger. And you will obey that order.'

'I have no fear of danger. Otherwise I would not have chosen the life I have. By all means order me to chart a perilous course; I will pursue it to whatever end it leads. But I will not follow a foolish order. I have come to know you well enough to understand that you are not one of those officers who play games with the lives of others. I trust your judgement, and I respect you. I do not say those things lightly, Prefect Cato.'

Cato weighed the other man's words carefully. It was possible that he was speaking the truth. Equally it was possible that he knew Cato well enough to attempt to appeal to his pride, but only after having won his respect, so that he might be more inclined to take praise at face value. Trying to follow the agent's line of reasoning was starting to twist Cato's mind and make his head hurt. Perhaps it was better to trust the man's actions rather than his motivations. After all, in the end it was deeds not thoughts that counted. Besides, such a teleological approach to his notional subordinate was easier to cope with. By the gods, he thought, had it come to that? Had his association with Apollonius caused him to twist his words into such tortuous sentences? He refocused his mind and cleared his throat.

'Very well. We understand each other.'

A movement caught his eye and he glanced round to see the clerk hurrying across the courtyard, accompanied by a centurion who was fastening the buckle of his sword belt over his scale armour vest. He was a short, wiry man, Cato observed, his grey hair fast receding around a thin, angular face and his expressive eyes were dark. As they entered the building, he and the clerk stood to attention and saluted.

'Centurion Massimilianus reporting, sir.'

Cato wagged a finger. 'At ease. My name is Prefect Quintus Licinius Cato. I have been appointed by the emperor to put down the brigands operating in this province. My authority exceeds that of the governor with respect to all military matters. That means that every soldier, marine and sailor on the island is answerable to me until my task has been achieved. Do you understand?'

Massimilianus took this in and nodded. 'Yes, sir.'

Cato gestured towards Apollonius. 'This is my, ah, master of scouts. He holds no official rank but he is to be treated as if he is a senior centurion.'

If Centurion Massimilianus had any reservation about the role of Apollonius, he was wise enough to keep his thoughts to himself and his expression neutral as he responded. 'Yes, sir.'

Apollonius tilted his head to one side. 'Master of scouts? That's a title I can live with.'

'Then let's hope you survive long enough to do so.' Cato turned his attention back to the centurion. 'I understand you are the senior centurion of the Sixth Gallic Cohort.'

'Yes, sir.'

'I take it that Prefect Vestinus is not much of a fixture at the fort.'

'Sir?'

'From what I have already gathered, the prefect prefers to spend most of his time in Carales.'

The centurion glanced quickly at the clerk standing beside him, but the latter continued to look fixedly ahead.

'Well?' Cato raised an eyebrow.

'Vestinus has frequent business in Carales, sir. I am supposed to be in command in his absence.'

'Frequent business?' Apollonius chuckled. 'Personal or pecuniary?'

'It's not for me to say . . . sir.'

'But you do know,' he probed. 'Don't you?'

There was a silence while the centurion struggled to compose a reply that did not drop his superior in trouble. That, at least, was a quality Cato could admire. All the same, he needed to know what Vestinus's game was in order to assess whether the prefect was going to be useful or a hindrance.

'I will find out one way or another, Massimilianus. You can either stall me now, for which I will not be forgiving, or you can tell it straight and save me wasting time having to find out for myself. What'll it be?'

The centurion made the decision with commendable speed. 'The prefect bought an estate outside Carales a year back, sir. He has salt pans on his land and exports to Rome. His family lives there as well.'

'Ah!' Apollonius chuckled. 'Pecuniary *and* personal. I was almost right.'

Cato's expression remained stern as he glared at Massimilianus. 'Then you are the one responsible for the condition of this fort. No?'

'I would be, sir, if the prefect did not insist on having me refer every decision on the running of the cohort to him in person.' The bitterness in the man's tone was unmistakable.

'Every decision?'

'I can barely take a shit without having to request permission in writing, sir.'

Apollonius intertwined his fingers and thrust his hands down

139

to crack the joints. 'Clearly the prefect is a man who likes to wield effluence from afar. Doesn't strike me as the best way of exercising his responsibilities.'

'No,' Cato said curtly. 'It won't do. Not at all. Clerk!'

The man stepped forward. 'Sir.'

'Send a message to Vestinus. Tell him I want him to return to the fort at once. What's the quickest means of getting the message to him?'

'By sea, sir. Coasters come and go almost every day.'

'Then draft the summons so I can attach my seal and then get it on the first vessel heading for Carales. Move!'

The clerk scurried to his desk, pulled out a tablet and set to work. Cato strode out of the building into the courtyard. 'Apollonius, Massimilianus, on me.'

They fell into step as they crossed the enclosed space, baking in the sunshine. From beyond the walls of the building came the sounds of shouts and the drumming of boots.

'I've ordered my officers to get the cohort to form up on the parade ground,' Cato explained to the centurion.

'Your officers, sir?'

'That's right. I've brought some good men with me from the Praetorian Guard. They're here to kick the garrison troops into shape so we can put an end to the brigands on this island.'

'Good . . .' Massimilianus grunted. 'It's about time.'

Cato shot him a quick glance and saw the glint in the centurion's eye. 'How long have you served with the Sixth Gallic?'

'Two years, sir.'

'And before that?'

'Twentieth Legion, sir. I was an optio. I was wounded on campaign in Britannia and got a promotion to centurion of

140

auxiliaries. Can't say it turned out to be the best decision I ever made.'

'Britannia, eh?' Cato smiled at him for the first time. 'That was where I cut my teeth. Second Legion.'

'You'll have been one of Vespasian's lads then? Fine unit that. Saved our arses outside Camulodunum when Caratacus set his trap for us.' Massimilianus's brow furrowed as he recalled the close-fought battle. 'It's an honour to serve with an officer of the Second Legion, sir.'

'I wasn't an officer back then. Just a freshly minted optio.'

Massimilianus gave him a searching look and thought a moment before he continued. 'You've done very well for yourself, sir. From optio to prefect in not much over ten years. Not bad at all.'

They marched out onto the fort's main thoroughfare and followed the last of the auxiliaries jogging towards the eastern gate and the parade ground beyond. As they approached the gate, Cato heard the sound of horses' hooves pounding along the baked earth and turned to see fifty or so riders emerging from the end of the stable block and cantering towards the gate. He waved his companions out of the way and watched as the cohort's mounted contingent passed by. The beasts were ill-fed and their uneasy gait indicated that they had been poorly exercised. Their hides were dull from lack of grooming and the saddles and bridles looked worn.

As the dust swirled in their wake, Apollonius covered his mouth with the back of his hand and made a muffled comment. 'It seems almost cruel to burden those broken-down wrecks with riders. I doubt they'd go more than a mile before they were blown and good for nothing more.'

Cato nodded grimly and turned to Massimilianus. 'What's your explanation for that lot?'

'As I said, I joined a couple of years back, sir. In that time the cohort has not had a single remount added to its strength. Most of those beasts are almost no use any more. The prefect has been too, er, preoccupied to request funds from the governor to purchase fresh ones. It's not as if the island is short of good mounts. They breed some of the finest horses in the Empire. I put in a request of my own a few months back but heard nothing back from the governor's office, and then the next time the prefect returned from Carales, he tore a strip off me for exceeding my authority.' He shrugged. 'That's how it goes here. Sardinia's been a backwater of the Empire for too long, I'm thinking.'

'That is going to change,' said Cato. 'Come on.'

They followed the small column of riders out of the fort and onto the levelled ground beyond. The men of the cohort were formed up in their centuries, with the mounted contingent taking their station on the right flank. Plancinus and the other Praetorians were waiting on the reviewing platform to one side of the parade ground. Cato did not join them immediately, but paced slowly along the front of the formation, pausing occasionally to look more closely at individuals and their kit. What was true of the horses seemed to go for many of the men as well. Some looked ancient, with wizened limbs and sunken eyes and the shrunken mouths of those who had lost all their teeth. Like most auxiliary units, their armour was a mixed bag of scale and iron rings. A few had segmented armour. It was heartening to see that at least some effort had been made to keep helmets polished and weapons and armour free of rust. Their oval shields bore personalised designs, a feature that Cato found less tolerable now that he had grown used to the standardised appearance of the Praetorian Guard.

As was common with mixed cohorts, the established strength

of the Sixth Gallic was supposed to be in the order of a thousand men. But there were always men who were sick, or on detached duties, or who had been given leave. In addition to the six squadrons of the mounted contingent, most of whom were formed up on foot behind those who still had horses, there were ten centuries of infantry, but none of them came close to having the full complement of eighty men. Cato calculated that only about half of the cohort's usual strength was standing before him.

'Massimilianus, I'll want full strength returns submitted to headquarters after the cohort is dismissed. All leave is cancelled and every man is to be recalled to the fort.'

'Yes, sir.'

He took one last look at the men formed up before him, then turned towards the reviewing platform and climbed the short flight of steps to join Plancinus and the other Praetorians. The standard-bearers of the cohort were formed up at the rear of the platform, and he was gratified to see decorations attached to the staff showing that the cohort had performed well at some point in its past.

Plancinus saluted and made his report. 'All available men on parade, sir. Not that they make for an impressive sight. I don't know what the brigands are going to make of them, but I've seen tougher-looking gangs of street kids back in Rome.'

'That may be.' Cato sighed. 'I only hope the other two cohorts are better than this lot.'

Centurion Massimilianus frowned and opened his mouth, then clamped it shut.

'You have something to say, Centurion?' Cato prompted.

'Only that the Sixth Gallic is the best cohort in the province, sir.'

'The best, you say?' He felt his burdened heart sink even further. 'The gods preserve us . . .'

'Let's hope it doesn't come to that,' Apollonius said lightly. 'In my experience the gods have demonstrated rather more insouciance than any desire to preserve their darlings.'

Cato turned to face the assembled men and stepped towards the edge of the reviewing platform, drawing a deep breath to begin his address.

'Soldiers of the Sixth Gallic Cohort! You will by now have realised that the garrison of Sardinia is under new management.'

He heard some chuckles from Plancinus and the others and was gratified to see amusement on the faces of some of the men before him. Better that than sullen expressions or resentful scowls.

'I am Prefect Cato, commander of the garrison. Our emperor has tasked me to lead you men in a campaign to wipe out the brigands who dare to defy the will of Rome. I will be honest with you from the outset. Since I reached the province, I have heard many say that these brigands are more than a match for the soldiers of Rome; that they have more cunning than foxes and cannot be caught. They say that this is the way it has always been and always will be. That kind of talk ends now. Rome will no longer tolerate the defiance of these criminals. They will be hunted down and destroyed. That is our mission, and we will carry it out!'

He paused for a beat. 'Doubtless some of you will dismiss my words as mere bravado, and believe that in the end I will be humiliated, like those who have tried to subdue the brigands before me. To those men I say: you had better pray to the gods that you live to see the day we secure a swift victory, because I will not rest until we do. Nor will any man under my command. Until that day I will demand the last ounce of effort and courage from every man here. And the gods have pity on those who fail in their duty, for I will show you no mercy and nor will our enemy. Centurion Massimilianus, dismiss your men.'

He joined the Praetorian officers as the centurion bellowed the orders that sent the men and horses back to barracks.

'Our new auxiliary friend has a fine set of lungs on him,' Apollonius observed. 'Almost as deafening as Macro. I dare say that's as far as a favourable comparison can go in most respects.'

'You're not wrong,' Cato muttered. 'But I'll give him the same chance I give any man to prove himself.'

He turned to Plancinus and the other officers. 'What do you think?'

'The address was a bit on the short side, sir.'

'I said all that I want to for now. I just needed to see them as a formation and let them know what to expect.'

Apollonius arched one of his fine eyebrows. 'And as a formation what do you make of the Sixth Gallic Cohort?'

'I've seen better.'

'Have you seen worse?'

Massimilianus had turned to join them, so Cato ignored the question and delivered his orders instead. 'Gentlemen, I want you to go over the fort and make a list of work that needs doing. Don't miss out a single detail. I want this place to bring a tearful gleam of pride to the eye of the most ardent centurion that ever lived. And I want that done within two days. Centurions Plancinus and Massimilianus, you're coming back to headquarters with me. There are plans to make.'

CHAPTER THIRTEEN

The office of Prefect Vestinus was well appointed, no doubt from the proceeds of the thriving business he ran as a sideline to his role as commander of the cohort. An ebony desk, inlaid with pearl and silver floral designs, sat in front of a large shuttered window that overlooked the courtyard, the fort walls and the port beyond. The sea sparkled brilliantly a mile off, and several cargo ships and fishing boats gracefully rode the gentle swell. One wall had been painted to represent a bucolic scene of a lake surrounded by trees and mountains, with a temple on the shore. A shepherd leaned on his crook as he regarded the splendid vista. It was a fine piece of work, Cato conceded. Worthy of the finest houses in Rome. The other furnishings of the office, cushioned benches and shelves for scrolls and waxed slates, were the work of craftsmen.

'Our host is a man of some taste, not to mention considerable means,' said Apollonius as he examined his surroundings. 'Given that he has chosen to spend most of his time elsewhere, I can't help wondering at the magnificence of his other accommodation.'

Cato searched the documents on the shelves until he found what he was looking for: a rolled-up map of the island. Opening it out on the desk, he weighted the corners with waxed slates and gestured to the others to gather round.

'You know this place, Massimilianus. Tell me where these brigands are located and where their attacks have been reported.'

The centurion leaned forward and indicated the centre of the island to the east of Tharros. 'There is a dense forest in this region that covers most of the plain between the hills that surround it. The Balari tribe control the area. In the winter, the ground is like a bog, but then you'll be used to that from your time in Britannia, sir.' He glanced at Cato with a quick smile before he continued. 'In summer, most of it dries out, but there are places where the marsh conditions persist and the air is thick with mosquitoes. Any patrol or column sent into the area is asking to be struck down by the falling sickness. I know that from experience, as I pursued a band into the forest two summers ago. Half the men from my century were in sickbeds for the best part of a month, and eight of them died.' He moved his finger over the parchment and tapped an area south of the forested plain. 'The other tribe causing us trouble are the Ilenses, here. This landscape is quite different. Hilly, almost mountainous in places.'

'There are towns marked there,' Apollonius intervened. 'Are they held by the enemy?'

'No. We still control the towns. For the moment. The brigands have started setting ambushes on the roads. That in turn has forced the merchants to travel in convoys of wagons and carts protected by hired men and even some gladiators hired out by the island's lanistas. There are military outposts along the main routes, manned by men from the three cohorts, which is one of the reasons why the ranks looked thin on the parade ground just now. I'd say a quarter of the province's total strength is tied down in guarding the roads passing through or close to the territory controlled by the Balari and the Ilenses. It worked well enough until they got more ambitious and started launching raids right across the island. They create havoc in one area just long enough for us to send a column up there to deal with them, then they run back for the forest and the hills. And while we're dealing with that, they strike somewhere else and we have to send another column to chase them off.' Massimilianus sucked his teeth in frustration. 'We've been chasing our tails all year, sir, and they've been striking at will and laughing their arses off each time we've tried to hunt them down.'

Cato nodded thoughtfully for a moment. 'We're not going to be able to do the job with the forces we have. We'll need more men.'

'Good luck with that, sir. The governor's shown no interest in paying for any, and I dare say you'll get the same response if you ask Rome.'

'Then we'll find the men and the money to pay them from other sources. If the merchants can pay to have their convoys guarded, they can afford to help man the outposts along the roads. That'll free up our soldiers for other duties.'

Plancinus scratched his chin. 'Other duties, sir?'

'That's right. I've been thinking about this problem since I was first given the job. We're going to do the same as we did in Britannia, when we took on the hill tribes. We march auxiliaries into an area and build a fort to control it, then move on and do the same again. Little by little we'll box the brigands in and destroy any of their settlements that we find. We'll also capture those people who are supplying them with food and shelter. They won't last long when they start getting hungry. Their bands will break up and then we'll track down the ringleaders and put an end to it.'

'You make it sound very simple,' said Apollonius.

'It is simple,' Cato agreed. 'It worked well enough in Britannia, on a bigger scale.' He indicated the map. 'Our main effort will come from the west, using the Sixth Gallic. The other two cohorts will push forward from the north and south, while I'll order the naval squadron to arm its sailors, and with the marines they can move in from the eastern coast. We'll hem the enemy in on all sides and slowly close in for the kill. Any questions?'

Massimilianus nodded. 'One thing. I've been dealing with those bastards long enough to know that they can outpace our men easily. On foot and on horseback. That'll come as no surprise now that you've seen the quality of the nags we have on our strength.'

'Then we'll need better horses,' said Cato. 'The best that we can find in the province.'

'Horses we can't afford, sir. Like I said, the governor's not going to open the coffers of the province's treasury. He wants as much of that as he can get his hands on for when his term of office is up and he returns to Rome.'

'The solution's obvious,' said Apollonius. 'We don't pay for the horses.'

'You're right.' Cato folded his arms. 'If we can't count on the governor, or the officials back in Rome, we'll have to take what we need from the resources available on the island. That means we'll need to requisition mounts from the horse breeders. We'll also need to make the merchants cough up money to hire men and pay for their kit. There will be local militia in the larger towns and ports. We'll rope them in too. They can man the forts and free up men to fill out the ranks of the pursuit columns. With good horses, we'll be able to match the pace our enemies move at.'

The others nodded their approval, before Plancinus spoke

up. 'The plan's sound enough, sir, but it's only as good as the men used to put it into effect. Many of those we rousted out and got on parade are in no condition to be running down brigands through forests and over hills.'

Cato nodded. 'So the first task is to weed out those too old or unfit to march with the pursuit columns. Massimilianus, I want the strength returns for the cohorts, then I want you to go through each century, man by man, and pick out the best. Same goes for the horses. I only want the fittest. Get rid of the rest. Sell 'em in the local market and get what you can for them. We'll make up the numbers from the horse breeders in the country around Tharros. But don't breathe a word about the way we're going to set about it. Is that clear?'

'Perfectly, sir.' Massimilianus grinned. 'I can't wait to see their faces when we come for their beasts.'

'Something occurs to me,' Apollonius intervened. 'I doubt the local landowners are going to take kindly to having their mounts commandeered. They will make their complaints known in Rome. I doubt the emperor will be happy to have dealt with the brigands only for a fresh problem to arise. I'd advise you to soften the blow by giving them a receipt for every horse and the promise of its safe return or fair compensation in the case of its loss. They might grumble, but that's as far as they will take it for the present. And when it's all over and you return to Rome, well, then it'll be someone else's problem.'

The two centurions stared at him with disdain before Massimilianus spoke. 'Can I ask where you found this one, sir? He's got a touch too much of the politician about him for my taste.'

Cato laughed. 'Just be grateful he's on our side. I'm sure you will value his particular talents as much as I do in the days to come.'

'If you say so, sir,' Massimilianus responded doubtfully.

Removing the waxed slates, Cato rolled up the map and replaced it on the shelf. 'You know how I plan to deal with the brigands. But first we need to get this cohort kicked into shape and ready to march against the enemy. I'm leaving that job in the hands of Plancinus and the other Praetorians. No offence to you, Massimilianus, but I want the men pushed hard, and they'll take it better from outsiders than from those officers who have been content to let standards slip. And I'll need you here at headquarters to advise me on the lie of the land.'

It was difficult to hand the training over to Plancinus and the other volunteers without impugning the professionalism of the cohort's senior centurion and the other officers, but they needed to be shaken up as much as the rank and file. Cato decided to move on to other matters before any objection could be made, and rejected, thereby adding to the umbrage of the local officers.

'What is your opinion of the other cohorts on the island?'

'I've not had that much to do with them, to be honest, sir. I've only had cause to visit their forts a few times over the last two years. They're in the same state as the men here. Of the two, I'd say that the lads of the Eighth Hispanic are in better shape. Their prefect was promoted from the legions, so he does his best to keep them on their toes. He's also got men serving in the outposts, so his cohort will be under strength as well. As for the Fourth Illyrian at Olbia . . . They've been here the longest, and I doubt there's much Illyrian blood left in any of them. You know how it is with long-term garrison troops. They get involved with the local women, and their kids join up in turn, and so it goes, one generation after another until the unit's original name is meaningless. Chances are some of them are closely related to the men they're going to be fighting.

151

That's not going to be helped by their commander. Prefect Tadius is the son of a senator who had the ear of the last emperor and who owns several large estates on the island. Tadius prefers an easy life to hard soldiering. Bit of a playboy, and he and Prefect Vestinus ain't exactly friends.'

'How so?'

'One of the reasons Vestinus spends so much time in Carales is to keep an eye on his wife. The rumour is that she and Tadius had a bit too much wine one night and misbehaved.'

'If that's true, then why not just bring her here to Tharros?'

'Because Carales is about the only town in Sardinia where there's enough going on to keep the nobility entertained. Even if someone might be knocking a slice off his missus, Vestinus likes his creature comforts enough to make the most of his time there.'

Cato puffed his cheeks out in irritation. 'So, we've got three third-rate cohorts, two of which are commanded by fifth-raters playing at being soldiers . . . I may have to knock their heads together when I summon them here to brief them on the campaign. Better deal with that as soon as possible. I'll get messages sent to all three commanders as soon as we're done here. Does anyone else have anything to say?'

He glanced round and Apollonius nodded.

'Just one more thing, sir. The small matter of this plague that's hit the south of the island. If that spreads, we're going to have all manner of additional problems.'

'That's true,' Cato conceded. 'But if it affects our men, chances are the enemy will suffer from it too. In any case, that's a matter for the governor to deal with. If Scurra has any sense, he'll quarantine any towns or villages where the sickness is getting out of hand. If he acts quickly enough, and firmly, there's a good chance it can be contained.'

Apollonius sneered derisively. 'He's a politician. The kind of politician who looks out for himself and tries not to cause any more trouble than he can afford. Have you ever known that kind of man to act quickly and decisively? Mark my words, sir. I fear the plague is going to be as much of a danger as the enemy.'

Cato considered his words and sighed. 'Let's hope you're wrong.'

CHAPTER FOURTEEN

The following day was cloudless and the sky was a depthless cerulean from which the sun blazed, painfully brilliant as it bleached the landscape either side of the road leading inland from Tharros. Cato, Apollonius and Massimilianus rode at the head of ten men mounted on the best of the cohort's horses. The men themselves had been hand-picked by their senior centurion and were fit and strong; the kind of soldiers who exemplified the uncompromising duty that Cato had chosen for them. Their armour and sword belts had been cleaned and buffed to a good shine and their horses had been groomed well enough to satisfy Cato's critical eye.

Behind them, outside the fort, the rest of the cohort was being drilled and exercised by Plancinus and the other Praetorians, who yelled orders and insults as they doubled the men around the dusty open space. The soldiers were carrying the wicker training shields and swords that were made to be heavier than the real kit in order to build muscle and increase endurance.

No one had been excluded from the morning training sessions in case some of the older soldiers were tough enough to keep up with their younger comrades. Equally, there were newer recruits who were puny, overweight or infirm who needed to be tested to see if they were capable of playing their part in the coming campaign. While the process might reduce the number of men available for the pursuit columns, Cato refused to allow the cohort to be held back by stragglers. Those not hardened to undertaking long marches and fighting at the end of them were better left behind to man the outposts and forts that would encircle the enemy's territory.

With the messages sent to the other cohort commanders and the trierarch in charge of the island's small squadron of biremes and their marine detachments, Cato felt content that his arrangements for the campaign were in hand. Gods willing, he would soon have enough men, horses and fortifications to close in on the brigands and cut them off from the supplies they needed. Hungry and caught in a trap, they would be forced to fight it out or surrender. Then, for the first time in two centuries, the province would be free of the brigands, and no outlying settlement, farm or villa would be at risk from raids. No longer would the people await the coming of nightfall in fear, nor tread the roads of the island glancing anxiously from side to side in anticipation of ambushes. If – when, Cato corrected himself – he succeeded, he would apply for a permanent posting as commander of a cohort in some quiet province and take his son with him. Lucius could grow into manhood while Cato retired to live out his life in comfort and contentment. Just as Macro would be doing when he and Petronella reached Britannia.

He felt a moment's sadness that Macro was no longer serving with him. The veteran would have dearly loved to kick the Sixth Gallic Cohort into shape and lead them into the fight. There were some men who seemed born to become soldiers, as wolves were born to hunt, and any other kind of life was unnatural to them. Macro was such a man, in Cato's estimation, and he could not help wondering if his long-time comrade and close friend would adapt to civilian life. He hoped so, for Petronella's sake mainly, but also out of consideration for Macro's age. The tough centurion he had first met in Germania had aged, as all must, and the injuries he had carried through his army years would increasingly take their toll on his joints and his ability to keep up with the younger men.

'It's a fine morning.' Apollonius cut cheerily into his thoughts. 'Just the thing to set a man up for a few days of equine larceny.'

'The term you are reaching for is requisitioning.'

'That may be the term you prefer, but I dare say our victims will pick a more choice word for what we are about.'

'Let them. If they can't see that they have to make sacrifices for the common good, making their lives somewhat easier in the long run, then I have no sympathy for them.'

'Such sacrifices are for the ordinary people. That's how it is with warfare. The poor go hungry. It's usually their farms that are looted and burned down, their women and daughters who are raped; and like as not they're all sold into slavery if their side loses. For the wealthy and the powerful it's a different matter. They like to talk up a good war but hardly ever pay the price for it, and often find some way for the gift of victory to shower them with new ways of enriching themselves as the poor struggle to rebuild their shattered lives . . .'

Cato saw that a dark expression had formed on his companion's face. Apollonius stirred self-consciously and laughed. 'Do pardon me for souring the mood of our happy rural excursion.'

'You seemed to speak from the heart,' said Cato. 'A rare moment of insight into your origins, perhaps.'

'I was just thinking aloud, that's all. I wouldn't read anything more into my words.'

'No?' Cato regarded him with amusement.

'No,' Apollonius concluded tersely, and turned to Massimilianus. 'Tell me, Centurion, which fortunate landowner is going to be the first to receive us?'

Massimilianus raised the vine cane that was resting across his thighs and pointed out a distant building atop a hill. The whitewashed walls of the extensive villa overlooked terraced slopes where olive trees grew in ordered lines. Behind the villa sprawled meadows contained within dry-stone walls, and the tiny shapes of goats and horses dotted the verdant pasture. 'That's where we'll start. The place is owned by some aristocrat in Rome and managed by a steward. There's a fine stable there with plenty of good mounts. They breed them for racing. Best we start with them before word gets round what we're about and they have a chance to take the horses somewhere and hide them.'

The road began to curve in easy loops as it climbed the slope towards the house, and an hour later, the party of horsemen reached the waist-high wall that ran around the estate. They turned into a long lane shaded by ancient poplars that towered above them like the wreathed columns of a temple. On either side the olive trees spread out as far as Cato could see before folding around the hill upon which the villa and the stud farm were built. Half a mile later, they came to a gate set into a high wall that enclosed the villa and its outbuildings. A figure squatted in the shade, a round shield and heavy spear propped up beside him. As he noticed the riders, he stirred and rose casually, picking up his spear and stepping forward to bar the gate.

'Jupiter's balls, but he's a giant,' said Massimilianus.

They were close enough for Cato to recognise the man as

157

one of Claudia Acte's German guards. Tall and broad-shouldered, he had fair hair and a beard that fell across his mail vest. His arms were powerfully muscled, and he had the haughty air of one raised to be a warrior.

'I had no idea we were to be reunited with these brutes so soon,' said Apollonius. 'I hope they don't cause us any trouble when their mistress discovers the reason for our visit. Much as I appreciate that the men at our backs are the pick of the cohort, the men ahead of us are the pick of the Empire.'

The German held up a hand and called out to them in his own tongue. The words might be strange but the intent was unmistakable, and Cato halted the other riders and walked his horse forward the last few paces towards the gate. He smiled a greeting and pointed in the direction of the villa, then at himself and his men. 'We've come to see Lady Claudia. Open the gates.'

He mimed the action and the German hesitated before nodding and striding to the gate to give it a heavy knock. A voice called out from the far side, and there was a brief exchange before the locking bar was slid back and the gates swung open. The German guard waved them through.

Beyond the gate was a large open space in front of the villa. To the left were the stables, with straw and feed piled to one side. On the right was the slave accommodation, a long, low block with regular doors and small shuttered windows, similar to the barracks of the legionary fortresses Cato was familiar with. There were other buildings arranged around the compound: barn, granary, smithy and storage sheds. The villa was a simple design, though large enough to be imposing. The front stretched for a hundred and fifty feet across the enclosure, and a balcony ran around the first floor to afford its residents a clear view over the surrounding countryside and the ability to take advantage of cooling breezes from any direction. Some of the villa's servants and slaves were at work in the stables, and a hammer rang from the direction of the smithy, where a thin column of smoke rose into the sky before gradually dissipating. Two of the Germans stood either side of the gate, while two more guarded the entrance to the villa. The rest were nowhere to be seen.

Cato rode across to a tethering rail in front of the stables and gave the order to dismount. As he flipped the reins over the wooden rail, he spoke quietly to Apollonius and Plancinus. 'While I find the lady and speak to her, you have a look over the stables and note the horses we want. Oh, and tack. Might as well get as much good kit as we can while we're at it.'

As he walked slowly towards the house, he rubbed his backside to ease the discomfort of being in the saddle. Ahead of him, the decurion in command of the German detachment emerged into the sunlight.

'Ah, Prefect Cato, good to see you again, sir. What can I do for you?'

'I'm here to see Lady Claudia.'

'She's inside, sir.' The decurion stood his ground. 'Can I tell her the reason for your visit?'

'I'll tell her myself, thanks. It's official business, so just take me to her, eh?'

'As you command, sir. Follow me. I should warn you the lady is not quite ready to receive formal visitors. Nor is the villa.'

Close to, Cato could see that the green paint on the shutters was faded and peeling in places. Clearly the owner of the property before Nero had gifted it to his mistress had not been concerned with its upkeep. The casual neglect was in evidence inside as well, with streaks of dust on the tiled floor and over

159

the furniture in the entrance hall. Claudia's baggage was heaped along the sides of the hall, and Cato saw slaves sweeping the floors and dusting off the cobwebs along the corridor that ran the length of the building. The decurion led him through a door into the enclosed garden at the rear. The flower beds were overgrown with weeds and wild shrubs and the pond in the middle had long since dried out and was full of debris and dead leaves. Several slaves were hard at work uprooting the weeds in the corner of the garden; in amongst them was a woman in a plain brown tunic and a mob cap, squatting over some exposed roots she had grasped in both hands and was straining to rip out of the ground.

'That's her?' asked Cato.

'Yes, sir.'

'I'll speak to her alone.'

The decurion looked uncertain, then nodded. 'Be gentle with her, sir. She's not had an easy time of it.'

'Really?' Cato gestured towards the rear of the villa. 'She seems to be doing rather well for herself. There aren't many former slaves who can boast such a fine home.'

'That may be so, sir. But Rome is where she was born; it's all she knows. She didn't ask to be handed over to Nero, and she had to work hard to keep him sweet. I saw the things he did to her . . . Like I said, I'd be grateful if you didn't make things any worse for her.'

Cato had not been expecting such sensitivity from one of the emperor's personal bodyguards. Was it possible the decurion's feelings towards his charge arose from some sort of tenderness? Did he have feelings for the exiled woman? Then a darker thought occurred to him. Perhaps the decurion had been given orders concerning Claudia that troubled his conscience.

'I mean her no harm, Decurion.'

'Thank you, sir. I'll be in our mess room if you need me.'

As the decurion made his way back to the villa, Cato continued towards the small party of gardeners. Claudia's attention was focused on the roots; she gritted her teeth and strained to tear them out as her visitor approached from the side.

'Would you like some help with that?'

She glanced round quickly, her brow creased into a frown that eased off slightly as she squinted up at him. 'Oh, it's you.'

'You seem to have picked on some kind of growth that has the advantage over you,' Cato said lightly. 'Here, let me deal with it.'

Without waiting for a response, he bent down, took the tough, twisted bundle of roots in both hands and pulled gently, then harder as they resisted his attempts to shift them. Claudia backed off a step and stood, hands on hips, watching him with an amused expression that piqued his pride. Trying not to betray his growing sense of frustration, he heaved with all his strength, the muscles of his forearms trembling with the effort. Without any warning, the roots came away with a soft crack, and he tumbled onto his back, trailing the bundle in his grip. The impact of his landing winded him slightly, and he heard her burst into laughter, followed by the others who had been working alongside her.

Throwing the roots to one side, he stood with as much dignity as he could muster and dusted the dirt off his fingers as he regarded her with a scowl.

'Sometimes you try too hard, my dear Prefect Cato!' She was smiling broadly, revealing good teeth, and there was a delighted twinkle to her countenance that spoke of no malice, merely delight at the unexpected humour of the incident. Some kindred impulse stirred in his heart, and he could not help smiling back.

'If the bloody roots of this island are too much for me, then the gods know how I'm going to deal with the brigands.'

She laughed again, then raised a hand apologetically. 'Forgive me; it's been a while since I have found anything so amusing.'

'Then it's my pleasure to have been the source of your amusement.'

They exchanged another smile before she suddenly glanced down at her tunic and touched a hand to the grimy cap on her head. 'Oh! What must I look like? You'll be peering down your nose at me, just like those snooty senators did back in Rome.'

'Snooty? Me?'

'I'm sorry. I meant no offence. Anyway, you understand what I mean. I'm sure you had the same thing to deal with the moment you rose to the equestrian class.'

Fortunately for Cato, a career in the army had largely spared him from such snobbery. Deeds tended to speak louder than family background amongst soldiers. But he could easily guess at the snide remarks that had been made behind Claudia's back, and occasionally to her face.

'Never mind.' She touched him gently on the arm. 'That life has been taken from me now. And good riddance too . . . It's hot, I could do with some refreshment. Come with me.'

She led him to the other side of the garden, where a trellis ran along the wall. An untended vine had taken over the framework, but enough had been cut back to clear a small area where a couch had been set up in front of a low table. Claudia called out to one of her slaves to bring them some water, and then sat down at one end of the couch. Cato hesitated, so she leaned over and patted the far end. 'I don't bite, Prefect.'

'Thank you, my lady.'

'You can call me Claudia. I'd prefer it if you did. I was

Claudia for far longer than I was "my lady", and now I am plain Claudia once again. And I shall call you Cato, if I may?'

He nodded as he sat down, thinking to himself that few would ever consider her to be plain, in spite of the fact that she was dressed like a servant of the villa rather than its owner.

She saw him looking over her attire and laughed again. 'Not quite what you expected the emperor's former sweetheart to be wearing. That's what you're thinking, eh?'

'Something like that.'

'This is how I dressed before Seneca noticed me and added me to his collection of young women. And then passed me on to Nero as if I was little more than a toy dressed up to delight a child. In truth, he was not much more than a child, even after he became emperor. Content to follow his own interests while the real power was exercised by his advisers, and that poisonous bitch, his mother. I tried to encourage him to stand up to her, but he hated being caught between the two of us. In the end, blood and snobbery proved to be thicker. She won – the senators won – and Nero sent me into exile. He cried when he told me. Cried like a baby while I held him in my arms. If the Senate and people of Rome could have seen him blubbing like a toddler, you can only imagine the disgust it would have provoked. All the time he told me he loved me and swore that I would live out my days like a princess and no harm would come to me. And now here I am, and I wonder how long his promise will hold true. I may as well keep myself busy and make this house into the comfortable gilded cage that it really is.'

The slave approached with a jug and two silver cups on a tray, which she set down carefully, then bowed and retreated back towards the villa. Claudia filled the first cup and held it out for Cato before filling her own.

'I'm sorry for troubling you with my woes. I never even asked you why you have come visiting. It's not a social call, I imagine.'

'Sadly not.' Cato would have liked to continue the small talk. He enjoyed discovering that there was more to Claudia Acte than the pampered imperial mistress he had first encountered. But this was only the first of the farming estates and villas he intended to call on this day, and there was little time to waste. 'As you know, I have been sent to deal with the brigands menacing the island. I haven't been given enough men to do the job, and those that I do have are in poor shape. The same goes for the horses of the mounted contingent. If I am to succeed in running the enemy to ground, I'll need good mounts. The difficulty is that the governor isn't likely to advance me the necessary funds from the provincial treasury, and in any case, I don't have the time to argue the toss with him. I need those horses now. Which is why I am here. This villa has a fine stud stable attached to it. Claudia, I need your horses.'

'You want to buy them from me?'

He shook his head. 'I cannot pay for them now. I can only give you a receipt for the horses I take and a promise that you will have them returned to you or paid for.'

She smiled cynically. 'I doubt they will be returned in the same fit state that they leave here. And in any case, what good is your promise if you are no longer around to honour it? I do not mean to say that you will be defeated and killed, although that is a possibility in your line of work. I refer to what happens if you are victorious and move on to new campaigns, leaving this island behind you. Who is to honour any promises you make then?'

Cato laughed self-consciously. 'You are a shrewd thinker,

Claudia. You have me there. All I can say is that my promise *will* be honoured, even if I have to pay for the horses myself. I have the means, back in Rome.'

'You'd do that?'

'I would not be able to live with myself otherwise.'

She stared at him, then took a sip of water and gently swilled it around her mouth as she reflected. 'I believe you,' she said eventually. 'You are not like the other men of your rank I knew in Rome.'

'I'm not quite sure how to take that.'

'I meant it as a compliment, Cato. Take it as such. You may have your pick of my horses. I have no attachment to the beasts. They are merely part of the property that Nero gifted me. Use them as you will and return those that live when you are done with them. Any money that is owed I can afford to wait for.'

'Thank you.' Cato drained his cup and stood up. 'I have to go. There are several more villas I need to visit before the day is over. I doubt that I will be received as well elsewhere.'

'I can imagine.' Claudia rose from her end of the couch. 'I'll let my steward know that you have my permission to take the horses. I hope we'll see more of each other before you march your men off to fight.'

'I hope so too.' Cato gave a polite bow in farewell before striding back to the doorway at the rear of the villa. He felt a warmth in his heart that he had not experienced for years; the recognition of a kindred spirit and intelligence. As he recalled the memory of his first wife, Julia, however, his mood instantly soured. If the daughter of a senator could play him so falsely, then why should he trust any feelings inspired by a cast-off mistress of the emperor? He was a fool to let himself be romantically distracted by Claudia. He resolved to steer clear of her. Put her out of his mind and focus on the preparations for

165

the campaign. She was worse than a distraction; she was potentially dangerous. Particularly if she was correct in her characterisation of Nero as a child. Children, he knew from his experience of Lucius, were prone to regard their playthings covetously, even if they did not play with them any more. His standing with the emperor was precarious enough. It would be foolhardy to stir up feelings of jealousy in the imperial breast. Yes, he resolved, he must keep his distance from the woman.

Once Cato had related the bare details of his agreement with Claudia, Massimilianus ordered his men to round up the chosen horses and the best of the saddles, harnesses and bridles while Apollonius wrote out the requisition receipt. When it was done, the agent handed it to Cato to sign his name and seal it with an impression of his equestrian ring.

'Take that to Claudia's steward,' Cato commanded.

Apollonius arched an eyebrow. 'Claudia, eh?'

Cato rounded on him. 'I have no time for your insinuations. Just do as I say, damn you.'

Apollonius smiled knowingly. 'As you command, sir.'

He sauntered off, leaving Cato furious with himself for giving away an insight into his dealings with Claudia. He thrust thoughts of her aside and joined the centurion as the horses were led out of the stable and roped together in loose strings.

'Twelve of them.' Massimilianus rubbed his hands together enthusiastically. 'Fine horseflesh, every one. If we get another seventy like this, we'll have the best mounted men in the entire army.'

Cato regarded the beasts and nodded. 'Good. Let's be on our way. It's going to be a long day or two before we can satisfy your ambition, Centurion.'

Massimilianus shouted the order to his men to mount up,

and once Apollonius had climbed into his saddle and taken up his reins, Cato waved his arm forward towards the gate and the small column of riders, swelled by their acquisitions, trotted out of the villa's enclosure. As he passed through the gate, he glanced back through the haze of dust and caught sight of Claudia in front of the entrance to the villa, watching them leave. She raised a hand in farewell, but before he could even think to respond, it was too late: he had passed through the gate, and the riders behind him had closed up and obscured his view. He turned away with a feeling of regret. She might be trouble, she might even be dangerous, but he found himself wondering how he might find a way to see her again. He felt himself to be on the threshold of a path that promised as many perils as it did pleasures, and yet he already knew he would take his first steps as soon as the situation allowed.

CHAPTER FIFTEEN

Over the next two days they secured enough horses to supply some eighty men of the mounted contingent with another twenty beasts to serve as remounts. Some of the horse-breeders had grudgingly assented to the requisition of their stock, but most had been hostile and Cato had been obliged to threaten to take the horses by force. They had shouted insults and threats after him as the growing column of men and horses trotted away. He was sanguine about any action they might take. If ever their complaints were aired by their friends in the Senate, by then he would have defeated the enemy and few would question the actions he had taken to achieve victory. If he failed, the complaints raised against him would be the least of his concerns.

While the horses were being gathered, Centurion Plancinus and the other Praetorian officers drilled the men of the cohort mercilessly. Some twenty of the older and less fit amongst the auxiliaries had already been admitted to the cohort's modest hospital, and more pallets had been set up in the neighbouring storeroom to treat the additional injured. The routine was the same served up to recruits to the legions. Up at dawn for a run around the fort before morning inspection of the barracks. Then a hastily cooked meal of a barley-based gruel that was held to be the best staple diet for men in training. The morning roll call on the parade ground was followed by weapons and formation drill. At midday they were formed up in their centuries, marching yokes loaded with the clothes and kit for campaigning, and then the cohort set off for a march along the coast road, returning along a strenuous track through the hills before reaching the fort exhausted. But there was little respite, with the evening meal to be cooked before cleaning of weapons and kit, ready to repeat the process as soon as dawn broke the next day.

Much as the men cursed their drill instructors under their breath, they took pride in their ability to keep up with the demanding training schedule and did not want to face the shame of straggling behind, or falling out injured and having to be picked up by the cart following the marching column. The discomfort of the heat was made worse by the dust kicked up by the nailed boots, which settled on the men and their kit so that they ended each day covered in a patina of grey that made them look prematurely aged as they paced stiffly to their barrack blocks.

Another time Cato might have trained and exercised with them, since he was of the school of thought that all officers should be as fit and handy with a sword as the men they commanded. But there were too many other tasks demanding his attention. Supplies needed to be requisitioned and sent to the forts and outposts surrounding the territory already claimed by the enemy. Each convoy had to be escorted by sufficient soldiers to deter the brigands from attack. Then there were the intelligence reports he requested from each outpost, as well as those garnered from merchants and the tribes still loyal to the Empire. The commander of the cohort at Tibula had asked for more time to prepare his men before he could meet his new superior, and Cato had been obliged to send him a terse message to come to Tharros at once. He was also worried about the handful of reports he had received about the sickness that now seemed to have the southern part of the island in its grip. He had passed the intelligence on to the governor, with advice to quarantine those towns and villages affected to prevent the pestilence spreading any further. Scurra had not responded and his silence was adding to Cato's concerns.

In those rare moments when his mind was not turning over the details of his new command and the plans he was making for the campaign, he found himself thinking about Claudia. It was strange the grip she had on his attention given the briefness of their acquaintance and the poor manner in which it had begun. He was tempted to send her a message asking if she would be interested in taking a ride into the hilly countryside around her villa, only to dismiss the notion as a fresh task cropped up at the fort. And so it happened, as these things will when a shrewd woman is involved, that they met, as if by chance, in the port on a fine afternoon several days after Cato had taken the horses from her villa.

He had just concluded his business with a grain merchant for a consignment of barley and olive oil and was strolling along the quay, his gaze wandering over the vessels moored alongside and the bustle of sailors, stevedores and idlers. Above, seagulls whirled and glided against the backdrop of a deep blue sky, and occasionally swooped down to snatch up a discarded or unattended morsel of food. Whistling a refrain from one of the marching songs he had picked up in the Second Legion many years before, he caught sight of Claudia walking in the other direction, with two of the German guards following, carrying baskets laden with her purchases. Dressed in a simple yellow stola and a straw sunhat, she saw him at the same moment.

The tune died on Cato's lips and he felt a surge of frustration that she had intruded on his good mood and put him on edge. And then she smiled at him and nodded a greeting, and at once the frustration disappeared. Before he could check himself, he had smiled back and they greeted each other as if they were old friends.

'You're looking cheerful this morning,' Claudia observed. 'It makes a nice change.'

Cato laughed. 'I'm not always a dour army officer, you know.'

'I had begun to wonder. But happiness suits you. You look like a different person.'

'What brings you here?'

'Shopping. I wanted some fruit and fish and the market here has a fine supply of both. My steward offered to send someone to buy what I needed, but where's the fun in that? It was a good chance to escape from the villa and see something of my nearest town. So here I am. How about you?'

Cato explained his presence, and there was a beat where they said nothing and just smiled.

'Come,' said Claudia. 'I've been told there's a fine inn with a terrace overlooking the port close to the end of the mole where the wine isn't watered down too badly and the food is digestible. If you can spare the time?'

Cato hesitated. He thought of the meeting he had arranged that afternoon with Plancinus to review the progress of the training, but there was plenty of time to spare since he had concluded his business with the merchant more quickly than he had anticipated.

'Why not? I should be delighted to. Rome can spare me for an hour or so.'

'I doubt the Empire will collapse in your absence,' she teased.

She took his arm as Cato steered a course through the throng towards the end of the mole. They were ushered inside by the owner of the inn, who glanced warily at the Germans before he ran through his patter about the food on offer that day.

'We'll have the prawns fried in garlic butter, bread, olive oil, garum and a jug of your local wine,' Cato said before pausing to glance at Claudia. 'If you are happy with that?'

'Just what I would have chosen. Garlic and all.'

'Fine. We'll eat on the terrace.'

The innkeeper bowed his head and indicated the stairs at the side of the building. Claudia gestured to the Germans to take one of the benches outside in the shade of an awning and followed Cato upstairs. The terrace had six tables with stools, and vines grew over the wooden beams, providing some shade and dappled light. Once Claudia had settled, she rested her elbows on the edge of the table and folded her hands together.

'So, how are your plans for the campaign developing?'

'As well as can be expected.'

'That badly?'

Cato gave a wry smile. 'I expect my concerns are the same as those of every commander throughout history. Do I have enough men? Is their equipment adequate? Are they adequately supplied? Is morale good? How can I know where the enemy is and what he is planning? At the moment, none of the answers to those questions is very encouraging. But that is changing, day by day.'

'Do soldiers always grumble so?'

'I'm speaking from the perspective of command. I can assure you the true masters of the art of grumbling are the rank and file.'

The innkeeper reappeared carrying their order on a large tray and set it down on the table. Cato took out his purse and paid the man, and added a generous tip, since he considered it appropriate for someone of the equestrian class to demonstrate a little largesse. The innkeeper grinned and nodded his thanks before disappearing down the stairs. There was a moment's awkwardness about who should make the first move before Cato served food onto Claudia's platter and then helped himself.

The meal was delicious and they ate in silent appreciation before Cato noticed that Claudia was looking past him, out to sea, a frown on her face.

'What is it?'

'Look, that ship.'

Cato turned to see a merchant vessel approaching the harbour. It was no more than a half-mile from the quay, and as they watched, the sail billowed, then flapped as the bows swung into the wind. A handful of figures on deck worked the sheets as the steersman struggled to get the ship back on course.

'They don't seem very competent, compared to the seamen on the boat that brought us from Ostia,' Claudia observed.

Cato grunted in agreement, shading his eyes and staring at the cargo ship as she swung off course once more. The sail flapped briefly before the vessel resumed its approach.

'Something's wrong,' he muttered.

Now he could see that a figure at the bow was wearing a red military cloak that rippled to the side as the wind caught it. A soldier . . . It struck him that this might be the ship from Carales with Vestinus and Prefect Bastillus of the Eighth Hispanic Cohort on board. Pushing his platter aside, he stood and moved to the rail running around the terrace, straining his eyes to make out the figures on the deck of the ship as it passed the end of the mole. As the vessel turned into the wind, the few crewmen on deck laboriously lowered the spar rather than climb up to haul in the folds of the sail. The bundled linen lay untidily across the deck, and a moment later the anchor splashed into the azure water and the ship swung slowly round into the breeze. There was no sign of any attempt to draw alongside the skiff that was tethered to the stern. Instead the soldier at the bows waved his hand from side to side to attract attention.

'I have to go,' said Cato, turning to Claudia. 'I'm sorry. I must see what's happening.'

She nodded. 'I'll wait for you here.'

He hurried down the stairs and out of the inn before striding over to the edge of the quay and looking about. A short distance away, two fishermen were landing the morning's catch, the scales of the fish in their baskets gleaming like freshly minted denarii.

'You there!' Cato pointed to them. 'Yes, you! Take me out to that ship. At once.'

One of the men lowered the basket he was holding and made to protest, but Cato had already scrambled down the crude stepladder and landed heavily on the deck of the small boat. It swayed slightly and he clutched the mast for support.

'Get moving. There's a sestertius for each of you if you do as I say.'

The man who had been holding the basket immediately told his companion to cast off the mooring, then the two of them took their places on the rowing benches and positioned their oars in the holding pins. With the first man calling the time, they eased the boat away from the quay. Once they had turned towards the anchored ship, they began to pull hard on the oars and the boat lurched into motion, surging across the light swell of the harbour. Cato glanced over his shoulder and saw that people along the quay had stopped to stare at the anchored cargo ship. On the terrace, Claudia was also watching.

As they approached, the soldier at the bows lowered his

arms and Cato heard a shout above the creak of the oars and the swish of the blades. Then the man suddenly stopped and slumped out of sight.

'Bring the boat alongside,' Cato ordered.

The fishermen did as they were told, expertly manoeuvring against the hull with a soft bump. Cato reached for the wooden boarding rails on the side of the cargo vessel and pulled himself up, climbing over the ship's rail and dropping onto the deck. He saw the bodies at once; some hunched up, others sprawled out. A few were still moving, and a handful of the crew were on their feet, swaying as they held on to the shrouds. There were streaks of vomit, puddles of urine and brown stains around most of the bodies. His first thought was that the crew had been attacked by pirates. But there was no sign of blood.

'Go!' a voice cried out plaintively. 'Get off the ship!'

He turned to the bows and saw the soldier sitting with his back to the side rail, his body trembling fitfully.

'Save yourself,' the man croaked.

Cato approached him warily, stepping round the body of another soldier lying on his back, staring at the sky, his mouth hanging open. A puff of wind blew a terrible acrid stench directly at him and he clasped a hand to his mouth and struggled to stop himself retching. Cato was two paces away from the soldier when he realised what had happened, and he felt the blood turn cold in his veins.

'The sickness killed those men?' he asked.

'Yes, sir.'

'Who are you?'

'Galerus, sir . . . senior centurion of the Eighth Hispanic Cohort.'

'You've come from Carales, then. Is Prefect Bastillus on board? And Vestinus?'

'Vestinus was sick the day he came aboard and died the second day out. One of the first to go, sir. The captain wanted to put into the nearest port, but the wind veered and took us out to sea for the next three days. More got sick and died as we waited for the wind to change. By the time it did, only half the crew were still on their feet, besides the captain.' He paused and let out a moan before convulsing and throwing up a bilious green fluid that splattered down his tunic and between his legs. When he had recovered, and wiped his lips on the back of his hand, Cato spoke again.

'What are the conditions in Carales?'

'Bad, sir. Hundreds dead by the time we left, and more dropping in the streets. The same in the fort. And here on the ship . . . You'd better go.'

The idea of abandoning the survivors on board the ship revolted Cato, but there was no telling how many lives would be lost if he allowed the sick to land at Tharros. And every moment that he remained aboard, he himself was at risk. Galerus was right. He must leave, swiftly. But first he must give the crew their orders. Turning to face the men watching anxiously from the stern, he called out to them.

'Which one of you is the captain?'

A short, skinny man with bow legs raised his hand. 'That's me, sir. Captain Alekandros.'

Avoiding the sick and the dead on deck, Cato approached so that his words would not be overheard. 'Alekandros. You cannot stay in this port. You must return to Carales, and remain there until the sickness has gone.'

The captain's jaw dropped, then he gestured to the men still living on the deck. 'How in Hades do you expect us to manage the ship short-handed, and care for those who are still alive? In any case, who are you to tell me what to do, eh?'

Cato could see the strain and fear in the man's expression and adopted as gentle a tone as he could. 'I am Prefect Cato, commander of the island's garrison. I am giving you an order. I cannot permit you to land here and risk spreading the sickness. Surely you understand that?'

Alekandros let out a bitter groan and scratched his head before his shoulders slumped. 'I understand, sir.'

'Have you or the other survivors shown any signs of the sickness?'

The captain shook his head. 'Stephanos had a fever before we left Carales, that's all.'

'Then you may have been spared the sickness. Is there anything you need before you leave? Water? Food?'

'We've more than enough.'

'Very well. I have one last thing to ask of you. When you reach Carales, report to the senior officer of the Eighth Cohort. Tell him he is to use what men he still has to close the town gates. No one is to enter or leave until the pestilence has disappeared or until there are fresh orders from me. Is that clear?'

The captain nodded.

'The gods be with you, Alekandros.'

Cato turned and made his way to the bow, pausing as he came to Galerus.

'Good luck, brother. I wish I could do more to help.'

'Go, sir . . . I'll be all right.' The centurion smiled weakly before his face contorted in agony and he retched and coughed violently. Cato felt some of the sputum spray onto his hand and forearm, and backed off a step. Galerus gritted his teeth and waved him away as a fresh bout of retching began.

There was nothing to be done for the man, and Cato hurried forward and climbed over the rail before dropping awkwardly into the fishing boat. He kept his distance from the men at the oars, sitting on the tiny weathered board at the prow.

'Cast off and get us back to the quay.'

The fishermen did as they were told. The nearest looked over his shoulder as he rowed. 'What happened on that ship, sir?'

Cato did not reply; he was looking at the droplets on his forearm. He reached hurriedly over the side and washed his hand and arm in seawater before he sat up again.

'Ease oars!'

The fishermen waited for an explanation. Cato was thinking hard. There was too much at stake for him to risk returning to the quay where he had boarded the fishing boat. He pointed to a flight of steps close to the end of the mole, where there was a small tower at the top of which a beacon burned at night to guide any ships still at sea to the harbour.

'Take me there.'

'Sir?'

'Don't argue. Just do it.'

The fisherman shrugged his muscled shoulders. 'It's your money, sir. Come on, my lad,' he called to his companion. 'Let's do as the gent says.'

As the small craft turned towards the end of the mole, Cato felt fear stirring in the pit of his stomach. If the sickness struck Tharros, many thousands would die. It was his duty to do all he could to prevent that, even at the cost of his own life.

CHAPTER SIXTEEN

C ato tossed the fishermen their coins and waited a moment to judge the movement of the boat before leaping across the narrow gap onto the small stone platform at the foot of the stairs. He climbed to the top and approached the tower. The keeper was outside, tending a griddle above the glow of charcoal. The smell of sardines wafted towards Cato as he stopped a short distance behind the man.

'You there!'

The keeper turned, his iron tongs raised in one hand.

'I need the tower. And I need you to run an errand for me.'

'What?' The man tilted his head to one side and frowned.

'I need you to do something for me,' Cato repeated in a louder voice.

'I'm busy. I'm cooking.' The keeper waved the tongs. 'Leave me alone.'

'I don't have the time for this.' Cato drew his sword and took a step closer. 'You'll do as I say or I'll cut you down to size.'

The two men faced each other for a beat before the keeper lowered his tongs and placed them by the grille.

'That's better.' Cato relaxed his posture and pointed to the terrace where Claudia was still watching events. 'See that woman. I want you to go to her and tell her I need to speak to her urgently. Go!'

The tower keeper shot a concerned look at his meal. 'Look after my fish.'

He hurried off down the mole. Cato watched him go and then sheathed his sword. He looked out over the harbour towards the cargo ship. He could see the three crewmen hauling at the anchor cable. A wash of glittering water showed as the iron flukes surged out of the sea and rose up the bow until the iron ring jammed against the hole and the cable was secured. The ship was drifting to windward in the direction of the mole, and Cato felt a fleeting surge of anxiety that it would run aground before the crew could get it under way. But then the spar rose from the deck, the sail flapping beneath it as it ascended the mast and filled, and the captain hurried to the stern to take charge of the tiller, easing the ship round until it was heading for the open sea. Cato could make out the figure of Galerus leaning against the side rail, and he raised his arm and waved. The auxiliary officer waved back and then slid onto the deck and sat hunched over his knees.

A sharp smell caught Cato's attention, and he saw that one of the sardines was burning. Snatching up the tongs, he moved the charred fish to the edge of the grille and turned the others over. Even though he had eaten not long before, the aroma was enticing, and he put three of the fish onto a wooden platter and sat down beside the door of the tower. Peeling the flesh off the fine bones, he ate with little relish as he watched the keeper reach the inn and call up to Claudia. There was a brief exchange before she emerged and hurried after him along the mole. The two Germans followed her, still holding the straw bags packed with her shopping.

Cato finished the fish and wiped his mouth with the back of his hand, then raised his arms.

'Stop! Don't come any closer!'

'What's happened to my bloody sardines?' the keeper demanded, striding forward.

'Stay back!' Cato ordered. 'Unless you want to die.'

The warning in his tone was enough to halt the man, and Cato continued to address the small group loudly enough that they would all hear him. 'That ship came from Carales. The town is in the grip of the sickness. Most of the men on the ship were dead or dying. That's why I sent them away. You must not come any closer to me. I went aboard; I was close to those who were sick. It may have spread to me already and I can't risk letting what is happening in Carales happen here.'

'What are you going to do?' asked Claudia. 'Shall I send for the cohort's surgeon?'

'No. I am going to stay here alone for the next ten days. If the sickness is already upon me, we'll know by then. If nothing has happened, we can assume it's safe for me to return to the fort. I'll take shelter in the tower. I want you to post one of your German friends at the other end of the mole. He's to let no one past, unless they are one of my men. Then I want you to get to the fort as soon as you can. Find Plancinus and Apollonius and tell them what's happened. I need to see them as soon as possible. Plancinus will have to take command whilst I am quarantined . . . Have you got all that?'

She nodded. 'Are you all right?'

'It's too early to say. I'll make sure someone lets you know if anything happens. Now please go . . . Wait. Can you find somewhere for this man while I use his tower?'

'He can stay at the villa.'

The keeper looked from one to the other. 'What's that?

181

Leave my home? No! I'm not going anywhere. I want you out. Leave me alone to finish what's left of my bloody sardines!'

Claudia took his arm and drew him away as he continued to protest. One of the German guards grabbed a fold of his tunic at the back of his neck and steered him firmly down the mole to the harbour front, where a small crowd had gathered to watch the unusual turn of events. Already, Cato imagined, rumours were spreading through the throng, quicker than any sickness but almost as dangerous in the longer term. It would not help his plans for the coming campaign for panic to grip the streets of Tharros. Of course, it would be worse if the sickness really did take hold of the port. Shops and businesses would close, people would retreat into their homes, and soon food would become scarce; and all the time the death toll would mount and the stench of putrefaction would add to the woes of the town's inhabitants. It was better that they knew the truth about the cargo ship from Carales, he decided. And that he had chosen to isolate himself rather than risk the lives of others. People needed to believe that those who led them shared the risks and put themselves in the same jeopardy as everyone else.

While he waited for Plancinus and Apollonius to arrive, he finished off the sardines and inspected the keeper's accommodation in the tower. The ground floor was used for the fuel for the signal beacon. Logs and kindling were neatly stacked along the walls, together with small tubs of pitch. A ladder led up to the living quarters on the next floor. The keeper was a neat man, and his spare clothes hung on pegs by the ladder leading to the top of the tower. There was a comfortable bed-roll and a stool beside a low table upon which lay an array of sharp knives, chisels and a small hammer, with the work in progress – a beautifully carved head and neck of a horse –

emerging from a block of wood. Climbing the last ladder, Cato came out onto the roof of the tower. A waist-high parapet was sheltered by a shingled roof with a vent in the middle. Beneath that was the brazier, an iron-framed basket four feet across. Logs and fuel were stacked in one corner and the fire had been prepared for the night. With a sinking feeling, Cato realised that it would fall to him to ensure that the signal beacon stayed alight each night of his quarantine.

Leaning on the parapet, he looked out to sea and saw Alekandros's ship steering across the ocean. It was already at least two miles away and had not yet turned south. Perhaps the captain was concerned to give himself plenty of sea room now that he was short-handed. Cato offered a quick prayer to Neptune to guide the vessel safely to its destination so that his orders could reach whoever was in command of the cohort at Carales. The gods only knew what havoc the sickness was playing in the south of the island, and it was vital that the region was quarantined as effectively as possible to spare the rest of the province, and to stop the pestilence spreading to Italia and beyond.

It was late in the afternoon before he saw Claudia returning with Plancinus and Apollonius. He had not been expecting her to come back but was pleased to see her. Climbing down the ladders, he emerged from the base of the tower and waited until they were close enough for him to be heard above the waves breaking on the far side of the mole.

'Stay back,' he ordered when they were twenty feet away. 'No closer.'

They stopped, and Plancinus frowned. 'Is this necessary, sir?'

'We have to play safe.'

'How close did you get to the infected men on the ship?' asked Apollonius.

'Close enough. I'll stay here until I'm certain there's no risk to anyone else. I'll need food and drink brought to me each day. And some spare clothes.'

'I can take care of that,' said Claudia.

'There's no need, my lady.' Plancinus shook his head. 'I'll get one of the men—'

'I said I'll do it,' she snapped. 'You and your men have better things to do with your time, I'm sure.'

'But—'

'Careful, Centurion.' Cato grinned. 'Her bite is worse than her bark.'

He ignored the scowl on her face as he recalled the duties for the two men that he had prepared in his head. He began by relating the orders he had given to Alekandros to pass on to the cohort at Carales. 'We can't count on the ship making it back to port, though. I want a message sent to the cohort ordering them to quarantine the town. Make sure the courier is instructed to keep his distance from anyone. If he is touched by anyone who looks as if they might be sick, he must stay in Carales until the pestilence has passed. I want mounted patrols sent to cover the roads leading north from the town. No one is to be permitted to leave. Anyone who tries is to be turned back. If they resist, then arrows or javelins are to be used on them. No sense in getting close enough for sword work. You need to impress upon the men of the patrols that the sickness can easily be passed on, and if it is, they will be left to fend for themselves.'

Plancinus sucked a breath in through his teeth. 'They'll not want to abandon their mates like that, sir.'

'I don't give a damn. It's up to you to make it clear to them the danger of letting the sickness spread throughout the island. It'll be their families and anyone who knows them that'll pay the price if they fuck up.'

'Yes, sir.'

'How does this affect the plans for the campaign?' asked Apollonius.

Cato considered this briefly. 'It shouldn't make too much difference. I want you to report to me daily. We'll talk through anything that requires attention and you can relay it back to Plancinus at the fort. You're in command in my absence, Centurion. I want you to keep training the infantry. Work 'em hard so that we're ready to move in on the enemy the moment my quarantine period is over. Get the supplies to the outposts in time for that. And when the prefect from the Fourth Illyrian cohort arrives, have him brought to me. Is all that clear?'

'Yes, sir.'

They stood silently for a beat before Cato spoke again. 'That's all for now. You'd better get on with it.'

'What about you?' asked Apollonius.

'I'll make myself comfortable here. I suspect I'll become adept at carving by the time the ten days are up.'

The agent cocked an eyebrow.

'Never mind.' Cato forced a smile. 'I'll be fine. I'd like some food brought in the morning and at the end of the day, when you can brief me. All right?'

Apollonius nodded and turned away, followed by Plancinus. Claudia lingered a moment and stared anxiously at him. 'You take good care of yourself, Cato. If you start to feel ill, tell me when I come with the food. I'll have the cohort's surgeon on the spot at once.'

He shook his head. 'If it happens, I'll deal with it myself. No one else. Understand? Not you. Not anyone.'

She chewed her lip, then sighed. 'As you wish.'

He nodded a curt farewell and went back into the tower, closing the door behind him.

★ ★ ★

For four days the quarantine regime ran smoothly. Claudia approached at daylight, carrying a basket of food. She brought a spare tunic on the first day, and then on the second morning a volume of poetry from her collection at the villa. She stayed for a while to talk each time, sitting cross-legged a safe distance away.

Cato opened the book and glanced at her with a wry smile. 'Catullus?'

'Why not? Can you think of better reading matter to warm a man's cockles while he is quarantined?'

'Any particular verses you would recommend?'

'Just those where the pages are more worn than elsewhere.'

They shared a laugh before Cato regarded her with a more serious expression. 'When this is over – the campaign, I mean – I'd like to get to know you better. You are an interesting person, Claudia Acte.'

'Interesting? Now that's a carefully chosen word.' She tapped a finger on her chin. 'What am I to make of it? Are you interested in my mind, my personality, my not inconsiderable fortune, my looks?'

'I would settle for any one of those qualities, and the rest I would treasure as a cornucopia of unexpected bonuses.'

She snorted with mirth and her smile lit up her face so that Cato could understand how she had once won over an emperor.

'My dear Prefect Cato, you have the gilded tongue of the oiliest of politicians. I am sure you will go even further in your career, given the chance.' She climbed to her feet. 'Now I must resist your blandishments and return to the villa. There is still plenty of work to do in the garden.'

'Will you not stay a little longer?'

'No. I find that men are most pliant when the things that give them pleasure are rationed.'

'You are playing with me.'

'Of course I am.' She smiled and walked away, slowly enough to ensure she had his attention all the way to the end of the mole.

When Apollonius approached later that afternoon, as the setting sun burnished the west coast of the island and made the tiles on the roofs of the town's buildings glow like the hearts of rubies, Cato was waiting for him. They exchanged the briefest of pleasantries before the agent reported on matters at the fort.

'The patrols have been sent to cut off Carales and the immediate area.'

'I hope they're in time to stop the sickness spreading.'

'We'll know soon enough. There was a messenger from Tibula. The prefect of the Fourth Illyrian is on his way. He apologises for the hold-up, but claims he was delayed by the governor. He should arrive tomorrow. I'll bring him straight to you.'

'Good.'

'Is there anything else you need here? Anything to help pass the time?'

Cato thought a moment, then shook his head wearily. 'I think I have all I need.'

'Very well. I'll see you tomorrow.'

As Apollonius walked away, Cato reached up and rubbed his forehead. His head ached. He put it down to sitting out for too long in the sunshine. Now that the sun was setting, he felt the first chills of the evening air and trembled for a moment before stepping into the tower to climb the ladder and prepare to light the beacon.

CHAPTER SEVENTEEN

Cato woke in the middle of the night, shivering and nauseous. Outside the wind moaned round the tower and waves crashed against the boulders of the mole with a steady rhythm. He sat up with a groan and pulled the tower keeper's blanket about his shoulders, then swung his feet round and tried to stand up. His limbs felt like jelly and trembled as he struggled to rise. After what seemed like a monumental effort, he stood, swaying, and had to reach out to the stone wall to steady himself.

'The beacon . . .' he mumbled to himself. The fire needed feeding and he knew he must climb the tower to carry out the task he had taken responsibility for. Shuffling to the ladder, he gritted his teeth in determination and began to climb, one effortful rung at a time, until he emerged onto the platform bathed in the red glow of the flames flickering in the iron basket. The warmth was some comfort against the chills that racked his body. He made his way to the piled logs and began to toss more into the middle of the fire, each one causing bursts of sparks to rise and swirl.

Once the blaze had built up, he moved to the corner closest to the open sea, heat soaking into his back. A crescent moon low in the sky away to the south-west cast a beam of glittering reflections across the waves rolling in from the darkness. The black mass of the coast on either side revealed no detail, just the faint sparkle of lamps at the windows of distant homes. He turned in the direction of Claudia's villa and strained his eyes for any sign of life there, but he could discern nothing and gazed back to sea, finding some comfort in the salty tang of the air, the sound of breaking waves and the steely shimmer of the water. Despite his fever, it was a serene moment and one he felt glad to have to himself.

Then he felt his guts clench tightly, and he leaned over the edge of the parapet and retched, retched again and then vomited repeatedly until he felt that he had been wrung out. He stooped there, mouth agape, straining to expel the last gobbet left inside his stomach. His head was pounding and the tranquillity of a moment before was consumed by wretched discomfort and self-pity. There was concern too. If this was the same sickness he had seen on the ship, he was a danger to the people of Tharros slumbering peacefully through the night. He had to make sure that he was awake when Claudia came with the food in the morning. The last thing he wanted was for her to call out to him and, when he did not reply, come into the tower to find him.

'Shit . . .' He groaned as he began to shiver again despite the warmth of the fire. He piled on enough logs to keep the blaze going until dawn, then braced himself to climb down the ladder to the keeper's accommodation. He paused at the bottom as a fresh wave of nausea made him feel dizzy, and closed his eyes momentarily, but that only seemed to make it worse. Releasing his grip on the risers, he staggered over to the opening to the storeroom. With great effort he climbed down and opened the door onto the mole, wedging it open with a log before glancing round and making out a pile of straw mats and old

189

reed baskets. He collapsed onto it, rolling up into a ball and pulling his military cloak over him.

He had never felt so ill before in his life and began to wonder if this was the end for him. The thought of dying alone in the home of a stranger added to his misery. As did the prospect of never seeing Lucius again. Not being able to watch him grow to manhood and share what wisdom he had accrued along the way. The thought of losing the chance to tell his son how much he loved and treasured him weighed down on him like a mountain. His misery plunged to new depths as he lay on his side, knees drawn up, wincing at every agonising throb in his head and struggling to stay awake till first light, when Claudia was due with the next day's rations.

An hour or so later, the chills became a heated fever and sweat pricked out on his face. He trembled and then flicked his covers off and lay stretched out on his back. His throat felt raw from the vomiting, and constricted, and when he poured himself some water, he found it difficult to swallow. The chills and shivering resumed and he groaned in despair as he pulled the blanket over his weakening body and closed his eyes, praying to the gods that his life might be spared, and that the pains that racked him would go . . .

'Cato . . .'

The soft voice penetrated the nightmare of slowly drowning in a dark pit, far from the distant light.

'Cato!'

It was closer, more urgent and distinctly female, and Cato stirred and let out a meaningless mumble. His mouth was dry and his tongue felt swollen and coarse. He tried to summon up some spit to moisten his tongue and lips so that he could speak clearly.

'Who . . . who is it?'

'It's Claudia. You look terrible.'

'Claudia . . .' His mind struggled to make sense of the name for a moment. It was an effort to think clearly, as if joining one thought onto another was the most demanding of tasks. He remembered her. He remembered the vitally important need to stay awake. But he had been weak and allowed himself to sleep. What was it that he needed to stay awake for? Someone was in danger . . . Then it hit him with a stab of lucid clarity and he opened his eyes and tried to sit up. He saw her squatting beside him, behind her the open door and beyond that the decurion of the German guard with two of his men holding a bed frame with a thick mattress tied to it. The sky was overcast and in the distance a single shaft of sunlight pierced the clouds to paint a patch of forested hillside a vivid green.

'Shh. Lie back and rest.' She gently pressed his shoulder to ease him onto the bedroll. Now he could smell the acrid stink of vomit, and worse, a faecal stench from soiling himself. He turned his face away in shame.

'Leave me. Go, before it's too late.'

'Don't be foolish. You need help. If you stay here alone in this condition, you'll surely die.'

'If you don't go now, you may share my fate. Get out of here.'

'I'm here now, so I'm staying.'

'No,' Cato said feebly, cursing himself for failing to stay awake to warn her off.

She rose and went to the door, calling out to the decurion. 'The prefect's sick.'

The decurion flinched, then gestured urgently to her. 'My lady, get away from him!'

'It's too late. I'm at risk now and must be quarantined as

well. You'll have to tell them at the fort. Before you go, leave the bed at the door. I'll take it inside from there. Have one of the men bring me fresh clothes from the villa, and spare tunics for the prefect. I'll also need blankets, a bucket, sponges and water. Have you got all that?'

'Yes, my lady, but—'

'I've told you what to do; now get on with it. The bed first.'

She backed away from the door as the decurion barked an order to the two Germans and they hurried forward with the bed, placing it outside the door before the decurion gave the order to head back down the mole. Claudia left the store-room and a moment later there was a grating noise and Cato turned to see her dragging the bed through the door. She manoeuvred it to the rear of the room and pushed it against the wall.

'There, that's the best I can do. We'll have to manage with this room as neither the bed nor you are going to make it up that ladder.'

Cato moistened his lips again. 'What are you doing, you fool?'

She stood, hands on hips, head to one side. 'That's no way to address the person who is going to be nursing you for the next few days. I'd suggest you improve your manners, Prefect.'

Regardless of his frustration at her presence, it was too late now to dismiss her, Cato realised. She would have to wait for several days to make sure that she did not become sick. The worst prospect was that she might fall ill alongside him. In his present state he would be able to do nothing for her.

'Claudia, you must have known something was wrong when I did not come out of the tower to meet you.'

'Of course I knew. That's why I came in to find you. Just as well that I did. You'll need looking after.'

Again Cato felt a surge of shame at the prospect. Then he was overcome with a fresh urge to vomit. At once she looked round, spotted a bucket and hurried to fetch it for him. He was too weak to sit up and lean over it, so she supported him with one arm and stroked his damp locks of hair as he rested between the bouts of retching that racked his trembling body.

'I'm here now, Cato. I'll look after you. Someone has to . . .'

When he was finished, she helped him over to the bed and laid him out on it. His breathing was laboured as she looked down at him with a sympathetic expression. 'First thing, I need to get you cleaned up. You look like something a street dog has dragged out of the Great Sewer in Rome.'

'Thank you very much,' Cato muttered.

She sighed. 'I'd better get some water heated then. You can sleep while you wait.'

She picked up some kindling and logs and went outside to lay a fresh fire in the hearth beneath the grille where the tower keeper had cooked his sardines. As she went to and fro, Cato watched for a moment before exhaustion overcame him and he fell into a deep, dreamless sleep.

Days and nights passed in a haze punctuated by bouts of pain, delirium and snatches of lucidity. At times Cato was conscious but floating free of the world he had known. Memories flowed seamlessly into nightmares and then back again. At one time his dead wife Julia came to him, her face twisted into a sneer as she mocked him on the subject of her lovers and then tried to smother him with a bolster. He woke suddenly and sat up, eyes wide and glancing nervously from side to side as he gulped air and sweat dripped from his brow. Something stirred in the darkness and hands eased him down before a cool, damp cloth soothed his forehead and he slipped into unconsciousness again, unsure if the last thing he was aware of was a kiss on his forehead, or if that was merely another dream.

One day he woke at noon, his mind clear and his thoughts cogent. As his eyes opened, he stared up at the beams crossing the ceiling of the storeroom. The raw cry of seagulls sounded from outside and he turned his head towards the door, wincing at the stiffness in his neck. The sky was cloudless and seemed impossibly blue. He was aware of voices outside.

Steeling himself, he turned on his side and propped himself up on an elbow. He saw that he was dressed in a soft blue wool tunic and lying on a bed. It was a moment before he recalled the Germans bringing it to the tower. Gritting his teeth, he eased himself up into a sitting position and lowered his feet to the floor. So far, so good. He was alive, and paused a moment to offer silent thanks to Asclepius, before he recalled Claudia and was gripped by a mixture of guilt over the risk she had taken in tending to him and gratitude for saving his life. Without her, he would most likely have succumbed to hunger and thirst while incapacitated by the fever.

Bracing his hands on the edge of the bed either side of his thighs, he pushed himself up and rose unsteadily to his feet. He was shocked at the uncontrollable trembling in his legs as he staggered across the room and leaned against the door frame. Outside he saw Claudia and Apollonius sitting apart on the edge of the mole, their backs towards him as they talked.

He cleared his throat. 'Any chance of a cup of wine?'

They turned round and Apollonius smiled broadly as he got to his feet. Cato's gaze shifted to Claudia, and he was shocked by how drawn her features were.

'You shouldn't be up,' she said. 'You look as weak as a kitten.'

'I'll be fine once I've sat down.' He stepped out of the tower and slid down onto the keeper's stool set against the wall. 'That's better.'

'How are you feeling?' asked Apollonius.

'Terrible. Next silly question?'

The agent laughed. 'Well enough to let what passes for your sense of humour make itself known at least.'

'If all you can do is insult me, then you can fuck off.'

Apollonius turned to Claudia with a mock expression of horror. 'I have to apologise for my superior. What he lacks in wit and good manners he makes up for with . . . some other quality that escapes me for the moment.'

Claudia came over to Cato and held her hand to his forehead. Her palm felt cool and soothing. 'The fever seems to have broken finally.'

Seeing that he was trembling, she went inside and came out with a cloak to settle around his shoulders.

'I don't need that. It's a warm day.'

'Just do it. For my peace of mind. I'll see to that wine now. I noticed some upstairs. Could use a cup myself.' She disappeared inside the tower and Cato heard the ladder creak as she climbed to the first storey.

'How many days has it been since I fell ill?' he asked.

'Five.'

He felt his pulse quicken anxiously. 'What's happened during my absence?'

'Let's see . . . Plancinus reckons the cohort is ready to march. The supplies have reached the forward outposts safely. There was an attempt to ambush the last convoy but the auxiliaries saw them off in style. I've chosen the men I want for my scouts. Ten in all. They're good riders and tough individuals. Some thought they were tough enough to get the better of me.' Apollonius gave one of his lopsided smiles. 'They learned otherwise.'

'I hope the lesson wasn't too painful.'

'Bruised pride and a few sore heads, that's all. I'm teaching them a few of my tricks to try out on the enemy if the chance arises. It's gratifying to see how readily they apply themselves to fighting dirty. I fear for the locals if they ever get into a brawl with my fellows.'

'What about the situation in Carales?'

Apollonius's smile faded. 'It's bad, I'm afraid. One of the mounted men reported back yesterday. Hundreds have died already. They're struggling to keep up with burning the bodies. However, the good news is that the ship got back to the port and passed on your orders. The town gates have been sealed and the mounted contingent have put up roadblocks on the routes leading away from Carales. That said, there have been some falling sick in the nearest villages and estates. They have been isolated and those around them told to stay where they are for ten days after the sick have recovered or died.'

Cato nodded with satisfaction. 'What about the port? Has that been closed too?'

'Yes. I made sure of it by sending an order in your name to the commander of the naval squadron at Olbia to send two of his biremes to block the harbour entrance. They're sending any arrivals back to their port of origin and preventing anyone from leaving. I trust you don't mind me usurping your authority.'

'Not on this occasion, but I'll thank you not to make a habit of it. Anything else?'

'The prefect of the Fourth Illyrian has arrived and is kicking his heels at the fort. I told him you'd speak to him as soon as you were well enough, but he's been threatening to head back to Tibula until you recover. He seemed more than a little concerned to discover you were sick.'

'Tell him I'll see him this afternoon.'

Apollonius raised an eyebrow. 'So soon? Are you sure?'

'It'll be a few days before I'm fit to march and fight, but my mind's clear enough to give the prefect his orders.'

'Very well. The last thing to note is that Scurra has sent a request to Rome for reinforcements to help deal with the enemy now that the cohort at Carales is no longer available.'

'I doubt he'll have much luck with that while the pestilence is loose in the province. Nero and his advisers aren't going to be happy about putting more men at risk. We'll have to make do with the forces we have left. Two thousand men or so. Half of them manning the outposts and forts around the enemy's territory. It's going to be tough work,' Cato mused.

'It's heartening to see that Rome is appointing the brightest and best of its strategists to positions of command,' Apollonius responded archly. Then he relented. 'It's good to see you have recovered. I'll be honest, I feared that with Plancinus in charge, things might not work out well. Don't get me wrong, he's a fine centurion, but he is no Prefect Cato, nor a Centurion Macro for that matter.'

'Things may not work out well all the same,' Cato cautioned. Something else occurred to him. 'Did Claudia have any assistance when she was looking after me? The cohort's surgeon, for example?'

'There was only Claudia. I brought the surgeon with me that first day, but his advice was so minimal as to be useless. She took it all on herself. You might want to consider offering her the surgeon's post. From what I've seen, she could do the job much better. But then maybe she was motivated by more personal considerations . . .'

Cato shot him a challenging stare. 'What do you mean?'

'What do you think I mean? A man would have to be uncommonly unobservant not to see that she is fond of you.

197

Very fond. And from our exchanges each day, I would add that a man would have to be uncommonly stupid not to be flattered by her attention and affection. She's a fine woman, Cato. You could do far worse. Forgive me, I forgot, you already have.'

He had gone too far and Cato growled at him. 'Before I lose my temper and do something I'll regret, you'd better go and tell Prefect Tadius to report to me once I return to the fort.'

'You are in no condition to make such threats, Prefect.' Apollonius tapped a finger to his forehead in farewell and turned to walk down the mole to the quay. Cato watched him with a sour expression. He had confided too much in Apollonius and the agent had obviously discovered more about Cato's previous life by himself. Enough to goad him, but to what end? Julia's treachery was going to be an open wound, it seemed. No matter how hard Cato tried to forget, let alone forgive, it would always be there, disfiguring even those memories of the happy moments they had once shared.

Then he recalled Claudia. She had gone to fetch him some wine and had not returned. Come to that, he had not heard a sound out of her since she had climbed the ladder to the tower keeper's quarters. He felt a cold stab of fear run down his spine and struggled to his feet, making his way inside as quickly as he could.

'Claudia?' he called.

There was no response, so he called out again and then began to climb the ladder, gritting his teeth at the effort it caused his weakened limbs. As his head rose above the opening, he saw that she was slumped over the table next to the carving the keeper had been at work on the day he was forced to leave his home. A small jar rested on the table before her and a cup lay on its side, knocked over. Wine was still dripping into the puddle on the floor, bright like blood in the sunlight streaming in through the open window.

'Are you all right?' he asked as he clambered up the last few rungs and crossed the room towards her, praying that she had not succumbed to the sickness.

She responded to the hand he placed on her shoulder with a disgruntled shift in position, and then her torso swelled as she took a deep breath and began snoring.

'My poor Claudia,' Cato said softly. He looked round and saw a cloak lying on top of a small chest. Easing her head up from the table, he slid the folds under her cheek. 'You rest . . . Sleep as long as you like. You have earned it. That, and my eternal gratitude.'

He hesitated, then bent to kiss the back of her head, breathing in the scent of her hair. She stirred slightly and mumbled something incoherent, then settled again. Cato regarded her fondly before climbing back down to the storeroom, his mind already turning to the prospect of the coming campaign against the province's enemies. The pestilence that had struck Carales had robbed him of a third of the men needed to put down the brigand tribes. It was almost as if he was fighting two enemies, he mused. Neither of them was the kind of conventional enemy he had been trained to face in battle, but both would need to be contained and eliminated. The question was, which of them would prove to be the greater danger? As things stood, he was anxious that while he might crush the brigands, the pestilence might never be defeated.

CHAPTER EIGHTEEN

Several hours passed before Cato felt himself well enough to leave the beacon tower. After sending for the decurion of the German bodyguards to take care of the exhausted Claudia, he hired a cart to take him back to the fort. The short journey proved to be a new form of torment, as the wheels thumped down into potholes and lurched in and out of the grooves worn into the flagstones of the streets leading through the town. Each jarring movement threatened to make him throw up or loosen his bowels. It was even worse when the cart left the town and took the turning onto a track that covered the mercifully short distance to the fort. He had the driver drop him outside the headquarters building and walked slowly through the entrance, acknowledging the salute of the sentry with a nod. His quarters were on the first storey and he had to pause halfway up the staircase as he did not trust his legs to carry him to the top without collapsing.

'Here, let me help,' said Apollonius as he hurried down to meet him. 'I was watching for you through your office window.'

'I can manage.'

'I don't think so. If anything, you look worse than you did this morning.'

He pulled Cato's arm across his shoulder and took his wrist

firmly, supporting the prefect's weight with his other hand as he helped him to climb the remaining stairs. Cato was too exhausted to refuse his help and allowed himself to be steered along the landing to his sleeping quarters opposite the office.

'The prefect of the Fourth Cohort is waiting in your office. I can't say that he's been happy about being kept there for most of the day.'

'I can imagine,' Cato responded as he indicated the chair beside the narrow window that looked out over the roofs of the barrack blocks. Once he was seated, he found that his limbs were trembling, and he clasped his hands together to try and still them. 'I'll see him in a moment. Just need to get my strength back.'

Apollonius regarded him critically. 'You look done in. Why not wait until the evening, or even tomorrow morning? He's not going anywhere.'

Cato shook his head. 'There's no time to spare. I've wasted enough of that already in recent days.'

'You were laid low by the sickness.' Apollonius frowned. 'It was hardly your choice to waste time. Stop being so hard on yourself for once. You are not Heracles or Achilles. You are mortal like the rest of us and should judge yourself by that standard rather than crushing yourself under the weight of the burdens you heap on yourself. What do you think you have to prove? I've not known you long, Cato, but I know your worth, and that's not something I say lightly.'

Cato sighed as he looked the agent in the eye. 'Have you finished?'

'Why, is there something I missed out?'

'You forget yourself, Apollonius. I am in command here. I will not brook insubordination from my officers. Not even Macro.'

'Macro is no longer here, and you sorely need someone you can trust to tell you the truth.'

'The truth? I can recall rather too many occasions since we first met when you proved to be evasive at best when you weren't being dishonest.'

'All the more reason for you to value the words I offer you now. And if you cannot stomach me being honest with you, then perhaps it might be best if I leave you to get on with your campaign without my assistance.'

There was a silence as both men stared at each other, grim-faced. Cato cleared his throat so that his voice would be firm. 'Is that what you really want?'

'No, damn you,' Apollonius replied softly. 'I want to serve a man I actually respect. I've served too many who were not worthy of my talents.'

'Such commendable modesty should not go unrewarded. I will allow you to remain in my service.'

Apollonius's eyes narrowed fractionally and Cato could not help the twitch at the corners of his mouth that betrayed his humorous intent, then both men laughed spontaneously in relief.

'You had me there, sir.'

'Yes, I did. For once. And it feels very satisfying.' Cato's expression became serious. 'I thank you for your honesty and I promise that I will always listen to your advice, but I cannot give you my word that I will act on it, nor that there can be any question of you disobeying my orders. That has to be understood between us. I should have made it clear before now. That is my mistake. Are we agreed?'

He held out his hand, and after the briefest of hesitations, Apollonius reached out and they clasped each other by the forearm. 'You have my word on it, sir.'

'Good, then you'd better let Tadius know that I will join him shortly.'

'Yes, sir.' Apollonius dipped his head in acknowledgement, which was the nearest he had yet come to a formal salute, and turned to leave the room, closing the door behind him.

Cato gathered his strength as he reflected on what the agent had said. It was heartening to be praised by a man whose skills and intelligence were at least a match for his own. And yet, being the cautious creature that he was, he was instinctively wary. To his mind, those individuals who offered him praise were either too easily pleased or lacked the perspicacity to see him as he truly was: a man riddled by self-doubt whose courage was born out of fear of being seen as a coward. If they only knew how his guts turned to ice every time he went into battle, and how he dreaded failure, their praise would swiftly turn to contempt.

He stood up and tested his footing before crossing to his travel chest and taking out a wide military belt. Fastening it about his waist, he grimaced as he saw that the buckle needed to be tightened two more notches to fit his diminished frame. Taking a deep breath, he left the room, crossed the corridor and entered the cohort commander's office.

As he paced steadily across the room to the desk, Prefect Tadius rose from the bench by the door and regarded him coldly. He was a thin, angular man who seemed to be little more than a frame upon which to hang his tunic and armour. He had dark eyes and lifeless brown hair that hung over his forehead, straight and glistening with some kind of oil.

'I've been kept waiting here all day,' he seethed, his accent nasal and well bred.

'So I understand. Then again, I've been waiting for you to come to Tharros for rather more than a few days, so you have little to complain about.' Cato stared back at the other officer, challenging him to display any further defiance. After a moment, Tadius's gaze shifted over Cato's shoulder, towards the nearest window.

'I had matters to attend to in Tibula.'

'Matters so important that you failed to obey my orders? What matters could those be precisely?'

'Governor Scurra required me to complete preparations for the defence of the town before I came here.'

'Defences? Against what? The nearest enemy is nearly a hundred miles from Tibula. That is not an acceptable excuse, Prefect. Furthermore, the military chain of command stops here.' Cato banged the top of the desk with his fist. 'You take orders from me, not Scurra. If you fail to obey me again, I will have you removed from your command and sent back to Rome.'

Tadius's jaw sagged in surprise. 'You would not dare. I have friends in Rome who—'

'Quiet! Do you imagine for one moment that you are the first man to make such a threat to me? I don't give a shit about what friends you and that fat dolt Scurra may have back in Rome. Chances are they are cut from the same cloth as you: indolent inbreds with an arrogant sense of entitlement to public office and military rank that should be the preserve of men with greater talent who have earned their right to hold those ranks . . .' Cato paused, angry with himself for letting his temper reveal his thoughts. He eased himself onto his chair before he continued, more calmly, 'You know where you stand now, Tadius. Do not test my patience or authority again. Is that clear?'

'Yes . . . sir.'

'Good. Now let's not waste any more time.' Cato went over

his campaign plan before turning to his specific orders for the Fourth Illyrian. 'Your cohort is to march from Tibula as soon as you return there. Take the local militia with you and collect any other forces from the towns you pass through.'

'The local magistrates aren't going to like that.'

'Doesn't matter. You tell them the orders come from me and I am the one to take it up with if they want to complain. Either way, the militia are to join you. Make it clear to them that they are to consider themselves subject to military discipline. Anyone who refuses to march with you, or who tries to run off, will be treated as a deserter and punished accordingly. No exceptions. Understand?'

Tadius nodded.

'You will make for Caput Tyrsi and construct a marching camp there. You will construct further outposts to cover all the roads and tracks between there and the sea. They will be garrisoned by the militia until the campaign is over. Your cohort will cover the outposts if they come under attack, but you are not to pursue the enemy. You and your fortifications will be the anvil to my men's hammer. With the marines covering the coastal settlements, my columns will force the enemy back towards you, destroying their settlements and camps as we advance. Once the trap closes, we'll crush them between us.'

Tadius reflected a moment before he responded. 'Seems simple enough.'

'I'm glad you think so, since there will be no excuse for any mistakes in carrying out my orders. If everyone plays their part, this should be over before autumn arrives.'

'And what of the spoils?'

'What about them?'

'Strikes me your columns will capture most of the enemy, as well as looting their settlements. What will the rest of us get out of it? Me and my men, as well as those from the naval squadron?'

'There'll be fair shares from the proceeds of the prisoner auctions and any large caches of treasure that fall into our hands. Satisfied?'

'Very.' Tadius smiled for the first time. 'What about the militia?'

'They'll get their share, just like everyone else,' said Cato. 'The prospect of reward might cure their resentment at being forced to leave their homes for a few months.'

Tadius's smile faded. 'It'll mean less for the rest of us.'

'True, but if I were you, I'd sleep better knowing the militia had a stake in covering my back . . . Anything else you want to say?'

'It occurs to me that there is one other factor you need to consider as far as your plan goes.'

'You mean the pestilence?'

'Yes, sir. From what I've heard since I reached Tharros, it's hit Carales badly and there's a danger it may spread across the island.' He cleared his throat. 'I was told that you were affected?'

'Yes, it's true. But I have recovered now.'

Tadius regarded him dubiously. 'If you say so, sir . . . If the pestilence does spread, it may affect our campaign.'

'Then let's hope we deal with the enemy first,' Cato said tersely. 'Anything else?'

The prefect thought briefly and shook his head.

'I'll have your written orders prepared and you can leave for Tibula the moment they are in your hands. There's a stockpile of supplies for your forces waiting at Caput Tyrsi. It should be enough for the next two months.' Cato gestured towards the door. 'You are dismissed, Prefect Tadius. I expect a message from you within the next ten days to say your men are in position at Caput Tyrsi. Don't disappoint me.'

'I'll do my best,' Tadius replied, and left the office.

Cato's shoulders slumped wearily as he leaned over his desk. He was frustrated that the briefest of meetings had fatigued him. How many more days must pass before he was fit enough to take the field?

There was a tap at the door and Apollonius entered without waiting for a response. 'I take it some sharp words were exchanged with Prefect Tadius, judging from his expression as he stormed down the corridor.'

'I said what needed to be said. I gave him his orders. Make sure he gets the written version before he leaves. I want the Fourth Illyrian ready to march as soon as possible. Pass that on to Plancinus. We'll leave for Augustis at first light. A half-century should be enough to hold the fort and reassure the locals. They are to be chosen from those too old or unfit for the campaign.'

'Speaking of fitness, are you sure you will be recovered enough by tomorrow?'

'One way or another. We need to strike at the enemy before the pestilence has a chance to spread to our forces. We'll need the mounted column back, so Centurion Ignatius will have to take one of the infantry centuries to replace it at the roadblocks around Carales.'

'Shall I send for him?'

'No. I need to rest. Pass the order on to him. He'll take command of the Sixth Century and head for Carales tomorrow. Tell him to pick up any militia he comes across along the way.'

Apollonius sucked his cheek. 'You're cutting things a bit fine, if I may say so. Stripping towns of their militia to fill out our ranks is going to leave them defenceless.'

'I'll have to take the risk. We need as many men as we can get to take the fight to the enemy. If we simply try to defend every town, fort and outpost, we'll only end up defending none of them once the enemy decides to pick them off one at a time.'

'That's true.'

'I'm glad you agree,' Cato responded drily as he stood up and made for the door. 'Now leave me be and pass the orders on.'

'Yes, sir.'

Once he had reached his sleeping quarters, he loosened the belt and let it slip to the floor before collapsing onto the bed. He was still wearing his boots and decided to rest a moment before removing them. Lying back, he closed his eyes. He could hear the orders barked by an officer as he drilled some troops not far from the headquarters building. This late in the afternoon, it was likely that the men in question were on a punishment detail for some infractions committed during the day. After the sounds of waves crashing against the rocks that had accompanied his fever over the last few days, the fort was strangely quiet by comparison. Cato's thoughts turned to what Apollonius had said about him being fit and ready to resume command. He feared that a good night's sleep would not be enough respite to prepare him for the hardships and dangers that lay ahead. For a few heartbeats his mind was troubled by his doubts and fears, and then he slipped into a deep sleep, still wearing his boots.

Long before the sun had risen over the peaks of the hills to the east of Tharros, the Sixth Gallic Cohort had marched out of the gate and down the track to the road that led from the town into the heart of the island. A short distance further on, another road branched south, and Ignatius and his small column of infantry peeled off from the tail of the cohort and marched to relieve

Centurion Massimilianus and his mounted squadron maintaining the quarantine of Carales.

Cato was riding at the head of the cohort, ahead of the colour party with its standards and the gilded image of Emperor Nero. It was not a great likeness, he mused, but then nearly all the men who served under the symbol would never see the emperor in the flesh, so they would never know. He smiled at the significance soldiers placed in such symbols, ready to shed their last drop of blood in their defence. There was no apparent logic to it, and at the same time Cato knew he would willingly do the same in a heartbeat. It was like the chariot races back in Rome. There were people who supported one of the teams and wore their colour as if their lives depended on it. Those who wore other colours were the enemy. People argued, fought and even died because of the colour of a strip of cloth, and yet to question the rationality of such blind loyalty was sufficient to provoke uncomprehending disdain at best.

As the sun rose and its rays flooded across the landscape around Tharros, Cato looked out across the rolling hills and verdant woods and picked out the distant villa that belonged to Claudia. The whitewashed walls gleamed like ivory in the direct sunshine, and he could not help his thoughts turning to the beguiling woman for whom his initial unfavourable impression had transmuted to growing affection and a desire to spend more time with her. Much more time. That must wait, he reminded himself. First he must destroy his enemy.

He turned his gaze away and directed it towards the line of hills stretching out on either side before him. On the far side of those hills lay the dense forests and mountain lairs of the tribesmen who were descended from the island's first inhabitants. Such people cleaved to their traditions and love of their land with the same fervour with which the soldiers of Rome venerated the standards beneath which they marched, fought and died. It would be a battle of convictions as much as a military struggle. In Cato's experience, such fanaticism could be the deciding factor in a conflict. So who would prove to have the most heart for the coming struggle? Those fighting for the lands that had been theirs for generations immemorial, or those paid to fight in the name of Emperor Nero? He was not encouraged by his answer to the question.

CHAPTER NINETEEN

The fort at Augustis was situated on a small plateau with steep sides that overlooked a vast rolling landscape of forest bounded by distant hills. The tree canopy was pierced by tall conical stone towers at regular intervals. Some of the structures were larger, with two or even three towers. It gave the illusion of some great city swallowed up by nature so that only its highest monuments lay visible. At the foot of the sheer cliff that dropped down from the eastern wall of the fort lay a river. Boulders and small rocks that had fallen from the cliff littered the bed so that the shallow current surged round them with unceasing bursts of spray and the soft roar reached up to those on sentry duty at the fort. At the time the fort had been constructed, nearly a hundred years earlier, the builders had ensured that it had a ready supply of water by carving out four large cisterns fed by the rains of autumn and winter. They lay beneath the barrack blocks at the highest point of the fort and were accessed by an inspection passage at the foot of a short flight of stairs.

To the west of the plateau lay the town of Augustis, sitting beside the junction of the road that ran from Carales to Tibula and a lesser route that crossed the island from Tharros to the minor port of Sulcis. Thanks to its position astride two trade routes, the town, though of modest size, was prosperous, boasting three bathhouses, a theatre where gladiator fights were held on occasion, and a wall high enough to deter brigands but no match for siege weapons.

As Cato and his column approached, a deputation of the town's councillors came to greet him. He ordered Plancinus to take the column on to the fort while he turned aside with Apollonius to confer with the small party. As introductions were made, he saw a mixture of relief and anger in the councillors' faces and braced himself to deal with their complaints. It had taken three days to march from Tharros, and he was bone weary.

The leader of the town council was a short, corpulent individual named Pinotus. He proudly wore his chain of office as if it was a military decoration for extreme valour, and raised it slightly between finger and thumb as he addressed Cato.

'It's about time Scurra sent some men to protect us from those bloody brigands. These last few months they've been ranging over our farming estates and mines at will. Now that you're here, there'll be soldiers on hand to defend our property. And it's about time. We pay our taxes and we deserve better than Scurra has done for us so far.'

His companions murmured their support for his robust complaint.

'The governor is not in command of this operation,' Cato explained.

'Ah!' Pinotus exclaimed happily. 'He's been replaced, then?'

'Scurra is still in office. I have been sent from Rome to take charge of the garrison and deal with the brigands. I intend to use my men to hunt down the enemy, not to spread them out to act as nightwatchmen for your property.'

'Ouch . . .' Apollonius muttered.

'You'll never succeed in hunting them down,' Pinotus protested. 'They know the forests and hills of this region better than the lines on their hands. They'll slip through your fingers just as they have with every Roman that ever tried to run them to ground.'

'We'll see about that. Tell me,' Cato nodded towards the town, 'is there a militia at Augustis?'

'Yes, enough to defend the town but not to protect the surrounding farms and villas, or to patrol the roads. That's why we're glad to see you and your soldiers.'

'How many men do you have in the militia?'

'Fifty or so. Barely enough to man the gates, let alone defend the walls.'

'I want them moved up to the fort immediately. They'll need their marching packs. See to it.'

Pinotus's jaw sagged before he laughed nervously. 'You are joking, of course.'

'Do I look as if I am?'

'But . . . but we need the militia to defend the town! What are we supposed to do without them?'

'Buy yourself a sword and learn how to use it would be my advice. Perhaps it will do you good to defend your property rather than paying others to do it for you. In any case, I need your men. All fifty of them. If they are not there by nightfall, I'll send Apollonius and his men to make up the shortfall, starting with you and your friends here.'

'This is an outrage!' Pinotus blustered, his fat cheeks shaking with rage. 'I shall protest to the governor!'

'Join the queue,' Apollonius said in an amused tone.

'Your protest is noted,' Cato concluded. 'Complain to whoever you like, but I will have those men by nightfall.'

He clicked his tongue and tugged his reins, turning his horse away to rejoin the passing column of dust-covered soldiers sweating freely under the burden of the kit fastened to their marching yokes. Apollonius lingered a moment longer to savour the discomfort of the men from the town.

'Until we meet again, gentlemen. Just make sure it isn't later this evening. I'll not be best pleased if I have to come down to round you up to fill out the ranks.' He dipped his head briefly in farewell and turned his mount to catch up with Cato.

From the track leading up to the fort the structure looked formidable enough, but as they reached the gate, Cato saw that there were piles of rubbish lying in the bottom of the ditch, and the foundations of the wall were crumbling in places, causing cracks to work their way up towards the ramparts. Stunted bushes were growing close to the ditch and down the slopes and along the bottom. That was of less concern since they would hinder any attacker. However, they made the fort look neglected and Cato resolved to have the cohort's base of operations repaired and smartened up, as much for the good it would do to discipline as to improve its defences.

The gates had been opened as soon as the approaching column was sighted by the half-century that had been sent to ready the barracks for occupation and to prepare the supply stockpiles. The optio in command, Fabius, had drawn up his men in two ranks on either side of the gate, and gave the order for them to salute as Cato emerged from under the gatehouse. He reined in and looked over his immediate surroundings. The barrack blocks seemed to be in good repair, and the fort was large enough to accommodate a standard auxiliary cohort of five hundred or so men. The column he had led from Tharros was half as big again, thanks to the two hundred largely reluctant militiamen he had collected along the route. The extra men would mean the fort would be overcrowded until the last of the militia had been sent to man the new outposts that were to be constructed around the enemy's lands.

He turned back to the optio. 'The outside of the fort seems to be in poor shape, Fabius.'

The man's face fell at the rebuke, then he swallowed and gave his response. 'We've been making good the interior, sir. I haven't had time to deal with the walls and ditches yet.'

'Hmm,' Cato growled. He did not approve of officers whose first instinct was to make excuses, no matter if they might be justified. As a Praetorian, Fabius should have taken the criticism on the chin. Now he had a mark against his name.

'Plancinus!'

'Sir?'

'Assign the men to their barracks. Have the militia distributed amongst the blocks with your men in.'

Plancinus looked uncomfortable. 'Is that wise, sir? It's bound to cause some friction, given that we're going to be doubling up on some of the accommodation.'

It was a fair point, but Cato had weighed it against other considerations. The men of the militia units were already grumbling about their conscription into the campaign, and it would be unwise to give them the opportunity to air their grievances to each other en masse, thereby undermining their morale. Better to disperse them amongst the auxiliaries, where the inter-unit frictions would keep their minds occupied and where they might even be encouraged to pick up some soldierly habits. As it was, they were mostly poorly trained and unfit, if their shambling along at the rear of the marching column was anything to go by. There had been too many stragglers, and only by sending back Centurions Cornelius and

Pelius to wield their vine canes had he managed to keep the column intact each day. The militia were only suited to garrison duty, where they would free up the auxiliary troops to strengthen the columns Cato planned to use to strike into the heart of the enemy's territory.

Plancinus coughed, and Cato realised that he had been distracted by his thoughts. He met the centurion's gaze. 'Have them bunk down with your men, like I said.'

'Yes, sir.'

'Once the men have settled in, pass the word for all officers to attend a briefing at headquarters as soon as the first hour of the night is sounded.'

'Very good, sir.'

Cato dismounted and handed his reins to one of Fabius's men. Signalling to Apollonius to join him on foot, he set off to walk through the fort to the far wall that ran along the top of the cliff above the river. With the sun at their backs, the rock upon which the fort was built cast a long shadow over the forest below. They regarded the vista in silence for a moment before Apollonius spoke.

'I fear that finding our brigand friends amongst all those trees is going to be like finding a glass bead in a grain store.'

'Quite. But if anyone can do it, you can. You've plenty of experience of scouting and spying.'

Apollonius smiled. 'Pardon me for pointing out the obvious, but there's something of a difference between the desert terrain of the eastern frontier and that dense woodland down there.'

'Granted. However, a man of your talents will always adapt to circumstances. Are your men ready?'

Apollonius nodded. 'As soon as you give the order.'

'Good. Then take whatever provisions you need from the

stores and leave at first light. I need you to map the routes through the forests, any settlements belonging to the enemy's tribes, as well as their camps. It's an intelligence-gathering operation, mind you. No heroics. Get me as much information as you can and report back here in ten days.'

'Spare me the lecture on heroics. I'm not Macro.'

'No. You're not. And he'll be missed when the time comes to stick it to the enemy.'

Apollonius looked at him searchingly. 'I suspect he is missed rather more often than that.'

'Maybe. But that can't be helped. Our ways have parted now and I'll have to manage by myself.'

'And how is that going for you?'

Cato rolled his head and cracked a stiff muscle in his neck. 'You ask too many questions.'

'That's what spies are supposed to do, Prefect. Fewer questions when we are trying to be unobtrusive, of course.'

'How about when you are merely being *in*trusive?'

'Oh, if that's our purpose, then as many as possible before our presence becomes intolerable.'

'I think we may just have reached that point . . .' Cato turned to him. 'You have your orders. Take no risks with your men's lives, nor your own. If you can capture a few prisoners for interrogation, so much the better. Dismissed.'

'Dismissed? Just like that.'

'It's how we do things in the army. Stick around long enough and you'll get used to it.'

'I'm not so sure I want to, but I'll play along for now.' Apollonius tapped a finger to his brow in an informal salute and turned to descend the wall.

Cato leaned on the parapet and stared at the forest as the daylight began to fade. He felt uneasy. It took a moment to pin the sensation down, and then he realised that he was recalling his time on the northern frontier many years ago. He recalled the chill in the air as night fell over the dense forests of Germania. It was as if the tall trees marked the frontier between civilisation and the mystery and depravity of the lands inhabited by barbarous tribes whose appetite for war was matched only by the savage cruelty with which they waged it. Varus and his three legions had marched into those forests half a century ago and, abandoned by their guides, had stumbled through the shadows beneath the boughs of ancient trees until they were trapped and annihilated. The handful of survivors had spent the rest of their lives haunted by the experience. Now Cato was looking out over another forest, wondering if the fates intended to treat him the same way.

He shivered and forced the prospect from his mind. Varus had been an incautious fool. Thanks to the relatively small number of men under his command, and the dubious quality of many of them, Cato was obliged to exercise caution. If he experienced one serious setback, he feared the campaign would fail at the first hurdle.

Apollonius and his men slipped out of the fort the following morning as soon as there was enough light to see by. Cato had found it difficult to sleep and was dressed in time to watch them ride down the slope and disappear into the forest. He was under few illusions about the dangers the party faced. If they were caught by the enemy, they would be held as hostages if they were lucky. If not, it was likely they would be killed to serve as an example to any Roman soldiers who dared to enter the territory the brigands claimed as their own. Yet the risk must be taken; it was vital to gain intelligence on the disposition of the enemy if they were to be hunted down and forced to fight.

Not long after the departure of the scouts, a trumpet sounded at headquarters as the first hint of the rising sun glimmered on the horizon and the daily routine began. Officers roused their men to fetch their section's rations from the quartermaster to cook the barley gruel that would fill their stomachs until the evening meal. The smell of woodsmoke filled the air for a while, then the fires were extinguished and the men formed up outside their barrack blocks ready for inspection. Eight carts had already been loaded with supplies and equipment for the two centuries Centurion Plancinus was leading to construct the first of the outposts on high points overlooking the forested hills.

A hundred of the militiamen were also marching with them to aid with the construction work, with ten men being left behind to garrison each outpost that was built. They would be provided with sufficient supplies to feed them for a month. The outposts would consist of a tower surrounded by a stockade and ditch. A beacon would be on the tower with a ready stock of wood and materials to make smoke. The signals were simple enough: an uninterrupted column of smoke if the outpost was attacked, and puffs if the enemy were spotted, plus four further signals to communicate the direction the brigands were headed. The militia units had a wide assortment of weapons and armour and their yokes were laden with an idiosyncratic variety of essentials and items that Cato suspected would be abandoned once the men struggled to keep up with the auxiliaries.

As soon as the inspection and roll call were completed, the first and second centuries of the cohort fetched the mules from the fort's stables and harnessed the teams to the carts before gathering up their marching yokes and taking their place in the column ahead of the loose formation of the militiamen.

Cato regarded them with an experienced eye and conceded

that, auxiliary troops though they were, they turned out well and looked ready for action. Plancinus and the other Praetorians had done a commendable job of training them in the short time available. He walked down the column inspecting the men, and nodded a greeting to Plancinus as he stood with Centurion Cornelius, the auxiliary officers of the two centuries and those in command of the militia contingents.

'Good morning, gentlemen!'

They exchanged salutes before he turned back to Plancinus.

'You know what to do. Stick to your orders. Get the forts built, assign the garrisons and then get back here to replenish your equipment and supplies for the next batch of outposts. If the enemy attack, you are not to pursue them, no matter how tempting it might be. I'll not have my men blundering about in the forests looking for shadows when they should be building forts. You'll get your chance to get stuck into the brigands soon enough, I promise.'

'Yes, sir.'

Cato switched his attention to the militia officers. Aside from better kit, they looked as unsoldierly as those they commanded. It was as well that he was only depending upon them to keep watch over the landscape around their outposts. He would not have trusted them to take their place in a battle line and hold firm when the fighting began. Nevertheless it was necessary to encourage them to be diligent, and he addressed them in a friendly tone.

'You men have the most important task of all. You are the eyes and ears of our column, so you must stay alert and give the signal if you see anything of importance. If any merchants or shepherds pass your position, talk to them and see if they have useful intelligence. Anything that isn't covered by the signal system we went over last night means you'll have to send one of your men back to the fort. What I said to Plancinus goes for you too. Carry out your orders and do nothing more than that. Is that clear?'

They nodded or mumbled their assent and Cato sighed inwardly at the frustration of being reliant on such men when he was used to the proficiency and confidence of the trained men of the legions and the Praetorian Guard.

'Good luck to you, gentlemen. Plancinus, I'll see you back here in a few days. As for you militiamen, I'll be making the rounds of the outposts once Centurion Massimilianus's mounted force reaches the fort. Make sure you check carefully when you challenge anyone approaching your outposts. I didn't survive the pestilence only to be skewered by some javelin-happy sentry.'

The officers laughed and smiled at the warning before Cato cleared his throat. 'May the gods march with you! Farewell.'

He left Plancinus to bellow the order to stand to and make ready to advance, and made his way back to headquarters. He was still feeling weak. Three days in the saddle and lack of sleep had taken its toll, and he knew he must not strain himself unduly if he was to be fit enough to lead his men into battle when the opportunity came. There were plenty of administrative tasks demanding his attention, but he was determined to rest and build his strength up over the following days while the ground was prepared to contain the enemy.

As he trudged back to headquarters between the barrack blocks, he could not help feeling some concern over the enemy's quiescence as the column had marched across the island towards the forts. There had been no news of further attacks, nor any attempt to ambush or even harass them, a surprising omission given the lack of mounted men to drive off and chase down any brigand horsemen. That did not bode well.

He sensed the enemy was up to something. Quite what their intentions might be, he did not know, but he must be ready to act the moment they revealed themselves.

CHAPTER TWENTY

It had been a long, hot day and Claudia's exposed skin tingled with sunburn as she eased off her headband, stained with sweat, and regarded the results of her work. The trellis ran along the length of the crumbling storehouse she had chosen to make into her study. It was perched on a terrace amid the olive groves of her small estate. Once used for agricultural tools, it had been neglected since a previous owner had decided to concentrate on breeding horses. It faced west, overlooking the sea a couple of miles in the distance, and provided a spectacular view of the sunset. She had cleared the rusted tools and debris from inside the building and had had a carpenter cut the wood for the trellis, which would provide a frame for a vine to create shade while she lay on a couch and read.

The task of erecting the supports and angled braces and fixing the beams in place to support the trellis had been beyond her, and the decurion had brought two of the Germans with him to provide the necessary manual labour. Claudia had overseen their efforts in between cleaning the interior ready to whitewash the walls inside and out. Now the work was done, she viewed it from every angle. Already she was thinking about the furnishings she would need to complete the place: a table and a spare couch for guests. As soon as she considered the prospect, her thoughts turned to Cato. She felt a stab of concern at his marching off with his men before he had fully recovered. That was foolish of him. He should have given himself time to build up his strength. She smiled at herself. In truth she had hoped he might delay leaving the fort so she could spend more time with him.

What Cato did not recall, but must surely suspect, was that she had seen every detail of his body while she had nursed him through his illness in the tower in the harbour. After she had gently stripped and washed him, she had stroked his skin as he slept or rested fitfully. Now and again she traced her fingers over his scars, wondering how he had come by them and what sights he must have seen in the years he had campaigned across the Empire. She herself had travelled very little, having been raised in Rome and kept there first by Seneca and then by Nero. Aside from two trips to the imperial palace at Baiae, crossing the sea to Sardinia was the furthest she had ever been. Given the strict terms of her exile, it was likely she would live the rest of her days on the island. She had known a handful of men's bodies as intimately as she knew Cato's, and it had only added to her attraction to him. If the gods were kind, he might spend some time at Tharros once his campaign was concluded and she could get to know him better. She had sensed that her feelings were reciprocated, and it gave her a warm thrill of pleasure to anticipate showing him her lodge and entertaining him there as they watched the sun set amid the scent of the flowers she would plant around the terrace.

'Is good?' one of the German bodyguards grunted.

Claudia turned to them. The decurion and his two men had stripped to the waist to work on the construction of the trellis, and their muscled torsos gleamed with perspiration in the honeyed glow of the late-afternoon sunshine. The Germans, larger than their decurion, had tied their long blond hair back with strips of cloth and regarded her with wide grins as they awaited her verdict.

'Is good, yes.'

'We finish now. Go . . .' The German paused and frowned with frustration before miming putting something in his mouth. 'Go and eat. Ha!'

Claudia laughed happily. 'Yes, we've all earned a good supper tonight. I'll have the cook make us something special.'

The Germans looked at her blankly, so she nodded to the decurion and he translated. Their eyes lit up at the prospect of food.

'Have your men put their tunics back on and pick up their weapons and tools and we'll head to the villa.'

'Yes, my lady.'

Claudia went inside the lodge and picked up the brushes and the bucket she had brought with her. A sudden chill caused her to shiver, and she draped a shawl around her shoulders. She decided she needed a good night's sleep to recover from her exertions. She took a last look around the interior. The only inconvenience associated with the building was the lack of water. There was no well nearby and any water needed would have to be carried up from the villa to fill the trough at the back of the lodge. That would be work for one of the house slaves, she decided. That reminded her to ask after the slave who had gone missing from the villa the previous day. One of the kitchen boys. He had been sent to pick wild herbs in the morning and had not been seen since. It was possible he had run away, although it was unlikely given the harsh beating he could expect for that if and when he was captured and returned. Claudia was more concerned that he might have fallen and injured himself, so she had sent three men from the stables to look for him. She made a mental note to ask for news the moment they reached the villa.

As she emerged with the bucket and brush, she saw that the men had put their tunics on and slung their sword belts over their shoulders. One of them carried the box with the hammers and nails while the other was holding the ladder across his broad shoulders. The decurion approached her and held out his hand.

'I'll take that for you, my lady.'

'Thank you,' Claudia replied. She handed it over, then turned to inspect their work one last time before setting off along the path that led through the olive trees towards the villa, no more than half a mile away.

The sun was low in the sky, and its slanted light bathed the tree trunks and boughs in a golden hue. The pleasant sense of well-being that came from a satisfactory day's labour filled her with a contentment she had not known in a long time. A short distance ahead, beside the track, grew a clump of magydaris, the mass of tiny white flowers glowing brilliantly in the angled light. She paused to reach down and pick some for her sleeping chamber in the villa. As she straightened up, she saw a face watching her over the top of the wall that ran around the estate. Her eyes moved on for an instant and then swept back to where she had seen it, but it was no longer visible.

The decurion and the Germans caught up and stopped a short distance behind her.

'What is it, my lady?'

'I . . .' She hesitated. There was nothing to be seen now and she might look foolish raising concern over seeing the face. More than likely it was a passing shepherd or some such. It certainly wasn't the boy who had disappeared the day before. As she tried to recall the brief glimpse in more detail, she realised there was something not quite right about it. Something not quite . . . human. She felt the first tingling apprehension at the back of her neck.

The decurion was scanning the olive trees in the direction he had seen her looking a moment earlier.

'What did you see, my lady?'

'I thought I saw a face. But it was probably just an animal of some kind. The evening light can play tricks sometimes.'

'Where did you see it?'

'Behind that wall over there, beyond the trees.'

The decurion strained his eyes as he stared at the spot. 'I see nothing.'

'Like I said, it was probably just a wild animal. Let's go. I want to be back at the villa before dusk.' Claudia was unsettled, and wanted to feel the security of having walls around her before it got dark. Having spent so much time in the city, she sometimes found the open country around her new home alien, even if it was beautiful and uncontaminated by the miasmic stench of Rome's streets.

They set off again, but now all four of them were more subdued, and watched the ground around them warily as they passed through the olive plantation and emerged at the foot of the hill upon which the villa stood. The grass grew sparsely on the slope, which was studded with shrubs, save for a small wooded area of sweet chestnuts a hundred paces to the side of the narrow track leading up to the villa. Claudia did not slow her pace as she began the climb. Her heart beat faster with the effort, and fresh beads of sweat broke out on her brow as they approached the crest of the hill. Behind them, out to sea, the sun had set over the horizon and the light had started to fade.

There was a sudden guttural comment, and Claudia stopped and looked back at the three men of her escort. One of the Germans was pointing towards the trees, and as he spoke hurriedly, the anxiety in his tone was palpable. She saw the decurion's hand slip to the pommel of his sword and his fingers clench slightly. That was the moment her unease crystallised into fear.

'What do you see?'

The decurion did not respond, and all three men stood still as they stared towards the trees. A moment later, there was a shrill warble, as if from the throat of a bird, and Claudia's gaze swept away from her escort, across the slope towards the wood, as several dark figures rose up from the grass in front of the chestnuts. They were clad in thick cloaks that seemed to cover their heads, where small horns protruded.

'Run!' the decurion shouted as he tossed the bucket into the grass.

There was no need to repeat the order in the tongue of his comrades, who dropped the ladder and tool box and surged up the path. Claudia hesitated, transfixed by the men breaking from cover and rushing up the hill at an angle to cut them off from the villa. More men were rising to their feet some distance to the other side of the track; there was no escape in that direction.

The decurion surged forward, grasping her by the wrist as he overtook her. 'Faster, miss! Run for your life!'

Claudia did as she was told, spurred on by the terror that gripped her heart as she glanced round and saw the strangely dressed men closing from either side. Apart from the scrabble of loose pebbles and laboured breathing, she heard nothing from them as they swept over the grass in silence. The top of the slope was no more than a hundred paces away, and she ran as hard as she could, drawn on by the decurion, the Germans following hard on her heels. She heard the dull thunder of hooves and saw a party of horsemen emerge from behind the chestnut trees and make for the crest of the hill. Ahead, she could see the top of the wall that surrounded the villa and its outbuildings, but a glance either side was enough to reveal that their pursuers were going to catch them before they gained the side gate at the end of the path.

The decurion snapped an order, and at once the two Germans stopped, drew their swords and strode out each side of the path to intercept the men rushing towards them. Now that they were closer, Claudia could see that they were wearing animal skins cut to cover their torsos and stretching up their necks to act as hoods. There was clearly some form of helmet beneath the hood to support the horns that protruded like small sets of antlers. Where their skin was exposed, it was covered in tattoos of animals with exaggerated claws, teeth, eyes and horns. They looked more like monsters from nightmares than human beings, and her blood ran cold with terror at the sight of them.

Still they made no noise, not even in response to the two Germans as they bellowed their war cries and challenges to their enemy.

'Keep going!' The decurion ran on, pulling her after him. The incline began to ease as they reached the brow of the hill, and the gate in the wall lay ahead. Claudia looked over her shoulder and saw one of the Germans charge forward, cutting down the first of the enemy with a savage blow to his shoulder. Pausing to wrench his sword free, he was set upon by three more men, who hacked at him as he raised his arm to shield his head. A flurry of blows drove him to his knees, and he collapsed out of sight in the grass. The other German was holding off two men, and was parrying their attacks when a spearman got behind him and thrust his weapon between the warrior's shoulder blades. It was all over in a few heartbeats, and then she and the decurion were at the side gate. It crashed back on its hinges as he burst through into the enclosure and thrust her towards the villa.

'Get inside and barricade the windows and doors. I'll deal with the main entrance. Go!'

She ran across the open ground as the decurion shut the side gate and slid the locking bar home then turned to shout, 'To arms! To arms! We're under attack!'

The other Germans in the enclosure instantly grasped the danger and ran to snatch up their shields and draw their weapons, while the villa's slaves and servants took up pitchforks and staves to defend themselves. The main gate to the enclosure was wide open, and the decurion had started running towards it to help the two servants who had recovered their wits enough to go to the assistance of the German guard on duty there. Before they could swing the heavy gates into position, however, the first of the enemy horsemen had galloped through the opening and reined in, spinning his mount around and striking down the nearest servant. He lived one heartbeat longer to celebrate his kill, as the guard grasped his spear in both hands and drove it upwards, under the rider's ribcage and deep into his chest, ripping the point free as his foe toppled from his saddle.

As more riders charged into the enclosure, the decurion realised that the first line of defence was lost. He turned and ran towards the main entrance of the villa, calling out to the surviving Germans and then to all the others of the household. 'On me! On me! Get back to the villa!'

The side gate shook under the impact of blows from outside. One of the riders galloped across to it and dropped nimbly to the ground before lifting the locking bar and casting it aside. The gate swung open and his comrades raced past him.

As soon as the decurion reached the entrance of the villa, he stopped and turned, chest heaving. His men formed up around him, shields raised, swords and spears angled towards the enemy. Those slaves who had been outside the villa rushed past them to the safety of the large building. Some were too slow and were cut down in the open ground. The decurion could hear shouts from inside as Claudia gave her orders, and there was the scraping of furniture and the crash of shutters being closed and barred. As the last of the fugitives pressed through the ranks of the Germans, he saw a group of the enemy forming up twenty paces away, preparing to attack.

CHAPTER TWENTY-ONE

'Inside!' the decurion called out to his men in their tongue, and the small force backed up and hurriedly closed and bolted the doors before dragging a heavy chest against them and then adding other items of furniture.

'Stay here!' he ordered, and hurried off to find Claudia. She had already got the door to the garden closed and bolted and was supervising barricading the shutters of the lower windows along the front of the house. He could see at once that the enemy would make short work of such obstacles.

'My lady, we can't stop them getting in. We need to fall back to a room we can defend.'

'The kitchen,' she suggested. 'There's only one door leading into the corridor and one to the outside, and the windows are set high in the wall.'

The decurion recalled the arrangement of the room and nodded. 'That'll have to do. Get everyone in there and barricade the outside wall. I'll hold the front door and we'll fall back if it gives way or we hear them getting in elsewhere.'

She nodded. 'Good luck.'

'We're going to need it, my lady.'

Claudia turned away to shout instructions to the house slaves, and they scurried down the corridor to the kitchen, terror etched into their expressions. She checked the rooms on the ground floor to make sure they were clear and then hurried after them, passing the atrium, where she saw the broad backs of the Germans as they stood a short distance from the door. Already the air was filled with the sounds of axes hacking at the timbers, and the first splinters flew inwards as she continued down the corridor.

'Steady, boys!' the decurion called out calmly as he tightened his grip on his sword. His shield and armour were still in his room, but there had been no time to fetch them. He glanced round and saw that he and his men were alone. More splinters shot past his head, and then there was a shattering crash and the doors burst in to reveal several of their attackers, holding the horse trough they had used as a battering ram.

'Get 'em!' the decurion yelled, and rushed the enemy, who had dropped the trough and were reaching for their weapons. He thrust his sword into the face of the nearest raider, smashing through his teeth and tearing through the top of his throat and the spine beyond. The man gave a guttural cry and staggered back as the decurion tore his blade free and hacked at the arm of the next man. The Germans crashed into the attackers outside the entrance, using their bulk to knock their foes back with their shields and slashing at them with their swords and axes, striking down several raiders in the first few heartbeats. The decurion felt a searing pain in his left arm as a spear tore at his bicep and pinned it to his chest. He swung his sword at his attacker and cut through the man's wrist, and the pressure of the spear against his ribs eased.

'Hold your ground!' he shouted to his men. 'Defend the entrance!'

He pulled back through the ruined door and sheathed his sword before grasping the shaft of the spear. With gritted teeth he pulled the point out of his chest and back through his arm, and cast it aside as blood pulsed from the wound. He took the strip of cloth he had been using as a headband and bound it tightly over the wound before tying it off with the aid of his teeth, then drew his sword again. He saw that the Germans had been pressed back. Only five remained on their feet and the body of one of their comrades lay across two of his enemies, his skull caved in by a sword blow. Beyond, the enclosure was filled with at least fifty more of the attackers, most of whom were running to join the fight for the entrance to the villa. The odds were massively against the Germans and the decurion knew they must retreat to the kitchen, where there was a better chance of holding the enemy off.

'Fall back! Fall back to the kitchen!'

He backed away into the corridor as his men unleashed a last series of blows, accompanied by full-throated roars, to encourage the enemy to recoil for an instant. Then they turned and ran, following the decurion along the corridor towards the kitchen door. He saw Claudia in the opening, beckoning to them frantically. Behind them, the attackers surged through the entrance and chased after them, accompanied by the sounds of hoarse breathing and bare and booted feet slapping and grating on the flagstones. Claudia ducked aside as the decurion was first through the door, instantly turning aside as the Germans rushed in and turned to defend the doorway. The attackers were ten paces back, racing towards them. One of the Germans grabbed the door and slammed it shut, throwing his weight against the sturdy timbers as Claudia slipped the key into the lock and turned it. The door shook under the impact of the first of the enemy to reach it, their weapons hammering against the far side.

'Get that table up against the door!' the decurion snapped,

pointing to it with his sword. The Germans soon had the bulky kitchen table on its end and thrust the scored surface against the door. A bench followed to wedge the table in place before the decurion was assured that entrance was denied to the men hacking at it from the other side.

He looked round. The kitchen was some sixty feet long by twenty wide. The ceiling was high and rose into a cone where the smoke from the ovens and griddles in the centre of the room could vent to the outside. Three windows, high up and covered with iron grilles, looked over the garden and afforded light during the day. Small braziers attached to the walls provided illumination at night. At the far end was a door leading out to the garden. It had been closed and barricaded with another of the tables, with heavy grain jars leaned against it to hold it in place. Besides his surviving men and Claudia, there were some forty others, household slaves and servants, some wounded, all looking to him for reassurance.

He cleared his throat and spat to one side. 'We're safe in here for now,' he called out, loudly enough for all to hear over the din of the pounding on the door.

It was a lie. It wouldn't take the attackers long to realise that the trough they had used to batter down the villa's entrance could as easily be deployed against the kitchen door. The decurion saw sacks of grain and flour lining the wall beneath the windows and sheathed his sword before he pointed them out.

'Get those over here and pack them against the table as tight as you can. Hurry!'

The harshness of his tone snapped the slaves out of their stupor and they got to work piling the sacks against the back of the table and over the bench, deadening the sound of the pounding on the door. A moment later the other door shook as the enemy set to it, but there was no immediate danger of them breaking that one in either, and for a moment the decurion dared to hope that they might yet get out of the precarious situation alive.

Abruptly the blows against the door to the corridor ceased, and shortly afterwards, the same happened at the garden door. Those in the kitchen looked at each other questioningly.

'Why have they stopped?' asked Claudia.

The decurion shook his head. 'I don't know.'

'Perhaps they've given up on us. Maybe they want what loot they can take from the villa.'

Both strained their ears for a moment, and then they heard orders being shouted from the direction of the garden.

'Help me with that table over there,' the decurion ordered one of his men, and they dragged the last of the unused tables over to the gap that had been made when the sacks had been removed. It was beneath the middle window, and the decurion clambered onto it and saw that he was still a foot below the bottom of the window. He turned and looked round, then pointed. 'Bring me that stool!'

As soon as he had positioned it against the wall, he carefully climbed onto it and reached up with his good hand to steady himself against the grille as he looked out. The light was fading, but he could see groups of raiders in the garden tearing up the wooden trellises and running to and from the timber store. He could hear voices close by, at the foot of the wall outside the kitchen, and he guessed their intent.

There was a shout, and he saw that one of the enemy carrying a bundle of logs had stopped twenty feet away, letting them tumble to his feet and raising an arm to point at him. A moment later, something streaked out of the gloom and struck the edge of the window, sending flecks of plaster into the decurion's face. He shut his eyes instinctively and ducked down as another arrow shot through the grille and across the kitchen to ricochet off the ceiling and drop to the floor. He released his grip and stepped off the stool, then jumped off the table.

'What did you see?' Claudia demanded. 'What are they up to?'

He steered her to a corner out of earshot of the others and lowered his voice. 'I fear they mean to set fire to the villa, my lady.'

Her eyes widened in fear. 'What's the point of that? Why not just take what they can loot and leave us?'

'I don't know.' The decurion was equally puzzled. It made no sense to go to such an effort to kill them this way if they were just after the riches of the villa and the horses that Prefect Cato had left behind. Why take the risk of setting the villa on fire and alerting everyone for miles around to their presence?

Those in the kitchen could hear the sounds outside as the wood was piled up.

Then a voice called out to them from the garden, just below the window.

'You inside! Open the door and come out.' The words were in Latin, but crudely accented. 'If you come out and surrender, I will let you live. Even those big hairy bastards who slew some of my men.'

Claudia exchanged a look with the decurion. 'What shall we do? Can we trust them to keep their word?'

'They didn't look too merciful when they attacked the entrance. They were out for our blood. I wouldn't trust them. Why would they want us alive? If they're prepared to burn the villa down and us in it, the only reason to get us to surrender is to make it easier and quicker to kill us.'

'What's your decision?' the raider demanded. 'I will not ask

237

you again. Come out now, or we'll burn you alive.'

One of the slaves gasped in horror and clasped her hands to her head. Over by the garden door, a male slave was already pulling back one of the benches braced against the barricade.

'You there! Stop that!' the decurion shouted. He ordered two of his men to stand by each barricaded door, then turned to the slaves now huddled against the windowless wall. 'I've told my men to kill anyone who attempts to remove the barricades. Stay where you are and keep quiet. I'll deal with this.'

'How?' one of the slaves demanded, taking a step towards him. 'You heard him. They'll burn us to death if we don't surrender straight away. I want to live. We all do!' He turned to the other slaves. 'Ain't that right?'

Some nodded. The bolder amongst them called out their support for him. The decurion strode over and raised his sword.

'Silence! One more word from any of you and I swear I'll cut you down where you stand!' He glared at them, defying any to oppose him.

'Open the doors now!' the raider outside shouted. 'Last chance.'

The decurion held his sword at eye level to the slaves and slowly moved it from side to side as he hissed, 'Stay where you are.'

The raiders wasted little time in setting light to the combustibles, and the first wisps of smoke curled around the barricades. The tops and sides of the window arches glowed red, and there was the crackle of kindling and logs as the flames took hold.

'Fire!' one of the slaves cried out. 'The villa is on fire!'

'For pity's sake.' A young woman sank to her knees in front of the decurion. 'Don't make us stay in here, master! Don't make us die. I beg you.'

He backed off and brandished his blade. 'Quiet! Be quiet! Let me think.'

Claudia had observed the confrontation from the corner of the room, and now she approached the decurion and spoke gently.

'If we stay in here, we'll all die. Choking on smoke or perishing in the flames. If we give in, they may spare us. Most of us perhaps.'

He looked at her and shook his head. His eyes were drawn to the first flicker of flames at the middle window, and the roar of the blaze was clearly audible. 'It's too late.'

'No, it's not,' she said firmly. 'We can use the wine from the jars to pour over the flames outside the door. Enough to extinguish them and give us a way out.'

'No.'

'You're supposed to guard me. Protect me. I'm giving you an order, Decurion.'

He gave a sad smile. 'You don't understand, my lady. My men and I were sent here not to protect you but to make sure you didn't try to escape. I was also told that I might receive orders from Rome to kill you.'

She stared at him for a moment, and then replied calmly, 'I see. Then do you intend to kill me, rather than let me try to save our lives?'

'I hoped the day would never come . . .'

'If I am to die, let it be by the hand of those men out there. Better that than fire.'

'You don't know what they will do to you.'

'It's my choice, Decurion. I choose the chance to live over certain death. And so, I imagine, does everyone else here.' She gestured towards the slaves watching them with terrified expressions.

239

The decurion clenched his jaw and thought quickly, then nodded. 'Your choice then . . .'

At once Claudia turned to her slaves. 'Get those wine jars by the garden door! You men, take the barricade down. Decurion, tell your men to help.'

As the smoke curled round the barricade blocking the corridor and began to billow in through the windows, the room grew warmer and sweat coursed from those removing the sacks and tables from the garden door. The decurion and his men choked on the smoke coming from underneath the barricade, and as they removed the last table, flames flared and drove them back from the blazing door.

'The wine!' Claudia urged, her voice catching as she breathed in smoke. 'On the flames . . .'

The decurion snatched up the first jar and pulled out the stopper. A familiar aroma reached his nose, and he muttered, 'Fucking waste of a decent Falernian . . .'

He approached as close as he could get before the stinging heat felt as if it was burning his skin, then began to slosh the wine over the door. The liquid sputtered on the hot surface and turned to steam, but some of the flames went out.

The decurion tossed the empty jar aside. 'Hand me another!'

Jug by jug he doused the flames, and at length there were only the charred timbers of the door left. He reached for the top bolt and snatched his hand back at once, his fingers seared by the heated metal. 'Shit . . .'

He drew his sword and used the tip to work the bolt free, then leaned down to do the same for the lower bolt as more smoke and flames began to work around the frame of the door and the cracks in its surface. The smoke coming through the windows was starting to fill the room, and those within covered their mouths, though the smoke still caught in their throats.

Above, lurid red lines glowed between the beams supporting the ceiling as the fire spread to the roof, and the first bits of burning debris – laths and reeds used for lining beneath the tiles – began to fall onto those within. A young boy screamed as his hair smouldered, and one of the Germans snatched up a rag from the floor and smothered the flames before using his body to shield the boy.

The second bolt snapped back and the decurion sprang away from the heat. 'It's done!'

'Then get it open,' ordered Claudia. 'Before the roof falls in!'

The decurion took a shield from one of his men, sheltering behind it as he approached the door. The flames outside shone brightly in the gaps burned through the timber as the decurion drew the shield back and punched it against the door. He heard a crash and some of the charred surface gave way. Again and again he smashed it until the door was shattered, revealing the burning logs heaped outside.

'More wine!' he shouted. 'Quickly!'

His men rushed forward, emptying the contents of the jars onto the flames, damping them down until the decurion could see into the garden beyond, where the enemy stood waiting, some fifty feet from the building.

'My lady.' He took Claudia's arm. 'Get your people out. I'll follow with my men. Go!'

She stood by the ruined door and beckoned to the slaves. 'Outside. Now!'

The nearest man hesitated, and she thrust him towards the gap. He shielded his head with his arms as he crouched and ran through the doorway, between the flames still burning on either side, and on towards the attackers waiting silently.

'Next!' Claudia pointed to a woman clutching two small

children at her side. 'Hold their hands and run!' The woman took a deep breath and rushed forward, the children crying in terror as they scrambled to stay on their feet.

Claudia continued to send them out one by one for fear of causing a panicked crush around the door. At length there were only a handful left besides the decurion and the Germans. Suddenly there was a resonant crack from above and a section of the ceiling collapsed in a shower of blazing debris, dust and smoke, half burying one of the Germans.

'Get out!' the decurion shouted. 'All of you, go! Run!'

Claudia snatched up some discarded sacking to protect her head and stood by the gap as the last of her slaves squeezed past and fled from the burning building. She turned to see the decurion and another of his men trying to clear the debris off their buried comrade while the others held their shields up to protect them from the steady shower of burning material and falling tiles from the collapsing roof. Claudia braced herself and darted through the gap, feeling the stinging heat as the flames raged around the exterior of the kitchen. The hem of her stola began to smoulder as she ran on towards the slaves, who stood at a safe distance, surrounded by the men who had attacked the villa. She removed the sacking from her head and beat out the small flame on her stola where it had started to burn.

A sudden roar of collapsing masonry and timber made her look round. The roof of the kitchen had caved in, taking a section of the wall with it. An explosion of sparks and flames leaped into the evening sky and a fresh wave of heat drove everyone back several paces.

'By the gods . . .' she muttered as she recalled her last sight of the decurion and his men. 'Oh no. No.'

A harsh shout broke into her grief and she saw a group of men approaching. They stopped a short distance away, one side of their bodies lit up by the lurid light of the flames consuming the villa, the rest shadowed. Their leader stepped forward, a length of rope in his left hand. He gave it a sharp tug and a small figure lurched out from between his companions and stumbled to his side. Claudia felt her heart quicken with anxiety as she recognised the face of the boy who had gone missing the day before. His eyes bulged and he trembled as he stood beside the leader of the band that had attacked the villa.

The man gestured at the grime-streaked faces of those who had escaped from the kitchen.

'Is she among them?' he demanded.

The boy's gaze flitted over the group and fixed on Claudia, and he nodded.

'Which one, boy? Point her out.' He let the rope run through his fingers as the boy walked slowly towards Claudia. Her eyes pleaded with him and she gave the slightest shake of the head. But he came on, stopped in front of her and reached his small hand out to touch her arm, then lowered his head in shame and let his hand drop. Claudia took a deep breath and gave his shoulder a gentle squeeze.

'It's all right . . . I'm sorry they put you up to this.' She reached to his neck and loosened the rope, slipped it over his head and threw it aside. 'Join the others.' Then she stepped past him, drew herself up and glared at the man with a mixture of defiance and contempt.

'You are Claudia Acte,' he stated.

'I am. What of it?'

'You are the emperor's whore.'

'Not any longer. He exiled me to the province. You are misinformed.'

'Maybe. Maybe not. But Nero will not want you to die at our hands.'

She could not help a bitter smile. 'He might not, but those who advise him would celebrate news of my death. I'm no good to you as a hostage. You're here on a fool's errand. My men died, along with yours, and you destroyed my home, all for no reason. I am worth nothing to you.'

Now it was his turn to smile as he spoke in a soft, rasping voice. 'You'd better pray that you are wrong, Claudia Acte.'

He picked up the rope she had removed from the boy and approached her. He forced the noose over her head, and before she could protest or react against him, he had yanked the rope so the noose tightened about her neck, permitting only a shocked gasp to escape her lips. Then he grabbed her shoulder, spun her around and pulled her hands behind her back, crossing the wrists over and tying them together. When she was securely bound, he eased the noose fractionally and took a step back. 'You are coming with us.'

'Where?'

'To our king.'

'King? What king? There is no king on this benighted island,' she sneered.

He slapped her hard across the cheek. 'Silence. You are not to speak until spoken to. You are not to escape. If you try to defy me, I will have you stripped and flogged.'

He turned to face the slaves before she could respond. He looked over them briefly before addressing them.

'You are free. You can choose to come with us and join our people. Or you can take your own path. If you choose to follow my band, you must keep up. We will not wait for stragglers. And when we reach our lands, you will swear an oath of loyalty to our king. If you break your oath, you will be put to death. Make your choice now. We are leaving.'

He shouted an order and it was relayed around the parties of brigands surrounding the burning villa. They formed up with the horses they had captured tied to the saddles of their own mounts. A handful of carts and their mule teams had been taken from the stables and piled with what loot had been gathered from the villa before it was set on fire. As darkness gathered, the leader barked an order and the motley column moved off.

Claudia had been placed in the charge of a rider in the middle of the column. He attached another length of rope to her bindings and looped the free end around one of the horns of his saddle. As the raiders marched away, the slaves stood still for a moment, before the first of them, a man, strode after them. Several more followed, while the rest looked on in silence. The column crossed the enclosure, bathed in the light from the blaze, and left by the main gateway before turning east, disappearing into the night.

CHAPTER TWENTY-TWO

Centurion Massimilianus's mounted force reached the fort at midday, two days after the main column had arrived. As soon as they were sighted by a sentry, Cato was alerted, and he rode out to meet the horsemen, reining in while they were still twenty paces off and raising his hand to halt them.

'Good to see you, Centurion.'

'And you, sir.'

'Before you get any closer to the fort, I have to ask, have any of your men been sick or shown signs of the sickness?'

'Yes, sir. I had to leave five men behind in Carales.'

'What happened to them? My orders were for your men to keep their distance and turn people back.'

'Yes, sir. One of the men knew of a good brothel in the town and talked some of his mates into sneaking inside the walls one night. By the time I heard of it, they had already left the camp. I was waiting for them when they crept back. I told them I'd have them speared if they tried to rejoin their comrades and ordered them to report to the fort at Carales. I let them know they'd be up on charges once this is all over, if they're still alive.'

'Good. Anyone else?'

'The rest of my lads are fine, sir. I've told them to report any sign of sickness. But there's been nothing. Not even a sprained ankle.'

'Well done.' Cato nodded and urged his horse forward. 'What was the situation in Carales when you left?'

'Not good. They were bringing the bodies out each morning and tipping them into a mass grave. Over a hundred a day, I'd estimate. Once word got round that we were turning people back, at spear point if necessary, they eventually stopped coming. We caught some who were trying to get past under cover of darkness and sent them back. But there'll be some that got through. Maybe the same ones who passed the pestilence on to a handful of the nearest villages. I had a word with their headmen not to let anyone leave until they'd had no deaths or sickness for ten days. I didn't have enough men to cover the villages as well as Carales, so all I could do was threaten them with dire consequences if I discovered one of them had allowed any of their people to spread the pestilence to another village.'

'That was the best you could have done in the circumstances. Come, let's ride on to the fort.'

Cato tugged his reins and waited for the centurion to fall in alongside him before clicking his tongue and walking his horse on.

'We're not going to be able to contain the pestilence, are we, sir?' Massimilianus said quietly.

There was no sense in pretence or misplaced optimism, thought Cato. That only ever made a man look a fool when a crisis was over and people looked back and asked questions of those in authority. 'I doubt it. We might have had a chance early on, if Scurra had quarantined people as soon as he heard they were sick. It's too late now. Carales will have to be left to its fate, and those villages where the sickness has spread. And since we have too few men to control people's movements *and* deal with the enemy, the sickness will make its way throughout the island eventually. And then it's just a question of burying the bodies.'

Massimilianus considered his words briefly and then nodded. 'It's just bad timing. The sickness and this business with the brigands happening all at once.'

'True, but that's how the Empire is run. Every unit on the frontier or garrisoned in the quieter provinces is stretched thinly. We can deal with one crisis well enough. But any more than that . . .' Cato shrugged and gestured vaguely at the surrounding landscape. 'That's how it goes. Which makes it more urgent that we deal with the enemy before the pestilence spreads to Augustis, as I am sure it will.' He shot Massimilianus a warning look. 'Keep that to yourself, by the way. I don't want men deserting for fear of the sickness, or out of worry that their families might be at risk. They won't understand that the best thing is to stay where they are for now. So not a word to anyone. Clear?'

'Yes, sir.'

'I'll need twenty of your men ready to ride at first light tomorrow. We'll be heading out to inspect the forward outposts that Plancinus has been constructing. Make sure the men and horses are fed well and have a sound sleep tonight.'

As evening settled over the forested landscape, Apollonius returned from his first patrol with his scouts and immediately made his way to headquarters to report to Cato. He wore a simple dull brown tunic with a sword belt customised with small sheaths for his dagger and throwing knives. A linen bandana of the same colour protected his head and neck from the sun and helped him to blend into the dry grass and shrubs of the terrain. The only concession to military attire was the thick woollen breeches and sturdy army boots he wore. His face and exposed flesh were streaked with grime and he stank of his own sweat, mingled with that of the horse he had been riding.

Cato, professional soldier that he was, could not help regarding him with a touch of disdain. 'You could attempt a more military demeanour now that you are serving with the army, you know.'

'I could, but I won't.'

'It might mean something to the men you command.'

'Do you think my scouts look any different? The first thing I did was order them to leave unnecessary kit in their barracks and get hold of some clothing that blends in with the landscape. You won't find them any more military in appearance than me.'

Cato tried not to wince at the prospect.

'We're not scouting ahead of an army, Prefect. Our job is to be as unobtrusive as possible in order to track down the enemy's lairs. It's up to me to provide you with intelligence the best way I see fit, and for you to make use of it.'

'Well, thanks for explaining my job to me,' Cato responded acidly. 'So what intelligence do you have? Take a seat.'

Apollonius smiled briefly at the barbed question, registering acknowledgement rather than amusement. 'Mind if I stand? My arse is still suffering from being too long in the saddle.'

'As you wish. Well?'

Apollonius reached into his sidebag and took out a roll of parchment, which he opened across Cato's desk. Instead of the usual itinerary maps used by the army, with distances marked between locations rather than any attempt to reproduce the features of the landscape, Apollonius had marked out the terrain in considerable detail, depicting prominent hills, rivers with crossing points, roads, tracks, settlements and other notations. Most of the space on the parchment was blank, however. Still, Cato conceded, it was impressive how much information the agent had gleaned in a matter of days.

Tapping the simple symbol of a fort at Augustis, the agent traced his finger across the parchment to where a ridge was marked, some distance to the east. 'That's the position I chose for our camp. There's one of the old towers there. It's been abandoned for a long time, judging from the condition, but it was possible to climb the stairs inside and reach the top. I had the men keeping watch from there. It makes a fine observation post; you can see for several miles in every direction. It was even possible to see this fort from there. I'd recommend that Plancinus and his men pay a visit to the tower and put up a palisade. It's well sited for signalling as well as observing. I left two of my men there to keep watch over the area. I'll be taking the rest back there in the morning, and then we'll push on deeper into the enemy's territory.'

'Very well, I'll tell Plancinus to fortify the tower when I catch up with him tomorrow.'

Apollonius raised an eyebrow. 'Tomorrow?'

'I'm taking the mounted contingent with some supplies for the outposts.'

'I see. Is it necessary for you to run errands like that?'

'I'll do as I damned well like. Besides, I want to inspect the works and see how the land lies. Did you see anything of the enemy?'

'Very little during the day. Some bands of horsemen, no more than ten at a time. A few parties on foot on the more difficult ground. There was no sign of smoke to give away their camps. We could make out some fires at night, but they were put out long before dawn, so we couldn't identify the source with any accuracy. They're smart. They hide their numbers and don't give away their position when they stop for the night. It's no wonder they have managed to slip through Rome's fingers for so long.'

Cato scratched his jaw as he considered what the agent had said. 'What we need is to take a prisoner. If you and your men can get one, the cohort's interrogator might be able to persuade him to tell us where we can find their lairs.'

'I should think we'll be able to grab one, given a few days to track down one of their bands.'

'Time is short,' Cato responded, and related what Massimilianus had told him about the situation around Carales. 'Find me a prisoner as soon as you can.'

'I'll do my best. And when I do, you'd better let me handle the interrogation. I have a few tricks I've picked up over the years. I imagine I'll have more chance of getting a prisoner to cough up the intelligence we need than some amateur from an auxiliary cohort.'

'I'm not sure I'd express that view too loudly around here.'

'I'll make sure to ask the best of my lads to give me a hand with the interrogation. He'll be happy enough to learn some new skills.'

Not for the first time, Cato wondered about Apollonius's previous life, which he was reticent about revealing in any great or reliable detail. He felt a cold tremor slink down his spine at the thought of the horrors the agent had in store for the hapless prisoner when the time came. It was a disturbing prospect. He could see the agent was watching him closely, almost as if he was reading his thoughts. He cleared his throat and patted the parchment map.

'You've done well so far. Catch me that prisoner and make him reveal the enemy's location so we can end this campaign before the pestilence catches up with us. Oh, and one other thing occurs to me. If the enemy gets wind that we have taken one of their men alive, they may abandon their lairs before we can act on any intelligence we get out of the prisoner.'

'That's true,' Apollonius conceded. 'If that happens, we'll have to take another prisoner and repeat the process. Even if we don't find out where they are, we'll be whittling them down one by one. There's always a bright side, Prefect,' he concluded with a dry laugh.

'If we live long enough to see it. You can take the opportunity to use the bathhouse and find some clean clothes before you get back into the field.'

'Nothing doing. There's a chance I might bump into some of the local people while I'm scouting around. I don't want to look like some freshly scrubbed Roman soldier trying to pass for an islander. The more grime I have on me and the more I stink, the less likely I am to arouse suspicion. Disguises come in many forms, some of them less salubrious than others. I'll report back again as soon as I have any news, or better still, a prisoner.'

He folded his map and tucked it into his sidebag before nodding a farewell and leaving Cato alone in the office. The light was starting to fade, and Cato called one of the clerks to bring him a lamp. As he sat in its wan glow, he pondered the implications of Apollonius's brief report. If the enemy were as elusive as the agent said, it was going to be difficult to force them into a position where they must fight. Very well, he decided, if the enemy bands were hard to pin down, he would turn his attention to their weak spot: the settlements of their people. If they could be destroyed and their inhabitants removed from the campaign area, the brigands would soon start to go hungry. That in turn would force them out of the forests and into the open, where they would more easily be spotted and run to ground. The question was what Cato would do with the tribespeople he removed from their villages. They would need to be kept under guard and fed. The fort at Tharros would serve as a temporary prison. He would need to assign men to guard them and supply them with food and water. There were the Germans guarding Claudia, he thought. Not all of them would be needed to ensure their charge did not abscond. They would do a fine job of terrifying the prisoners enough to forestall any notion of revolt or escape.

Thoughts of the Germans led on to a moment's reverie over the prospect of renewing his acquaintance with Claudia once the campaign was concluded. That raised a fresh difficulty. She had been sent into exile possibly for the rest of her life, unless Nero relented. Even if she chose to return to Rome, she had made an enemy of the emperor's mother, and no doubt any future mistress or wife of Nero would see her as a potential rival. For Claudia, Rome would be an even more dangerous place than she had left it. In which case it would be safest for her to remain unobtrusively in exile on the island. If, as Cato hoped, there was any chance of their friendship developing into something more, he would be faced with a choice of spending his life in Sardinia with Claudia, or abandoning her to continue advancing his army career elsewhere in the Empire. Weighing up the options, he found himself yearning for the prospect of an intelligent, honest wife he could share his life with, as Macro had chosen to do with Petronella. Yes, he thought, Claudia was such a woman. He looked forward to returning to her fine villa on the hill above Tharros and sitting with her in that garden she had been working to restore to its former glory. He pictured her in his mind. At this time she would probably be on her balcony, watching the sun set

253

over the sea. He smiled. It felt good to think of her enjoying her peaceful surroundings, far from any of the challenges and dangers he himself was facing.

The dawn air was blissfully cool as Cato joined Massimilianus and his mounted squadron inside the fort's gate. The four supply wagons were in place on the other side of the main thoroughfare that bisected the fort, and the mules stood calmly in their traces, long ears twitching lethargically as they stared ahead with the fatalistic ambience of their breed. There had been a brief shower of rain an hour or so earlier, and a thin mist hung in the vales and valleys between the forested hills. The air was still, the quiet broken only by birdsong, the soft chink of the horses' bridles and the muted chatter of the soldiers as they stood by their mounts.

'Morning, sir,' Massimilianus greeted him. 'The men and wagons are ready. Just give the word.'

Cato slung his sleeping roll, canteen and sidebag over the horns of his saddle and made to pull himself up. His arm muscles failed him at the first attempt and he gritted his teeth and strained every sinew to rise up enough to sling his leg over the horse's rump. It was shocking to discover he had still not fully recovered from his illness. He sat for a few breaths recovering his composure before he addressed the centurion. 'Give the order to mount up.'

'Yes, sir.' Massimilianus eased his shoulders back as he drew a deep breath. 'Squadron . . . mount!'

The centurion and his men climbed into their saddles and steadied their horses. Massimilianus waited until the last of them had his horse under control, then called out to the two sentries beneath the gate tower. 'Open up!'

The men removed the locking bar and eased each gate open

in turn, standing to the side as Cato walked his horse out of the fort, over the ramp that crossed the defensive ditch and down the track towards the road that led from Augustis to the coast. Massimilianus followed him at the head of his squadron, with the wagons bringing up the rear. When the last of them had rumbled out of the fort, the gates closed and there was a dull rumble as the locking bar was replaced.

Cato looked up at the sky and saw that the last of the night's clouds were receding to the south. A fine day lay ahead. That might be a pleasing prospect were he not facing a long day's march through the forest. The hot air would close in around the men of the small column and they would stew in their thick tunics and heavy armour as the sun blazed down on them. He knew from experience that it was far more comfortable to march under an overcast sky with a light breeze blowing.

They turned east onto the road, which was little more than a well-worn track that described a gentle series of turns until it reached the foot of the hill. From there they headed into the forest that sprawled across the hilly terrain stretching from Augustis to the sea. On either side the trees, a mixture of oak and pine, closed in right up to the edge of the track; in places the canopy extended across the road and left the riders and the wagons in the dappled shadows beneath. In other provinces of the Empire that Cato had served in, the army's engineers would have cleared a wide margin either side of the road to make ambushes more difficult. There was no sign that this had happened here. Instead, ancient trees with gnarled and twisted limbs crowded in on them, and the stillness and shadows worked on the nerves of Cato's men as they stared into the depths of the forest about them.

Massimilianus edged his horse alongside Cato's and muttered, 'I don't like this terrain, sir. You could hide ten legions in these

255

forests and no one would ever know. How in Hades are we supposed to find the enemy in this wilderness?'

'Is this the first time you have travelled this route?'

'Yes, sir. This region's been left to the tribes for as long as I can remember. I know that merchants used it until recently, and had to pay the brigands handsomely for the privilege. The forests belong to the enemy.'

'That's going to end now. Sardinia is a Roman province, every inch of it, and we're not leaving until the enemy are destroyed. You'd better get used to the sight of trees, Centurion.'

They rode on in silence for a while before Cato's hubris gave way to caution and he issued an order. 'Have ten of your men fall back to cover the rear of the wagons.'

'Yes, sir.'

'And two more can ride fifty paces ahead.'

Massimilianus nodded and reined in his horse briefly to relay Cato's instructions.

At noon they came across a clearing at the edge of a shallow gorge, and Cato halted the column for a rest. As the auxiliaries and mule drivers talked quietly, he walked on a short distance and climbed a pile of boulders that had fallen beside the road. From the top he could see a low ridge perhaps five miles off, and his spirits rose as he saw the dark shape of a watchtower peeping above the trees on the ridge. That must be the first of the outposts constructed by Plancinus, a day's march from the fort at Augustis. If there were no delays, the column would reach the outpost before nightfall, he calculated with satisfaction. He took the stopper out of his canteen and took a quick swig of the lukewarm water. As he put the stopper back and lowered the canteen, he scanned his surroundings again. Apart from the distant watchtower, there was no sign of habitation.

He climbed down from the rocks and was walking back to

the dismounted men and wagons when he was aware of movement to his right. He turned quickly, straining his eyes. All was still. And yet he felt an icy tingling in his scalp as he made himself calmly resume walking back along the road. It had only been the briefest of movements, but he was certain it had been a man, spying on them from the depths of the forest.

CHAPTER TWENTY-THREE

'We're being watched,' Cato said quietly as he approached Massimilianus. 'Don't react, just listen. I saw someone to the left of the road, forty or so feet back in the trees.'

The centurion kept facing Cato but his eyes turned to the area indicated. 'How many of them, sir?'

'I only saw one. There could be more.'

'What do we do?'

Cato thought quickly. They were closer to the outpost than the fort. If the man he had seen was one of the enemy, there could be more of them concealed amongst the trees, possibly preparing an ambush. Or it might just be a scout, shadowing the column before reporting its presence to his leader. If so, it might be possible to take him prisoner. The thought of sending several of his soldiers charging into the forest after a brigand who knew the ground far better than the Roman interlopers filled Cato with dread, and he discounted the idea.

'Who is your best man?'

'Sir?'

'I need someone strong who can move quietly.'

The centurion glanced over the auxiliaries standing beside their horses and pointed out a thin man standing alone. 'Lupis. He was a hunter before he joined up.'

'Good. I want you to send him to me in a moment. My plan is for us to make for the outpost. We'll need to be on our guard. Tell the men to put their feed bags and the rest of their kit on the wagons. I want them unencumbered and ready to fight if we have to. And assign two men to protect each wagon. Make it clear to them they are responsible for its safety. That leaves us six men to cover the front of the column and four to the rear. You take charge at the rear. Whatever happens, we must try to save the wagons and get them through to the outpost.'

'Yes, sir.' Massimilianus gave a curt nod and moved through the men, giving his orders quietly. The auxiliaries loaded their feed sacks and saddlebags onto the wagons. The centurion spoke briefly to Lupis and the latter hurried over to Cato and saluted.

'The centurion said you wanted me, sir.'

'I hear you used to be a hunter.'

'Yes, sir.'

'A good one?'

'Good enough,' the auxiliary replied warily.

'So why did you join the army?'

'I wanted more from life than tracking down wild boar, sir.'

'Then you should have joined the legions rather than a garrison cohort in an imperial backwater like Sardinia.'

'Hindsight's a wonderful fucking thing, sir.'

Cato smiled thinly before his expression became earnest. 'I need a good hunter. Someone is watching us. It could be one man. Could be more. That's what I need you to find out. The column is going to move on in a moment. When it does, I want you to wait at the rear until we are out of the clearing, and then slip into the trees to the left of the road. Find out who is watching us. If there's only one man, take him prisoner if you can and bring him to me. Otherwise, report to me as soon as you are certain of their numbers.' He let Lupis digest the orders before he continued. 'Can you do that without being seen?'

'I wouldn't be much of a hunter if I couldn't, sir.'

'Fine, then I'll see you again later. If the enemy attack us first, make your way back to the fort at Augustis and report what has happened.'

'Yes, sir.'

'May the gods watch over you, Lupis.'

The auxiliary flashed a reassuring grin and rejoined his comrades. Cato took a last look around the clearing before calling out calmly to his men. 'Time to get the column moving again, lads!'

Massimilianus gave the order to mount, and the men climbed into the saddle and walked their horses to their appointed positions, with pairs of riders interspersed between wagons. When all was ready, Cato casually swept his arm forward and urged his horse down the track at a walk. The riders behind him, two abreast, rippled forward, and then the heavy wooden wheels of the wagons rumbled over the baked earth. The din of hooves and wheels seemed almost deafening, smothering any sounds that might have emanated from the trees as the column left the clearing behind. Cato glanced back to see if Lupis was still with them, but he could see nothing through the haze of dust raised by the leading horses and wagons.

For the next hour or so, the column continued along the route. The creeping boredom of the first part of the day had given way to a tense watchfulness that seemed to stretch out each heartbeat and breath. The taut atmosphere was made worse by the stillness of the air around them. They rode mostly in the direct glare of the sun, while insects swirled around the heads of the horses and mules and did their best to irritate the freely sweating men in the saddles. Cato's eyes constantly swept the route ahead of them and the trees on either side, straining to penetrate the shadows. At the same time his ears tried to detect any suspicious sound that might be heard above the noises made by the horses, mules and wagons.

The strain was wearing on his nerves, and he was aware of the danger of the tricks that a tired mind could play. Occasionally he detected movement, and once a shape crashed out of the trees onto the track a scant twenty feet in front of him. He had snatched out his sword before he realised it was a boar. The beast turned its bristling head towards him briefly before charging off into the trees on the other side of the track. Cato sheathed his weapon sheepishly as his heart pounded. The auxiliary riding behind him clicked his tongue.

'That one would have made a fine meal. Shame.'

Cato took a deep breath and tapped his heels to make his horse walk on. His thoughts were far from any notion of a roast pork supper. Something had startled the boar and caused it to flee across their path. He glanced into the trees, but there was no sign of movement. A short distance ahead, the route curved round a bare, boulder-strewn hillock. As Cato approached the bend, a man stumbled out of the trees and staggered to a halt. Behind him came Lupis, sword in hand, tip pointed at his captive's spine.

Cato halted the column and dismounted, striding ahead to meet Lupis and his prisoner. The latter was wearing a dark woolly pelt belted over a brown tunic. There were tattoos on his cheeks and forehead; strange angular designs quite unlike the elegant swirls that Cato had seen on the skin of the Celts he had faced in Britannia years before. A small fringe of hair grew along his jawline. Blood ran down from his left temple, where the hair was matted with gore. Close to, Cato could see that he was a youth, no more than fifteen or sixteen.

'He was tracking us, like you said, sir,' Lupis announced as he kicked the lad in the back of the leg, causing him to drop to his knees in front of Cato. 'I picked up his trail and watched him leapfrogging the column for a while to make sure he was alone before I dealt with him. He needed a clip round the ear with the flat of my sword before he gave in. Seems to have his senses about him, so no real damage done . . . yet.'

Cato looked at the youth. His face was downcast and his hands were trembling.

'What's your name, son?'

The youth did not reply, and Lupis cuffed the back of his head with his spare hand. 'Answer the prefect, you fucking cur.'

Cato gave the auxiliary a sharp look and a quick shake of the head before he turned his gaze back to the captive and spoke gently.

'Look at me.'

The youth raised his head hesitantly.

'Tell me your name.'

The prisoner licked his lips and muttered something Cato could not catch.

'Speak up.'

'Calgarno.'

'Calgarno,' Cato repeated. 'You were caught spying on us. Are there any more of you hiding in the trees? Do you understand me? You speak Latin?'

The youth did not reply, but Cato could see the fear haunting his expression and decided to play on it. 'I'm not going to waste time asking you politely for information. If you don't answer me directly, then I'll have my man there beat it out of you.

You'll suffer badly, and sooner or later you'll tell me what I need to know. The choice is about how much agony you want to experience before you speak up. I'll ask you again, are there any others out there?'

The boy clenched his jaw and stared back with a show of defiance. Cato sighed and addressed Lupis. 'Soldier, take your dagger out and cut off this fellow's ears.'

Lupis grinned as he sheathed his sword and drew his dagger. He grabbed a fistful of the youth's locks in his left hand, yanked his head savagely to one side and raised his dagger.

'No!' Calgarno shrieked, struggling to break free. 'No!'

Cato raised his hand to stop Lupis. 'Answer my questions. Truthfully. I know when I'm being lied to. I can smell deceit.' He made himself sneer. 'You'll tell me everything. If not, you'll lose your ears . . . then your eyes . . . then your balls.'

The youth let out a pained whine and his shoulders slumped.

'Are you alone?'

Calgarno nodded.

'Speak up. Alone? Yes or no?'

'Yes.'

'Did you chance upon us, or were you sent to watch us?'

'I was hunting with my father.' His accent was guttural, but Cato followed it readily enough.

'Where is he?'

'He told me to follow you while he went to get the others.'

'Others? What others?'

'The rest of the war band.'

Cato felt his pulse quicken. 'How many of you are in the war band?'

Calgarno looked at him blankly, and Cato guessed that he was innumerate. He tried a different approach. 'As many men as I have? Or more?'

'More. Many more.'

'Where are they? How far away?' asked Cato, before realising that the question might be meaningless to the captive. 'A day's march? Half a day?'

'Less than that.'

'How long ago did your father leave to fetch your friends?'

'As soon as we saw your column.'

'And when was that?'

'After you entered the forest.'

Lupis cursed softly. 'That was hours ago, sir. They could be on us at any moment. Or lying in wait ahead.'

'Quiet!' Cato was thinking. The man was right. He put himself in the place of the enemy and considered their options. Better to get ahead of the convoy and take time to prepare the ambush rather than rush the wagons and their escort at the first opportunity. If the enemy had responded at once to the news of their presence, they might not have reached the track yet. If the convoy moved swiftly, they might get ahead of them.

'Lupis, get the boy's hands and feet tied up and load him onto one of the wagons.'

'Yes, sir.' Lupis released Calgarno's hair and prodded him in the back with the tip of his dagger. 'On your feet! Move yourself!' He marched the youth back down the track towards the rear of the column.

Cato called Massimilianus forward. The centurion trotted up and dismounted, and Cato briefed him quickly and pointed out the hillock he had spotted. 'I'm riding ahead to see the lie of the land. You take charge here. Get the column moving. Have the mule drivers pick up the pace and we might get ahead of the enemy.'

'And if we don't?'

'Then we're going to have to fight our way through to the outpost. Make sure the men are ready for that.'

'Yes, sir.'

Cato returned to his mount and pulled himself up into the saddle, surprised at his new lease of energy. Taking up the reins, he urged the horse into a canter and set off down the track. When he reached the foot of the hillock, he saw that its slopes were littered with boulders and small rocks, with clumps of dry grass and stunted shrubs covering the open ground. He tugged the reins and steered his mount up the slope, making his way to the level ground on the crest, where he stopped and swept his gaze over the surrounding terrain. The top of the hillock afforded him a view of the track ahead for at least two miles, he estimated. Here and there it disappeared beneath the forest canopy, or into a fold in the ground, before it climbed out of the forest towards the ridge upon which the outpost had been constructed a mile beyond. From his vantage point, Cato could see swathes of ground where saplings were growing amid the faded ashes and blackened stumps left behind by forest fires. There was no sign of any people, and he allowed himself a moment's hope that the column would reach safety before Calgarno's father and his war band caught up with them. At the foot of the hill, the horsemen and wagons passed by with the mule drivers trotting beside their teams, driving them on with flicks of their slender whips.

Cato tightened his grip on his reins and was about to turn his mount back down the slope when a flicker of movement caught his eye. 'Easy there.' He pulled up sharply and half turned in his saddle, raising a hand to shade his eyes. No more than a mile away, a line of men were emerging from the trees to cross one of the areas cleared by fire. At once he dismounted and led his horse behind the nearest boulder, so that he would not give his position away as he observed the enemy.

'Forty . . . fifty . . .' he muttered as he estimated their numbers. 'Sixty . . .'

Several more came out before the full force was in sight. Odds of three to one. Cato grimaced. He gauged the progress of his men and the direction and fast marching pace of the enemy, and calculated that if they continued in the direction they were headed, they would reach a point on the track at almost the same time as the column.

'Shit . . .'

CHAPTER TWENTY-FOUR

Cato gave the order to increase the pace the moment he returned to the column, and related what he had seen to Massimilianus as they rode together behind the last wagon.

'Any chance of avoiding them, sir?'

'There's a chance,' Cato replied. 'But only if we get far enough ahead of them by the time they reach the road that they can't be certain if we have passed that point or not. If I was in command of that war party, I'd send men in both directions to scout the track. Even if they don't catch sight of us, it'll be obvious soon enough that we have got ahead of them. Then it's a straight race to the outpost. The mules won't be able to keep this pace up for long. When they slow down, the enemy will quickly make up the ground. It's likely that we'll have a fight on our hands, one way or another.'

'Good.' Massimilianus nodded with satisfaction. 'About time we had the chance to face those bastards in a stand-up fight.'

'I want you at the front of the column,' Cato decided. 'I'll take charge here.'

The centurion turned to his superior with a frown. 'Why, sir?'

Cato briefly considered telling him to obey orders, but it

was imperative that the man understood Cato's thinking.

'I need you to set the pace and keep the men and mules going. If there's contact with the enemy, I'll take command of the rearguard and delay them as long as possible. With luck, that might buy you enough time to get the wagons to the safety of the outpost. If fighting starts, you are not to stop for anything. Keep the wagons moving and only deal with any of the enemy that threaten to stop you or slow you down. Is that clear?'

'Yes, sir,' Massimilianus replied grudgingly.

'Then go.'

As the centurion cantered off, Cato tested his sword to ensure it slid smoothly within the scabbard, then settled his helmet securely on his head and rocked gently backwards and forwards against the horns of the saddle to make sure they held him firmly. Then he called ahead to the men assigned to protect the wagons to join the rear of the column so that he would have a force large enough to be effective if the fighting started. Individually, mounted men could easily be defeated, but even a small force could terrify and charge down a much larger group of infantry, especially if they had not been trained to deal with cavalry.

The column continued at pace along the road, the mules braying in protest as their drivers forced them on, flicking their whips at the rump of any beast that attempted to slow down. The cacophony of the mules, the rumble of wheels and the clopping and snorting of the horses seemed certain to betray their presence long before the enemy caught sight of them. Fortunately, the trees about them grew densely enough to hide the dust kicked up as the column moved along the road.

As they neared the point where Cato had estimated the two forces might clash, his gaze focused on the treeline to their left. Nothing moved there, as far as he could see. The road continued straight for a few hundred paces before climbing to rising ground over a mile away where the forest gave way to scattered boulders and stunted shrubs close to one of the ruins of one of the island's ancient towers. If they could make it there, they would have the advantage of more open ground to fight the enemy, and they would be much closer to the safety of the outpost on top of the ridge beyond. For a moment his attention was drawn to the figure of Calgarno, jolting up and down on a pile of tools at the rear of the wagon he had been loaded onto. The youth grimaced at his discomfort but Cato could not spare any more thought for his prisoner's pain while every pace between the column and their pursuers might make the difference between life and death.

The column rumbled around the bend in the road and Cato waved on the mounted men at the rear as he steered his horse to the side of the road and looked back the way they had come. The dust was settling in their wake, and a few heartbeats later there was no sign that they had passed this way shortly before. The enemy had not yet come into view, and he felt a surge of hope as he turned his horse and cantered to catch up with the others.

There was a shout of alarm as he approached the men of the rearguard, and the hope of a moment before quickly transformed into fearful anxiety. He called an order to clear the path ahead, and his men steered their horses to the side of the road to make way for him. He saw the figure of the boy rise up in the rear of the wagon, his ankles and hands trailing the frayed ends of the bonds he had managed to cut through. Calgarno snatched up a pick and hurled it at the nearest rider, striking the horse on the brow so that it gave a panicked whinny and reared up, forcing Cato to yank his reins to avoid a collision.

Calgarno leaped nimbly from the back of the wagon as it

269

continued on, the mule driver oblivious to the drama taking place behind him.

'Stop him!' Cato yelled. 'The boy's escaping!'

The nearest of the auxiliaries wrenched out his long-bladed sword and spurred his horse forward as the youth ran for the trees. Calgarno ducked and rolled over as the rider loomed above him and the blade flashed down savagely. The tip caught him on the shoulder, ripping through his tunic and scoring a shallow cut across the flesh above his shoulder blade. He let out a sharp cry of pain as he scrambled on all fours into the shadow beneath the lowest boughs of a young oak tree. The rider who had wounded him swore in frustration and swung his leg over the saddle, dropping to the ground to finish the job. Calgarno was already back on his feet, running through the trees, and the auxiliary raced after him, swerving and ducking under branches. Cato could see that it was already too late. The boy knew the ground better than his pursuer and would soon outdistance him. All that would happen was that the soldier would blunder around helplessly until the enemy found and killed him.

'Leave him!' Cato shouted as he rode back towards the wagon. 'Get back on your horse!'

The soldier stopped, swooped to pick up a rock and hurled it uselessly after the retreating figure, then rejoined his comrades. Glancing into the wagon, Cato noticed the edge of a saw protruding from the tools lying there and silently cursed Lupis for not placing the boy in a more secure position. He turned to the man whose horse had been hit by the pick.

'Get forward and tell Massimilianus that the boy has escaped and we can expect the enemy to come after us sooner than I'd hoped. We push on and stop for nothing from now on.'

The man nodded and spurred his mount down the road, swerving to overtake the wagons. As the dismounted man reached for the saddle horns and pulled himself back astride his mount, Cato's racing mind was considering his choices. The simplest course would be to form up across the track and hold the enemy off for as long as possible. But it would be easy for men on foot to outflank them through the trees the moment they caught sight of the Roman mounted soldiers waiting for them. He needed a plan. Something to shock them and break their morale long enough to win some time. The present position was not suitable for what he had in mind, so he called the men to form up and they set off after the wagons.

By the time they had reached the foot of the gentle slope that led to the more open ground that Cato had spied earlier, it was clear that the mule teams were tiring and could no longer keep up the same pace. Their sides rose and sank with each laboured breath, and as they began to strain into the incline, they slowed to a walk. Cato ground his teeth in frustration at the prospect of the enemy steadily closing in on them. He glanced from side to side as the trees thinned out and exposed rocky outcrops littered the slope. Ordering his men to follow the wagons for the moment, he turned his horse off the road and trotted a short distance up the slope, then turned parallel to the road and picked his way through the shrubs and rocks. A hundred paces further on, he found what he was looking for. A cluster of large rocks lay close to the road, with the ground between relatively even and open. He turned to look back down the road and saw no sign of the enemy.

'On me!' he called to the mounted rearguard. 'Over here, quickly!'

The men tugged their reins and trotted their horses towards him. Cato indicated the rocks and the gaps between them. 'We'll dismount and hide there, lads. There won't be much time, so when I give the order to charge, I want you in the

271

saddle and shouting your fucking hearts out as we ride down and take the enemy in the flank. There may be more of them than us, but the shock and speed of our attack will give 'em the shits before they realise it. When we hit them, go in hard. Ride them down, cut them down, but stop and re-form on me the moment I give the order to break off the attack. Any man who fails to obey and gets himself killed will have me to answer to when I eventually join him in the afterlife.' He made himself smile slightly to put heart into them, then gestured towards the rocks. 'Now get in there, stay out of sight and keep silent.'

The men rode their horses in amongst the rocks and boulders and slipped to the ground, standing by their mounts' heads, reins in one hand, as they calmed the beasts to still them. Cato glanced towards the wagons climbing the slope behind Massimilianus and his small party of horsemen. The mules were advancing at a slow walking pace, and no amount of cajoling by the drivers could make them go any faster. Looking the other way, he saw that there was no sign of the enemy yet. He took his place in the centre of the roughly aligned riders of the rearguard, leading his horse to the edge of a rock where a large spiky shrub grew, big enough to conceal him, but allowing him to see through it to make out the road no more than thirty paces away. A glance to either side showed that his men were hidden and standing by in readiness for his order to attack.

The rumble of the wagons' wheels, the crack of whips, the shouts of the muleteers and the occasional braying from amongst their teams began to fade into the distance as the column climbed towards the brow of the hill. As the noises diminished and the blood in Cato's ears pulsed more calmly, he was aware of the steady drone of flies and buzz of bees amongst the sparse wild flowers growing across the slope. The sun beat down mercilessly and the air was hot and still, save for the shimmering on the ground in the distance beyond the road. Sweat pricked out on his forehead and trickled down his brow before dripping onto his cheek, tickling his skin so that he brushed his face irritably. His ears strained to pick up any sound of the approaching enemy, and he saw the tense expressions of his men as they stood silently, swatting away the odd insect. The wagons, meanwhile, had reached the top of the hill and disappeared over the crest one by one; all that remained to indicate their passage was a haze of dust hanging in the air.

The enemy moved quietly and were almost upon the waiting soldiers before Cato became aware of their presence. Two files of men were emerging from the trees either side of the road, where the ground was not rutted and was more forgiving. Despite the heat, they were wearing animal hides belted over their dark tunics. Many had extensive tattoos on their skin and sported crudely trimmed beards. They wore their long hair in rope-like plaits, and most had leather skullcaps reinforced by iron rims and cross-pieces. Some had animal horns protruding from their caps; a mixture taken from rams, cattle and deer that added to the barbarous nature of their appearance. They were armed with spears, axes and swords, and a few had shields across their backs, slung from broad leather straps. Cato could easily imagine the terror their appearance caused when they emerged from the night to attack merchants' convoys and the more isolated villas across the province. Scanning their ranks, he saw Calgarno, now armed with a spear.

He tightened his grip on the reins of his horse and stroked its neck as he whispered soothingly, 'Quiet now . . . Not a sound or sudden movement, eh?'

There was a shout from one of the men at the head of the loose formation, and he thrust his arm towards the last of the haze hanging in the air at the top of the hill. At once, one of the men with antlered headgear ran forward to his side and shielded his eyes as he stared up the hill.

Cato could guess at the enemy leader's excitement now that his prey was in sight. Any moment he would halt his men and give orders for the attack. The time for Cato to strike was now, before the war band was poised to charge up the road to fall on the wagons. Steeling his nerves, he eased himself up into the saddle, bending low to stay in concealment. Then he drew his sword from its scabbard and sucked in a deep breath.

'Mount up!'

On either side came the shuffle of hooves and grunts of men as they clambered onto their horses and readied their weapons. Cato looked both ways quickly and saw that they had made ready to attack in the space of a few heartbeats. He rose up in his saddle and raised his sword. Over the bush he could see the faces of those amongst the enemy who had heard his order and now glanced anxiously at the rocks to their left.

'Charge!' he roared, the cry tearing at his throat as he arced his sword down towards the war band strung out along the road. He kicked his heels in, steering his horse around the bush and out into the open before urging it into a gallop across the narrow stretch of open ground. On either side his men emerged from the rocks, bellowing their war cries as they raised the glinting blades of the cavalry swords.

For an instant the brigands were shocked into stillness as they stared in horror at the men charging down on them. One recovered quickly enough to hurl his spear at Cato, and it was only with a deft change of direction that he avoided the long shaft as it shot past his side and tore into the ground a short distance behind him. As the riders bore down on them, a few of the brigands turned and ran, some making for the cover of the boulders on the other side of the road, others fleeing back down the road towards the trees.

A few heartbeats later and the riders burst through the nearest file of the enemy, slashing at their heads and shoulders. Cato made for one of the brigands with antlered headgear; a tall man with heavy shoulders who had drawn his sword and unslung his shield. His teeth bared in a snarl as he raised his sword to block the blow, and there was a sharp clang and scraping of metal as the edge of Cato's short sword struck the flat of the brigand's blade and slid harmlessly towards the point as Cato's mount carried him on. He recovered his weapon and held it up, handle level with his shoulder, as he looked for a fresh opponent. The second file of brigands had broken ranks, and blades flashed in the sunlight while horses snorted and whinnied and men shouted as they hacked at the enemy around them amid the swirling dust and flying grit kicked up from the surface of the road.

Cato caught sight of Calgarno ten feet away. The youth lowered the point of his spear and ran forward, plunging the tip into the chest of the horse to Cato's right. The beast flung its head up and shook it from side to side with a shrill braying before it lurched aside, snatching the shaft of the spear from the youth's hands. Before Cato could swerve his horse to attack the boy, a man ran at him on his unguarded left side with an axe raised to strike. He yanked his reins hard and his horse collided with the brigand, forcing him to stumble to one side. Before the man could recover his balance, Cato twisted in his saddle and swung his sword down, cutting deeply into his foe's skull. The jarring impact threatened to loosen his grip on the handle, and he clenched his fingers tightly and freed the blade as the brigand swayed, blood pouring from his wound, before he released his axe and his legs collapsed beneath him.

Holding his sword up, Cato looked round quickly and saw that none of the brigands were in striking distance. Some were still standing their ground and attempting to fight off the mounted men, but most had broken and were fleeing. His men were bellowing hoarsely as they struck out at any of the enemy who came within reach of their swords. Cato looked for the man he had taken to be their leader, and saw him by the rocks, calling out to his men and trying to rally them. Several had already formed up round him, and their example was shaming and inspiring others to join them and face the auxiliaries. The advantage granted by the initial surprise of the attack was fading, and soon the enemy would have the numbers and the boldness to close round Cato and his men and pull them off their saddles to butcher them on the ground. It was time to break off the attack.

'On me!' he called out above the din made by his men. 'On me! Now!'

The nearest of the riders heard his cry and disengaged, warily edging their mounts towards their commander. Others were still caught up in the frenzied exhilaration of the charge and continued to urge their mounts across the slope on the other side of the rocks. One horse stood still, flanks heaving as blood coursed from a broken shaft protruding from its chest. Pink froth was bubbling from its flaring nostrils as the beast refused to respond to the urgings of its rider. Then one of the enemy ran up behind it and savagely swung his axe at the auxiliary's exposed back above the saddle horns. The heavy curved edge of the weapon shattered the rider's spine, and he convulsed and dropped his sword. His attacker grasped his arm and hauled him violently out of his saddle so that he tumbled to the ground with an explosive gasp. Then the brigand raised his axe and swung it down to batter his victim's head, driving a dent into his helmet before the second blow found the man's face and pulverised the nose and jaw. More blows swiftly reduced the auxiliary's features to a gory pulp.

Cato saw it all in the time it took to draw a few breaths before he called to the other men to break off and rejoin him. One by one they obeyed. He observed that two other men had been lost, and another was leaning forward in his saddle, sword hand clasped over a wound in his side, though he still had the strength to hold his reins and steer his mount towards Cato. As the last of them abandoned his pursuit of those who had fled back down the road, Cato sheathed his blade and pointed to the crest of the hill.

'Follow me!'

He spurred his mount into a canter and the others followed. He kept the pace up until they reached the crest and saw the wagons, a quarter of a mile away at the bottom of the gentle reverse slope of the hill. Two miles further on lay the outpost, blissfully unaware of the savage skirmish that had taken place. Massimilianus was riding alongside the wagons, urging the muleteers to push their tiring beasts into one last effort to reach the safety of the stockade that ran around the outpost. If the enemy recovered swiftly and came on apace, Cato realised, there was still a danger that they might overtake the wagons.

He raised his arm and halted the surviving men of the rearguard. 'Turn and form a line across the road!'

The men walked their beasts into position astride the rutted track, facing down the hill towards the enemy. Cato saw that their leader had already rallied over twenty of his men, and more were making their way over the broken ground to join their comrades. The bodies of the dead and injured marked the place where Cato and his men had charged home. As soon as most of them had formed up around him, the leader pointed towards the crest and waved them forward. Cato noticed that some hesitated to approach the small line of horsemen. Clearly they were still unnerved, and that could be turned to the mounted party's advantage.

Drawing his sword again, he called out, 'At the walk, advance!'

The line of horsemen rippled forward, moving down the slope towards the brigands. The sight caused many of the war band to draw up warily, and the cohesion of the group began to fall apart at the prospect of another mounted charge. Cato, however, had no intention of ordering another attack. This time the enemy were ready for them and had sufficient numbers to be sure to overwhelm them. He slowed the pace of his horse as he calmly issued another order.

'Dress the line! On me.'

His men obediently adjusted their pace and the horsemen steadily approached the enemy in good formation. Cato saw more of the brigands draw up, and their leader paused to shout and punch his spear in the air as he tried to instil some courage into them.

'At the trot!' Cato called out, and tapped his heels in to urge his horse forward. The other men followed suit, rising and falling in their saddles, their accoutrements jingling. They were now within two hundred paces of the war band, and the sight of the mounted auxiliaries increasing their speed did the trick. The first of the brigands backed off and turned to retreat down the slope, breaking into a run after just a few strides. Those with greater courage stood by their leader, closing ranks, with the spearmen amongst them presenting their points to the oncoming cavalry.

When they were a hundred paces from the enemy, Cato threw his arm up. 'Halt!'

The riders reined in, and for a moment the two sides confronted each other in silence before the brigand leader shouted an order. Several of his men lowered their weapons, and Cato saw them uncoiling something from around their waists before they reached into their sidebags and stepped out in front of their comrades. He grasped the danger at once and sheathed his sword. Drawing a quick breath, he snapped an order to his men. 'Retreat! Back to the crest of the hill! Go!'

The riders drew sharply on their reins, turned their mounts and spurred them into a gallop as the first slingshot zipped through the air close by. One hit the ground a short distance in front of Cato and bounced up to strike his mount on the flank. The horse let out a sharp whinny and lurched to the side, and Cato had to clamp his thighs tightly and snatch at the saddle horn to stop himself from being thrown.

At the sight of the retreating horsemen, a ragged chorus of jeers sounded from the war band.

'Easy . . . easy there.' Cato spoke soothingly as he steered the horse uphill and urged it into a canter. He saw that one of his men had been hit; the shot had smashed his knee, and blood streamed down his calf and over his boot as he used his other leg to guide his horse round to follow the others. Another slingshot crashed into the back of his helmet and snapped his head forward. His shield, reins and sword slipped from his grasp, and Cato could see that he was in danger of falling from his saddle. Redirecting his own mount, he made for the man and took up the loose reins, leading the horse up the slope as swiftly as he could while keeping the man in his saddle.

More slingshots whizzed past. Instinctively, Cato hunched his shoulders forward to try to make himself a more difficult target. He rode on, expecting the dreadful impact of a shot to strike him at any moment. But the distance between himself and the slingers quickly opened up, and soon he was out of range and the enemy gave up. He eased the pace of his mount and turned to see the auxiliary's head lolling from side to side.

When he reached the other men waiting on the crest of the hill, he held out the reins to the nearest rider. 'Take this horse. We'll look at his wounds once we've put some distance between us and the enemy.'

The other man eased his mount alongside his stricken comrade and slung his shield across his shoulder before he took the reins.

Cato saw that the wagons were already on the first leg of the zigzag route leading up to the outpost. They should be safe enough now, he calculated. There was no need for any further charges to delay the enemy.

'Sir, he's dead.'

He looked round to see the rider nodding at the man in the saddle beside him. He leaned over to raise the man's head and saw the glazed, unblinking eyes and the blood oozing from his nostrils and ears. There was no sign of movement, or breath, and Cato sighed bitterly. 'We can't afford to lose the horse. You take charge of it.'

'What about Amelius, sir?'

'Amelius?' Cato realised that he had never learned the name of the dead man. There was no time to feel bad about that now, and no time to spare to strap his body to the horse. 'Leave his body here.'

'Sir?' The auxiliary looked surprised. 'Leave him for the enemy? He don't deserve that. We need to give him proper funeral rites, sir.'

Cato grasped the dead man's harness and wrenched him from his saddle, letting the body fall to the ground. 'Take the horse and make for the wagons.'

The auxiliary's eyes blazed with anger and he made to swing his leg over the saddle horns to dismount.

'Stay in your saddle!' Cato snarled at him. 'And get out of here! Or I swear by all the gods I'll have you flogged.'

They stared at each other for a beat before the man spat to the side in disgust and did as he was ordered.

'All of you, get forward to the wagons!' Cato called out.

The riders peeled away from the crest and trotted down the road. Cato waited, looking back to see the enemy leader running up the slope, followed by the rest of his men, including those who had lost their nerve only moments before. As the horsemen disappeared from view, the brigands let out a triumphant cry.

'Enjoy this small victory,' Cato muttered with a sneer of contempt before his gaze fixed on the body sprawled in the dry grass. 'You will be avenged, brother. I swear it.'

He wheeled his horse around and galloped down the road to catch up with the rest of his men.

CHAPTER TWENTY-FIVE

As the last of the wagons rumbled into the stockade, the optio in charge of the militia detachment manning the outpost gave the order to close the gates. The rough-hewn timbers were heaved into place and secured with the locking bar, and Cato felt his heart lift with relief. He exchanged a salute with the optio, Micus, before examining the layout of the modest fortification.

A wooden tower stood in the middle, some thirty feet high, with a platform ten feet square on top. The sides of the platform were protected by hoardings, as was the ladder that scaled one corner of the structure. A length of rope ran beneath a sturdy post and through an iron ring before trailing to the ground, where a stock of wood and green foliage for the signal fire was ready for use. Two timber structures with shingle roofs served as accommodation and storage for the small garrison. A rectangular stockade, twelve feet high, ran around the enclosed space. Earth-covered rocks formed a crude sentry walk on the inside, while a ditch surrounded the exterior, save for the narrow causeway in front of the gates. The horses, mules and carts filled most of the interior, and one glance at the garrison's water butt was enough for Cato to realise there would not be enough for the thirsty men and the exhausted beasts as well as Micus and his section of militia troops. In every other respect, however, Plancinus and his party had done a competent job of siting and constructing the outpost.

His brief inspection was interrupted by the distant jeers of the brigands, who had pursued them to the outpost, but not quickly enough to overtake and destroy the small supply convoy. Followed by Micus and Massimilianus, he crossed to the rampart to the right of the gate and climbed onto the walkway, looking out over the open ground that fell away in front of the gates. For a distance of fifty paces the vegetation had been cut away, and all that remained protruding from the soil were the stumps of the trees felled to provide timber for the construction of the outpost. Further out, stunted shrubs and trees grew as far down the slope as the treeline of the great forest that covered the landscape beyond. The enemy stood beyond javelin range in a loose arc, brandishing their weapons and shaking their fists as they hurled insults at those in the outpost.

'I count fifty or so of them, sir,' Micus observed. 'Not enough to take this place.'

'Not yet,' Cato responded. 'But I dare say they'll have sent for reinforcements. We'll soon know if they can gather enough men to try an assault. Meanwhile we've got more pressing needs.' He pointed to the water butt. 'Is that all the water you have?'

'No, sir. There's two more in the store hut there.'

'Still not enough for our needs. Where's the nearest water supply?'

'There's a spring at the bottom of the slope behind the outpost, sir.'

'How far?'

The optio made a brief calculation. 'A quarter of a mile, maybe more.'

'If we move quickly, we could send men down there to fill some waterskins before any reinforcements pitch up,' Massimilianus suggested.

Cato considered the idea and shook his head. 'By the time they return, the enemy might have surrounded the outpost. It's too much of a risk. We'll have to make do with the water that's already here. In the meantime, we need to alert Plancinus and the fort. Micus, get the smoke signal going. There's a few hours to go before nightfall, plenty of time for it to be seen.'

The optio called orders to two of the militiamen to load fuel and leaves into the wicker basket at the bottom of the hoist. By the time Micus had climbed the ladder to the lookout platform, the first batch of combustibles had been swung in and added to the supply already in place. Another of his men was gently feeding kindling onto the glowing embers in the iron basket in the middle of the platform. As the small flames eagerly consumed the bundles of dry grass and twigs, he began to add split logs until the flames were licking up above the sides of the basket. Small, freshly cut leafed branches were heaped onto the flames, and soon smoke billowed up from the tower and extended into a curling column reaching into the sky.

'There we go, sir,' Massimilianus smiled. 'As clear a signal as could be.'

Cato nodded, then turned his attention to the enemy below the outpost. They were gathered around their leader, who was gesturing animatedly as he issued his orders. Once he had finished, he turned to the outpost while groups of his followers spread out and began to surround it, as Cato had anticipated. As he watched, there was a shout from the tower and he looked up to see Micus pointing west towards the road cutting through the forest.

'More of the enemy sighted!'

Cato and Massimilianus stared in the direction indicated but could see only the trees.

'Damn it,' Cato growled, scrambling down the rampart and hurrying across to the ladder. He climbed as quickly as he could. By the time he reached the platform, his heart was beating wildly and he had to pause a moment to catch his breath before he made his way around the flames in the signal pyre to join Micus.

'Where are they?'

'There, sir. See that outcrop of rocks on the hill? Two miles off, I'd say.'

Cato shaded his eyes and squinted. For a moment he saw nothing, and then a tiny movement drew his attention to a line of dots moving towards the road.

'By the gods, your eyesight is little short of miraculous, Optio.'

Micus beamed with pride.

'How many of them can you make out?' asked Cato.

Micus stared silently into the distance for a moment before he responded. 'Another hundred, perhaps a hundred and fifty of them, sir.'

Cato sucked in a breath through his teeth. That was bad news. The odds had shifted to six to one in the enemy's favour. The reinforcements would reach the outpost before nightfall, long before its defenders could expect any help to arrive.

'There's more of 'em, sir.' Micus pointed to the crags on a ridge to the south, where Cato could easily make out the distant figures of more men against the backdrop of the clear sky. At least another fifty of them were picking their way to the end of the crags and descending a precarious-looking path to the blanket of trees below.

'Looks like they've decided to make an example of the

outpost and us along with it,' Cato mused. He looked down into the packed space within the rampart. The auxiliaries had tethered their horses to a rail beside the store hut. Those who had already removed their saddles were manhandling the wagons close to the rampart in order to make more room. The mule drivers had unharnessed their teams and tied the mules' halters to a rope that had been set up opposite the wagons. They had taken some feed from one of the carts and were distributing it to their animals. Massimilianus was ordering some of the auxiliaries to do the same for the horses, as well as using buckets to draw water from the butt to fill a small trough by the horse line. The mounts pressed round and drank greedily until the trough was nearly empty and the centurion had to order more water to be fetched.

'Massimilianus!' Cato called down to him. 'That's enough water for the horses. Have your men move the trough over to the mules. They can have what's left in the butt. No more than that for now. We'll need the rest.'

'Yes, sir.'

Cato stepped back from the wooden hoarding and rubbed the small of his back, stiff from the day's riding. As he gazed to the western horizon of hills and forest, his eyes picked out what he was looking for. A thin, dark smear against the sky many miles off in the direction of Augustis.

'Sir!' Micus pointed.

'I see it already. The fort's seen our signal. We can expect help from them in a day's time. Plancinus and his men may be closer if they're still working on the next outpost to the north. We should see their signal any moment . . .'

The sun sank slowly to the west and had begun to slip below the horizon before the response came from Plancinus. A column of smoke was spotted several miles to the north, from the crest of another ridge. Cato was concerned by the delay in the response. The signal from the outpost should have been easily visible from Plancinus's position. It was possible that poor watch-keeping was responsible, or another equally unacceptable reason. Or, Cato grimaced, there was a more sinister possibility. It would be best to keep such thoughts to himself. It was likely that the men in their outpost would soon be fighting off an attack from the brigands. It was important to keep their spirits up. Drawing a deep breath, he called out so that every man within the rampart would hear him.

'Plancinus has responded to the signal, lads! More help is on the way! It's up to us to keep those bastards outside the stockade until then. If they're foolish enough to try and attack the outpost, we'll show them what happens to anyone who dares to take on the Sixth Gallic Cohort!'

A handful of weary cheers sounded in response, and Cato turned to address Micus. 'I'm taking command of the outpost until it is relieved.'

'Yes, sir.'

Was there a hint of relief in the optio's voice? Cato wondered. If so, perhaps it had been wrong to give him an independent command. Experience had taught him that some men might be fine officers in a subordinate role, but they lacked the confidence and competence to act independently, even in a capacity as limited as commanding this outpost.

He quickly took stock of the situation. He had Massimilianus and nineteen of his men, trained soldiers and well armed. In addition, there was Optio Micus, who seemed dependable. Then there were the eight militiamen assigned to garrison the outpost. Cato regarded them with misgivings. They were typical of their kind: poorly paid men tasked with guarding town gates and collecting the tolls, as well as adding to the lustre of dignitaries at public events. Although they were equipped with weapons and armour, they maintained them poorly and undertook minimal military training. The closest they were likely to come to fighting in a battle was sorting out rowdy drunks or dealing out heavy-handed treatment to some mob that might form to protest about rising grain prices. In most cases, they were little more than armed civilians. No doubt they bitterly resented being ordered to serve under Cato, and now they were facing a dangerous enemy for the first time. They would be fearful, he reflected. As would the five mule drivers who had been contracted to carry the supplies from Augustis. They had been paid handsomely and told they would be protected by the army. That promise must seem empty to them now. Besides their whips, they carried only daggers; better weapons needed to be found for them to help with the defence of the outpost. Like the militia, they were not trained as soldiers, but if it came to fighting for their lives, it was possible they might make a useful contribution.

There was no artillery at the outpost. Even a single bolt-thrower would have been useful in harassing the brigands standing nonchalantly across the slope. Nor were there any bows, or javelins. Some slings might be fashioned from the coils of rope that formed part of the supplies in the wagons. But there was no lead shot for them. The only missiles available would be stones plucked from the ground. Still, Cato decided, a few makeshift slings would help tilt the odds a little in their favour. A lucky shot might take down one of the brigands' leaders.

He paused to put himself in the enemy's position. To destroy the outpost, its garrison, a squadron of cavalry and a supply convoy would deliver a severe blow to Roman prestige and hearten those who still resisted the governor's authority. It would surely encourage more men to join the ranks of the brigands, and with the pestilence already weakening Scurra's control of the province, the time might be right for a more general uprising against Roman rule. An attack was inevitable. Most likely under cover of darkness, he concluded. In which case, the defenders needed to be prepared.

As dusk fell, Cato could make out the figures gathering around the outpost. Shortly before, the sound of axes cutting wood inside the forest had fallen silent, and the only noises coming from lower down the slope were those of orders being given and the occasional raucous exchanges of men drunk on the certainty of victory. Inside the outpost, Cato had ordered two of the carts to be placed hard up against the inside of the gates, their wheels wedged with rocks. The leader of the mule drivers, a thin man with hollow cheeks and deep-set eyes, was also the owner of the wagons, and he accosted Cato as soon as he realised why his vehicles were being repositioned.

'Now just a minute, Legate. You ain't putting my property in the way of danger. Not unless you're prepared to pay for it first.'

'I'm not a legate,' Cato replied with forced patience as he regarded the man. 'Barcano, isn't it?'

'Yes, sir.'

'What good do you think your property is going to do you if the enemy fight their way into the stockade? They'll cut you down alongside us and take your wagons. It's better that they are used to improve our defences. For your sake as much as my soldiers'.'

'That's as may be, but I've got to think about my livelihood if we get through this alive. When the fighting's over, it's me that's going to be out of pocket if there's any damage done to my wagons, ain't it?'

'Then let's hope the enemy doesn't get close enough to damage them, eh? Where's your weapon?' Cato looked over at the rest of the mule drivers sitting together in front of the other carts. 'Why aren't your men armed? I gave orders that every man was going to take his place on the battle line.'

'Ah, well now, that's another matter.' Barcano jabbed his thumb into his bony chest. 'We're paid to haul supplies, not to fight. If you're asking me and the lads to take up arms, that'll cost extra.'

'I'm not asking you. I'm ordering you.'

Barcano shook his head. 'You ain't got the right. We're not your soldiers.'

Cato was tired and fast losing his patience. It seemed incredible that he should be discussing such a matter while they were surrounded by an enemy determined to wipe them out. 'You'll do as I say. Now report to Optio Micus and get some weapons for your men.'

He was about to turn away, but Barcano sidestepped neatly into his path. 'Nothing doing. Not until we agree terms.'

'Fuck it,' Cato growled. He grabbed the folds of the man's tunic and forced him back several paces until he slammed into one of the posts of the watchtower. 'I'll tell you my terms. You'll do exactly as I bloody say. If you don't, or you give me any more trouble, I'll have you and your men thrown out of the fort and you can take the matter up with the enemy. Do you understand me?'

Barcano's eyes were wide with fear and he nodded vigorously. 'Y-yes, sir. No need to threaten me. I'm just a businessman trying to earn a living.'

'Then fucking earn it and get yourself a weapon, or living is the last thing you'll be doing.'

Cato released his grip and thrust himself away from the man with a snort of disgust. He turned and made his way up onto the rampart beside the gate, where Massimilianus was leaning on the rail between two of the hoardings.

'Anything to report, Centurion?'

'No, sir. It's gone quiet down there. Won't stay that way for long, I'd imagine.'

Cato looked up at the velvet sky. The brightest of the stars were already visible, but there would be no moon for a few nights. That worked in favour of the enemy, who would be able to get close to the fort before being spotted. The timing of any attack was a less certain matter. A patient leader would let his men eat and rest during the night while he sent skirmishers forward in feints, forcing the defenders to stay alert so they would be tense and exhausted when the real attack was unleashed. However, the leader of the brigand war band would be aware that the smoke signal from the outpost had been answered and that relief columns might already be marching to the aid of the defenders, forestalling any chance of a dawn attack.

'I think they'll keep us on our toes for a few hours before they attempt anything. Make sure the men and animals are fed.'

'Yes, sir.' Massimilianus turned to indicate the mules, which were braying loudly from the corner of the outpost where they had been tethered. 'The trough's run dry and those beggars have a raging thirst. They'll keep that up, and it'll get worse the thirstier they get.'

Cato had not been thinking of the welfare of the draught animals. 'So?'

'The more noise they make, the harder it will be for us to hear the enemy when they approach the fort.'

'Ah . . . That's not good.'

'No. So we can either give them some more water, or put up with the noise, or silence them.'

'We may need whatever water we have left,' Cato responded. 'They'll have to go without. If we get through the night, we'll need them. We'll leave them be for now. Make sure you tell the sentries to keep their ears open. And have some bundles of kindling tied up with rags, in case we need illumination in front of the defences.'

'Yes, sir.'

Cato looked over the rampart towards the enemy for a moment before he continued. 'Post two men on each wall and two in the tower. The remainder can rest at the foot of the rampart. We'll change the watch around midnight. You take the first watch.'

'Very good, sir.'

They exchanged a nod and Cato climbed down to the interior of the outpost and crossed to the stores hut, where Micus and his militia were eating around a small iron stove. They scrambled to their feet as he approached.

'Stand easy. Any spare rations to be had?'

Micus offered him his own mess tin and Cato nodded his thanks. He raised it and sniffed, then tried a spoonful of the thick stew, chewing on a lump of meat and swallowing. 'Is that pork?'

'Wild boar, sir. There's some in the forest by the spring. I took down a sow yesterday and we found her piglets at the same time. The carcasses are hanging at the back of the store shed.'

'And you forgot to tell Massimilianus and his men about them?'

Micus smiled. 'He didn't ask, sir.'

'Then I suggest you be a good comrade and let his men share the meat. It's important to have a good meal before a fight.'

'Yes, sir, I'll see to it.'

Cato ate quickly, surprised to find that the seasoning of the stew lent it a fine flavour. He scraped the bottom and sides of the mess tin for his last spoonful and returned it to Micus. 'Thanks. I'll sleep that off. Don't forget what I said about the meat.'

'Of course, sir.'

He found himself a place at the foot of the rampart where he could be seen by the light of the flames beneath the stove, then settled back and closed his eyes. He kept still and breathed easily. Tired as he was, his mind was racing, yet he knew that it set a poor example to the men if they saw him fretting and keeping a constant lookout for an attack. Better that they saw him calmly take a nap.

Though his eyes were closed, his ears missed little. Besides the braying of the mules and the gentle crackle of flames from the cooking stove and the signal brazier, there was the murmur of conversation between the men inside the crowded interior of the outpost. Some of the voices were anxious, but most sounded calm, and there was even some laughter before someone broke into a bawdy song about a cuckolded miller and his lecherous young wife. His comrades joined in until it reached the humorous conclusion and all of them roared with laughter. Cato half opened his eyes and saw one of Micus's men carrying two small boar carcasses across to the auxiliaries, who were busy lighting their own cooking fire. The fresh meat was accepted gratefully and the auxiliaries shared their wineskin with the militiaman. Cato's lips raised slightly in a satisfied smile at the prospect of the two groups of men bonding.

He closed his eyes again and breathed deeply as the night closed in over the outpost. Overhead, a multitude of stars glittered serenely as a lone bird began to call out somewhere in the distance. On another night, it would have been the epitome of tranquillity, he mused. His thoughts drifted, and soon he was thinking of Claudia once again, and then he was fast asleep, snoring loudly enough to draw smiles from the militiamen nearby.

Cato woke gradually, so that the dream he'd been having vied with the reality around him for a few moments before his head cleared and he sat up quickly. The cooking fire had died down to a few glowing embers and the night air was cool enough to make him shiver. He rose stiffly to his feet and looked around. All was quiet. Even the mules had fallen silent. The sentries on the rampart were just visible, as were the men sitting or lying around the inside of the stockade. There was a glow at the top of the watchtower from the signal brazier, which was kept alight at all times. He could make out the transverse crest of Massimilianus's helmet above the rear wall of the stockade. Climbing up the rampart, he joined the centurion as the latter stared intently into the darkness.

'Anything to report?'

'Not much. There was some movement about an hour ago, down by the edge of the forest. Nothing since then, apart from the odd outbreak of shouting. Sounds like they're having something of a party. Probably filling their guts with wine to build up some Tungrian courage.'

A vague sense of foreboding gripped Cato. He tried to shake it off. It would not do him or his men any good to spend the night jumping at shadows.

'How long have I been asleep?'

'Four, maybe five hours, sir.'

'Then it's time you were relieved. Send the next watch up to replace the sentries.'

'Yes, sir.'

The centurion climbed down and went round the outpost waking some of the sleeping men. One by one those on watch were relieved and descended from the stockade to find a place to rest. Cato leaned on the rail and stared into the darkness, ears straining to detect any sound that might be cause for alarm. He heard a chorus of shouts, roars of laughter, and then a group of men burst into song.

He eased himself up and walked slowly along the rampart, checking that all the sentries had been replaced by men from the second watch and that the latter were fully awake. As he made his way along the stretch of the stockade leading to the gate, he glanced out and was about to take his next step when he heard a faint noise – a light, almost animal grunt. He froze and leaned his head towards the sound. But there was nothing more and he wondered if he had imagined it. There it was again, the sense of foreboding he had felt earlier, nagging at his thoughts. He was tempted to dismiss it once more, but something felt different. He turned to the rail of the stockade and half concealed himself behind one of the protective hoardings, then listened again. The sound of singing from the bottom of the slope at the rear of the outpost swelled in volume.

'I don't like it,' he whispered to himself. He turned to the nearest sentry. 'Bring me a taper from the cooking fire embers, and one of the kindling faggots.'

'Yes, sir.'

'Be quick about it.'

While he waited, he continued watching the ground in

front of the outpost but could make out no movement. When the auxiliary returned, Cato drew his sword and stabbed it into the tightly bound bundle of sticks, then held it up and ordered the other man to light the kindling. It took a moment for the spark to spread to the bundle, but the dried twigs were soon eagerly consumed by small flames, and smoke curled up. When it was properly ablaze, Cato stretched his sword arm back and hurled it forward, and the bundle slipped off the blade and flew in a flaring shallow arc for a short distance before hitting the ground in a burst of sparks and rolling down the slope.

The bright yellow flames illuminated a group of crouching men some fifty paces away, staring intently at the blazing bundle as it passed close by them and lit up another huddle of brigands a short distance further on.

Cato cupped a hand to his mouth and turned to shout at his men. 'To arms! To arms!'

CHAPTER TWENTY-SIX

'They're coming!' Cato bellowed. 'Bring up the rest of the faggots! Light 'em up and get them over the walls!'

The men who had been resting a moment earlier scrambled to their feet, snatched up their weapons and surged up the rampart to take their positions along the stockade. Cato saw Barcano hesitate before one of his men thrust him forward. As more of the faggots were set alight, a cacophony of cheers and war cries rose up from the darkness around the outpost. Cato gripped the edge of the wooden rail as he saw the enemy swarming up towards the ditch that surrounded the stockade. The first wave consisted of a dispersed line of men armed with arrows and slings. Behind them came groups with shields to protect the ladder-bearers hurrying after them. There was a bright flare and a crackle of flames as another faggot arced over the stockade. It struck the ground and rolled down the slope, forcing two of the brigand skirmishers to dive aside, its vivid glow revealing another party of men with a ladder. There was a brief burst of sparks and spurts of flame as the faggot hit a tree stump, and by their light Cato glimpsed an even bigger party of men packed tightly together further down the slope. Then the glow faded and they were lost from sight.

'Beware! Slingshot!' Massimilianus called out. 'Get down!'

297

Most of the men along the stockade hunched or ducked behind the hoardings, but some were slow to react. Shot whipped out of the darkness, splintering the wooden stockade or shooting overhead to thud into the opposite rampart, or going high and passing right over the outpost. There were arrows too, dark shafts shivering as the points bit into the timber. Cato saw one of the mule drivers lurch as an arrow struck him in the shoulder. He stumbled back a pace before slipping and rolling down the rampart, howling as the shaft snagged and jarred the arrowhead before it snapped. A constant ragged chorus of sharp raps sounded across the outpost as missiles continued to strike home. Cato crouched behind the parapet in grim frustration at being forced to keep his head down, unable to keep an eye on the enemy. He could hear them above the din of the bombardment, cheering as they surged towards the ditch.

There was a cry of pain from the far side of the outpost, and he turned to see that one of the militiamen had been struck in the back of his thigh by an arrow. Even as he watched, there was a burst of grit as a slingshot slammed into the rampart nearby. He saw the danger he had missed at once, and cupped his hands to his mouth as he bellowed, 'Keep your shields up, facing into the outpost!'

His men hurried to obey, while the mule drivers huddled up close to the soldiers to try to shelter from the barrage of arrows and shot. It was the first time Cato had been subjected to an all-round deluge of missiles in such a confined space, and he sat tensed up, convinced that he would be struck at any moment. Nor were the men the only ones at risk. An arrow pierced the neck of one of the horses and it reared back, forelegs kicking as its head swung wildly from side to side, straining to break free from the tethered reins. Its shrill whinnies and frantic movements frightened the horses on either side. An instant later, one of the mules was hit in the rump and added its agonised braying to the noise swelling up within the small fortification. The only thing that compensated for the danger and terror of the storm of missiles flying at and over the stockade was the realisation that the overshoots were as much a danger to the enemy. Cato wondered if they had neglected to consider that in their burning desire to destroy the outpost, or whether they simply considered it a risk worth taking.

He heard a shout close by, beyond the ditch, then the rattle of the arrows and slingshot against the stockade began to ease. He braced himself and stood up. On the other side of the ditch he could see the enemy pouring forward out of the pools of light cast by the faggots. As the first group reached the ditch, he saw that the ladder they were carrying was longer than he had thought, and he felt his guts knot with anxiety as he shouted the warning.

'Stand up! They're using ladders!'

The defenders rose, shields towards the enemy, as the nearest brigands grounded the base of the ladder and fed it forwards, out over the ditch, at an angle towards the top of the parapet. Cato drew his sword and stepped closer as the arms of the ladder clattered onto the wooden rail. At once the first of the attackers began to scramble up the shallow angle, the rungs bowing slightly under his weight. He was hampered by the spear in his right hand, and Cato could hear his laboured breathing as he approached. The man slowed as he caught sight of the Roman officer waiting for him, sword raised; then, grasping the riser firmly with his left hand, he braced his feet and made a one-handed thrust.

Cato parried the spearhead easily and leaned forward to slash at his opponent's left hand. The point tore through the flesh about the brigand's wrist and he loosened his grip on the riser.

His body collapsed onto the ladder and then rolled over the edge, and he fell into the ditch, still clutching his spear in his good hand.

Cato lifted the top of the ladder and tried to thrust it back, but the base was solidly positioned and resisted his efforts to dislodge it. Already another man, armed with an axe, had climbed onto it and was making his way across to the palisade, more nimbly than his predecessor. Cato began to hack at the nearest rung, splintering the wood. At the fifth blow it split in the middle and he leaned out to strike at the second rung.

His new opponent saw the danger and scurried forward, raising his axe to slash at Cato's extended arm. At that moment the ladder lurched and the brigand was forced to release the haft of his axe to grab at one of the risers, letting the weapon swing from his wrist by the leather strap. Cato hacked savagely until the second rung splintered, then quickly sheathed his sword to grasp the end of the ladder and rock it from side to side. The brigand could do nothing but cling on desperately and shout over his shoulder. One of his comrades came forward, hefting a spear, and raised it above his shoulder as he took aim at Cato. Straining his muscles, Cato gritted his teeth in a last desperate effort, and was rewarded as one of the risers shifted an arm's length from the stockade. The ladder twisted to the side and the man with the axe clung on with one hand for a heartbeat before letting himself drop into the ditch, rolling to the bottom.

There was no time for Cato to register his small victory as he glimpsed the spearman's arm sweep back. He ducked behind a hoarding and the point of the spear smashed through the rough-hewn board and showered his face with splinters. He blinked as a piece stabbed into his eyelid close to the top of his cheekbone. Reaching up with his left hand, he pulled at the finger-length splinter and tugged it out. The vision in his eye was blurry and the sharp pain almost agonising.

'Sir!' Micus was half crouching beside him. 'You're wounded.'

Cato shook his head. 'It can wait.'

He glanced round the interior of the outpost and saw several of the men battling to dislodge ladders or keep the enemy from gaining the palisade. For the moment the defenders were holding their own. Even with their small numbers, they had enough men to cover the perimeter of the stockade. Massimilianus had taken command of the rear of the outpost, and Cato grasped Micus's arm. 'Get to the other side of the gate and take charge there. We can't afford to let any of those bastards get over the parapet.'

'Yes, sir.' The optio scuttled down the rampart and ran past the wagons bolstering the gate to take his position on the far side. Cato blinked rapidly to try and rid himself of the sensation of grit in his left eye, and then swore in frustration as it still refused to focus. He drew his sword again and peered round the hoarding to see that the ladder he had hacked up now lay abandoned and the party of men who had carried it up the slope were running along the edge of the ditch to join another group. He turned to look in the other direction, and by the light of one of the burning bundles of kindling twigs he saw the large party he had glimpsed earlier climbing resolutely towards the gates. Now he could see that they were carrying a ram fashioned from the trunk of a tree, and his blood ran cold. They were no more than fifty feet from the causeway across the ditch.

Dipping his head, he ran to the nearest group of defenders who were not in combat. He picked three of them – two auxiliaries and one of the mule drivers, a heavyset man with a pockmarked face whose ugliness was exaggerated by the firelight.

'Follow me!'

Two of the wounded horses had broken loose and were careering around the interior of the outpost, and Cato and his small band had to work their way round them to avoid being trampled. Reaching the wagons behind the gate, Cato climbed onto the right-hand one and beckoned to the mule driver. 'With me.' He nodded to the other wagon. 'You two in there.'

Pulling himself up onto the driver's bench, he clambered over the sacks of grain and chests of tools and made his way to the rear of the vehicle, where it had been backed onto the gate. At that moment the timbers shook and there was a loud crash as the ram slammed into the gate. The shock of the impact shifted the wagon beneath Cato's boots as he balanced on a pile of coiled ropes. A hand grabbed him by the shoulder and steadied him, and then the mule driver moved round to stand at his side.

Cato nodded his thanks and indicated the ropes. 'Get these out of the way. We'll need a firm footing.'

'Yes, sir.'

The driver handed Cato the spear he had been armed with and bent to his task, throwing the coils towards the bench until he had cleared enough space for them to stand side by side.

'What's your name?' asked Cato.

'Vespillo, sir,' the driver replied without looking up as he continued clearing the rope away.

'Have you been in a fight before?'

'Plenty of fights. I used to be a boxer.'

'A successful one, I hope.'

Vespillo cleared away the last coil and responded in a wry tone. 'Why do you think I'm a bloody mule driver, sir?'

302

Cato handed the spear back to him and they stood waiting as the ram crashed home several more times. In between, Cato could hear a scraping sound, and he saw fingers curl over the top of the gate in front of him. The fingers clenched tightly and then a head appeared. Cato swung his sword at the nearest of the man's hands before he could release his grip, and the blade cut through the knuckle and severed the little finger, which fell into the wagon as the man dropped out of sight. Vespillo laughed hoarsely and ducked down to retrieve the finger, looking at it with bemusement.

'There'll be time for gathering trophies later,' said Cato. Vespillo tossed the bloodied digit over the gate.

A few blows later, the ram shattered one of the timbers in front of Cato, who looked down instantly to avoid the splinters. When he looked up again, he saw that there was a small opening where the head of the ram had punched through. The next blow smashed the locking bar behind the gate in two, and one end dropped to the ground at the rear of the wagon.

'They'll be through any moment,' he said. 'Be ready to strike at the first one through the gap.'

There were several more blows, and then an order was shouted and those manning the ram ceased their assault. Axes cleared away the loose shards of shattered timber, and what was left of the gate was wrenched outwards until there was a gap large enough for a man to slip through. The first of the brigands to enter the outpost was a huge warrior swathed in the fur of a large bear, the skin of its head covering the man's helmet. He carried a round shield and a long club studded with iron nails.

'Stick him, Vespillo!' Cato shouted.

The mule driver raised his spear and made a powerful overarm thrust at the warrior's neck, but the man snatched his shield up and deflected the blow. Before Vespillo could react, his opponent swung his club down on the shaft of the spear and battered it out of his grasp so that the weapon flew to the side and struck Cato's left arm a numbing blow. With a roar of triumph, the warrior drew his club back to strike again. Vespillo recoiled, his heel catching the nearest heap of ropes, and he lost his balance and fell backwards. Cato lashed out, but was blocked by the shield as the man raised his club to finish Vespillo off. The mule driver was saved by one of the auxiliaries in the next wagon, who thrust his cavalry sword into the warrior's bicep and tore open a gaping wound before wrenching his blade free. The brigand bellowed with pain and rage and stepped back through the gap, his axe hanging uselessly at the end of his maimed arm.

Cato helped Vespillo to his feet and the mule driver retrieved his spear as the enemy began to break down the shattered remains of the gate to allow more men to pass through and attack the defenders in the wagons. By the wavering glow from the cooking fire, Cato could make out the seething mass of brigands stretching down the slope as they waited to surge into the outpost and butcher those within. Lengths of timber were smashed apart with axes and wrenched aside until a gap nearly six feet across had been cleared and the first of the enemy surged forward. Cato and the others defending the wagons had the advantage of height as they fought it out in the narrow space. As the Romans rained sword blows on the shields of the enemy warriors below them, Vespillo thrust his spear at any exposed limbs, piking one of the first men inside the ruined gate in the shoulder. Another was struck down as one of the auxiliaries hacked at the side of his head, slicing off his ear before the blade went on to cleave his collarbone.

More men pressed forward over the bodies of their comrades, and those with spears stabbed them at the men on the wagons.

Cato cut at the head of a man who dropped to the ground to avoid the blow and did not come up again. A quick glance down the narrow gap between the wagons revealed movement, and he stepped back to shout a warning.

'Massimilianus! They're under the wagons! Stop them!'

As he turned back to join Vespillo in holding back the enemy, he heard the centurion bark an order and glanced across to see Massimilianus and one of his men stooping to hack at the brigands trying to crawl into the outpost.

Vespillo suddenly gasped and stumbled back, blood gushing from a wound in his thigh, and Cato sheathed his sword and snatched the spear from the mule driver. Grasping the shaft in both hands, he made a quick series of brutal thrusts, driving the point into shields to force the attackers back and aiming at any exposed target. He caught one man in the face, plunging the point into his eye and thrusting the tip deep into his skull before ripping it free. Driven wild by agony the brigand turned and fled, sweeping his comrades aside and knocking two of them off the causeway before disappearing from view. Taking advantage of the brief distraction, Cato had long enough to grasp that the three men left on the wagons could not hold off the enemy horde for long. It was only a matter of time before they too were wounded, and there were not enough men in the outpost to replace them and still defend the rest of the stockade.

'Massimilianus!'

'Sir!' The centurion rose up at the front of the wagon.

'Set fire to the wagons.'

'Do what, sir?'

'Set fire to the bloody wagons, man! Do it now!'

There was no time for further words. The enemy were once again pushing forward, one spearman duelling with Cato as one of his comrades made to climb onto the bed of the wagon.

'No you fucking don't!' Cato snarled as he smashed the first man's spear aside and lashed out with his boot, the studded sole raking the other brigand's face and thrusting him back onto his comrades. Behind him, Cato could hear Massimilianus shouting orders for one of the injured men to set light to the faggots and push them under the wagons. At the same time two brigands with shields raised to protect their heads and upper bodies stabbed spears at Cato's feet and legs, forcing him to retreat onto the ropes. He breathed in a waft of smoke and coughed as he braced his feet and jabbed the head of the spear at the man clambering onto the back of the wagon. The brigand took each blow on his shield and made ready to spring at Cato while his companion climbed up to join him.

The gap between the wagons began to glow as the bundles of kindling burned fiercely and the smoke billowed up and swirled around the men fighting for control of the outpost's gate. Cato could feel the heat from beneath and saw the bright glitter in the narrow gaps between the boards on the bottom and sides of the wagon. There was an alarmed shout from the man at the rear of the wagon, and his companion snorted with derision as he rose to his feet to confront Cato. There was an instant of stillness as the two men weighed each other up, and the brigand smiled thinly as he realised that the advantage lay with him, armed as he was with a shield as well as a spear. Cato punched his own spear forward with the kind of savage snarl that Macro had often used to good effect. The brigand retreated a step as he absorbed the blow on his shield, deflected it and then surged forward to smash the shield into Cato's body before the latter could recover the weapon for another thrust. The shield boss caught Cato on the medal harness over his sternum as the top of it struck his helmet.

The impact drove him backwards, and he tumbled onto the piled ropes, the brigand rolling down beside him. Gasping for breath, Cato released his grip on his spear and drew his dagger as he threw himself on his opponent. The brigand too released his spear, but his other arm was caught in the strap of his shield and he only had one hand with which to defend himself, his fingers scrabbling for his opponent's face as Cato stabbed him in the chest and stomach again and again. With a last burst of strength, the brigand clawed at Cato and a finger gouged his injured eye. He felt the agonising pressure and jerked his head away; then, pulling his bloodied dagger free, he reached up and forced the blade into the soft tissue under the brigand's jawline and punched up into his skull, twisting the handle savagely as the man gurgled frantically, spurting blood into Cato's face.

As his stricken opponent spasmed, Cato rolled aside and sat up. His left eye felt like it was burning in the socket and he had no sight in it now. Some of the rope beneath the dying brigand was smouldering, and flames were licking up through the widening gaps in the bed of the wagon. More flames blazed at the end of the vehicle, forcing the enemy away from the ruined gate. Cato struggled to his feet, swaying as he tried to cope with the pain raging through his head.

'Sir!' Massimilianus called out to him. 'Get out of there!'

The heat from the blaze beneath and around him began to singe his legs, and he stumbled across the smouldering heap of ropes and tool boxes, clenching his eyes shut as he fought off a fresh wave of agony and nausea. Hands gripped his harness and hauled him over the driver's bench and onto the ground. As he was dragged a few paces further away from the heat of the flames, he heard the centurion shouting orders for his men to save what they could from the burning wagons. He was dimly aware that the sounds of fighting were fading away, and then there were just the shouts within the fort as the defenders dealt with the fire to prevent it spreading to the stockade on either side.

He eased himself up, supporting his weight on his right hand as he raised his left to tenderly examine his injured eye. The slightest pressure instantly increased the searing pain. With his other eye he could see several more wounded men around him, close to the cooking fire. A militiaman was tying off a dressing over the head wound of one of the mule drivers. He picked up a basket and came over to Cato, gently turning his head to the light.

'Hold still, sir, I need to remove your helmet.'

He undid the straps under Cato's chin and lifted the helmet off and placed it on the ground. Once he had eased off the felt skullcap, he examined the wound briefly before taking out a wad of folded linen from the basket and carefully positioning it over the left eye socket. Cato gritted his teeth at a fresh burst of pain as the man began to wind a long strip of cloth around his head to hold the wad in place. He secured it with a simple knot and tucked the loose ends into the folds of cloth at the back of Cato's head.

'That's all I can do for now, sir.'

'It'll do, thank you,' Cato responded, relieved that the man's ministrations were complete. 'See to the others.'

As the militiaman moved on to deal with Vespillo's thigh wound, Cato forced himself to his feet and looked round the outpost. The interior was brightly lit by the flames at the gate. There were a handful of bodies on the rampart, and several men were still in position, sheltering behind the hoardings as they kept watch for a fresh assault. Others were busy controlling the horses and mules, which were stamping in fear at the flames. A handful of animals had been wounded by arrows and slingshot, and two lay dead. He saw Massimilianus on the rampart a safe distance from the flames. The centurion stared down the slope in front of the gate for a moment before turning away and slithering down the rampart.

'What are they up to, Massimilianus?'

'They've fallen back fifty paces or so. They'll wait until the fire burns down before they make another attempt.'

'What's the butcher's bill?' Cato asked.

'Three of my men are dead. Four wounded. Micus is dead, along with one of the militia. Another is wounded. The mule driver there is the only casualty from Barcano's lot. Then there's you. How are you doing, sir?'

'I'll live.' Cato struggled to clear his head. 'We need to be ready for the next attack if it comes. Have more faggots prepared to roll down the slope. Can't afford to let them use the darkness to get close to the ditch. Meanwhile, we'll keep feeding the fire in the gateway. Just enough to discourage them. I don't want to burn down the fucking stockade.'

'No, that wouldn't be helpful, sir.' Massimilianus grinned for a moment before his expression resumed its grim look. He lowered his voice. 'We only just fought them off this time, sir. If they make another attempt, I don't think there's much chance of keeping them out.'

'Not much chance?' Cato sighed. 'There's no chance at all.'

CHAPTER TWENTY-SEVEN

The wagons burned fiercely for over an hour before the flames began to die down. Massimilianus had pairs of men on both sides, smothering any flames that spread to the stockade with lengths of sacking soaked with water from the limited supply that remained. It was tiring work and the auxiliaries could not bear the heat from the fire for long before they were driven back and the next relay took their place. The wagons were soon no more than charred frameworks held up by the thick timber of their axles and their solid iron-rimmed wheels.

Most of the remaining men still fit enough to fight manned the stockade, keeping low in order not to attract any fresh arrows or slingshot. One of the mule drivers was sent up the watchtower to keep the signal beacon alight, and the wounded had been moved to the shelter of the garrison's small hut. As Cato surveyed the men at their places around the interior of the outpost, he felt a small measure of satisfaction. They had kept the enemy out, for now. More casualties had been inflicted than suffered; the bodies in the ditch and on the slopes beyond were testament to the fortitude of the defenders. The bodies of Micus and the others had been laid out beneath the tower.

Dawn was still some hours away. Cato strained his weary mind to focus on the forces in play. There were barely twenty men still fit enough to fight, and if the brigands struck from all sides simultaneously, there was little chance of being able to defend the entire line of the stockade. That would mean falling back to defend a shorter line. He looked at the two sheds backing onto the side of the outpost, then called Massimilianus away from directing the men controlling the burning wagons.

The centurion unfastened the chin straps of his helmet as he approached and removed it to mop his brow and scratch his scalp.

'The fire's not going to last until dawn, sir. They'll be able to get across the embers easily when the time comes.'

'We'll do what we can to keep it alight. Feed it from the stock of fuel for the signal beacon, enough to discourage our friends outside. There will be a brief respite when the fire dies down and before we build it up. Use that to get the remaining wagons lined up in front of the sheds. Two will cover it. The third will protect the exposed end. The supplies can be put between the wheels to stop the brigands getting underneath. And we can block the walkway above the corner of the stockade, and there at the end of the shed. If the stockade falls, we can pull back to the wagons. Five men in each and the rest covering the stockade behind will give us a much shorter line to defend.'

'True . . .' Massimilianus turned to him and arched an eyebrow. 'Last stand?'

'Let's hope it doesn't come to that.'

'What odds would you give me that it won't?'

'Where would I send the money if you win the bet, Centurion?'

They shared a brief laugh at the old joke before Cato sighed wearily. 'Never thought it would all end fighting for a flimsy outpost in a quiet backwater of the Empire . . .'

'Rather than sticking it to a barbarian army in battle, eh?' Massimilianus smiled knowingly. 'In my experience, soldiers rarely get the death they would wish for, sir. You could have died from the sickness back in Tharros.'

'True. That would have been a wretched way to go.' He punched the centurion on the shoulder. 'If it happens here, we'll make a fight of it. Something to make Horatius proud!'

There was a faint rumble and both men turned to the gate as what was left of the wagon on the right collapsed in a burst of sparks and swirling flames.

'Better start work on our last redoubt . . .'

Massimilianus bowed his head in salute and turned away to give the orders to his men. Cato turned his attention to the mule teams and the horses, considering whether it might be best to have them slaughtered so that they did not fall into the brigands' hands. His conscience revolted at the notion. Besides, they might yet serve some purpose. There might be a chance for some of the men to attempt to break through the enemy surrounding them and escape. Those left behind would face certain death. Cato was not prepared to abandon them to such a fate. And if this was the place where fate had decided he should die, then so be it. A fresh burst of throbbing in his wounded eye drove the melancholy from his thoughts and he gritted his teeth as he paced up and down by the light of the fire, trying to fight off the pain.

The hours of the night passed with aching slowness. From time to time small groups of the enemy approached the outpost and loosed a volley of arrows before retreating. A shouted warning was enough to ensure that the defenders scrambled for shelter before the shafts dropped inside the stockade. Two more of the horses and one of the mules were hit. They thrashed about in pain and threatened to set off a wider panic amongst the beasts tethered tightly together, and Cato was obliged to have them cut loose and led across to the opposite rampart to be killed with a merciful blow from a hammer driving an iron spike into the area between their eyes and ears. They went down, legs collapsing beneath them and long necks stretched out as their tongues lolled between their bristly muzzles.

The men who had been detailed to prevent the fire spreading to the stockade were now tasked with keeping the blaze going by feeding it with logs from the fuel store beneath the watchtower. As long as the flames lasted, Cato hoped the enemy would keep their distance and wait for what they thought were the wagons to burn out and open the way for their final assault. They would not be fooled for long when the flames refused to die down, he reasoned. A couple of ladders covered with dampened foliage would be sufficient to lay across the logs and provide a way for the enemy to rush across the fire.

He took a last look around at their preparations and then climbed up the rampart to the walkway and sat down beside one of the hoardings close to the gate. It was a cool night and he was comforted by the warmth generated by the ongoing blaze where the wagons had once stood. The pain in his left eye had subsided into a steady throb, and now that he had time to think clearly, he wondered how serious the injury was. It was possible he might lose the sight in the eye. The prospect of being a half-blind soldier caused him great concern. If he lost the other eye, what quality of life would remain? He might never see Lucius grow into a man, nor see any children that his son might father. Gone would be the ability to read, to relish the glorious pageant of the seasons . . . He smiled at himself for thinking so far ahead when he might be dead ere the sun rose again.

His thoughts were interrupted as he saw movement on the slope in front of the gateway. Three men, including one wearing the antler headgear of one of the brigand leaders, were approaching warily. They stopped twenty paces from the ditch and scrutinised the fire and the stockade on either side, talking in low tones that Cato could barely make out above the steady crackle of the flames. They took a final look at the gate before making off, disappearing into the darkness beyond the orange loom of the fire. He felt no wiser about their purpose. They might have been planning their next attack, but it was possible that they might conclude that further action could result in more deaths than taking the outpost was worth. All the same, it was better to be prepared for the worst. Carefully pressing his felt skullcap over the dressing, Cato eased his helmet on and fastened the chin strap, adjusting it to make sure it sat securely and comfortably. Then, in order to fight off his tiredness, he made a slow circuit of the stockade, ensuring the men were alert, offering them words of encouragement and exchanging an occasional quiet joke to keep their spirits up.

The brigands came on again in the last hour of the night, swarming up the hill on all four sides. The mule driver in the watchtower was the first to see them and gave an anxious cry of alarm.

'Stand to!' Cato called out as he drew his sword and lifted the shield he had taken from one of the injured auxiliaries. The remaining defenders rose to their feet and stood ready along the line of the stockade. Cato looked to make sure each man was at his post and none were shirking. He gave a grunt of approval as he saw that even Barcano and his mule drivers were ready to make their stand.

'Light the faggots!' he ordered.

Massimilianus and one of his men scampered around the stockade with tapers to set fire to the bundles before they were pitched over to illuminate the slope. As the enemy surged forward into the glow of the flames, they bellowed their war cries and the sound assaulted the ears of the defenders from every side. From his position, Cato could see a force of at least a hundred men making for the gate, carrying several ladders with them.

'Assault ladders!' he shouted. 'Don't let them over the stockade!'

A shout from the rear of the outpost drew his attention and he saw the risers of a ladder rap down on the palisade. Barcano and one of his men ran to the spot to dislodge the ladder before any of the enemy could scale it. As the first of the brigands scurried into sight, the mule drivers managed to twist the ladder and heave it into the ditch.

'Good work!' Cato muttered, then turned to face the enemy to his front. They had separated into three streams: two making for the ditch either side of the gate, while the main group headed for the causeway and the fire beyond. Closer to, Cato could see that they had stretched dripping furs over their ladders. It was as he had feared, and there was little he could do to delay the inevitable loss of the gateway.

'Massimilianus!'

'Sir?'

'I need four men inside the gate. Be quick about it.'

As the centurion reeled off the names, Cato called out to the next man along the wall from him. 'You cover that ladder. Let no one over the parapet!'

'Y-yes, sir.' The auxiliary nodded. By the glow of the fire Cato could see the fear in his expression and softened his tone as he addressed the soldier.

'Hold your ground and trust your comrades to do the same, and we'll come out of this alive. Understand?'

'Yes, sir.'

Hoping he had reassured the man, whatever the truth might be, Cato ran down the rampart and over to Massimilianus and the four auxiliaries detailed to defend the gate. Already he could see the brigands on the other side of the flames as they began to feed through the first of the skin-covered ladders. It was clear that they would take the outpost now. There was no other possibility. He turned to Massimilianus.

'Hamstring the horses and mules. I won't let them fall into the enemy's hands. Do it quickly.'

The centurion hesitated, then grasped his superior's thinking and nodded soberly before he made off to carry out his instructions.

'Two of you on either side,' Cato ordered. 'Close shields!'

The auxiliaries did as they were told, leaving a gap between their shields wide enough to thrust their swords, and Cato led them as close to the flames as they could bear before halting. The first ladder dropped onto the burning logs, the soaked skins damping down the flames with a sharp hiss. The second followed quickly, and fell to one side, narrowly overlapping the first to create a path through the flames nearly four feet across.

'Here they come!' Cato warned the men beside him as the first terrified whinnies sounded from the horse lines.

As a third ladder was extended over the blaze, the first of the enemy charged across. He carried a buckler, and an axe raised above his head, and his lips were stretched back, revealing his bared teeth. Cato braced his feet apart and slightly bent his leading leg to absorb the impact of the man's charge. An instant later, the edge of the axe shattered the upper trim of his shield and bit into the layered wood. He controlled the recoil from the impact and then shoved back as hard as he could, slamming his oval shield into his opponent's. The brigand stumbled back towards the flames beside the ladders, then howled with pain and reeled forward onto the point of the sword of the auxiliary to Cato's left. The blade was thrust home deep into the man's guts, then twisted and wrenched back. The brigand staggered into the path of the second man to cross the ladders and was knocked aside, falling into the blaze, where he screamed and writhed as the flames consumed him. The second man, like those behind him, was also carrying a shield and an axe, and Cato realised that they had been hand-picked for close combat to lead the attack. The man moved at once to Cato's left to hack at the auxiliary there and create space for the next of his comrades, who went to the right. The third made for Cato.

The top of his shield took more damage as an axe splintered the edge close to the first cut. Again Cato thrust back, but this time his opponent was more deliberate in his movements and absorbed the blow, then they both leaned into their shields, feet braced as they heaved. Cato held his ground, but as more brigands piled in behind the first ranks and thrust at the defenders, he was forced backwards, the auxiliaries retreating with him. The fight for the gate was lost . . .

'No!' Cato snarled at himself. He ripped his shield back, punched it forward and stabbed with his sword at the same time. He felt the point pierce flesh and then lurch into bone, and he twisted it violently from side to side before tearing it free. Then he swivelled at the waist to throw his weight behind the shield and knock his wounded opponent back. A quick stab to his right caught the next man in the thigh, no more than a flesh wound, but enough to cause him to recoil from the fight, blocking the men hurrying to cross the fire and escape the searing heat of the flames on either side.

'Fall back!' Massimilianus shouted from behind him. 'They're over the wall! Fall back!'

Cato roared and punched his shield forward, quickly glancing over his shoulder. He saw some auxiliaries and two of the mule drivers dashing past the bottom of the tower towards the makeshift barricade in front of the two sheds. More men were running from the stockade, Massimilianus amongst them as he waved them towards the redoubt. Cato turned back and saw that a fourth ladder had widened the path across the fire, and now a large group of men had started to cross over.

'When I give the order, charge home. Once you've hit your man, turn and run for the wagons. Ready . . .' He allowed a beat for the auxiliaries on either side to brace themselves, then roared, 'Charge!'

The five of them burst forward, shoulders bracing their shields, and slammed into the leading rank of the brigands, knocking them back, to the side, and down onto their knees, and forcing their comrades behind them to stop in their tracks.

'Break off!' Cato shouted.

The auxiliaries turned and ran. But Cato held his ground, standing in a crouch, leaning slightly forward with his shield to his left and his sword held level at waist height, ready to pounce again. The brigands before him hesitated, none willing to take on the bandaged officer in front of them, his single eye sparkling as it reflected the glare of the fire at their backs. His face was contorted in a savage snarl and blood dripped from the tip of his sword as it wavered slightly from side to side.

'Who's first?' he growled. 'Come on, you ugly bastards . . . who's first?'

When none of them moved, he stepped forward and slashed to his right, hammering a blow across his opponent's shield boss. Then he surged to the left behind his shield and slammed

318

it into the side of another brigand, driving him into the charred remains of the side of the gate. Before he could recover, another brigand ran at him, and Cato dropped to one knee and slashed his sword out in a low arc, cutting an angle into his opponent's shin and shattering the bone. The man pitched forward, his full weight colliding with Cato's shoulder and the side of his helmet. The impact drove him off his feet and he fell heavily to the ground, driving the air from his lungs with an explosive gasp. The brigand landed on top of him, but immediately rolled to the side and released his axe as he reached for his injured shin with a pained groan.

Cato's sword had flown from his grip as he fell, and lay two paces away, out of his reach. He still held the shield, and raised it as he struggled to his feet. With no one to stop them now, the brigands poured across the ladders and into the outpost, with several spilling out to surround Cato, shields and weapons raised. He turned quickly, one way, then the next, his right hand balled into a fist, determined to fight on with bare hands, and then his teeth if need be. He caught a glimpse of Massimilianus standing in the middle wagon, beckoning frantically to him as the defenders on either side looked on. In front of them the interior of the outpost was swarming with men in skins ready to charge the last line of defence and overrun those behind.

'Here, sir! Run for it!'

He shook his head and filled his lungs as he bellowed one last time, 'For Rome, lads! Fight to the last for Rome!' Then he braced himself and charged headlong at the nearest of his enemies. He knocked the man back, then hurled his shield at another before throwing his hands around the first man's neck to choke him. His opponent tried to pull himself free, clutching at Cato's hands, then he punched Cato in the face before digging his fingers into his cheek and jaw.

Cato snarled and lunged and bit into the man's hand, feeling flesh and bone give way beneath his teeth. The man howled in pain and Cato hung on, shaking his head like he had seen Cassius do when he hunted down his prey. He sensed a figure at his shoulder, and then a deep voice snapped, 'Enough!'

The blow to his helmet set off an explosion of brilliant flashes of light, and then there was darkness. The last words Cato heard himself say before he lost consciousness were 'Lucius . . . my son . . .'

CHAPTER TWENTY-EIGHT

He came round with a start as a bucket of water was thrown into his face. He winced and jolted his head to the side. A numbing, nauseating pain filled his skull and made him retch. A boot kicked him in the side.

'Get up, Roman!'

He blinked and his uncovered eye opened a crack. There was light in the sky overhead, and only the brightest of the stars twinkled in the pre-dawn heavens. He lay there for a moment, sensing the bruises across his body and the crust of dried blood on his lips and face. His helmet had been removed, along with his sword belt and his dagger and sheath. He could taste blood in his mouth and recalled the man he had bitten, and turned his head to spit in disgust.

He was kicked again, harder this time, and let out a moan.

'Get up, I said!'

He forced himself to roll over onto his hands and knees and push himself up until he was standing unsteadily by the base of the watchtower. His head was still pounding, and he leaned forward and vomited while the brigands around him jeered. When his guts were empty, he stepped aside to avoid the stench rising from the puddle beneath him. Straightening up, he stared at the man who had spoken to him. The brigand leader was a wiry man of middle age with a dark beard streaked with grey. He wore a leather cuirass along with a wolf skin, the forepaws of which were fastened by a gold brooch at his neck. His helmet was made of bronze, with a slender nose guard and hinged flaps to protect the cheeks. A set of large ram's horns and a plume of dark horsehair decorated the top of the helmet. He regarded Cato with no obvious feeling before he spoke again in heavily accented Latin.

'You are the Roman commander.'

Cato did not know if it was a question or a statement and kept his silence.

'I know who you are. I found out from one of your soldiers before we killed him.'

Glancing round the interior of the outpost for the first time since he had regained consciousness, he saw the destruction that had taken place after he had been knocked cold. There were bodies strewn on the ground and on top of the three wagons in front of the sheds. The fire in the gateway was no more than smouldering embers buried beneath the skin-covered ladders, which had burned through in places. Some of the horses and mules had been butchered and lay in pitiful heaps along the lines they had been tethered to. Those that Massimilianus had not managed to hamstring had been roped together and were being led from the outpost by some of the younger brigands. One of them looked round and shot him a look of triumph, and Cato recognised him as Calgarno, the boy they had captured. Other men were filing out of the outpost carrying supplies and equipment looted from the wagons and the bodies of the defenders. There were no more than ten of the brigands left within the ruined outpost. The bodies of two men, no longer recognisable, had been bound back to back around one of the legs of the tower. Stripped to their loincloths, they had been crudely tortured with blades and were covered with the blood that had flowed from shallow cuts to their faces and torsos. Bound to another leg of the tower was Centurion Massimilianus. He had a dressing tied over his right arm and his face was cut and bruised. Like Cato, his helmet had been removed, along with his weapons.

Cato swallowed and cleared his throat. 'I am Prefect Quintus Licinius Cato, commander of the forces on this island.'

'Not any more you're not.' The brigand's mouth twitched briefly in amusement. 'You are now the prisoner of the King of the Mountains.'

'King of the Mountains?' Now it was Cato's turn to force a smile. 'That's a grand title for the leader of a gang of robbers.'

'We have overcome this outpost and wiped out its garrison, and we've already brought fear to every corner of this province.' The brigand leader cocked his head slightly to one side. 'Not bad for a gang of robbers.'

'What's your name?' Cato demanded.

The other man hesitated and shrugged. 'Benicus. Of the Ilenses.'

'Why have you spared me and my centurion?'

'Why do you think? The commander of the Roman forces on the island and one of his senior officers are bound to be worth a considerable ransom. We'll send a message to the governor once we reach our camp. We'll give him ten days to meet our demands, and if he refuses, we'll send him the centurion's head. If there's no reply after another ten days, we'll send one of your hands . . .'

Cato doubted whether Scurra – or more importantly, his steward – would agree to any ransom demand that would have to be paid out of the treasury so assiduously amassed for the personal benefit of the governor. That prospect was best not related to the brigand leader. Cato indicated the wagons where the defenders had made their last stand. 'Are any more of my men alive?'

'None. We killed most in the attack. A handful surrendered. We saved two to question and cut the throats of the others. Now that we've got all the plunder we can carry, and you're awake, we're leaving.' Benicus snapped an order and two of his men came towards Cato with a length of rope. While one pinned his arms behind his back, the other bound his wrists tightly and ran the rope up his back and around his neck, tying a loop and leaving enough for a leash some six feet in length. They did the same to Massimilianus and led him to Cato's side.

The two men exchanged a sad nod.

'Glad you made it, sir,' the centurion muttered.

'What happened to you?'

There was a brief silence as the centurion lowered his head in shame. It was the custom for centurions to lead their men into battle and be the last to leave the field, fighting to the death if needed. Capture was the ultimate shame for the men of the centurionate.

'We held the middle wagon for as long as we could. I was pulled off it and thrown to the ground and piked. Would have died there if this one hadn't called his dogs off. Any idea why we were spared, sir?'

'Ransom, he says.' Cato did not go into the details of the possible fate of his companion.

'That's enough talk!' Benicus interrupted. He looked round the outpost and called out to the men still remaining within, pointing to the blackened gateway. At that moment Calgarno came running back across the causeway, shouting in alarm as he gestured down the slope. There was a hurried exchange before

Benicus raced up the ladder of the watchtower. Cato could hear shouting in the distance.

'What's going on?' asked Massimilianus.

'Don't know. Doesn't sound good for our friends, though.'

More of the brigands came running back into the outpost, the youths amongst them, having abandoned the mules. The fear in their expressions was clear to see. A horn blared and all turned towards the sound.

'It's the relief column!' Massimilianus's bruised face split into a grin. 'By the gods, they must have marched quickly. We're saved, sir!'

'I wouldn't count on that just yet . . .'

Benicus leaned over the rail of the watchtower and bellowed orders to his men. At once, several of them ran towards the three surviving carts and began to drag the bodies aside. Others hurried up the rampart to take positions along the palisade. As soon as the way was clear, the first group manoeuvred one of the wagons over to the gate and rolled it into place above the charred timbers and still smoking embers. Another wagon was heaved beside it and the men climbed on top of the vehicles and readied their weapons.

'What goes around . . .' Massimilianus chuckled, relishing the abrupt reversal of fortune. 'Looks like these barbarian lads have caught themselves in the same trap they set for us, sir.'

'It seems that way,' Cato conceded. He did not want to give the centurion, or himself, any false hope. They were still bound securely and were the prisoners of Benicus and his men. He was under no illusion about their fate if it looked like the brigands' position was hopeless. They would be dead before the first soldier of the relief column set foot inside the outpost. He spoke softly. 'Don't make any noise about it. Let's keep quiet for the moment.'

Massimilianus stared at him questioningly, then, observing Cato's look of warning, he gave a nod and lowered his head a fraction to avoid meeting the glances of any of the enemy.

Benicus swung himself down onto the ladder and descended. He paused, his fist tapping his chin, then rounded on Cato.

'Your warning signal yesterday has been answered, Prefect. Your men are surrounding the outpost. Fortunately, most of mine have already escaped into the forest with their loot.'

'But not you and these others.'

'No.'

'You can't hold out. You have fewer men than I did, and no gate to protect you. Better to surrender. If you choose to fight, you will surely die. You and all your men.'

'And you as well.' Benicus tapped the ivory handle of the dagger tucked into his belt, and Cato recognised it as the one taken from him while he was unconscious. 'I'll slit your throats long before your troops cut me down . . . But let's hope it doesn't come to that, eh? I have no intention of dying here, nor surrendering to you Romans.'

'How do you think you'll escape?'

'My men and I will walk out of here with you as hostages. Your men are hardly likely to risk your lives by stopping us.'

Given what he knew about the likelihood of the governor paying any ransom, Cato realised that they were as likely to die as prisoners in the enemy camp as here in the outpost. It was just a question of time.

The rumble of hooves sounded outside the stockade and a voice called out. 'You in the outpost! Who speaks for you?'

Cato recognised the voice of Apollonius. So it was the men

from the fort at Augustis who had answered the signal first. Too late to save the outpost, but timely enough to avenge the small garrison, which had fought to the last.

Benicus hurried to the rampart and climbed up to the walkway. 'I am in command here.'

'What's your name?' asked Apollonius. 'How am I to address you?'

'Benicus of the Ilenses. Lieutenant of the King of the Mountains.'

'Listen to me, Benicus. I will offer you and your men your lives if you lay down your weapons and surrender. Slaves you will be, but you will live. If you do not surrender, we will take the fort and kill you all.'

'We have hostages,' Benicus responded.

'Survivors of the garrison? How many?'

Benicus turned and shouted an order. Two of his men grabbed Cato and Massimilianus's leashes and led them over to join the brigand leader. Benicus shoved his prisoners up against the edge of the palisade. Cato saw Apollonius and several mounted auxiliaries some fifty feet from the outer ditch. A hundred paces further down the slope was the rest of the mounted contingent. Sections of infantry were positioned at roughly equal distances around the outpost.

'Good morning, sir,' Apollonius called out. 'Centurion Massimilianus. Good to see you both still alive.'

'They will remain alive if you do as I say,' Benicus intervened. 'Pull your soldiers back to the edge of the forest and stay there while I lead my men out. If you make any attempt to stop us, I will kill your officers. Do you understand?'

Apollonius gave a nonchalant shrug. 'I only take orders from my prefect. You must hand our officers over alive and then surrender.'

'Fool,' Benicus spat. 'You are in no position to make demands if you want them to live.'

'I will speak for my men,' Cato interrupted. 'You negotiate with me and me alone, Benicus.'

'Silence!'

He snatched a breath. 'Apollonius! If they don't surrender, kill them all. I will not be a hostage!'

'Shut your mouth!' Benicus slapped Cato hard across the back of the head. 'One more word without my say-so and I'll cut your tongue out.'

He jerked their leashes and swung them away from the palisade, shoving them down the rampart. Both men rolled and tumbled to the ground inside the outpost. As he lay winded, Cato heard Apollonius's response.

'You speak to my prefect. I will wait for the outcome. If I hear nothing from him by noon, we will attack. Farewell, Benicus.'

He heard the sound of hooves receding as he struggled to sit up alongside Massimilianus. Benicus watched the mounted men ride away and turned to stare at his prisoners before he spoke.

'You've made things rather difficult for me, Prefect. I can't use you to leave this place now. You've seen to that. It seems I may have to kill you here.'

'That is not necessary. Why not choose to surrender and live?'

'Live as a slave, you mean?' Benicus shook his head. 'That's no life.'

'It's a good life for some. Not everyone ends up in a chain gang working in a mine. Many live comfortably. Some even win or buy their freedom.'

'Some . . . I imagine that most don't. I will not be a slave, Prefect. Nor will any of these men with me.'

328

'I wonder what they would say if the choice was put to them?'

'You don't understand us. We are a proud people. We always have been, since long before the Romans came. We have never bowed to your Empire and we never will. That is our way.'

'Then you are doomed. If you kill me, the emperor will be enraged. He will send more men under another commander. They will complete the destruction of your people. It is only a matter of time. There is still time to save yourselves. Surrender now and set me and the centurion free. I will let you return to your king, and you can tell him that if he swears allegiance to Emperor Nero, confines his people to their lands and ceases raiding other parts of the province, I will withdraw my men from your territory. I give you my word that no patrols will enter the king's lands. No Roman officials of any kind.'

It was a desperate bluff and Cato silently prayed to Mendacius that the brigand would not see through his deception about the extent of his powers.

'What if your emperor decides not to guarantee your word?'

'The emperor only requires a demonstration of obeisance. Give him that and he will allow your king to rule unhindered. Just as Rome has done for many others.'

Benicus looked pained as he thought over Cato's words. Pride warred with a desire to live and the prospect of peace.

'If you refuse, there is only death for you and your people. You may go to that death proudly, but you will still die. You will leave nothing behind but your graves and what is left of your villages and secret camps. In time, your people will be forgotten and all that will remain is a few overgrown ruins whose names have passed from memory. Or you can choose to survive and thrive in your part of this island.'

The brigand leader screwed up his face and let out a long, deep sigh of resignation. 'You give me your word that you will let me and my men leave this place unharmed if I set you and the centurion free?'

'I give you my word before all my gods, and this man is my witness,' Cato replied earnestly.

Benicus gave him a searching look with his dark, piercing eyes, then nodded. 'Very well.'

He drew Cato's dagger and stepped behind them to cut their bonds. Cato stretched his fingers and rubbed his wrists. 'Thank you. I'll send word when you can leave the outpost safely. Stay inside until then. Come, Massimilianus.'

He led the way to the wagons blocking the gateway and climbed onto one of them, picking his way between the brigands standing on the bed and jumping down on the other side. Then he and Massimilianus walked steadily down the slope towards Apollonius and the mounted men waiting behind him.

'Thank fuck for that,' the centurion said softly. 'I thought we were dead men. I feared you would never talk him round.'

'To tell the truth, so did I.'

Massimilianus laughed. 'You have balls of solid iron, sir. Solid iron.'

As they approached, Apollonius dismounted. He put his hands on his hips and tilted his head to one side as he examined Cato. 'You've looked better. What happened to your head?'

'Wound to the eye.'

'You need to get that seen to. I'll send for the surgeon.'

'I'll deal with that later.' Cato puffed his cheeks. 'You made good time.'

'Not good enough to save the outpost.'

Cato recalled the auxiliaries, Micus and his men and the

mule drivers, all of them dead. 'No . . . but you saved me and Massimilianus. For that I thank you.' He glanced at the groups of infantry positioned around the outpost. 'Did they march from the fort too?'

Apollonius shook his head. 'Those are Plancinus's men. They appeared on the scene at almost the same time. He's on the far side of the hill. So why did they set you free?'

Cato explained briefly, and then ordered Massimilianus to send one of his men to tell Plancinus to allow Benicus and his brigands to pass by unhindered.

'You intend to keep your word, then?' Apollonius mused.

'Of course. We might yet find a way to resolve this without further bloodshed.'

'Ever the optimist.'

Cato shook his head wearily. 'I'm growing tired of bloodshed.'

'Then you are a strange kind of soldier.'

'Even soldiers eventually see too much of it. Some of us, at least. I've had my fill.'

He turned to Massimilianus again. 'Get up there and let Benicus know he can leave now. Once the brigands are on the move, take your men and bury our dead.'

'Yes, sir.'

As the centurion made for the line of horses, Cato felt a fresh burst of pain in his left eye and clutched his palm over the dressing.

'You'd better send for that surgeon now.'

Apollonius let out a low whistle. 'Should have taken me up on the offer when I made it.'

'Just bloody well send for the man, before you need him too.'

★ ★ ★

331

Cato sat on a stump as the cohort's surgeon carefully undid the dressing. The blood from around the wound had dried and soaked into the linen, causing the layers to stick together, and Cato cursed as searing pain shot through his eyeball.

'Sorry, sir. I'm doing my best.'

'Yes, well, do it carefully,' Cato growled through clenched teeth. 'I don't want you to pluck it out of the socket.'

'Let's hope it doesn't come to that.' Apollonius smiled. 'Not a good look for the ladies. What would Claudia say?'

Cato batted the surgeon's hands away and turned to stab a finger at the agent. 'One more crack like that and you'll pay for it.'

'Apologies, Prefect . . . Sometimes I speak before I think.'

'Come the day. Meanwhile, I'd advise you not to push your luck.'

'Noted. Ah, here they come.'

Cato shifted to look up the slope, and the surgeon hissed before speaking with forced deference. 'If you wouldn't mind keeping still, sir, this would be easier and less painful, I can assure you.'

Keeping his head motionless, Cato watched as Benicus and his men emerged from the outpost and filed past the mounted auxiliaries waiting a short distance away. They moved warily until they were clear of the horsemen, and then increased their pace as they headed down the slope towards the forest half a mile away. Massimilianus waited until they were clear before ordering half his men to dismount and leading them towards the gateway.

'Last bit . . .' the surgeon muttered as he eased off the wad of linen.

'There's nothing. I can see nothing with it,' Cato said.

'You wouldn't, sir. It's covered in crusted blood. The lids

are stuck together. There's swelling too.' The man took out his canteen and poured some water on a clean roll of linen from the dressing chest, then began to dab around the socket. 'That's better, it's coming off . . .' He worked at it for a while longer, then leaned back. 'Try opening it, sir.'

Cato tensed himself as he attempted to raise his eyelid, with no success. He became aware of the wince in the surgeon's expression.

'What? What's the matter?'

'There's a lot of damage there, sir. I'll need to give it a proper examination back at the hospital, and you'll need plenty of rest.'

'Bollocks. Will it recover? Will I be able to see with it again?'

'I . . . I don't know, sir. Only time will tell.'

'Well, you're no bloody good to me. Get a fresh dressing on it and we'll deal with it when we return to Augustis.'

'Yes, sir.'

The surgeon carefully packed some light cloth around the socket, applied a wad of linen and wrapped a new dressing around Cato's head. As he tied the final knot, there was an outburst of shouting from the outpost. A moment later, several auxiliaries burst out of the fort and ran towards their horses. There was a brief exchange before they and most of the men who had been waiting outside spurred their mounts into a gallop down the slope towards the brigands, who were still two hundred paces or so from the treeline.

'What in Hades . . . ?' Cato stood up. 'What is Massimilianus up to?'

Apollonius was squinting at the riders. 'I don't see him. Must still be inside the outpost. No! There he is.'

Cato recognised the centurion by his crested helmet as he ran from the gateway and clambered onto his horse. He snatched up the reins and charged after the men, who had a good head start on him.

'Oh no . . .' Cato recalled the scene inside the outpost. The slaughtered horses, the bodies of the slain, and the two men who had been tortured to death. He burst into a sprint across the slope as he bellowed, 'Halt! You fools! Halt! I order you to halt!'

But his words were drowned out by the drumming of hooves and the savage war cries of the auxiliaries as they drew their long swords, then the shouts of alarm from the brigands as they turned to look back and saw the horsemen galloping towards them. Benicus gestured urgently to his followers and they broke into a run, but Cato could see that they were not going to reach the safety of the trees in time. He felt his lungs burning with the effort of sprinting in his armour, and his heart pounded wildly against his ribs.

The first of the auxiliaries caught up with the rearmost brigand. His sword rose and then slashed down at his prey and cut deep into the man's neck, almost severing the head. The brigand fell, and the rider galloped on towards the next man.

As Cato ran, he could only look on in horror as the auxiliaries charged amongst the brigands, hacking at them. Only Benicus and a handful of others made it to the trees, disappearing into the shadows. By the time Cato reached the scene, the rest of the brigands were dead, killed outright or butchered savagely as they lay wounded on the slope. Massimilianus reined in on the fringe of the massacre, his face white with rage.

'What have you done?' Cato bellowed as he drew up, his arms spread wide, fists clenched. He gulped several deep breaths. 'You fucking idiots! I gave my word they wouldn't be harmed. You have dishonoured me . . . dishonoured Rome!' He shook his head helplessly.

The auxiliaries stared back, bloodied swords in their hands. One of them brandished his weapon. 'They had it coming, sir. You saw what they did up there!'

'Shut your mouth!' Cato roared. 'You fool! We could have had peace with them. We could have saved lives. Now?' He bunched his fists to his forehead. 'Now, they will fight to the bitter end. There can be no peace. Just bloodshed . . . blood staining the whole island, until this is over.' He glared round at his men. 'Curse you, you fools. Curse every one of you for what you have brought on us all!'

'Wait!' Massimilianus pointed to one of the brigands whom Cato had thought was dead. He was inching away from the scene through the clumps of grass as the centurion made for him. 'This one's still alive!'

He leaned down to roll the brigand onto his back. 'It's Calgarno.'

CHAPTER TWENTY-NINE

The following morning, the surgeon carefully removed the poultice and tilted Cato's head up to the light coming through the window of the fort's modest hospital block. He scrutinised the eye for a moment before he gave his verdict. 'The wound itself is healing. You'll be left with a fresh scar to impress the ladies. But you still can't see anything, you say?'

'Just darkness to the left, and the rest is a dull blur,' Cato replied.

'I think you may never recover any vision in that eye, I'm afraid, sir.' The surgeon leaned closer, keeping his head out of the light. 'The initial wound tore up your eyelid and the splinter went on to pierce the eyeball at the edge of the pupil. I've seen similar wounds before. The best you can hope for is a partial recovery of eyesight, but don't pin your hopes on it.'

He removed his hands from the sides of Cato's head and straightened up. 'There's nothing more I can do for you. Fresh air will help heal the wound. Keep it clean and don't touch it in case you cause it to open again. I'd advise you to get a patch for it until the healing is complete. After that, keep it on if you find the eye and the area around it becomes sensitive. Could make you look quite rakish.'

'A patch?' Cato sighed. He had seen army veterans in Rome

wearing patches and remembered the pity he had felt for them. Now he in turn would be an object of pity, and the shame of it twisted his guts. He tried to persuade himself that people might see it as just another scar, as much proof of his good service as the medals on his harness. What would Claudia make of it when they next met? he wondered.

'What about the prisoner? Calgarno.' He nodded towards the adjoining room. 'How's he doing?'

'He took a sword cut to his shoulder. It's a flesh wound. The blow to the head that knocked him down was glancing, but it sliced off most of his ear. He'll recover. Not going to be a pretty sight, mind you.'

That did not concern Cato. What mattered was that they had captured one of the enemy. Calgarno must be persuaded to reveal the location of the brigands' camp. Better still, the location of the stronghold from where the self-styled King of the Mountains conducted his campaign of resistance to Rome.

'Have a patch made for me,' he ordered as he stood up.

He left the room and stepped outside onto the covered walkway that ran the length of the hospital block. It was still early in the day and it would be at least another hour before the heat became uncomfortable. The door into the room where the prisoner was held was open, and he stepped under the lintel and acknowledged the salute of the auxiliary standing guard.

Calgarno had been tied down to the bed. He raised his head to see who had entered, squinting slightly at the light-filled doorway. Cato approached and glanced at the bloodstained dressings that covered the boy's shoulder and the top and side of his head. 'The surgeon reckons your wounds will heal well.'

'That's more than can be said for your eye, Prefect.'

Cato's hand began to rise and he forced it to fall back to his side. Calgarno had noticed the gesture and smiled. 'You'll carry that scar with you for the rest of your life. Something to remember my tribe by.'

'It may be *all* that is left to remember your tribe by if they don't come to their senses and give up their pointless struggle.'

'Pointless?' Calgarno chuckled. 'We've defied Rome for two hundred years. What makes you think you'll succeed this time? We took your outpost and killed your men.'

'How many of your war band were lost to achieve that? How many more did you lose when you were cut down as you fled? Do you think you can afford to sacrifice that many men each time you attack one of our outposts?'

'Each outpost we destroy inspires another hundred warriors to join us.'

'Another hundred men who will give up their lives for a hopeless cause.' Cato sighed. 'What is it that you hope to achieve, lad? Do you think you and your friends can defeat Rome? Do you think anyone outside of these mountains and forests regards your leader as a real king? Do you even have the slightest idea how big the Empire is? How many men it can call on to crush your insignificant band of brigands? Well?'

'If Rome is as powerful as you say, why are my people still here? Why are we still the masters of these lands?'

'I'll tell you precisely why,' Cato responded wearily. 'It's because you have been too insignificant to merit any serious attention. Up until recently you have contented yourself with a little cattle-raiding from time to time. Occasionally you might have held up a merchant and demanded money for free passage through your lands. That sort of thing happens across the Empire. For every petty brigand we can be troubled to hunt down and crucify, another is born. And so it goes on. As long as people like you are sensible enough to limit your activities and keep them below the threshold of our interest, you survive.

But the moment you step over the line, the moment you get too greedy or ambitious, you provoke Rome into action and she does not rest until those who defy her are dead or on their knees begging to be spared.

'Make no mistake, that is how it will end here on this island, Calgarno. You and your people will be slaughtered or enslaved and within a generation no one will ever know your tribe existed. All that the man who calls himself your king will have achieved is the destruction of everything you hold dear. You, your family, your friends, your tribespeople, all gone. For what? To satisfy the arrogance of a hairy-arsed brigand who was insane enough to even consider taking on the most powerful empire in the world. You are not the masters of these lands. You never were once Rome claimed Sardinia for a province. You were shadows flitting through the forests. You were no more than an irritation. The bite of the lowliest of insects, not even irritating enough to scratch. Thanks to your leader, that has changed and Rome will not rest until you are wiped out.' He paused to let his words sink in and was gratified to see that all trace of mocking hubris had drained from the youth's expression. Cato sat on the edge of the bed and looked at the flagstone floor. 'I have witnessed enough bloodshed for more than one lifetime. It is one thing to fight barbarian armies in the wilds of Britannia, or face the Parthian hordes in the desert wastes of the east; it is quite another to massacre bands of brigands and the small tribes foolish enough to support them. There is no glory in it for either side. Just dealing out and suffering death. I am sick of it.'

'Then leave, Roman. Send your men back to their forts and go back to Rome. Leave these lands to us.'

'I can't. Your leader has made that impossible. All I can do is try and limit the damage to us all. If I could speak with your leader, I might persuade him to put an end to his futile ambitions.

He would need to surrender, and he and his men must lay down their arms and swear allegiance to Emperor Nero and accept our laws.'

'You don't ask for much,' Calgarno responded cynically.

'I ask what I must. If he would agree to terms, then I would give my word that there would be no repercussions. No crucifixions, no one forced into slavery.'

'I've seen what your word is worth. Benicus was promised safe passage. Your men tried to cut us all down. The gods be praised that he and some others escaped to spread news of your treachery. Now our people will know how worthless the word of Rome is.'

'The attack on your people was regrettable,' Cato conceded. 'My soldiers saw the bodies of the men you had tortured. They wanted to avenge their comrades and acted before they could be stopped. For that they will be punished.'

'Do I have your word on it?'

The mocking tone had returned and Cato felt his heart sink heavily. There was no point in trying to reason with the youth any further. It was time to make the situation clear to him. He stood and stared down at him in silence for a few heartbeats before he spoke.

'I need to know where your leader is camped. I need to know how many men he has. If you tell me now, I will see that you are spared from slavery and rewarded besides. There is not much time. If your people have not already moved to another stronghold, I dare say they will soon. If you don't agree to tell me what I want, and you refuse to lead me to them, right now, I will have one of my men torture you until you do. I should warn you, Calgarno, that Rome trains its torturers well. There is no degree of agony they cannot inflict on you. The man I will call on to break you is one of the best. Perhaps you think you are brave. Perhaps you think you can hold out long enough for your people to decide to abandon their current position. I can assure you that neither of those things is true. You will give in. And you will do it sooner than you think. You will beg me to end your suffering. You will be willing to tell me everything to put an end to it. All you will have achieved will be the slightest of delays, at the cost of torment that will haunt you to your dying day, and you will bear the scars of it for all to see. Is that what you want, Calgarno?'

The youth swallowed and turned his face away as he answered. 'I will tell you nothing.'

'I am sorry to hear that, truly.' Cato turned to the guard, and all trace of gentleness disappeared from his voice. 'Take the prisoner to headquarters. Chain him to the discipline post, and then send for Apollonius.'

The courtyard of the fort's headquarters block was forty feet across, with smooth flagstones covering the ground. The air was still and the sun beat down from a clear sky. The punishment post, a tall, thick piece of timber held up by cross-supports, had been set in the centre of the courtyard, and Calgarno had been fastened to it, his hands bound and tied to the iron ring on top of the post. Stripped naked, he had been left to hang by his arms, his toes dangling a few inches from the ground. The wound to his shoulder made the stressful position even more painful, and he moaned from time to time when he could no longer contain his suffering.

From beyond the walls of the courtyard came the sounds of another supply convoy being loaded up to feed the column that Cato intended to lead against the brigands. The entire force at the fort, together with the small companies of militiamen drawn from the nearest towns, would be marching out as soon as he gave the order. A messenger had been sent to the Fourth Cohort to release two centuries to march down and garrison the fort in the column's absence, to reassure the people of Augustis.

Two sentries had been left to guard the prisoner, more to prevent Calgarno from finding some way to kill himself than to stop any attempt at escape. Other than the three of them, there was no one else in the courtyard. Apollonius had ordered the gate onto the main thoroughfare to be closed and for the clerks to use the door at the rear of the main building.

'A bit of stillness does a good job of unnerving the recipient,' he explained to Cato as they looked out over the courtyard from a second-storey window.

'Recipient? A strange choice of word.'

'I am more comfortable with it than calling him a victim.'

Cato regarded the agent with surprise. 'Don't tell me you are squeamish.'

'Hardly, given what you know about me. Let's say I do have some standards. I am no mere torturer.'

'You're about to be,' Cato pointed out.

'I think of it not so much in terms of torture as enhanced interrogation.'

Cato shook his head. 'By the gods, you are wasted in this line of work. Have you considered becoming a lawyer?'

Apollonius looked at him coldly. 'Like I said, I have standards . . . I think our young friend has had enough time to let fear work on his imagination. I'll make a start on him.'

Cato was about to respond when he saw a clerk hurrying towards him, a grime-streaked auxiliary at his shoulder.

'Sir, beg to report an urgent message has come from Tharros.'

'Let's have it, then.' Cato held out his hand, and the auxiliary reached into his sidebag and took out a capped leather tube.

'From the chief magistrate of the town council, sir.'

Cato nodded as he broke the seal over the cap and removed it to expose the end of a scroll.

'Wait there,' he ordered the clerk and the messenger, then stepped to the window to read the dispatch in good light. The contents were brief. After a short greeting, the magistrate reported that the brigands had launched a number of raids on farming estates across the region surrounding the town. In particular . . . Cato's fingers clenched slightly as he finished reading the dispatch, then reread the concluding section again with dread deliberation.

'Bad news?' Apollonius prompted.

Cato nodded slowly as he rolled the scroll up and tucked it back in the tube, then dismissed the two men with a curt wave of the hand.

'The enemy raided the land around Tharros after the cohort marched for Augustis.' He swallowed and forced himself to speak calmly. 'They attacked Claudia Acte's estate. Burned it to the ground. Killed her bodyguards but left some survivors. According to whom, their mistress was taken away as a hostage . . .'

Apollonius began to reach out a hand towards Cato's shoulder, then withdrew it and let it drop as he framed his response. 'I'm sorry to hear that. I know she means something to you. At least she's alive.'

'For now,' Cato replied woodenly. He recalled the terms Benicus had outlined when he had talked of holding Cato and Massimilianus hostage, and felt a surge of icy terror flow through his veins at the mortal danger that faced Claudia. He chewed his lip and muttered, 'I swear by all the gods, if they harm her then I shall make these hills echo with the death cries of the brigands and all their folk.'

He turned his gaze to Apollonius, and though his left eye looked lifeless, his right blazed intently. 'We must find their lair before they can harm her. Do whatever you have to. Spare the boy nothing and make him talk as quickly as you can. Understand?'

'Yes, sir. You can rely on me.'

Cato stared at him a moment longer before he looked away. 'I know. Do it. Do it now.'

The agent nodded and turned towards the stairs at the end of the building. As Cato made to follow him, Apollonius held up a hand to stop him. 'It's best if you don't get involved.'

'I want to hear it from his own lips,' Cato said firmly.

Apollonius saw the dangerous expression on his superior's face and nodded warily. 'As you wish. But if you want me to find out where the enemy may have taken Claudia Acte, stay back, say nothing and let me do my job.'

Cato watched as Apollonius stepped back from the small table he had set up in front of the post. An array of knives, hooks and hinged devices were spread out across the top, in full view of Calgarno. The youth stared at them, eyes wide with terror, but he managed to keep his jaws clenched together and his lips compressed in a thin line.

'These are the tools of my trade,' Apollonius said fondly as he ran his fingers over the torture implements. 'With them I can cut the finest of slits in your flesh, or gaping wounds. These hooks can be used to peel back the skin from your muscle and bone, while these tools can crush your fingers, toes and balls into a pulp. I know how to use every one of them to inflict the slightest discomfort or the most unbearable agony you could possibly imagine. Before I am through with you, I will have all the information I need. You may not believe me, but I can assure you that you will beg for death long before I am finished.' He paused and stepped out of Calgarno's line of sight before winking at Cato. Then he leaned close to the youth's ear and spoke softly. 'So what's it to be, boy? Save yourself and answer my questions straight up?'

Calgarno drew a deep breath and cleared his throat before he responded. 'I'll say nothing to you. I will not betray my kin! Long live the King of the Mountains!'

'I wouldn't put too much faith in his longevity.' Apollonius smiled faintly.

Moving over to the table, he ran his fingers over the tools before settling on a set of iron bars joined by a hinge. He lifted them to Calgarno's face.

'Here we are. One of my favourites. Now, I'll ask a question you can answer without giving anything away. What's more important to you? Being able to walk, or being able to hold a weapon?'

Despite the agent's earlier instructions, Cato felt impatience swelling inside him. He wished the man would get on with his job and extract answers. Every moment of delay in being able to find and rescue Claudia was a torment. Yet he had sufficient faith in Apollonius's abilities and darker skills to keep quiet.

'Well?' demanded the agent. 'Feet or hands?'

The youth trembled as he stared at the instrument Apollonius was holding. He shook his head and closed his eyes tightly, and his lips moved in silent prayer.

'All right. I'll make the decision for you.' Apollonius turned to the nearest auxiliary. 'Hold his legs still.'

The soldier set his shield and spear down and grasped Calgarno's limbs, pulling them down tightly and holding the heels against the bottom of the post. The youth struggled but lacked the strength to put up an effective fight. Apollonius

345

kneeled down and opened the iron bars wide enough to fit his victim's big toe close to the hinge. Then he grasped the handles at the end of the bars and closed them over the toe, gripping it firmly. He glanced up. 'Where is your king's stronghold?'

Calgarno tilted his head back and continued praying.

'Your choice, my young friend,' Apollonius said as he began to press the bars together. Calgarno gasped, then clenched his jaw tightly. Cato could see that every muscle in his slim body was tensed and quivering.

'Aaahhhhhhhhh!' His cry cut through the hot, still air trapped in the courtyard, and he began to urinate, spattering the shoulders and helmet of the auxiliary holding his legs in place.

'What the fuck?' The soldier started to move, and Apollonius snapped harshly at him to keep still as he began to twist the rods from side to side to increase the youth's agony. Cato kept himself still and his face expressionless as he looked on, willing Calgarno to give up the information he needed.

Apollonius eased the pressure and removed the instrument from the mangled toe, then fitted it to the other foot and repeated the process. Calgarno howled with agony as the torment continued, toe by toe, until the ends of his feet were reduced to gory shreds of flesh and splintered bone.

'For pity's sake,' Cato whispered to himself. 'Speak, boy . . . speak.'

But Calgarno had passed out. Apollonius gestured to the auxiliary to release his hold and step aside. He regarded the youth for a moment, then glanced towards Cato.

'He's a tough lad.'

'It's a pity he's not on our side.'

Apollonius looked at the auxiliary. 'Fetch me a pail of water.'

As the soldier trotted off, the agent put the bars down and grasped the youth's shoulders, giving him a firm shake. 'Wake up, boy . . . Wake up, I said!'

Calgarno stirred and moaned, his head lolling on his breast. The agent shook him again and slapped him hard on the cheek. 'Open your eyes!'

As Calgarno's eyelids flickered open and his eyes rolled, the auxiliary returned with the water. Apollonius took the pail from him and threw the contents into the youth's face.

'Wh-what?' Calgarno spluttered, shaking his head as he returned to consciousness. At once his face creased in pain.

'That's better,' said Apollonius. 'I've done with your feet, so it's time for your hands now. Unless you have something to tell us?'

Calgarno raised his head and whispered softly.

'What's that, lad?' Apollonius cocked an ear towards him and the youth's lips moved again.

Cato took a step towards the post. 'What's he saying?'

Calgarno breathed deeply and spoke as steadily as he could. 'I said, fuck you. Fuck your emperor. Fuck Rome.' His eyes shifted to his torturer. 'But mostly, fuck you.'

Apollonius laughed. 'Oh, I do like this one!' He tousled Calgarno's sweaty dark hair. 'You're a tough lad . . . but that isn't going to save you. Time for your fingers.'

As he loosened the rope that ran up through the iron ring and down to Calgarno's wrists, the youth slumped to his knees. Without any hesitation, Apollonius fitted the boy's left thumb in between the bars and began to crush it. A series of howls and shrieks filled the courtyard and echoed dully off the facade of the headquarters building.

Cato cleared his throat. 'I'll be in my office. Inform me the moment he tells you what we need to know.'

'I'll tell you nothing!' Calgarno snarled through gritted teeth.

'Yes, you will,' Cato replied. 'I can assure you of that. It's only a question of when. Carry on, Apollonius.'

He strode towards the headquarters entrance and disappeared into the welcome shade within. The cries from the courtyard pursued him even as far as the commander's office at the end of the corridor upstairs. He crossed to a side table, where a jug and cups sat, and poured himself some water as he tried to focus his thoughts and push the sounds of torment aside. He forced himself to concentrate on the peril facing Claudia and told himself that the scene being played out in the courtyard was justified by her abduction and the other miseries inflicted on the province by the brigands. He was surprised by the strength of his concern for her and his desire to see her set free.

As his imagination took over and conjured up images of her suffering at the hands of his enemies, a cold rage filled his heart, and for a moment he indulged himself in the acts of retribution he would carry out against the brigands if they had harmed her. 'Bastards . . .' he muttered, draining his cup and setting it down with a sharp rap.

Sitting at his desk, he turned his attention to the administrative tasks that had accumulated during his brief absence. As the morning wore on, his mind became drowsier from the exhaustion of the recent action at the outpost and his lack of sleep. Pushing aside a waxed slate reporting the latest extent of the pestilence creeping across the island, he closed his eyes and rested his head in his hands, covering his ears. There was a moment of calm, as if a warm cloud had settled over his mind, easing him towards the welcome prospect of sleep.

'Sir . . . Sir!'

He sat up, his head snapping back, and saw one of the clerks standing in front of his desk.

'What is it?' he demanded.

'The optio in command of the morning watch begs to report that a message has been delivered by a man sent by the senior magistrate of Augustis, sir.'

'Well? Where is he?'

'Outside the fort's main gate, sir.'

'What the hell is he doing there? If he has a message for me, he can deliver it in person.'

'No, sir. The message is that the pestilence has reached Augustis. The first cases were reported this morning.'

Cato's exhaustion fell away in a heartbeat as his mind raced through the implications of the news. The future of the campaign was under threat, and with it the life of Claudia, and the men under his command. 'Is the messenger still outside the gate?'

'Yes, sir.'

Cato pushed a blank waxed tablet across the desk towards the clerk. 'Take this down. Firstly, I want the man to return to Augustis at once and tell the council they are to shut the gates and seal the city off until further orders. No one is to enter or leave without my permission. Secondly, I want all the men who have been into the town in the last two days to report to the hospital block. Tell the surgeon I want them quarantined there until further notice. Thirdly, any man who is showing any sign of sickness is to be assigned to one of the empty barrack blocks. Tell the surgeon he can treat that as an overflow for the hospital . . . That's all for the moment. Read it back to me.'

Once Cato was satisfied that the clerk had accurately noted down the orders, he dismissed the man to pass the instructions on. Alone, he reflected on the situation in a more deliberate manner. If the pestilence spread to the men at the fort, it would whittle down the already under-strength units under his command. The best thing to do would be to get the men clear of Augustis and march the column against the enemy as soon as possible in the hope of achieving a decisive result before the sickness struck.

He was still thinking his plans through when Apollonius entered the office. The front of his tunic was spattered with blood and he was wiping his hands on a stained strip of cloth.

'Our boy broke down in the end,' he announced. 'He told me where the enemy stronghold is. Two days' march east of here. We've got them, sir.'

CHAPTER THIRTY

Centurion Cornelius entered the office and stood to attention. 'You sent for me, sir.'

'I did.' Cato looked up from the report he was writing to the province's governor relating the events that had recently taken place and detailing his plan to attack the enemy's stronghold. He set down his stylus and folded his hands together, cracking his knuckles. 'I am leaving you here to command the fort when the column marches. I'm leaving twenty men from the militia contingent to serve as garrison. Not the best of soldiers – if they can be called that – but if you draw some kit from the stores you can at least make them look like regulars. Should be good enough to fool any spies watching the fort. As you will have heard, the pestilence has reached Augustis. I've already sent orders to the council to keep the town gates closed. You are not to permit any civilians to enter the fort. Nor will any of your men be allowed out. There are six men in the quarantine block showing signs of the sickness. They will need to be fed, but make sure their rations are left outside the door. None of your men is allowed to enter. If any of the garrison show signs of sickness, they are to be placed in quarantine at once. That includes you. Do you understand?'

'Yes, sir.'

'Any questions?'

'Yes, sir. Couldn't one of the auxiliary officers be given the job? If it comes to a fight, you'll need the best men at your side.'

'Indeed. But this fort is too important to be trusted to anyone else. I need someone I can depend on to make sure it stays in our hands. Are you up to the job, Cornelius?'

'Yes, sir.'

'Good. If anything goes wrong and the column is defeated, you are to hold out here until a relief force arrives. You are not to make any attempt to break out. Clear?'

Cornelius nodded, then replied sourly, 'As you command.'

Cato could guess at the reason for his mood. The garrison and its commander would miss out on the loot that would come the way of those of their comrades who took the enemy stronghold. Given the months of raids the brigands had carried out across the island, it was likely that there were considerable riches to be had once the enemy was defeated. But Cornelius's disappointment was irrelevant to the wider task of crushing the self-titled King of the Mountains and his followers. Soldiers were inclined to see things in more immediate terms, Cato reflected. Unlike their commanders, who were driven by more significant concerns . . . unless there was a lot of loot at stake. Cato smiled to himself. Pompey the Great hadn't become one of the wealthiest men in Roman history out of pious devotion to what was good for Rome.

He sighed. 'I'll see to it that you and the men left behind get an equal cut of any loot and sale of prisoners. Sound fair?'

'Yes, sir.' Cornelius grinned. 'Very fair indeed.'

'I wonder if those doing the fighting will feel the same way?'

'I've done more than my share of the fighting in recent years, sir. You know that better than anyone. I ain't got much to show for it, while these auxiliaries have been sitting on their arses here in Sardinia.'

'Point made, and taken. Dismissed.'

After the centurion had left, Cato quickly completed his report, pressed his seal into the wax and closed the tablet, then called for a clerk to have it sent north to Scurra at his refuge in Tibula. Although how much longer the governor and his retinue would be able to avoid the pestilence was hard to determine given the pace at which it was spreading. He arranged the patch he had been given over his left eye and tied the thongs securely at the back of his head, then, picking up his saddle-bags, sword belt and helmet, he left headquarters and made his way towards the column of riders, infantry and wagons lining the main thoroughfare that stretched across the interior of the fort.

His officers and Apollonius were waiting for him inside the gate. A donkey was tethered to the saddle horn of the agent's horse, and Calgarno was bound to the saddle on the animal's back. His feet and hands were bandaged and his face glistened with sweat as he fought to contain the pain that racked his ravaged fingers and toes.

Cato heaved his saddlebags over the horse being held for him by one of the militiamen. He put his helmet on, fastened the straps and pulled himself up into the saddle, then took up his reins and nodded to Plancinus. The centurion puffed out his chest. 'Open the gates!' he bellowed. 'Column will prepare to advance . . . Advance!'

As they passed Augustis, Cato was gratified to see that the gates were closed and one of the town's militia stood watch on top of the gatehouse. There were several more people visible along the wall, and one old crone screeched incomprehensibly at the column as it made for the road leading into the forest-covered hills to the east. Cato forced the pace, anxious to leave the pestilence behind and to close with the enemy as soon as possible. The location Calgarno had described sounded formidable: a valley protected by sheer cliffs and accessible only by a narrow gorge, the location of which was known to just a handful of people.

Any other time Cato would have been content to starve the enemy into submission, but with Claudia held captive within and the sickness spreading without, time was too precious to waste on laying siege to the brigands' stronghold. It was possible that the enemy's fortifications in the gorge might prove insubstantial enough to justify a frontal attack. If so, the brigands might use Claudia and any other prisoners as a human shield. If they did that, Cato doubted he had sufficient steel in his soul to order an attack. But if he prevaricated, there was a good chance the sickness would find its way into his camp and destroy whatever advantage he had over the enemy in terms of numbers. Unless he could find some other way of destroying the stronghold, the brigands might yet survive to continue terrorising the province and challenging the authority of Rome. Such an outcome would put an end to Cato's career as surely as a sword thrust.

'A sestertius for your thoughts . . .'

Cato glanced round and saw that Apollonius had edged his horse alongside. It was tempting to confide in the agent and share his burden, but Cato had long ago made it a rule not to reveal any weakness to his subordinates. He still burned with shame over his collapse some two years earlier into a dark well of exhaustion, fear and self-loathing. Macro had been there to shield him from others while he recovered. But Macro had gone now, and Cato did not trust Apollonius. The possibility of the agent discovering his weakness and banking the information for use against him at a later date was unnerving.

Cato cleared his throat. 'I was thinking . . . Sardinian boars are bigger than you realise.'

Apollonius's forehead creased into a frown and he was silent for a moment before he nodded. 'I suppose they are. Is there anything else on your mind?'

'No.' Cato tapped his heels into his horse's flanks and urged it on as he called out. 'Centurion Plancinus! Let's pick up the pace!'

As they marched into the depths of the forest, Cato ordered a squadron of mounted men to scout ahead of the main column. The infantry closed up and the small baggage train of ten wagons carrying rations, tents and heavy equipment was guarded by a century of auxiliaries, with one section assigned to each wagon. The four bolt-throwers that had been mounted on the towers of the fort had been broken down for transport, along with a small onager. They constituted the only artillery available to Cato, but they were field weapons and of little use in prosecuting a siege.

They halted for the night on a barren hilltop some eight miles from the fort, digging a ditch and throwing up a rampart before settling down behind their defences. A slim crescent moon provided little illumination to aid the sentries as they stared out at the dark landscape, watching and listening for any sign of the enemy. But there was nothing apart from the shrill cry of night birds and the occasional crackle of twigs and rustling of bushes as animals made their way through the forest.

Inside the command tent he shared a simple meal of stew and bread with Apollonius by the light of a pair of oil lamps.

'How is our guide doing?' asked Cato.

'He's in a great deal of pain, but he'll live. Long enough for our needs at any rate.'

'Where is he now?'

'I've got him chained to the headquarters wagon outside.'

'Under guard?'

Apollonius nodded. 'Not that he's going to be able to attempt to escape. Even if his hands were in fit shape to free up the locking pin, he's not going anywhere on what's left of his feet.'

'Make sure he understands that if he does not take us to their stronghold, or he leads us into a trap, he will be put to death. As painfully as possible.'

'Don't worry. He understands what's at stake.'

'Good.' Cato pushed his mess tin aside, his meal unfinished. The agent gestured to it with his spoon. 'Mind if I . . . ?'

'Help yourself.'

Apollonius scraped the leftovers into his own tin and took a few spoonfuls before fixing Cato with a searching look. 'You fear for Claudia Acte.'

'Of course.'

'She should be safe enough, assuming they think she is still the emperor's mistress rather than another of his exiles. The brigands will look after her. She's worth a lot more to them alive. The only time she might be in danger is if we break into their stronghold. Then they might choose to kill her as a final act of defiance.'

'That's what I fear,' Cato conceded. 'I cannot give in to any demands they might make, and I doubt they will surrender, so it looks as if we may have to take their position by force. If that's the case, I need to find a way to get her out safely before the attack begins. Or at least have her moved somewhere safe within the stronghold until the fighting is over. That means we'll need to have someone inside the defences who can locate and protect her. As things stand, I doubt we can count on one of the enemy to come over to our side. So it'll be a case of sending someone in to do the job.'

'Easier said than done, according to Calgarno. He claims there is only one way into the valley. Of course, he could be lying.'

'Or there is a way he does not know about.'

'If he doesn't know about it, then how are we supposed to find such a route, even if it does exist?'

'Quite . . . But unless we discover another way into the valley and get Claudia to safety, it's almost certain she will die. I doubt Nero will take the news of her death well.'

Apollonius clicked his tongue. 'It's no secret that your feelings for her are of more immediate consideration than the reaction of the man who cast her off. The real question is which do you consider a higher priority: saving her life or defeating the enemy?'

Cato folded his hands together and rested his jaw on them. That was the nub of it. But Apollonius was wrong. There was no question of priorities as far as Cato's duty was concerned. He looked up at his companion. 'My orders are to defeat the enemy. If Claudia dies in the process, then I will have to answer for that to the emperor.'

The agent bit his lip and an amused expression formed on his face. 'I would have put money on you saying that. But I can't help being a bit disappointed that you regard her life as the lesser priority.'

'Oh?' Cato felt the familiar apprehension at having Apollonius probe at his personality and thoughts.

'You play the part of a soldier as well as the finest actor in Rome. It's an accomplished performance. Yet you are a man who holds himself apart as far as pursuits of the mind go. You are a rational thinker, Prefect Cato, but more than that, I have suspected for a while now that you harbour a romantic streak. Not just for the love of a strong good woman, but for all the ideals you hold dear.' He turned his face slightly as he gave Cato a challenging look. 'Am I wrong?'

'It is no performance. I am a soldier.'

'And much more besides, else you would not have achieved all that you have.'

Cato stirred, uncomfortable with the line the conversation was taking. He decided to turn it round. 'And you, Apollonius? Do you ever question your own motives? Your own values? What are they, I wonder?'

'I have very few values, because the more I have learned, the more I encounter questions and doubts rather than knowledge and answers. In such a world, a reasonable man realises that the honest thing to do is to be wary of values. I am an observer of life. I watch people. I listen to what they say they believe and then observe how they behave in practice. The correlation between the two is something of a rare commodity. The charlatans who control Rome pretend to others that they stand behind their words. You are cut from a different cloth. You don't talk in terms of ideals, and often affect a cynical world-weariness, yet I believe you are really little more than a romantic idealist, disappointed that so few match up to the qualities you desire of them. For you, their moral failures are lapses, whereas for me they are the norm. Most people are wolves disguised as sheep. But you, Prefect Cato, with your values, are more like a sheep trying to pass itself off as a wolf. Frankly, I am fascinated to see how long you can carry that off. It's a wonder that a man with your moral core has managed to survive as long as you have. I consider you something of a fascinating experiment in

358

that regard. How far can a good man succeed in a corrupt world? I'd like to know the answer to that.'

Cato took the agent's comments in and then chuckled dismissively. 'Stick around, Apollonius. Serve with me long enough and maybe some of it will rub off on you.'

The agent's expression remained thoughtful. 'That's what worries me.'

At noon two days later, the column approached a formation of steep-sided hills that towered above the surrounding landscape. In many places sheer cliffs and crags rose to the ridgeline. The forest gave way to more open country dotted with scrub and stunted trees and rocks. After two days of marching along tracks bordered by ancient trees where ambushers might be waiting in the shadows, Cato and his men were relieved to enter less dangerous terrain.

Their approach to the enemy's stronghold would come as no surprise to the brigands, Cato reflected as he gazed up at the ridges. On the second day, the riders scouting ahead of the column had reported seeing distant groups of men watching them from hilltops. At first Cato had ordered that they be chased down, but by the time the mounted auxiliaries reached the spot where the enemy had been sighted, they had already fled and melted away amid the trees. After that, the Romans had been content to leave the enemy alone as they made for the lair of the King of the Mountains. Close to the range of hills, Cato could see tiny figures watching them from the safety of the ridge crests. If what Calgarno had told them was true, the enemy watch-keepers would be confident that the Roman column, like so many before it, would march past without ever being aware of the secret route into their hidden valley.

'Bring the boy forward,' he ordered.

Apollonius urged his mount to Cato's side and drew in the lead that was tied to the saddle of Calgarno's donkey until the youth rode between them. Cato indicated the ridges.

'This is the place you told us of. The enemy camp is in the valley on the far side, you say?'

'My people, yes.'

'Then now is the time for you to show us where the entrance to the valley is.'

Calgarno made no comment, but sat in his saddle with his shoulders hunched.

'You've brought us this far,' Cato continued. 'It's too late to play dumb now. If you think you've suffered enough already, I can assure you that Apollonius knows even more painful methods of making you speak up. You'll tell us all we need to know sooner or later; the only question you have to ask yourself is how much more torment you can endure before you give in. So, tell us where we must go.'

'To the darkest depths of Hades!' Calgarno snapped. He kicked his heels in, howling with pain as the shock of the impact jarred his toes, and urged his donkey forward, only to be drawn up sharply as the lead snapped taut and stopped the beast. The youth jerked frantically in his saddle, trying to break free, then slumped forward, his shoulders shaking violently as he wept. There was something profoundly ridiculous and pathetic about his attempt to escape, and Cato felt moved to pity and shame. He motioned Apollonius to leave the youth alone and edged his mount towards Calgarno, addressing him more gently.

'You're a brave lad and you have my respect. But you must know that you cannot escape us. I will not have you killed if you try, only punished. There is no honourable death for you now. You have already revealed too much for that. But you can live through this, and so can your people if they choose to surrender. Otherwise there is only death for all of you. Now cease your tears.' Cato pointed to the end of the ridge a mile or so distant. 'I imagine the entrance to the valley is not so far away, is it?'

Calgarno nodded.

'Good, then let's find it and put an end to this business.'

Cato glanced over his shoulder and gestured to Apollonius to come forward. 'Keep him on a tighter lead from now on.'

'Yes, sir.'

Late in the afternoon they reached the end of the ridge where it dropped precipitously into a large area of jumbled rock and craggy outcrops between which clumps of stunted trees grew on the dry, gritty soil. The towering rock formations seemed to continue unbroken before they rose to form another ridge almost parallel with the first. The track they had been following continued past the hills and turned east towards the coast.

Cato halted the column and gave the order to make camp. As the officers bellowed at the auxiliaries, the men downed their marching yokes. Plancinus and one of the headquarters clerks marked out the limits of the camp on a more or less even stretch of ground two hundred paces away. Then, as one of the centuries and the mounted contingent were assigned picket duty around the site, their comrades set to work with their picks, breaking up the ground to dig out a ditch and using the spoil to form the rampart that acted as the second line of defence for the camp. A small stream ran out from amongst the rocks in a shallow cutting that passed close by the campsite; it would provide sufficient water for the men and horses.

As the work progressed, Cato dismounted along with Apollonius and the prisoner and the three of them sat down on some rocks in the shadow of an ancient cork oak. Cato shared his canteen with Apollonius and then Calgarno. The latter was hesitant and Cato eased the canteen into his bandaged hands, now loosely bound. No such precaution was needed for his feet, as he could only manage a painful hobbling gait.

'Go on,' he urged. 'It's been a hot day and you could use a drink.'

Calgarno raised the canteen carefully to his lips and took several mouthfuls before returning it to Cato with a grateful nod.

They sat in silence, staring at the confusion of impenetrable-looking rock formations and the steep cliffs beyond. Cato wondered once again if their prisoner was leading them astray. It seemed improbable that such a place as he described existed. Maybe he was playing for time and directing them away from the stronghold. Perhaps he was braver than he appeared, Cato reflected as he studied the youth. Calgarno was staring away from the rocks towards the camp, his gaze fixed and unwavering and his body quite still. There was something unnatural about the pose, and for an instant Cato could not determine what was wrong. He glanced at Apollonius and saw that the agent was scrutinising the dramatic rocky landscape curiously. Then it hit him. Calgarno was studiously avoiding looking in the very direction that excited most attention.

Cato cleared his throat and Apollonius turned to look at him. Cato gestured subtly at their prisoner and then spoke.

'Calgarno, we're at the entrance to the valley right here, aren't we?'

The youth did not reply, but gave a slight grimace that was enough to betray the truth.

'Apollonius, bring me ten men.'

The agent hurried over to the camp and returned shortly afterwards with the auxiliaries. Cato assigned one of them to guard the prisoner, then led Apollonius and the others towards where the rocks and trees began, a few hundred paces away. The sun hung low in the sky and the shadows were already stretching out some distance across the rose-hued landscape. As the sounds of the camp construction gradually faded behind them, they moved warily into the trees and threaded their way through the rocks and crags towards the point where the two ridges met. The crunch of their boots echoed off the rock faces and the trapped air was still and hot. There was little sign of life. The first of the evening's bats flitted through the air like scraps of black cloth carried on a stiff breeze.

'I'm not sure it's wise for us to search this place mob-handed, sir,' Apollonius commented quietly. 'We're making too much noise.'

'True,' Cato responded, and ordered the auxiliaries to halt. 'Remain here. Don't make any noise. If I call for you, come running. Otherwise wait.'

He waved Apollonius ahead of him. 'Two eyes are better than one.'

They continued cautiously, eyes and ears scrutinising every shadow, every sound, but there was no sign of anything other than the handful of animals that lived in the vicinity. Fifty paces on, the way ahead was blocked by a low cliff, and Cato took a last look back as they made their way around its base and lost sight of the auxiliaries. On the far side they came across what looked like a goat track, meandering through the sparse vegetation.

'Shall we follow it?' asked Apollonius. 'It seems to head in the right direction.'

'Fair enough.'

After a hundred paces or so, Cato became aware that there were cliffs rising up on either side of them, and he felt his heart beat more quickly as he and Apollonius crept forward. Suddenly the agent froze and snapped his hand up to halt him.

All was quiet for a moment and Cato whispered, 'What's the matter?'

'Shh. Listen.' Apollonius cocked his head slightly. 'There, do you hear it?'

Cato could hear the faint pounding of blood in his head, and then . . . voices. Very faint, but still identifiable. They came from above and ahead, where the cliffs closed and seemed to come together.

Moving slowly, the two men left the track and hugged the bottom of the rock face to their left. As they rounded a corner, a narrow gorge was revealed between the two cliffs. It ran for a short distance before starting to broaden out again, giving onto an open patch of ground that looked like a dried-up riverbed. Fifty paces away, a stone wall topped with a wooden palisade extended across the gap between the two cliffs for a distance of around sixty feet. There was an open gate in the middle of the wall with a walkway above it and a small tower on either side. Two men were on duty in the towers and two more stood inside the gatehouse. The structure was shaded by the cliff, as was the ground before it, and Cato eased himself into a crouch to try and stay out of sight as he examined the enemy's defences. Then he turned to Apollonius with an excited expression.

'We've found them!'

CHAPTER THIRTY-ONE

There was a shout from high above, and Cato craned his neck to see a figure on the edge of the cliff pointing down at them. Those in the tower turned to scan the shadows at the foot of the cliff.

'We have to go.' Apollonius grasped his arm. 'Now!'

Already several men were gathering by the gate.

'Just a moment,' Cato replied, quickly looking over the defences and then the gorge around them, committing the details to memory. As he did so, the figures at the gate rushed out towards them.

'Sir!' Apollonius pulled him round and thrust him back the way they had come, and both men sprinted along the gorge, their pursuers racing after them. Cato could hear further shouts from the lookouts on top of the crags as they kept pace above.

A short distance ahead was a fall of loose gravel, and Cato yelled a warning as he thrust the agent against the wall of the cliff. An instant later a rock the size of a large wine jar crashed to the ground near them. As dust swirled round it, Cato thrust Apollonius forward and they continued to flee. The gorge widened for a stretch before it narrowed to four feet and then gave out onto the scattered rock formations and trees beyond. Cato could hear the footsteps of their pursuers echoing off the cliffs on either side, amplifying the sound and making it seem as if they were being chased from every direction. Another boulder, poorly aimed this time, struck the ground ten feet behind them, and he winced at the sound.

They reached the end of the gap and cleared the gorge, racing on through the trees and round the rocks as the enemy steadily drew closer. Cato's heart was beating wildly and his tired legs burned with the effort of running. He took a quick glance over his shoulder and saw that the brigands were fifty feet behind them. Through the trees ahead he glimpsed the camp, and the auxiliaries sitting on the ground as they shared a wineskin.

A spear passed close overhead with a soft rush of air and clattered onto the ground.

'Weave!' Cato gasped at Apollonius, and both men began to dart in one direction, then another, to put off the aim of their pursuers. Another spear struck the ground close to Cato, the point burying itself in the loose soil. Apollonius had pulled ahead and now bellowed to the auxiliaries.

'On me! On me!'

They glanced round towards him and there was a heartbeat's frozen surprise before they jumped to their feet, snatched up their shields and spears and charged towards the two officers and the enemy rapidly closing on them.

'Come on, Cato!' Apollonius called out. 'One last effort!'

At that moment, Cato felt a glancing blow on his side as another spear passed under his arm and dropped away, its energy spent. The impact spun him slightly round, enough for his trailing leg to trip over the other calf. He fell heavily and rolled over, the breath driven from his lungs. As he scrambled to his feet and fumbled for his sword, Apollonius turned, drew his weapon and sprang forward to put himself between Cato and the enemy. The brigands, elated at knocking Cato down, let out triumphant whoops as they charged on, then slowed uncertainly as they saw Apollonius, feet braced and sword ready in one hand as he drew a dagger with the other.

'Go, Cato! Run! I'll hold 'em!'

For Cato, there was no time for thought, only perceptions: a glimpse of the auxiliaries running towards them, the dust swirling, pink in the slanted light of the setting sun, the grim expression on the agent's face and the brigands surging forward, weapons raised. He drew his sword and crouched, struggling for breath, as he made ready to fight.

Three men were a few paces ahead of their companions. Two were armed with spears and the third carried a heavy curved sword. This last made for Cato as the others turned on Apollonius with levelled spear points. Cato saw his comrade deftly parry the first thrust with his sword and step inside his opponent's reach to slash at his arm with the keen edge of his dagger, slicing open the flesh with a precise incision. He continued the fluid attack by swivelling his hip and shoulder, the point of the dagger striking home in the side of the second man, whose impetus had carried him too far to strike with his spear.

The swordsman swung wildly at Cato, the blade sweeping round in a gleaming arc as the edge caught the rays of the dying sun. Cato raised his own sword tip and swept the blade to the side to block the blow. The weapons clashed with a sharp metallic ring and sparks flew as the heavier sword drove Cato back a step. He managed to keep his balance and shot his left hand out to grab his attacker by the wrist and pull him in and down, lowering the point of his weapon and driving it into the man's stomach, piercing his sheepskin jacket and the flesh beneath. Twisting the blade, he ripped it free, then let go of the man's wrist and struck his face with the back of his hand. The brigand staggered back, dazed and bleeding from his wound, and was roughly shouldered aside by one of his companions.

This time, the odds were firmly against Cato. Hefting an axe, the brigand shifted his shield to the front and surged forward. Cato slashed at the man's head, but his foe raised his shield and took the blow near the rim. As Cato's blade deflected to the side, the brigand swung his axe, the broad edge slicing through the air towards Cato's midriff. He acted instinctively and threw his body forward, leading with his left shoulder. As he crashed into his enemy, the man's forearm slapped harmlessly against the small of Cato's back and the axe blade missed its target. Cato drove on, thrusting the man back, causing him to stumble and keep retreating in an effort to remain on his feet.

With a last powerful thrust, Cato stepped back alongside Apollonius. The agent had downed the two spearmen and now three brigands with shields faced him, forcing the agent to turn and stare down each man in turn, daring them to attack. The axeman had recovered and approached Cato cautiously, then paused, looking past him, and frowned. He barked an order and his men drew back a few paces before turning and trotting towards the entrance of the gorge, leaving their stricken comrades behind. The man Cato had injured sheathed his blade, clamped a hand over the bloody patch on his sheepskin jacket and hurried after his comrades.

Cato and Apollonius stood, chests heaving, blood dripping from their weapons, as the thud of army boots approached from behind. The first of the auxiliaries ran by, chasing after the enemy.

'Leave them . . .' Cato rasped, then forced a deeper breath and called out, 'Let them go!'

The auxiliaries stopped and turned away reluctantly as the

rest of their comrades formed a protective line in front of Cato and Apollonius. The latter finished off the two spearmen on the ground with quick thrusts to their throats, then he and Cato wiped their blades clean and sheathed their weapons.

'Now we know,' said Apollonius.

Cato nodded. 'We've got them . . .'

As soon as he returned to the site of the camp, Cato gave orders for a ditch and rampart to be constructed to block the entrance to the gorge, sufficiently far back from the crags to ensure that his men were beyond the range of any missiles loosed at them from above. Once the camp was completed, two centuries marched out into the twilight to begin work on the fortification, while Cato conferred with his senior officers in the command tent.

Plancinus and Massimilianus sat on camp stools on the opposite side of the trestle table. The side of the tent had been rolled up to provide what little illumination remained as Cato sketched out what he could recall of the enemy's defences. Apollonius stood to one side, leaning on a tent post, looking on.

'There are two choke points,' Cato indicated his diagram, 'here at the entrance to the gorge, and here where they have built a wall. Only two of our men at a time can get through the first, and we'll be vulnerable to rocks, arrows, javelins, slingshot and whatever else they choose to throw down from the cliffs on either side. After that, there's the question of assaulting the wall and gate.' He paused to recall the structure. 'I'd say the wall is at least fifteen feet from ground to palisade. It's made of undressed rocks and seems substantial. The wooden gatehouse is the only weak point, but we'll not have the chance to test that with our catapult since it will be impossible to get it close enough to try. So the only means of attack is a frontal assault with scaling ladders. Given the narrow front we'll be fighting on, I doubt those who survive the gauntlet of missiles in the gorge will be able to take the wall. It looks like we're going to have to starve the enemy out. Once the forward siege line is constructed and we sow the approaches with caltrops, we'll have them bottled up. Then we wait until they surrender or attempt to fight their way out.'

Plancinus scratched his jaw as he thought it over. 'Is there any other entrance to the valley?'

'Not according to our prisoner. But he could be lying, so I'll be sending Apollonius and the scouts out at first light.' Cato turned to the agent. 'I want you to make a circuit of these hills. Look for any sign of another way into the valley and report back. Be thorough; we can't afford to miss anything.'

'I'll make sure of it, sir. If there's another entrance, I'll find it.'

'You'd better. Rome will not be pleased if we let the brigands slip through our fingers, as they have so many times before. Their resistance ends here, gentlemen. Whatever it takes.' He paused and cleared his throat. 'There is another matter we need to be aware of. The enemy have taken Claudia Acte. There may be other hostages as well. I want them recovered alive if possible.'

Massimilianus looked at him. 'If the enemy run short of supplies, chances are they'll not be concerned about the hostages. If we try and starve the brigands out, we may cause the hostages to die from hunger, or the enemy may kill them to save having more mouths to feed.'

'I'm aware of that. Let's hope it doesn't come to that. I'll be asking for the brigands' surrender the moment the forward fortifications are complete.'

'On what terms, sir?' asked Plancinus.

'They hand over their loot. The men are sold into slavery and the rest are settled amongst the coastal tribes. None will be permitted to remain in their traditional lands.'

Massimilianus sighed. 'They won't like that, sir.'

'They don't have to like it,' Cato responded curtly. 'They just have to accept it, or die.'

'You're missing my point, sir. I've served on this island long enough to know something about these people. They're as proud as can be. Their ancestors ruled this island long before Rome was even founded. They'd rather die than become slaves and give up their land.'

'That may be true,' Cato conceded. 'But there is no other arrangement I can offer them. Their dominance of the interior must be crushed and their tribes broken up. Nothing else will do. Unless you have a suggestion to make concerning the terms of their surrender?'

Massimilianus paused, then shook his head.

'Very well,' Cato concluded. 'If they don't surrender, they starve. If they try to break out, they must be stopped. That's all. Now if there's anything else anyone has to add—'

The flap leading through to the clerks' tent was swept aside as one of the headquarters clerks entered and saluted.

'What is it?' Cato demanded.

'The surgeon's here to see you, sir. Says it's urgent.'

'Urgent?' Cato frowned. 'Oh, bloody hell, send him through.'

'Yes, sir.' The clerk stepped aside and waved the cohort's surgeon through the flap. As soon as he saw the fearful expression on the man's face, Cato felt his stomach twist with anxiety.

'Is it the prisoner?'

The surgeon shook his head. 'He's fine, sir. I changed his

dressings while the camp was under construction. His hands and fingers will heal after a fashion, though he'll never regain full use of them.' He glanced at Apollonius before he continued pointedly. 'Your interrogator made a thorough job of it, sir.'

Apollonius shrugged. 'If you're going to do a job it's best to do it well, eh?'

'Enough!' Cato cut in. 'What have you come here to report?'

The surgeon hesitated before he answered. 'It's the sickness, sir. I think it's caught up with us.'

'What do you mean? We kept well clear of Augustis when we set off from the fort.'

'One of the men must have caught it from the town before then, sir. That's my guess. He turned up at my tent complaining of a headache and weakness. I had him put on a stretcher. That's when he started vomiting.'

Cato recalled the long days of the sickness he himself had endured, and the lingering weakness it had left in its wake. He could not afford the pestilence to strike down the men of his column. He needed every one of them to maintain the siege or to assault the enemy's defences if that became necessary.

'You'll have to establish a quarantine area inside the fort. Set up a tent in one corner and cordon it off, and place it under guard.'

'Yes, sir.'

'Where is the man you saw earlier now?'

'I ordered him to stay in the hospital tent while I reported to you, sir.'

'Good. With luck the sickness will run its course with this poor fellow without risking it spreading through the camp.'

'That's just it, sir.' The surgeon ran a hand over his head. 'Two more men came to see me before I set off to report to you. They had similar symptoms and I told them to wait with the first man. The truth is that I'm concerned the sickness is already spreading through the ranks.'

'I see . . .' The weight of another burden of command settled heavily on Cato's shoulders. It took a moment for the full implications of the news to occur to his tired mind. If his men started falling sick, the ability of the column to maintain the siege would steadily decrease. He would not be able to call on reinforcements from the Fourth Cohort or the marine detachment for fear of putting additional men at risk. The most important thing at that moment was to take stringent precautions to prevent the spread of the sickness.

'Change of plan. I want the quarantine area to be outside the fort. At least a hundred paces away. Get those who have already reported sick out there at once. Any fresh cases are to report to you there directly. You'll stay with them until the sickness has passed. Make arrangements with the quartermaster for rations and water to be left a safe distance away. You'll need a separate latrine ditch. Massimilianus?'

'Sir?'

'Assign a work party for that, and for a stockade to be erected around the quarantine area. I don't want any of the men tempted to pay a visit to their mates. And I don't want the area left exposed to any brigands who may still be outside the valley. Assign a half-section to guard it.'

'Yes, sir.'

Cato regarded the surgeon with an intent expression. 'It is vital that you do everything you can to contain the sickness. The success of this campaign depends on having enough men to see it through. If half the cohort goes down with the pestilence, all is lost. Do you understand?'

'Yes, sir. I know my duty.'

'Then don't let me down. You'd better see to the arrangements at once. Dismissed.'

As the surgeon left the tent, Cato folded his hands together and chewed his lip.

'That changes the situation somewhat,' Apollonius commented.

'Quite.'

'The choice is between launching an assault at once while you still have enough men and taking heavy losses, or sticking to your original plan and hoping that the sickness does not spread through the cohort and make it incapable of maintaining a siege, let alone mounting any attack.' Apollonius arched an eyebrow. 'I wonder what you will choose to do?'

Cato felt a prickly resentment that the agent was testing him again and trying to get under his skin. He bit back on the urge to snap at the man to be silent. He was saved by Plancinus's intervention.

'I say we go in and attack them at dawn, sir. Before they have a chance to improve their defences.'

'I disagree,' Massimilianus responded. 'You heard what the prefect said about the approach to the wall. We'd lose half our men just getting through the gorge. We've got them trapped. We can bide our time and starve them out.'

Cato shook his head. 'We can't bide our time. We've seen what this sickness can do. Whatever precautions the surgeon takes, I think the odds are against us containing it. We have three men down this evening. I'll wager there will be more at dawn. And those we identify are more than likely to have passed the sickness on to their comrades. We have to assume the worst. That means we must attack as soon as possible. At the same time, we must be certain that there is no way out of the trap they're caught in. That's down to Apollonius.' He turned to the agent. 'If you and your scouts can find another way into the valley, we may be able to break into their stronghold without having to negotiate the gorge. At the very least, we'll be able to post men to prevent them escaping.'

He paused for a moment and then yawned. 'There it is, gentlemen. We have to attack them within the next few days. There's no more to be said tonight. Keep a close eye on the men. Some may want to avoid quarantine quarters even if they are sick. If you have any doubts, send them to the surgeon at once. Clear?'

'Yes, sir,' the two centurions replied, then rose to leave the tent. Apollonius eased himself away from the tent pole, stretched his back and shoulders and sat opposite Cato.

'Tricky choice, but for my money you are right.'

'Thank you for the vote of confidence,' Cato said drily.

'How do you intend to go about it? Apart from quickly?'

Cato considered this for a moment before he replied. 'With fire . . .'

CHAPTER THIRTY-TWO

The fortifications blocking the entrance to the gorge were completed late the following afternoon. By that time, another six of Cato's men had fallen sick and reported to quarantine quarters. As dusk thickened, he walked the line of the rampart with Plancinus and Massimilianus, pausing every so often to commend good work and give instructions for improvements. The rampart, topped with a palisade, was not continuous but included outcrops of rock to save time in completing the fortifications, which stretched for some four hundred yards before they were bounded by the crags at the end of each ridge. Sharpened stakes had been driven into the base of the rampart, angling down at the ditch. The open ground beyond the ditch had been sown with caltrops. If the enemy attempted to charge the defences in a bid to break out of the trap, they risked impaling their feet on the sharp iron spikes hidden amid the tufts of dry grass. A watchtower had been erected to cover each stretch of the fortifications, and a single gated causeway crossed the ditch. Sentries patrolled between the towers, and two sections manned the gate and the fighting platform above it.

'Your men have done a good job,' Cato told Massimilianus. 'Considering how little practice most garrison units have in fieldcraft.'

'Thank you, sir,' the centurion replied with a proud smile. 'Those brigand bastards aren't going to get past my lads.'

'I trust I can hold you to that,' Cato responded. 'If the attack fails, we'll be counting on these fortifications to keep the trap closed long enough for the enemy to run out of provisions.'

At mention of the coming assault on the enemy's defences, all three men turned to the piles of faggots stacked close to the gate. Plancinus had taken a large forage party out to the nearest forest to bring back dry branches and twigs, which had been bound into bundles. If Cato's plan worked, the follow-up assault should carry the wall and what was left of the gate without too much difficulty.

'Any sign of the enemy while you were in the forest?' Cato asked.

'None,' Plancinus replied. 'I thought we might see some scouts, or a war band. But there was no one.'

'It's more than likely they had plenty of warning of our approach,' said Cato. 'Enough time to call their people into the safety of their lair. And not just their warriors. I'd imagine they moved everyone inside, including such herds of animals as they could take with them. That's good for us. It'd make the men jumpy if they thought they might be attacked from the rear while they were keeping watch over the approaches to the gorge. In fact, have the message passed to every man in the column to reassure them that the only brigands we have to deal with are trapped in that valley.'

He led the two officers across to the covered wooden frames that lay next to the stacked faggots. Tent leather had been stretched over the sturdy timbers and the latticework of smaller branches that had been cut and closely interwoven across the frames. They would not stand up to being struck by any boulder larger than a watermelon, but they would protect the men

377

beneath from smaller rocks and other missiles. Cato tested his weight on one of the shelters and judged that it was robust enough to protect the men who would be carrying it over the heads of their faggot-laden comrades.

'Let's hope Apollonius has good news for us when he returns.' He stepped back from the shelters. 'Much as I think our attack should be successful, I hope he can find us a different way into the valley. He should be returning to camp before nightfall.'

Massimilianus looked doubtful. 'I wouldn't pin your hopes on that, sir. If he finds anything that quickly, I dare say the enemy will already know about it. Seems to me they picked this place because there was only one way in and it would be easy to defend the choke point they chose for their defences. I don't see there's much hope of any alternative to the frontal attack you've planned.'

Cato gave a non-committal grunt in response as he looked back towards the camp. A centurion was leading his men out of the gate to relieve the unit on watch. From the slightly elevated ground where he stood, Cato could see over the rampart into the fort, and regarded the distant figures with an experienced eye. All seemed normal enough. The sentries went about their beat, the first of the evening campfires had been lit and tendrils of smoke were rising gracefully into the still air, and the men of the mounted contingent were leading their horses out to feed and water them from the nearby stream. His gaze shifted to the small stockade a short distance further down the slope. Aside from the two men outside the gate, there was no sign of life, and he could only imagine the scenes within. If his own experience of the sickness was anything to go by, the surgeon would have his hands full dealing with the patients. If many more men were quarantined, Cato decided, he would have to release at least one of the medical orderlies to assist the surgeon. That in turn would stretch the capacity of those remaining in the camp to deal with the casualties from the assault. Of course, if those tending the sick fell ill, he would have to review the arrangement.

Plancinus cleared his throat. 'So when do you intend the attack to go in, sir?'

Cato refocused his thoughts. 'The first phase will be to burn their defences. That we will do before dawn tomorrow. Once the flames have done their work, we'll launch the assault. It's possible the enemy may make some repairs, so have your men prepare scaling ladders in case they are needed in the follow-up attack.'

'Yes, sir.' Plancinus nodded, then paused before he continued. 'There's the question of who leads the fire party. If it's all the same to you, sir, I'd like the honour of taking the first crack at the enemy.'

'This is purely a wrecking exercise tonight. I want the gate burned down, along with the watchtowers and palisade. That's all. There's to be no attempt at engaging the brigands, Centurion. Is that clear?'

'Yes, sir.'

'That being the case, you can lead the fire party.'

'Yes, sir. Thank you.'

As he regarded the man's pleased expression, Cato could not help marvelling at the way the best of the army's centurions willingly put themselves in danger. Plancinus was cut from the same cloth as Macro. For them, the danger and excitement of action was like some kind of addiction. It was a wonder there were any such men left in the army, given their taste for peril. For Cato, it was different. He was cursed with a vivid imagination, and every time he was confronted with the prospect of

379

danger, his mind was filled with fearful premonitions of the myriad ways in which he might be killed or receive a crippling injury. Such dreadful thoughts plagued him until the very moment he was called on to risk his life. Then, as raw instinct, quick reflexes and years of hard training took over, all troubling thoughts were swept away in order to overcome the enemy and claim victory . . . or survive and retreat to fight another day. Afterwards, as reason returned, he always felt shaken by the transition from one state of mind to the other, and back again. It used to puzzle him how Macro seemed to take it all in his stride, and he knew that that was what marked the crucial difference between them. Macro was a soldier to the bone, whereas Cato felt as if he was something of an imposter, playing the part of a soldier. In recent years that feeling had dimmed a little, but he was still conscious of the gulf between himself and men like Macro and Plancinus. Perhaps one day he might feel truly at home in his uniform at the head of the men he commanded.

If he lived that long. Which brought his thoughts to a further matter.

'Massimilianus, you are to take Plancinus's place if he falls. And overall command if anything should happen to me.'

'Yes, sir.'

Cato reached up and stroked his brow close to the eye patch. The area around the socket felt bruised and tender to the touch. His eye still throbbed and so far his sight had shown no sign of improvement. It was hard to accept that he might be blind in that eye for the rest of his life, and for an instant the cold terror of losing his other eye caused an icy tingle to creep up his neck. To be blind seemed to him like a fate worse than death.

'You'd better prepare your men then, Centurion.'

Plancinus saluted and strode back towards the fort. Cato

returned to the rampart, accompanied by Massimilianus. There was no sign of movement amongst the rocks and trees in front of the ditch, but he saw a group of figures standing on top of the crags above the gorge, starkly outlined against the sky as they surveyed the Roman lines.

'They'll be ready for us when we come,' said Massimilianus.

'That can't be helped. The darkness will conceal Plancinus and his men for some of the way. But the moment the alarm is raised, they'll hit our lads from every side.'

As the two officers made their way back to the camp, Cato heard the sound of horses approaching, and he turned to see Apollonius and his party cantering along the track the column had marched the day before. Dust swirled behind them as they made towards the fort. When the agent caught sight of Cato, he threw up his arm and ordered the other riders to halt, then swung his leg over the saddle and dropped to the ground before running across to his superior, excitement evident in his expression.

'Any luck?' Cato asked.

'You must be one of the gods' favoured few, sir.' Apollonius grinned. 'There's another way into the valley, no more than a mile from here. Not that you'd ever know. We missed it completely when we rode by. That was before we came across the shepherd.'

'Shepherd?'

Apollonius called out, and one of the horsemen came forward. At first Cato thought there was a bundle of rags lying across the horse in front of the saddle, and then he saw movement and limbs flapping against the beast's flank. The rider dismounted and unceremoniously hauled his burden to the ground. There was a cry of pain and a shrill stream of curses as a wizened old man dressed in rags and a tattered sheepskin stirred and climbed stiffly to his feet. His bald pate was burned a deep brown by the sun so that it had the soft gleam of polished wood. A scraggy beard lined his jaw, and as he berated the rider who had dumped him on the ground, Cato saw that he had only a few teeth. His face, hands and feet were filthy and his sunken eyes were watery. His face was bruised and scabbed and his beard was matted with what looked like dried blood.

'What manner of creature is this?' Cato chuckled. 'A shepherd, you say?'

Apollonius grinned. 'That's what he claimed when we surprised him. He was leading a nanny goat off into the trees, so who can tell the truth of it? I thought he might have something of use to tell us and we stopped for a chat. It turns out that Milopus here knows of a goat path that leads up to the top of the ridge. He showed me where it began. I followed it up for a short distance. It seems practicable.'

Cato felt his pulse race as he turned to the old man. 'Is this true?'

Milopus narrowed his eyes and raised a gnarled finger, stabbing it towards Cato as he spoke in a barely comprehensible accent. 'Thissun said you'd reward me if I tell you!'

'Reward? Of course. Just show us this path.'

'What'll you give me? That first.'

'Name it and it's yours,' Cato replied impatiently.

The old man looked him up and down shrewdly and cocked his head to one side, like a bird. 'Fifty coins . . .'

It occurred to Cato that the man had little grasp of the value of his request. 'Asses, sestertii or denarii? Your choice.'

Milopus scratched his beard before he spoke up. 'Whichever is best.'

'Fifty denarii, then. Silver coins.'

'And a donkey.'

'A donkey, agreed.'

Greed glinted in the old man's eyes. 'Two donkeys!'

'Don't push your luck, old man. The coins and a donkey are yours if you can guide us up the path.'

Milopus winced. 'I show you the path. But I'll not go up there. Bad people. Cruel people. They beat Milopus. Take his herd. Only one goat left. I show you the path. You go. I stay.'

'No. You will come with us. And no tricks, or there'll be no coins. No donkey. And we'll show you how cruel people can really be . . .'

The shepherd's features screwed up so that his face looked like a large walnut, and he gave a reluctant nod. 'I agree. But hungry now. You feed me?'

Cato indicated Massimilianus. 'The centurion here will take you to the fort and give you some food. Go with him.'

Massimilianus bit back his disgust at the filthy specimen of humanity and beckoned to the shepherd. Milopus hesitated, then squinted suspiciously at Cato. 'Coins and donkey. Not forget.'

As he shambled away, Cato and Apollonius stared after him. 'Quite the discovery, isn't he?' said the agent. 'When we caught him, he refused to speak at first but just gave a sort of pained howl. I wonder what the brigands did to him that made him so terrified. He quietened down when I offered him some dried meat and a few sips from the wineskin. After that, it all came tumbling out. A river of words. The gist of it is that he's been living alone in a cave at the foot of the ridge for most of his life, tending a small herd of goats and keeping out of people's way. Until the brigands came across him a few days ago. Poor bastard.'

'Did he tell them about the path?'

'I asked him that. He says not.'

'Do you believe him?'

Apollonius shrugged. 'You saw. He's half mad. But at least the path is there. That much is true. Well worth fifty denarii and a donkey, I'd say. When should we try it? If it leads where he says, we might be able to get enough men into the valley to take the enemy from two sides.'

It would be dark soon and there would be no moon that night. It would be dangerous to attempt the path in darkness. Besides, plans had already been made for Plancinus and his men. The fire would divert the enemy's attention. All eyes would be on the gate and the wall.

'Tomorrow. After the first attack. As soon as there's enough light.'

Plancinus emerged from the darkness behind the rampart, the crest of his helmet black against the starlit heavens.

'The men are ready, sir,' he reported.

'Very good,' Cato replied. 'You may begin the attack. May Fortuna watch over you and your men.'

'Thank you, sir.'

'I'll be with the reserves,' Cato added unnecessarily. They had been over the plan a number of times and his words betrayed some of the anxiety he felt. The reserves would be on hand in case the enemy sallied out in force to attack Plancinus and his men. He cleared his throat lightly and spoke again. 'Remember, the second attack goes ahead the moment the fire has done its work, regardless of whether Apollonius and I have returned by then or not. Understand?'

'Yes, sir,' Plancinus responded in a patient tone.

'Carry on.'

They exchanged a salute and Plancinus took his place at the

head of the column. Behind him a dark line trailed back towards the fort, and Cato could pick out the shapes of the screens and the bundles of faggots carried on yokes. Here and there he could make out the glimmer of the incendiary pots, within which burned the oil lamps that would be used to light the tapers to set fire to the faggots.

Plancinus spoke softly as he gave the command to advance, and the line began to move through the gate and cross the ditch, leaving a gap of ten paces between each party to prevent them bunching up and providing an easy target if they were spotted making their way through the gorge. Pickets had been sent forward at nightfall to ensure that the way ahead was cleared of any enemy lookouts who might raise the alarm. There had been a brief skirmish before the brigands had fallen back through the gorge to the safety of the wall at the far end.

As the last of the incendiary parties moved off, Cato turned to Apollonius. 'Have a horse ready for me as soon as I return.'

'Yes, sir.'

'And make sure that shepherd doesn't slip away.'

'I've got two men guarding him. I've made it clear what I'll do to them if he makes a break for it, or comes to any harm.'

'Then I'll see you shortly.'

'Take care of yourself, Prefect.'

'I always do.'

Apollonius gave a light laugh. There was nothing more to be said, so Cato nodded to him and paced over to the forty auxiliaries from the Sixth Century moving up to the gate. He slipped into position ahead of the optio and followed the rear of Plancinus's force, visible a short distance ahead. It occurred to him that it might have been wise to arrange for the column to be linked by a length of rope to ensure there was no chance of men being separated, but it was too late for that now and all he could do was keep the group of men ahead of him in sight.

Because of the sheltered nature of the terrain, the night felt warm, and in the stillness the faint crunch of the auxiliaries' boots and the creak of leather straps seemed alarmingly loud to Cato's straining ears. The column threaded its way through the rock outcrops and clusters of trees towards the looming mass of the cliffs at the entrance to the gorge. Cato crept forward, waiting for the first shout of alarm from one of the enemy lookouts on the cliffs. There was no possibility of the brigands failing to detect Plancinus and his men before they emerged from the gorge. The only question was how far they would get before they were discovered.

The cliffs on either side began to close in, and it was impossible to determine where precisely the gorge cut between them. Cato saw that the rearmost section of Plancinus's column was tending to the right as they reached the foot of a large boulder and began to work their way around it. The quiet of the night was abruptly shattered by a shout from above, and a moment later a horn blared a single sustained note. As it faded, another horn answered it in the distance, muffled by the cliffs in between. Plancinus's voice called out.

'Fire party! At the double!'

An instant later the group ahead of Cato surged forward, and he feared he might lose sight of them as he shouted over his shoulder, 'Sixth Century! On me!'

He broke into a trot to catch up with the men ahead of him. There were shouts from ahead and above and the pounding of boots and the grunts of men labouring under their burdens as they hurried through the night. Cato rounded the rock and saw the black maw of the entrance to the gorge fifty feet ahead. The sounds of the men working their way through the constricted space echoed off the rocks overhead and amplified the din that had broken out only a moment earlier. Then there was a new sound: the faint rush of tumbling shingle and the crash of a rock bouncing off the cliff before continuing down to strike the floor of the gorge with a deep, echoing thud. More rocks followed, and this time Cato heard wood shattering and a cry of pain that was cut short as an officer bellowed at the casualty to shut his mouth.

The incendiary party ahead of Cato drew up at the sound, and he had to quickly halt the men from the Sixth Century before he ran forward.

'What are you stopping for?' he snapped. 'Get moving! Keep going forward. Move, damn you!'

In the dark the unnerved soldiers could defy him anonymously, and no one obeyed his order. Cato grabbed the arm of the man nearest the entrance to the gorge and gave him a firm shove towards it before moving on to the next. 'Follow me, you bastards!'

Now that the first two were moving again, the rest followed, and Cato moved to the head of the party and led them forward. It was almost pitch black as they entered the gorge, and the sound of more rocks falling, the cries of terror and pain and the clatter of the screens striking and scraping along the cliffs on either side filled his ears.

Thirty paces into the gorge, he ran into the back of an auxiliary, and both men stumbled to keep their balance. As Cato recovered, he groped for the man and pushed him on. 'Don't stop!'

'No!' a frightened voice responded. 'They're killing us. Fall back!'

Cato snarled. 'Go forward, or I swear I will cut you down where you stand. Keep moving. There're only two kinds of men stuck in this gorge. Those who are dead, and those who are going to be. If you want to live, push on!'

His hands made contact again with the man ahead of him, and he firmly steered him towards the far end of the gorge, from where he could make out Plancinus's voice as the centurion bellowed encouragement from the front of the column.

A shower of pebbles and grit rained down on Cato's head and shoulders and he shouted a warning and threw himself to the side of the gorge. A heartbeat later, a rock slammed into the ground close by. He continued moving along the gorge, his left hand staying in contact with the cliff face so that he could keep his bearings. More rocks tumbled down, and the terror of not being able to see them added to the nightmare being enacted in the confines of the gorge.

'Make way!' a voice called out a short distance ahead. 'Injured man coming through!'

'Move to the side,' Cato ordered, and the auxiliaries pressed against the cliff as a handful of men, some assisted by unwounded comrades, edged past. While he waited for the last of them to stumble by, Cato tried to recall how far the gorge extended. But he could not estimate his position.

The wounded made towards the rear and he moved on, nearly tripping over a body, thrusting a hand down to stay on his feet. His fingers dipped into a warm mass of bloodied flesh and he recoiled in disgust. He encountered the remains of one of the screens, smashed by a direct impact, and picked his way through the ruined siege equipment and abandoned faggots before stepping over another body. The dangers of being jammed into the gorge had become apparent to the men ahead of him, and there was no further bunching up as the auxiliaries hurried along, desperate to escape the gorge.

When he spotted a glimmer of red a short distance ahead,

bounded by two towering masses of black, he realised the end of the gorge was in sight.

'Almost there, boys! Just a little further. Keep moving.'

As he closed up on the end of the gorge, he could see the small stretch of open ground in front of the brigands' wall and gate. Plancinus had wasted no time, and fires lit up the area and the rocks above as flames consumed the tightly bound bundles of sticks that had been heaped up against the gate and the foot of the wall. His men were busy setting fresh fires while their comrades sheltered them as best they could with the wooden frames. The defenders lining the wall were clearly visible in the lurid red glow as they hurled small rocks and loosed arrows and slingshot at the attackers. They had downed several auxiliaries already, and their bodies, the dead motionless and the wounded writhing, were scattered along the route Plancinus and his men had taken.

The centurion was standing in the open, directing his men's efforts as they ducked out from the protective screens angled towards the enemy and hurled their faggots onto the growing blaze. The roaring flames grew in intensity and began to force the defenders from the wall so that only those in the two towers and above the gate remained, though even they would not be able to bear the searing heat for much longer. There was still plenty of danger from those on the cliffs above the gorge, who kept hurling rocks and rolling heavy stones onto the attackers.

Cato picked up a shield lying beside the body of an auxiliary whose head had been crushed as he stood at the end of the gorge. Taking a firm grip, he trotted forward to join Plancinus.

'Good work, Centurion!'

'Sir? What are you doing here? You're supposed to be with the reserves.'

'Easy there. I'm not taking charge. This is your show.'

'Fair enough.' Plancinus nodded and gestured towards the gates. 'That'll go up nicely when the fire spreads to those timbers.'

Cato regarded the blaze running most of the length of the wall. The stonework would be undamaged by the fire, but the heat would prevent the enemy from occupying the parapet. By the same token, there was no chance of using the assault ladders now. 'As soon as you've used up the last of the faggots, throw the ladders and screens onto the flames and get your men out of here. You can pick up the casualties as you fall back.'

'Yes, sir.'

Cato was mindful of the need to make sure he joined Apollonius and the shepherd to climb the goat track as soon as there was enough light to see their way up the ridge. He patted Plancinus on the shoulder. 'There's no need for the reserves. I'll lead them back to our lines and see you at the fort.'

As the centurion raised his hand to salute, his head snapped back, his arms went limp and he crashed to the ground on his back. At once Cato crouched, holding the shield up to protect Plancinus and himself. By the light of the flames he saw the gaping wound where the slingshot had smashed through the centurion's brow above the bridge of his nose. Blood coursed from the wound as Plancinus began to tremble violently. Cato grabbed the leather strap at the top of the centurion's harness and dragged his body to the base of the nearest cliff, covering them both with the shield as best he could. As he propped him up, he saw that Plancinus had lost consciousness.

One of the auxiliaries who had added his faggot to the fire and was now heading for the gorge made to move past.

'You!' Cato stood and blocked his path. 'Get the centurion to the rear.'

He helped lift Plancinus onto the auxiliary's shoulders and

steered him towards the opening of the gorge, then turned back and cupped his hands to his mouth. 'Optio Caudus!'

Behind the screen closest to the blazing gate, a figure turned.

'Caudus!' Cato waved his arms. 'Over here!'

The optio bolted from cover and sprinted across the open ground. Cato knew Caudus only by sight, and the anxious-looking junior officer crouching beside him did not appear up to the task of taking the place of his superior.

'Centurion Plancinus has been wounded. He's been taken to the rear. You're in command of the First Century now.'

Cato repeated the orders he had given to Plancinus only a few moments before, and stared intently into the younger man's face. 'Do you understand what you must do?'

'Yes, sir. I think so.'

'Don't think. Just do it,' Cato responded harshly, and gave him a shove towards the gate. 'Go!'

The optio scurried to his position and Cato waited until he saw him issue his orders, sending the first section back through the gorge. Satisfied that Caudus was capable of commanding the withdrawal, he took up the shield again and trotted into the narrow passage with the other men. Rocks continued to crash down from above, killing and wounding more soldiers as they blindly filed back towards their lines. Cato kept pace with them, urging them to keep moving as calmly as he could manage, aware that any panic might cause a stampede in the confined space that would only lead to chaos and more casualties.

At length he emerged from the gorge and joined the loose throng streaming through the rocks towards the safety of the ditch and rampart that blocked the enemy into their stronghold. Once through the gate, he set his shield down and found Massimilianus to inform him that Plancinus had been wounded.

'You are in command here now.'

'Yes, sir.'

Cato regarded him by the light of the fire in the nearby brazier. There was surprise and anxiety in the auxiliary officer's expression, but Cato knew the man well enough to be confident in his abilities. 'You know what to do. If for any reason I have not returned by the time the fire has burned itself out, you must lead the attack into the valley.'

'I understand, sir. I won't let you down.'

Apollonius was waiting for him a short distance behind the gate. The shepherd was already in the saddle atop a pony, and looked nervous and uncomfortable. Apollonius handed Cato the reins of his horse without a word being exchanged, and then swung himself up onto his own mount. The sky along the eastern horizon was already evincing the first pale band of the coming dawn. Over in the direction of the gorge, a red hue gleamed against the black cliffs as the fire raged.

As soon as Cato was in the saddle, the agent grasped the pony's reins and nodded to the west. 'This way!'

They made for the track that ran past the ridge, increasing their pace once they were on firmer ground. While the goat path might not be suitable for a large body of men, Cato prayed the three of them might be able to follow it and determine from the vantage point of the crest of the ridge where Claudia and the other hostages were being held, and if possible, save them.

CHAPTER THIRTY-THREE

'Are you certain about this?' Cato asked as he tilted his head and looked up the face of the cliff. In the thin light of dawn he could see clumps of grass and the odd shrub or small tree clinging precariously amid the rocks. A flicker of movement caught his eye and he made out a goat, hundreds of feet further up, seemingly stuck to the side of the cliff face. 'I can't see any bloody path at all, let alone a practicable one like you claimed.'

'It's there all right,' said Apollonius, pointing towards a finger of rock close to the base of the cliff. 'It starts behind that. Show him, Milopus.'

The shepherd shuffled forward, leading the other two men towards the rock, which Cato had assumed was part of the cliff when they had dismounted shortly before. It was only when he was close that he could see there was a gap behind it. Milopus suddenly ran ahead and then beckoned to them.

'See? See?'

As they moved round the rock, the start of the path was revealed. It was barely wide enough for a goat to pick its way up the side of the cliff, and sufficiently steep to make the climb exhausting.

Cato clicked his tongue. 'No wonder the brigands haven't come across it. Even if they had, I dare say they'd never believe anyone would try to use this route. It's impassable.'

'No.' Milopus shook his head violently. 'I climb it. Many times. The truth.'

'Fine. You go first then.' Cato began to unbuckle his sword belt and harness, then stripped off his armour, retaining only his dagger on the belt around his tunic. He piled his kit out of sight behind the rock. 'I'm ready. Up you go, Milopus.'

The shepherd needed no further encouragement. His earlier reticence had vanished the moment Cato had promised him a second donkey to seal the deal. Now he moved with a nimbleness that belied his age. Or was it that he was younger than he seemed under the unkempt hair and grime-streaked skin? He moved swiftly, his left hand seeking out one handhold after another as he climbed. Cato followed, doing his best to keep up, while Apollonius took the rear. It was easier going than it had looked from the bottom of the cliff, and soon they had ascended over two hundred feet. Cato paused to catch his breath. From his vantage point he could already see for miles over the forested hills that stretched out from the ridge. Then he made the mistake of looking down, and felt his head swim with nausea as his boot shifted and a shower of grit and tiny stones fell down the side of the cliff.

'You all right?' asked Apollonius.

'Fine.' Cato swallowed. 'Let's keep moving.'

'Come!' Milopus waved them on. 'Still far to go. Rest at the top.'

He continued climbing, pausing now and again to make sure that his less sure-footed companions were keeping up. By the time they were halfway up, as far as Cato could judge it, the sun had risen over the mountains to the west and the ridge cast a long shadow over the forest. Sweat was trickling from his brow and under his tunic, while his heart was beating fast from the exertion of his aching limbs. All thought of using the path as a means to deliver a force of men into the enemy's stronghold had been dashed. An armoured man carrying weapons would find it impossible to scale the cliff. The only value to Cato was the chance that they would be able to discover the layout of the brigands' stronghold and the number of men they could call on to defend what remained of the wall when the fire died down. That, and hopefully the location of the prisoners held by the enemy.

By the time they were two thirds of the way up the cliff, Cato began to wonder if he had the strength to reach the top. But a glance back the way they had come made him realise that it would be almost as tiring when the time came to make the descent. He flattened himself against the rock to take a brief rest. Apollonius joined him, chest heaving as he took several deep breaths.

'Where in Hades does our friend get the strength to climb this path?'

Cato shrugged. 'He knows it well and he's lean enough. Must be a hard living in these mountains. It's made him as tough as old boots.'

The shepherd had stopped twenty feet further up and was muttering to himself between tearing off fragments from a strip of dried goat meat that had appeared from within his tunic. He turned towards Cato with a guilty expression and hesitantly extended the snack towards him. 'Hungry?'

'No, thanks,' Cato called back. 'Thirsty.'

Milopus shook his head. 'No water. Maybe later.' He tucked the dried meat away and pointed ahead. 'Up!'

Without waiting for a response, he resumed the climb. Cato gritted his teeth and followed.

★ ★ ★

395

By the time the slope inclined towards the ridge and the going became easier and safer, the morning was well advanced and the warm air betokened another hot day. Cato's throat was parched and his tongue felt like it was sticking to the roof of his mouth. But he could see the ridgeline now, scarcely fifty paces above, and found a reserve of strength to complete the climb at a faster pace. The path gave onto the grassy crest of the ridge, and he saw several goats chewing stunted bushes a quarter of a mile or so away. He pointed them out.

'Yours?'

The shepherd nodded proudly.

'I thought you said the brigands had stolen your flock,' Apollonius said accusingly.

'My goats in the forest, yes. Not my mountain goats.'

'Stay here,' Cato ordered, and gestured to Apollonius to accompany him to the ridgeline.

They moved warily, unsure of what the position would reveal. As the ground flattened out, Cato slowed his pace and looked round before spying a cluster of rocks to his left.

'Over there, but keep out of sight of the far slope.'

On the other side of the rocks, the view of the valley below opened up before them. A quarter of a mile at its widest, it extended for a mile from the start of the gorge to the point where the ridges tended towards each other and merged. A dry stream bed ran along the valley and into a natural pool not far from the gorge. It seemed to lie in perpetual shadow, which was why the contents had not evaporated, Cato surmised. A hundred paces below their position, a spur projected into the valley. The enemy's stronghold extended from the spur to the wall they had constructed inside the end of the gorge. The fire was still burning and smoke billowed into the sky. A chain of tiny figures passed buckets from the pool to the wall, where others were trying to douse the flames that seemed to have all but consumed the gateway. Cato smiled at the irony of the enemy toiling to extinguish the flames that would only hasten the Roman assault. An assault that would have to be led by Massimilianus, he realised. There was no chance of descending the precipitous goat track and returning to the fort before the attack began. It was down to the centurion and his men to do the job, and Cato would be an onlooker.

Apart from the men fighting the fire, there was little movement in the rest of the camp, which comprised stone-walled huts and storerooms covered with wooden shingle roofs. There were over a hundred such structures, Cato estimated, along with a number of animal pens and small terraces where modest crops grew. A hundred paces from the huts was a large pit with what appeared to be a row of logs arranged across the bottom. As he watched, two men emerged from the brigands' settlement carrying some burden between them. When they reached the edge of the pit, they climbed down and laid out what Cato could now discern was a body wrapped in a dark cloth. Then they scrambled up and hurried away.

'Do you see?' He pointed out the pit to Apollonius. 'Must be a mass grave.'

The agent nodded before scrutinising the rest of the enemy position. There were people slumped or sprawled outside many of the huts, unmoving.

'Sweet Jupiter, it must be the sickness. They've got it bad. Worse than us.'

Cato nodded. Now the reason for other unusual aspects of the scene was clear. The lack of smoke from cooking fires. The untended goats picking their way through the terraced crops, and the sense of quiet and stillness about the buildings. 'One of their raiding parties must have brought it back with them. If we'd tried to starve them out, that's what the fort would have looked like before too long.'

'Seems the real victor of the campaign is going to be the pestilence,' Apollonius said. 'It will end up having killed far more on both sides than any combat. If we'd known in time, we could have let it do the job for us and saved Rome the trouble of this campaign.'

'The brigands aren't finished off yet.' Cato gazed towards the figures in the firefighting chain, and the groups of armed men waiting in the shade close to the wall. 'There are at least two hundred of them still capable of fighting. It could go either way.'

He scanned the settlement again and spotted two men standing outside an animal pen close to the largest building, as if guarding something within. When he strained his eyes, he could make out a handful of figures sitting inside the pen, and he felt his heart give a lurch. 'I can see prisoners. There, in the pen by the big hut.'

'I see them . . .'

'Can you make any of them out?'

Apollonius shook his head. 'Too far. If she's still alive, that's where we're likely to find her.' He leaned against a rock as he regarded the prefect speculatively. 'What do you intend to do?'

'Since we can't get back to the fort in time for the attack, we must try and rescue Claudia Acte and the other hostages.'

'I see. How do you propose we do that? All we have between us is a pair of daggers. Not going to give us much of an edge, if you'll pardon the pun, when we go down there and try to set them free.'

'The enemy's attention will be on Massimilianus and his lads. It'll be the best chance we get. If we leave it too late, they may kill the hostages before the fighting is over.' Cato regarded his companion coolly. 'You don't have to come with me if you're not prepared to take the risk. I can manage by myself while you and the shepherd go back down the cliff.'

'What? Stay here with that wizened derelict and miss all the fun? I don't think so, Prefect. In any case, I baulk at the prospect of letting a half-blind romantic blunder about in the heart of the enemy stronghold armed only with a dagger. I'm coming with you.'

Cato was relieved, but was damned if he would betray it to the agent. He shrugged dismissively. 'As you wish. But you'll do as I say.'

'Yes . . . sir.'

He looked over the enemy settlement and the surrounding terrain once more before he made his decision. 'We'll make our way down the far side of that spur and approach from the rear the moment Massimilianus launches the attack.'

'What about the shepherd?'

'What about him?'

'It would be dangerous to take him with us. You've seen what he's like. Half mad, I'd say. He could give us away.'

'Then he stays here until it's all over. I'll send someone up to fetch him.'

'What if he doesn't stay put? What if he gets curious and moves into the open and someone sees him?'

Cato did not like the conclusion to which Apollonius was steering him and addressed the agent firmly. 'He showed us the path. We'll honour our side of the deal.'

'As you wish. But I'll tie him up. That way we can be sure he won't do us any harm.'

'We haven't got a rope,' Cato pointed out.

Apollonius drew his dagger. 'I'll cut strips from that rag of a tunic he's wearing. Won't be long.'

He turned away before Cato could say any more and disappeared amongst the rocks. Left alone, Cato returned his gaze to the gate and saw that the flames had died down slightly and he could more easily make out the scale of the damage caused by the fire. Both of the towers were no more than charred frames as far as the scorched stone foundations. Between them the gate had been largely destroyed and was being steadily consumed despite the efforts of the brigands on the bucket chain. Surely it would not be much longer before Massimilianus gave the order to attack.

A crunch of scree close behind made him start and instinctively grasp the handle of his dagger before he saw that it was Apollonius.

'You were quick.'

'I work fast,' Apollonius replied. As he hunched down, Cato saw that there was a streak of blood across the agent's knuckles. At almost the same instant the other man saw what Cato had spotted. 'He didn't want to be left tied up here. I had to knock him down before I dealt with him.' He shaded his eyes and stared towards the gate. 'Won't be long now. We'd better make for the spur.'

Cato hesitated, not certain he could trust the agent's word that he had left Milopus alive. But what good would come of wasting the time to check? And if Apollonius had harmed the man, what could Cato do about it? Nothing. Not until they had succeeded in saving the hostages, or perishing in the attempt. It was a matter that could be dealt with later, if need be.

Keeping low, the two men moved stealthily towards the spur, using the rocks and bushes to screen them from anyone in the valley. When they had passed behind the crest of the spur, they hurried on down the slope, keeping a lookout for any of the brigands who might have been stationed to keep watch over the rest of the small valley. At the bottom of the spur, they approached the slight rise that would give them a vantage point from where to plan their approach to the hostages. Cato crouched and led the way forward, then eased himself onto his stomach as he crawled towards the shade beneath a clump of bushes. He stopped there and Apollonius crept up to his side.

Before them lay the grave pit. It was a hundred feet away, and yet Cato was sure he caught a waft of sickly decay from the bodies within. The ground was sparsely covered with dry grass and provided little cover. To the right, the dried stream bed curved round the end of the spur and meandered towards the settlement before passing round it in the direction of the pool.

'That's our way in,' Cato decided, indicating the course of the stream bed. 'We'll follow it to where it's closest to the hut by the pen.'

'What then?'

'We take down the guards, free the hostages and bring them here until the fighting is over. If the attack fails, we'll take them up the spur to Milopus and use the goat path to escape.'

'You make it sound so simple.'

'Unless you have a better idea, we'll stick with simple,' Cato responded curtly.

Before Apollonius could reply, there was the sound of a distant trumpet, easily identifiable to Cato's experienced ear as a Roman horn. He ran his tongue over his dry lips and took a deep breath as he felt his muscles tense, ready for action. 'That's the signal for the attack. Here we go . . .'

CHAPTER THIRTY-FOUR

As the last shrill note from the bucina faded, Centurion Massimilianus swept his arm forward and led off the first century of his cohort in columns of two. In his other hand he carried the end of the first assault ladder. Like the rest of his men, he was only armed with a sword, since spears would be too cumbersome to use in the attack and had been left in the fort. The opening to the gorge seemed narrow in daylight, and he could imagine the fear it would have induced in the dark. Most of the men in the century marching behind him had been part of Plancinus's column and would need to be led with a firm hand to get them through the gorge a second time. Glancing up, he saw the enemy's lookouts calling to their comrades to warn them of the soldiers advancing on them.

After he had been left in command of the cohort, Massimilianus had questioned Optio Caudus about the layout of the gorge and the dangers from above. He had decided to advance with the narrowest of columns from the outset to limit the possibility of his men bunching up and causing chaos, as well as being an easy target for the enemy. He had also ordered the men to lash their shields to the assault ladders to give them the most robust shelter possible from the deluge of missiles they faced as they passed through the gorge. Such measures had never been part of his training, let alone put into practice during his time as a soldier. Yet necessity had driven a creative approach to the problem, and he was satisfied that his men were as well protected as they could be for the approach to what was left of the brigands' defences.

The scout who had been left to observe the fire had come running back to report the moment the flames had died down enough to make an assault possible. Massimilianus had been hoping that Prefect Cato and his henchman would return in time to lead the attack. But that hope had been dashed the moment the scout had given his report. It was down to him now. As a long-standing garrison unit, this was the first time the men of the cohort had faced battle as a complete formation. Indeed, it was the first time Massimilianus himself had taken part in combat on this scale, and he was determined that he and his men would perform as well as any other auxiliary unit in the army. Succeed, he told himself, and perhaps the cohort would add a battle honour to its standard.

An arrow shaft pierced the soil ten feet in front of him, and Massimilianus snatched a breath and called out the order. 'Shields up!'

He and the seven men behind him swung the ladders overhead and gripped the risers as the shield-laden shelters advanced side by side. Now the enemy could see that the Romans were in range, they began to loose more arrows that slashed down from the top of the gorge and rattled off shields or hit the ground on either side. The first stone, the size of a fist, thudded down a short distance in front of the gorge, and Massimilianus quickened his pace. Now would come the test of the orders he had given. The ladder party to his left began to fall behind, as intended, so that they would reach the gorge to the rear of, rather than alongside, the centurion and the men leading the attack.

There was a sharp crash on his shield and the blow drove the ladder down a few inches as another rock struck home. Then he was inside the gorge and the cool air closed in around him as the cliffs cut off the bright morning sunshine. There were signs of the earlier attack along the length of the gorge: several bodies, horribly mutilated by crushing injuries; discarded weapons and kit; damaged screens and pulverised faggots. Occasional rocks continued to fall from above, but the vagaries of the cliff surfaces made it difficult for the brigands to see the men passing through the gorge, let alone take deliberate aim at them. Only two more struck the makeshift shelter before Massimilianus and the first group emerged from the far end.

Ahead, he saw more bodies and damaged and abandoned kit on the ground in front of the wall and on the stonework that remained beneath the trails of smoke rising into the clear sky. A few charred timbers amid the dying flames was all that was left of the gate, and through the gap he could see the enemy warriors forming up to defend their stronghold. The attack had been timed well; none of the brigands had been able to cross the searing heat emitted by the embers to contest the mouth of the gorge.

As the second ladder party emerged, Massimilianus directed them to unlash their shields and form up in lines hugging the base of the cliffs. Once the first century was through the gorge and ready to advance, he calmly gave the order.

'Ladder parties! Forward!'

The line surged from cover at a dead run across the open ground, ladders held up in their sword hands as they kept their shields raised overhead. A deluge of rocks, arrows and slingshot rained down from the enemy on the cliffs as they caught sight of the Romans advancing on the smouldering remains of the wall. Massimilianus winced at a splintering impact on the edge of his shield but did not falter as he made for the left of the ruined gateway. He stopped at the foot of the wall and ordered the nearest men to set their ladder up. The risers followed an easy arc to clatter against the scorched stonework, and the first man began to climb the rungs. On either side more ladders were raised.

Massimilianus thrust his way past the second man and scaled the ladder. The auxiliary ahead of him had turned to the right, and the centurion went in the other direction, drawing his sword as he crouched behind his shield. As he had hoped, the enemy had assumed the attackers would make for the gateway, and there were only a few brigands on the remains of the wall. The fire that had consumed the nearest tower and burned the palisade had baked the stones, and now the heat rising from beneath Massimilianus was sweltering as he charged towards a brigand who was wrestling to dislodge the risers of the next ladder along. The man caught sight of him and hurriedly drew an axe from his belt as he turned to face the threat. Swinging it from side to side as Massimilianus closed in, he turned his hips to draw the weapon back as far as possible, and brought it round in an arc with all his strength.

It was a well-timed blow that shattered the trim on the edge of the Roman's shield and cut deeply into the wood, slicing open the muscles of his upper arm. The shield absorbed the main force of the impact, and while the wound was serious, the bone was not broken. Nonetheless, the blood flowed freely as the brigand extracted his axe and immediately drew it back to strike again. Massimilianus felt his arm starting to go numb, and his grip on the shield handle loosened. Summoning his failing strength, he slammed into his opponent and followed up by stabbing his sword into the man's midriff. The blow unbalanced the brigand and he fell from the wall and was instantly cut down by one of the auxiliaries below waiting to climb the ladder.

Massimilianus's shield slipped from his grasp. With blood dripping down his limp arm, he looked round and saw that over a score of his men were already on the wall, outnumbering the defenders, and more were climbing up all the time. Behind the gateway a solid body of enemy infantry stood waiting for the auxiliaries to burst through the remaining charred timbers of the gate. Massimilianus picked out their leader, standing at the rear beside his standard, a long strip of cloth fashioned in the design of a wolf's head, which the bearer swirled from side to side in the still air.

Calling out to the loose line of men standing further back, the leader thrust his arm towards the wall. With a cheer, his more lightly armed reserves swept forward, clambering up the ramps and steps towards where the Romans waited to hold their ground. Massimilianus tucked the hand of his wounded arm into his belt and hefted his sword as he faced the enemy.

'Stand firm! Let the lads get up the ladders to even the odds!'

The men on either side presented their shields and readied their swords as they faced the wave of brigands sweeping towards them.

Three hundred paces away, Cato and Apollonius were watching over the edge of the dry stream bed as the attack unfolded. They could see some of the brigands defending the gate, and a section of the wall where the auxiliaries were battling to keep their position. The rest of the view was blocked by the huts on either side. There was no way to determine whether the attack was succeeding, but it had drawn off almost all the able-bodied men in the stronghold. Only the two sentries guarding the prisoners in the pen were still in sight. There were others, though, a handful of women, children and older men mostly sitting listlessly outside their huts. Those with the strength to do so had wandered closer to the wall to follow the course of the conflict there.

Cato looked over the ground between their place of concealment and the pen. Armed as lightly as they were, a frontal charge would be suicidal, even allowing for the agent's prowess with his blade. A more stealthy approach was needed. Not far from the rear of the pen was a long, low log pile that extended towards the dip where Cato and Apollonius were concealed. If they could reach the logs without being seen, they could crawl behind them to the far end of the pile and surprise the sentries from there. Or . . . Cato saw that the top of the pen was no more than six feet tall, and there was a small section where the sharpened tops of the wooden posts angled away from each other to create a gap.

'There's our way inside.' He indicated. 'We get a decent-sized log up against that and you can hoist me up and over. Then climb over after me.'

Apollonius looked across the ground and nodded. 'It'll work. What then?'

'If we can get inside the pen, we can hold the brigands off until Massimilianus and his men overrun the camp.'

'Assuming they do. And if the attack fails?'

'Then our friends will doubtless discover that they have two more hostages than they thought.'

'That's not very encouraging,' Apollonius muttered.

Cato eased himself over the lip of the depression and kept flat as he crawled slowly towards the end of the wood pile. The clumps of dry grass provided some concealment as the two men eased forward. The sounds of the fighting along the wall carried in the hot, still air, but it was impossible to tell which side had the upper hand. As he reached the end of the pile, Cato rose into a crouch, keeping his head below the level of the uppermost layer of logs. He moved a short distance along to make space for Apollonius, then rose to peer over the top.

On the other side lay a patch of beaten ground where a dog was sitting with its back to them, chewing on a large bone. Twenty feet beyond was a hut. A woman was lying to one side of the entrance, coughing. A young child with a mop of untidy dark hair was squatting beside the woman, using a stick to draw patterns in the dust. There were other huts a short distance further off, but no sign of any other people. Not living people at least. Cato saw a line of bodies lying outside the largest hut in the settlement: three children, a woman and a man. The latter was lying on a bier, with a shield, a helmet and an array of weapons arranged around him.

Satisfied that they would not be observed, Cato worked his way along the woodpile towards the pen, Apollonius following. As they approached the far end, the child he had seen drawing in the dust toddled into view, stopping as soon as it saw the two men. Cato realised it was a girl, perhaps three or four years old. She stared at them, sucking the two middle fingers of her right hand and scratching her scalp with the twig in her left. He froze, unsure of what to do and worried that any quick movement might cause the girl to panic and run off, alerting others to their presence. Apollonius began to edge round him, his fingers closing on the handle of his dagger.

'What a pretty girl you are.' He smiled. 'Do you want me to tell you a story? Just come closer.'

'No,' Cato interrupted firmly. 'Leave her to me.'

He beckoned to her, forcing a smile as he pointed to the stick. 'You like to draw, don't you? So do I. Let me have your stick.' He held out his hand.

The girl did not move and stared at them with the blank expression of a very young child who had not yet learned enough to be afraid. Then she casually held the stick out to him.

'Thank you.' Cato cleared a patch of ground with the palm of his left hand and drew a simple illustration of a dog. He looked up at her. 'Do you see what this is?'

She stepped closer and squatted on her haunches to look at the image, then smiled with delight. Cato gently took her hand and put the twig into it, pointing to the smoothed soil beside the drawing. 'Now see if you can do one just as good. Go on, I'm sure you can,' he coaxed her. 'See how many you can draw. Do some small ones as well. Puppies.'

'Puppies,' she repeated hesitantly, then smiled and set to work.

Cato moved on past her, cocking an eyebrow at his companion as he selected a solid-looking log. 'There you go. Sometimes the stylus is more effective than the dagger.'

Apollonius sniffed. 'I doubt that will ever be an axiom.'

They kept low as they scurried to the rear of the pen and Cato set the log down, thrusting it firmly into the angle between the two stakes. He could hear moaning from within the pen and the rustle of movement on straw or bracken. Climbing onto the log, he reached up and grasped the tops of the stakes, holding a foot up ready for Apollonius to give him a boost. With a sniff of disgruntlement, the agent bent to his task, and with a powerful heave he lifted Cato high enough for him to swing a leg over the fence. As quietly as he could Cato scrambled over and leaned back to help the agent across after him. Both men dropped to the ground inside.

There were six hostages within the small space. Four of them lay still, one on his back, mouth open, staring up sightlessly as flies buzzed about his face. The others who appeared to be lifeless were two more men and an older woman dressed in rags. Dried-out puddles of vomit and diarrhoea streaked and spattered with blood surrounded them. The air was thick with the foulest stench Cato had ever encountered, and he and Apollonius recoiled, instinctively holding their hands to their mouths. On the far side of the pen were two more hostages, a thin young boy wrapped in the arms of the woman sitting behind him. They too were dressed in rags, and their eyes opened at the sound of the intruders. The woman swallowed and croaked softly, 'Cato . . . ?'

If she had not used his name, Cato would never have recognised her. He whispered to the agent, 'By the gods, it's Claudia.'

He indicated to Apollonius to cross to the gate and keep watch while he stepped round the bodies and squatted down in front of Claudia and the boy. Her once fine hair and smooth complexion were streaked with filth and dried blood from the scratches and cuts on her face and scalp. She had lost weight, and there was a terrible pallor to her face and an emptiness in her eyes. It was the same with the emaciated young boy who lolled in her embrace, his head slumped against his shoulder as he panted with shallow breaths. He let out a pained cry and struggled feebly as Claudia stroked his hair.

She looked up at Cato. 'He's dying. Like these people and the others outside. So many dead . . . My fault . . .'

'You're ill,' said Cato. 'Is it the sickness?'

She nodded and tried to speak, but her tongue made a dry clicking noise as she mumbled incoherently. Frustrated, she raised her hand and pointed. Cato turned and saw a waterskin hanging from an iron hook close to the door of the pen. He padded over to fetch it and pulled the stopper, offering the mouthpiece up to Claudia's lips. She managed a few sips and swallowed, a dribble trickling from the corner of her mouth.

'That's better.' She smiled weakly. 'It was me who brought the pestilence here. After I nursed you. All these people dead because of me.' Her eyes moistened. 'Because of me.'

'It's not your fault,' he insisted. 'They took you hostage.'

She closed her eyes and sighed, then frowned and reached a quivering hand up to his face. 'What happened to your eye?'

'I'll tell you later,' Cato said urgently as he heard the sounds of fighting more distinctly now. Closer. 'Listen. We're here to save you. My men are fighting their way into the valley. They'll reach us soon. But the brigands may try to use you to escape, or kill you. We must stop them. Me and Apollonius.' He pressed the waterskin into her hand, cupped her cheek and nodded to the boy. 'Look after him.'

He turned, drew his dagger and took up his position on the opposite side of the entrance to Apollonius. Both of them waited, listening intently to the swelling sounds of shouting and the clatter of weapons. They heard footsteps padding by at a run, women and children crying in alarm, and the unmistakable sound of the studded boots of the auxiliaries further off. As Apollonius opened his mouth to call out, Cato shook his head desperately and hissed, 'No!'

It was too late: a strangled cry blurted from the agent's lips. He snarled at himself for his stupidity and raised his dagger, ready to strike. There was a quick exchange outside, then the sound of a group of men approaching, and an order was shouted to open the pen. Cato flattened himself against the posts and kept still in case any movement betrayed him through the chinks in the fence. A chain rattled, and an instant later the door, no more than four feet high, swung outwards.

'Kill them,' a voice ordered. 'Kill all the hostages.'

411

A brigand armed with a spear ducked his head down and stepped across the threshold. Apollonius drove his dagger between the man's shoulder blades and he dropped to his knees like an ox felled with a spiked hammer. Cato snatched the spear from his hands and flipped it round so the point was now facing towards the open doorway. He glimpsed a couple of figures crouching to see what had happened to their comrade and thrust the spear at them, feeling it strike home, then snatched it back before any of the brigands could grab the shaft.

A moment later, a wide-leaf spearhead darted towards him, and he just had time to step aside and dodge the strike. He stabbed again as he saw a leg to the side of the doorway, but the man jumped back out of reach. There was a hurried exchange outside, too quiet to be heard over the other sounds raging across the settlement, then a shield appeared at the opening. An oval auxiliary pattern, presumably looted from the body of a Roman. Cato stabbed at it, driving it back. The brigand came on again, and this time Cato's spear glanced off the shield. A sword shot out from behind it and hacked at the spear shaft, driving it down and almost tearing it from Cato's grasp. By the time he had recovered it, his opponent had rushed inside the pen, where Apollonius was lying in wait for him.

The agent grasped the rim of the shield near the top with his left hand and ripped it towards him, levering the bottom to strike the brigand across his knees. At the same time he raised his dagger and plunged it diagonally into the notch at the base of the man's throat. Hot gore welled up and the man slumped to his knees, dropping his shield and sword and clamping his hands over the wound in a futile attempt to stem the flow. Apollonius kicked him in the chest to send him sprawling back into the opening, then snatched up his shield and sword. Immediately another brigand wielding an axe charged inside and hacked at the shield with savage blows that splintered the trim and split the surface halfway to the boss and the handle behind it.

'Cato!'

Cato turned and saw Claudia pointing to the rear of the pen. A man was climbing over, using the log that the Romans had put in place. He dropped down and drew his sword as Cato swung his spear round to confront him. There was no chance to support Apollonius as he tried to hold his ground against the furious onslaught of the axeman. All Cato's attention was on the new threat. Already a second man was pulling himself up over the fence posts. Cato let out a throaty roar and jabbed at the swordsman's chest. His opponent raised his weapon to parry the strike and easily deflected it before hacking at Cato's leading hand. He had no choice but to let go of the spear. The point dropped to the ground and the sword glanced off it before Cato pulled it back swiftly with his other hand and struck again.

This time the brigand's parry was rushed and the point of the spear deflected down and caught him in the thigh, tearing through muscle and grating on the bone. He let out a gasp and then cried out as Cato worked the spear around to open the wound before tearing the point free and turning to confront the second man. But before he could bring his weapon to bear, the brigand had leaped from his position on top of the posts. The impact smashed Cato off his feet and he slammed back across one of the dead bodies, the crushing weight of his foe driving the air from his lungs and cracking a rib.

The agony was instant, and he strained to breathe as the brigand swung a fist at the side of his head, landing a glancing blow, then reached for Cato's throat, his thumbs feeling for the Roman officer's windpipe. Cato grabbed the brigand's wrist with his right hand and tried to loosen his grip. His left groped down the man's side, over his sheepskin jerkin, closing on the handle of the sword. With a desperate effort he drew the blade and made a clumsy cut at the back of the man's head. The blade made contact, but barely hard enough to draw blood. He struck again, with more power this time, and felt the edge connect with his enemy's skull. Above him the brigand's face twisted with agony, and his grip loosened enough for Cato to tear the hand away from his throat. He twisted and bucked under his attacker and then struck again. This time it was hard enough to knock the man out, and he slumped aside, dazed. Cato heaved him off and scrambled towards his dagger lying nearby.

He snatched it up and leaped at the man, aiming a series of savage blows at his stomach, then, as the brigand lowered his hands to protect his torso, switching to his face, stabbing into his jaw, cheeks, eyes and mouth in a frenzied attack. His opponent had no chance of warding off the blows, and his hands flailed as blood splattered around them.

'Cato!' Apollonius shouted. 'They're after the woman.'

Looking up, Cato saw that the man with the wounded thigh was dragging himself towards Claudia. The boy she was cradling was coughing violently, gasping for air to stave off his inevitable death. The brigand shortened his agony with a sword thrust under his ribcage into his heart, then turned his attention to Claudia, sitting weak and helpless against the side of the pen. There was no time to think. Cato launched himself onto the man's back and flattened him against the ground.

Wounded or not, the brigand was strong and fit, and he shrugged Cato off, then rose, feet braced, and drew his sword back to strike Claudia. Cato, despairing that he could not intervene to save her, threw out his hand, fingers splayed in a beseeching gesture. The surprised brigand hesitated for a beat, and in that moment, Apollonius hurled his sword across the pen. It flew end over end in a blur before the point caught the man in the midriff, piercing his vital organs. The impact knocked him back, and he hit the posts and slid down, the sword protruding from his chest as he bled out. Outside there were shouts and a brief clash of weapons, then they heard Massimilianus's voice.

'Keep after 'em, lads. Let none escape. If any refuse to surrender, kill 'em!'

'In here!' Apollonius shouted. 'Prefect Cato's in here, with the hostages.'

A moment later, Massimilianus cautiously entered the pen. A medical orderly hurried in after him and retrieved the end of the dressing he had started to wind around the centurion's wounded arm. Massimilianus smiled in relieved delight when he saw Cato, Apollonius and Claudia. His smile faded briefly as he looked at the bodies of the other hostages. Then he turned back to Cato and saluted.

'Beg to report, sir, the Sixth Gallic Cohort has taken the enemy fortifications and their settlement. My men are mopping up the last of the enemy warriors and taking the rest of their people captive.'

'Good job, Centurion,' Cato managed, still short of breath. 'Have the orderly tend to Claudia Acte when he's tied that dressing.'

'What about you, sir.'

'I'll be fine.'

'You don't look it. You look like shit, sir.' Massimilianus frowned and wrinkled his nose. 'And by all that's holy, you stink of shit too.'

There was a beat, and Apollonius laughed, then Cato joined in too, as nervous relief flooded through him.

CHAPTER THIRTY-FIVE

Rome, a month later

As Claudia's eyes opened and she glanced around the sleeping chamber, Cato leaned over and kissed her. She did not resist, but neither did she respond, so he drew back and propped himself up on his elbow, looking down on her face framed by the soft gleam of her hair spread over the bolster.

'How do you feel this morning?' he asked.

She hesitated before answering. 'Better . . . A lot better. I think I'm getting my strength back.'

'It'll take some time before you fully recover, as I know all too well. Rest as much as you can meanwhile.'

She smiled. 'I will.'

They did not talk for a moment and she became conscious of the muted sounds of the city drifting in through the shuttered window.

'I never thought I'd return to Rome.' She frowned. 'I'm not sure how safe it is for me to be here.'

'The only people who know you are here have been sworn to secrecy,' Cato reminded her. 'As far as anyone else is concerned, you fell sick and died along with the other hostages in the brigands' camp. That's what I'll be saying when I make my report at the palace later on.'

Claudia regarded him anxiously. 'What if they don't believe you?'

'Why wouldn't they? By the time the pestilence had run its course in that part of the island, most of the brigands were dead, along with nearly a third of the cohort. There's no reason to doubt you would not have been amongst them.'

'I might as well have been. The brigands destroyed my property, and killed, freed or carried off most of my slaves. They left me with nothing.' She reached her hand up and stroked his cheek. 'If it hadn't been for you, I *would* be dead. Thank you.'

Cato chuckled and shifted his mouth to kiss her palm softly. 'We've moved on rather more than a polite thank you, wouldn't you say?'

She put her hand on his shoulder and drew him down so she could kiss him on the lips, and Cato closed his eyes in bliss. When the kiss ended, he resumed his position at her side.

'You're taking a big risk, Cato. You can't keep me hidden in your house for ever. Someone will recognise me. Someone will talk, and Nero and his advisers will know I have broken the terms of my exile. The consequences will be . . . severe.'

'We'll find a solution. Something that keeps us both safe. I promise. You shouldn't be worrying about that. Concentrate on getting your strength back for now.'

'What about the people in your household?'

'Only my steward and Apollonius know you are here. I've told him that the sleeping quarters are out of bounds to everyone for the present. The only people in this wing are the two of us and Apollonius.'

'What about your son?'

Cato laughed. 'What sane parent sleeps within earshot of an over-exuberant child if he can avoid it? Lucius has a room on

417

the ground floor, next to his nanny. But I'll introduce you at some point. I think you'll like him.'

'If he's your son, then I am sure I will.'

Cato clicked his tongue. 'Best to reserve judgement, in my experience. And then there's the dog, of course.'

'Dog? You haven't mentioned a dog before.'

'Didn't want to put you off. Cassius is an ugly beast, but he has a loyal heart. I picked him up on campaign in Armenia.'

'Seems you make a habit of rescuing creatures in need.'

'I suppose I do.' Cato shrugged. 'Hadn't really thought about it. I hope you settle in as well as the dog has . . .'

'Oh, you!' She dug her elbow into his ribs and they kissed again.

Another moment of silent reflection passed between them before she asked him what he was thinking.

'About the campaign,' Cato responded. 'About the men I came to know, the men I already knew and came to know better. About the men who died . . .'

They had entered the city the previous evening, Cato and Apollonius seated on the driver's bench of the rented cart, with Claudia lying on two bedrolls under the shelter of the leather canopy. The surviving volunteers from the Praetorian cohort had marched behind, leading the mules that carried their kit and the shrouded body of Plancinus. The group had parted ways as they reached the Forum. After Cato had ordered one of his men to inform the palace of their return, and that he would make his report the next morning, the Praetorians made for the camp on the city wall, while Cato and the others headed for his home. It had been a sad parting, all the more so following Plancinus's death soon after the ship had put to sea, leaving Sardinia behind. The centurion had survived his terrible wound

418

for several days, alternating between unconsciousness and pro-gressively worse bouts of deranged screaming. He had refused food and water and grown weaker all the while before he finally lapsed into a deep sleep, his breathing shallow and laboured, until at length it gave out. He had been a fine officer, and a popular one, and there would be many in the ranks of the Praetorian Guard who would grieve at the news of his death.

By the time the wagon entered the stable yard at the rear of Cato's home, the sun had set and Lucius had already gone to bed. Cato ordered a meal to be prepared and served to himself, Apollonius and Claudia by the steward in person once the other slaves had been sent to their quarters for the night. None of them had seen Claudia enter the house. She would be safe as long as she remained out of sight. But she could not live that way for long. Sooner or later she would be seen. A slave would gossip. Word that Cato was keeping a woman hidden in his home would reach the ears of someone at the palace and questions would be asked. If the answers were not satisfactory, a squad of Praetorians would turn up at his door with orders to search his house, and Cato and Claudia Acte would be taken before the emperor and asked to account for the presence of a person exiled from Rome on pain of death.

Cato sat up and swung his legs over the side of the bed, his back to Claudia. 'I have to wash and get dressed. I need to see Lucius before heading to the palace.'

'Of course you must. Go. I'll be fine here.'

He glanced over his shoulder and looked at her sadly. He felt the burden of pain that came to those who had found a new love, only for the wider world to threaten to crush it at the outset. The feeling was true enough for him to know already that he would fight for it come what may, even if they were doomed. In that event, all that remained was to ensure that Lucius was safe. He had distant relatives on his mother's side who could raise him.

Cato stood up and stretched his shoulders until he felt the muscles crack, then crossed the room to his clothes chest to put on a loincloth and tunic. When he was dressed, he came back to the bed and bent down to kiss Claudia one last time.

'I'll return as soon as I can.'

'May Fortuna watch over you.'

'She has so far,' Cato smiled.

He made his way down to the water trough at the end of the landing. It was fed by a pipe that ran to the nearest feeder block, which was in turn fed by the Claudian aqueduct. The water that flowed into the trough had run down from the hills during the night and was cool and invigorating as Cato doused his face and sponged off the grime that he had missed the night before. As he was completing his ablutions, he was interrupted by the sound of Lucius shouting, and he made his way around the landing to the covered walkway overlooking the garden. His son was throwing a stick for the dog as the steward sat close by offering encouragement. As yet, Lucius's arms were not sufficiently developed to hurl the stick more than a short distance, and the dog only had to lope a few paces before snatching it up and bounding back to him. Rather than dropping it, Cassius stood, forepaws apart, tail wagging, until Lucius tried to grab it. Then he would twist aside, run round the boy and stop to tease him again. Each time Lucius laughed and pretended to scold the animal.

Cato hurried down the steps and out into the garden. At the sound of his footsteps, Cassius raised his nose and sniffed, then dropped the stick and charged towards him, jumping up, his paws resting on Cato's chest as his muzzle stretched and his long pink tongue licked his master's face.

'Daddy!' Lucius cried, and came running as the steward stood and hurried after him. The boy slowed as he took in the eye patch. 'What's happened to your eye, Daddy?'

'I lost it,' Cato said simply, suppressing the memory of the attack on the outpost. He forced a smile. 'So I'll be able to pass as a Cyclops from now on.'

He thrust the dog off, and scooped Lucius up, holding him high as he examined him. 'By the gods, have you grown another inch already since I've been away?'

Lucius nodded vigorously. 'I'm a big boy now.'

'And getting bigger all the time!' Cato set him down and affected a stern look. 'And have you been a good student in my absence?'

'Very good, master,' said the steward. 'His tutor says he is very quick.'

'Glad to hear it. Now let's go and have something to eat while you tell me all about it.'

They went to the informal dining room next to the kitchen and Lucius babbled about all the things he had learned and seen in the capital over the last few months. As the bread, cheese and honey was brought to them by the steward, Apollonius joined them and Lucius launched into a long monologue, repeating everything he had just told his father, while the agent good-naturedly feigned deep interest. When Lucius turned to his food and began to devour a bun smothered with honey, Apollonius glanced at Cato.

'You'll be making for the palace soon, I imagine.'

Cato nodded. 'Once we've eaten.'

'I'll come with you part of the way.'

'There's no need.'

'I have business of my own in the city. I know a senator who has one of the finest libraries in Rome. I've been intending to look him up and see if he'll let me borrow some of his books. I'll accompany you as far as the Forum.'

Cato thought it over. The company would be a distraction from his anxiety over having to present his report at the imperial palace. 'Very well.'

They set off at the second hour as the early-morning sunlight began to warm the city. Cato was dressed in a fresh tunic and his boots had been cleaned and polished. Due to the formal nature of his visit to the palace, he wore a soft leather cuirass over his tunic and his medal harness on top of that. He looped a simple belt about his middle but left his sword and dagger in their sheaths at home. His appearance was military and smart enough to present himself to the emperor and his advisers.

As they strode down the hill into the heart of the city, Apollonius spoke first.

'How do you think it will go?'

'We completed the tasks we were given. Claudia Acte was escorted into exile and the brigands were defeated. I'll try and keep it short and sweet.'

'I'm sure you will. What do you intend to do about Claudia?'

'I don't know.'

'You can't hope to keep her presence a secret for ever.'

'I know that,' Cato responded irritably.

'Your Praetorian friends might have given their word about saying nothing, but you know how it goes when they're in their cups. You'll have to do something about her as soon as possible.'

'Since we're asking questions, there's something I've been meaning to ask you.'

'Oh?'

'That shepherd, Milopus.'

'What about him?'

'You said you left him tied up behind the rocks before we made for the pen on the day of the attack. You were going to go back to release him afterwards.'

'That's right.'

'Is that true?' Cato glanced sidelong at his companion. 'Did you do that?'

'I dealt with him, yes.' Apollonius stopped abruptly as they reached the next crossroads. 'I'm heading that way. I hope all goes well at the palace.'

Cato fixed him steadily with his good eye. 'Did you free him?'

'I've answered your question, Prefect. The matter is closed.' Apollonius nodded in farewell. 'Until later.'

He turned off the street into an alley and strode away. Cato regarded him warily for a moment before he continued on his way.

Once he had reported to the chief clerk of the imperial secretariat, Cato was directed towards the large hall outside Nero's audience chamber, where a number of people were waiting for the chance to submit their petitions or plead their cases. He moved to the side and leaned against the wall as he scanned the modest crowd. He saw Rhianarius, and met his gaze just as the man looked in his direction. At once Cato glanced down and made a close study of his fingernails.

'Prefect Cato!' a voice called across the room.

'Oh bollocks,' Cato growled to himself.

'Prefect Cato, I thought it was you!' The shipowner bustled through the crowd towards him and Cato looked up with a polite smile of recognition.

423

'With the eye patch I couldn't be sure at first,' Rhianarius continued. 'I take it your work in Sardinia is complete?'

'I'm afraid my report is for the ears of the emperor first.'

'Well, of course. Of course it is. I wouldn't presume to encourage you to breach protocol.' He leaned closer to Cato and lowered his voice. 'But since you've just returned from Sardinia, you can tell me if the rumour from Ostia is true. Are they going to quarantine the island until the pestilence has passed?'

'Like I said, I can't comment.'

'But I need to know. That sort of thing could ruin my shipping business.'

'That would be a great pity, I'm sure,' Cato replied wryly.

The door to the audience chamber opened and a clerk slid through. All those waiting turned in anticipation. The clerk cleared his throat and announced, 'Prefect Cato!'

'Here!' Cato stepped away from the wall, conscious of the deflated expressions of those around him, and the scowls of those who resented having waited for hours only for a latecomer to jump the queue. He made his way towards the door, but the clerk indicated a smaller door to the side of the antechamber.

'This way, sir.'

'My report is for the emperor.'

'Yes, sir. But the emperor is dealing with another matter. Senator Seneca will see you instead. If you'd follow me.'

The clerk led him into a narrow corridor that ran alongside the imperial audience chamber and was lined with small rooms where clerks pored over documents. From the other side of the corridor Cato caught snatches of the business being carried out in the chamber.

'. . . and if they want to erect a statue to me in Rhodes, then you tell them it has to be made of gold.' That was Nero's voice.

'But Imperial Majesty—'

'Gold, I said. And gold it shall be . . .'

The voices faded as the clerk reached a larger room at the end of the corridor and announced, 'Prefect Quintus Licinius Cato, sir.'

Seneca was sitting on a couch beside the room's only window. The shutters had been opened and sunlight poured in, illuminating painted walls that depicted the adventures of Aeneas.

'Good to see you again, Prefect.' Seneca gave a smile that was neither warm nor sincere, merely the reflex expression of a long-term politician. 'I take it your return to Rome marks the end of our Sardinian difficulties, pestilence aside. But don't stand there. Come and sit here by the window.'

Seneca shifted to the far end of the couch, and Cato crossed the room to sit as far from the senator as he could.

'I've come to make my report to the emperor, sir.'

'Nero is busy with other matters.' Seneca looked at him shrewdly. 'I imagine you overheard some of that out in the corridor.'

'Enough to know that the people of Rhodes are not going to be happy about the outcome.'

'They're Greeks. They'll find a way to work round Nero's demands. They want a marble statue erected. Nero demands gold. They'll compromise on silver, and even if work on it actually begins, Nero will have long forgotten it was ever discussed. Such are the weighty concerns of emperors. Which is why I am tasked with the slighter business of overseeing the campaigns that make the Empire safe while wiser heads haggle over slight matters such as sculptural materials.' He gave a conspiratorial smirk, then hesitated. 'You seem to have one eye fewer than when we last met.'

Cato gestured to the patch. 'This? Just a wound. Nothing of concern to those dealing with weighty matters, or even slight ones.'

'Your point is made. Now let's have the report.'

Cato briefly related the details of the conditions he had encountered on arriving in Sardinia, and the campaign that had culminated in the destruction of the brigands and their stronghold. Seneca listened intently and nodded once he had concluded.

'Good work. Though it seems that the pestilence did half the job for you.'

'It hit the enemy before it began to work its way through my men. If it had been the other way round . . .'

'Quite. You were lucky it didn't claim you.'

'I had the sickness. It seems that as many recover from it as die, and some seem impervious. However, by the time I left the province, it had killed many of my men, and thousands of civilians, as well as the enemy. In fact, it's likely that without the intervention of the sickness, the brigands would have had the upper hand.'

Seneca nodded thoughtfully. 'It's strange, isn't it? Rome is the greatest power in the world, and yet we are powerless before an invisible enemy that moves and strikes us down with impunity.'

'There's one other thing I must tell you.' Cato braced himself for the lie he must tell, and tell convincingly. 'Claudia Acte is dead. She was taken hostage by the brigands and died from the sickness while held in their camp. We buried her there with the other dead.'

'Was she already dead when you discovered her?'

Cato hesitated before he replied, concerned that Seneca knew more than he had yet revealed. 'No. But it was too late to save her. Before she died, she did say that she had brought the sickness into the enemy's camp.'

'Ah, then she did us a final favour before her death. She was doomed either way. I was on the point of persuading Nero to sign the order for her execution. She had to go. He'd made a fool of himself by falling for her charms. We couldn't allow a woman from such common stock to exert influence at the highest levels of power and survive to tell any tales. She has saved me the bother of arranging an unfortunate end to her life. Still, I dare say Nero may feel a passing grief for her loss, though for those of us who have to advise him, the news is something of a relief.'

A cold dread filled Cato's heart as he considered the senator's words. There would be no mercy shown to Claudia if she was discovered alive, let alone alive in Rome.

'Almost as much of a relief as hearing that that blustering clown Scurra has been claimed by the pestilence.'

'Scurra, dead?'

Seneca smiled. 'Ah, you haven't heard then? I suppose not, since I only received the news from Tibula yesterday. Puts an end to his incompetent governorship of the province. I'll find a better man for the job easily enough. After all, it's not as if I could set the bar much lower . . . But that's work for another day. The question is how to reward you now. Reappointment to the Praetorian Guard should be possible once a suitable vacancy comes up.'

It was a tempting prospect, but for the fact that it would require Cato to remain in Rome. If he was to protect Claudia, the city was not a safe place to be.

'Thank you. I'll give it some consideration.'

Seneca frowned. 'I would have thought the prospect would have delighted you. It seems I am wrong. Have I missed something?'

427

'It's just that I am still recovering from the sickness,' Cato replied.

'You don't look ill.'

'I am still feeling weak. I have recurring bouts of exhaustion. I had hoped to rest a while and fully recover before I return to duty. Of course, I'd be grateful for the honour of serving in the guard again some day.'

'I see . . .' Seneca regarded him thoughtfully, then reached over and patted him on the shoulder. 'You know best what is right for you. Take as much time as you like; you've earned it. Why not hire a villa down at Baiae? The sea air will do you good. It's a beautiful place. I have a villa there myself.'

Cato nodded. 'That's a sound idea. I'll think it over.'

'Do that. And let me know when you are ready to return to duty. The Empire needs men of your calibre guarding our frontiers.' Seneca stood up and waved towards the door in an unmistakable gesture of dismissal. 'Now, I am afraid I must return to the emperor before the lad compromises too much and the Rhodians persuade him to accept a bronze statue.'

Cato bowed his head in farewell and left the room, conscious of the senator's scrutinising gaze as he strode away. He increased his pace as he headed back down the corridor and left the palace, eager to return home as swiftly as possible and make his plans.

CHAPTER THIRTY-SIX

'We have to leave Rome,' Cato announced as he sat at the desk in his study with Claudia and Apollonius. Cassius was lying close to Cato, his head resting on his master's foot as he stared blissfully into the middle distance with half-closed eyes. Cato's steward had brought them a jug of watered wine before leaving them alone to confer.

'Why?' Apollonius asked. 'We've only just arrived here.'

Cato related what he had learned from his meeting with Senator Seneca. He finished and looked anxiously at Claudia. 'Your life is in danger every moment you remain in the capital.'

'And yours,' she said quietly. 'And maybe your son's too.'

Cato's silence was confirmation enough for her.

'I must leave your home, Cato. I'm putting you and everyone else here in danger.'

'That may be so,' said Apollonius. 'But where else can you go? Who can you rely on to keep you safe and not betray you to Seneca or his agents? Can you think of anyone you would trust with your life?'

She thought a moment and shook her head. 'I'll have to leave Rome alone.'

'And go where?' the agent insisted. 'And how will you survive without coin or connections?'

'I'll think of something.'

Cato leaned forward and took her hand. 'You're not going anywhere without me. I'll look after you. It's the least I can do after you saved my life.'

She smiled softly. 'All I did was nurse you, Cato.'

'At great risk to your own life. I was the one who passed the sickness on to you.'

'You don't know that for certain.'

'No? Then if not me, who?'

She squeezed his hand affectionately. 'How long have you known me, Cato?'

'Long enough to know what I feel for you. And long enough to know that I do not want to live without you. I will protect you with my life. Just as I did when we rescued you from the pen.'

She stiffened at the memory. 'If you choose to protect me again, there is a good chance that this time it may cost you your life. I can't live with that on my conscience.'

'Any more than I can live with the idea of abandoning you to whatever dangers you may face alone. I won't do it.'

Claudia withdrew her hand and looked to Apollonius for support. 'Tell him I'm right. You know him well enough to know the right words to persuade him.'

Apollonius laughed and shook his head. 'Just when I think I do know him, the prefect says or does something that surprises me. But I think his mind is made up this time. And when it is, nothing on earth can turn him from the course he is decided upon. That much I know.'

'Oh, thank you,' she responded bitterly. 'You're a great help.'

She turned her gaze to Cato, pleadingly. 'Please, my dearest Cato. You know I love you . . . Yes, that's true. I admit it freely and wholeheartedly. But that's precisely why I must leave you. I could not bear to see you come to harm on my account. As long as I know you are safe, I will be happy.'

'How can you be happy if you love me and choose to forsake me?'

She thought for a moment and sighed. 'It is the way it has to be.'

'No,' Cato said firmly. 'There is another way. Like I said, we must leave Rome. You, me and Lucius. We must go somewhere there is little chance of you being recognised. Somewhere far from here. Somewhere we can be among people we trust with your secret.'

'And where would that be? I have been seen at Nero's side in Rome, Baiae, Capreae and every place he has ranged across Italia. Nowhere is safe for me.'

'Then we go further. As far from Rome as possible. To the very frontiers of the Empire if necessary.' Cato paused and took her hand again. 'There are some people I can trust with your secret. There's someone in particular I trust without reservation. A man who would give his life for me as freely as I would give mine for him.'

'Who is this man?'

'His name is Centurion Macro. I met him when I joined the army and we have fought side by side until this last campaign. He is the bravest man I have ever met. And the most honest. We'll be safe with Macro, I swear it.'

'And where will we find this paragon of soldierly virtues?'

'In Britannia.'

'Britannia? I've heard it's an island peopled by ignorant barbarians intent on spurning every benefit the Empire has to offer them.'

'That's true,' Cato conceded. 'But what better place to hide from those who know you? We can stay with Macro until we are ready to make our home there. I have more than enough money to buy some property. A farming estate in the south of the island will do. That part of the province has been subdued. We'll be safe there. I'll get a tutor for Lucius . . .' His mind raced with possibilities, each one confirming the rightness of his decision.

'Oh, my dear Cato!' Claudia laughed. 'One step at a time.'

She turned to Apollonius. 'Do you know this man Macro?'

'Oh yes. He's delightfully uncomplicated. Unlike our friend Cato.'

'But is he trustworthy? Is he a man of principle?'

Apollonius made a face. 'How would you define principle exactly?'

Cato scowled and made to speak, but the agent got in before him. 'Macro is as Cato has described him. You could not ask for a better man to have at your side in a dangerous spot. That much I know.'

Cato's umbrage subsided at the comment. It was the first time he had heard Apollonius describe Macro with such unqualified praise, and he was moved by his words.

'That being the case,' said Claudia, 'I should very much like to meet this Centurion Macro.'

'Then you'll come to Britannia with Lucius and me?'

'Gladly.'

'In that case, we'll need to make preparations, though nothing that gives away my intention to leave Rome for good, or at least until the danger to you has passed. It would be best that you leave the city as soon as possible. I have a small farm in the north. You can stay there while I settle my affairs in Rome.'

'I wouldn't leave it more than a few days,' Apollonius said

to her. 'If Seneca has not set his spies to watching this house already, I am sure he will before too long. Any man of Cato's rank who puts off the chance for a position in the Praetorian Guard is bound to provoke unwanted curiosity.'

'I fear you are right. I should have accepted his offer.'

'If you had, and then left for Britannia, that would only cause more suspicion. You said the right thing, Prefect.'

'I suppose so.'

Apollonius cleared his throat gently. 'There is one thing you haven't mentioned yet.'

'Oh? What's that?'

'Where do I fit in with your plans?'

Cato was surprised by the question. While Apollonius had chosen to serve under him, the agent was his own master. It had not occurred to Cato that he might wish to accompany them to Britannia. He would have expected him to want to remain in Rome and find himself another man on the make to attach himself to.

'What do you mean?' he asked warily.

'What do you think I mean?'

'You are welcome to use this house as your home in my absence, if you wish.'

'That's very kind of you, and I appreciate it,' Apollonius responded wryly. 'I had in mind a more adventurous experience. I've never been to Britannia. I must admit to being intrigued by what you and Centurion Macro had to say about the place. If you would permit me to travel with you as far as Londinium, I would be pleased to renew my acquaintance with Macro and see this new frontier province for myself.'

Cato did not need to consider the request for any longer than a heartbeat. If there were dangers to be faced on the journey to Britannia, then in the absence of Macro, the agent was the next best man to have at his side. With the two of them travelling together, Claudia and Lucius would be safer.

'I would be delighted if you came with us.'

'Good!' Apollonius smiled. 'Then it's settled.'

Cato nodded. 'Indeed. That calls for a toast, I think.'

He reached for the jug and filled their cups. As Apollonius and Claudia raised theirs expectantly, Cato thought for a moment. 'To a safe journey, and to being reunited with old friends. And a long future together for us all!'

They shared a smile and tapped their cups together, then emptied them swiftly before setting them down with a sharp rap on the desk.

Cato felt the dog stir at his feet, and a moment later Cassius's muzzle appeared on his lap, eyes rolled upwards as his tail wagged. He stroked the dog's head and patted him on the neck. 'That's right, boy, we're going to see Macro again.'

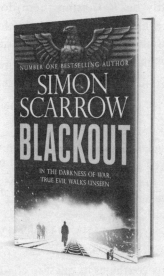

THE EAGLES OF THE EMPIRE SERIES

The Britannia Campaign

UNDER THE EAGLE
AD 42–43, Britannia

New recruit Cato arrives in Germany to serve under the command of Centurion Macro in the notoriously tough Second Legion. Soon the long march west for a brutal campaign in Britannia begins . . .

THE EAGLE'S CONQUEST
AD 43, Britannia

The invasion of Britannia is underway, but the Roman army is desperately outnumbered by the savage Britons. Centurion Macro and young optio Cato begin a treacherous battle against the enemy . . .

WHEN THE EAGLE HUNTS
AD 44, Britannia

Camulodunum has fallen to the Roman army, but the joy of victory is short-lived as the family of General Plautius has been captured by the vicious Druids. Cato and Macro must race against time to find them . . .

THE EAGLE AND THE WOLVES
AD 44, Britannia

As the Roman army continues its quest to conquer the ferocious Britons, it is weakened by its own split forces. The Romans must recruit native tribesmen to fight, and Macro and Cato must train them fast before they are destroyed by the enemy . . .

THE EAGLE'S PREY
AD 44, Britannia

The campaign in Britannia has been far bloodier than predicted, and Emperor Claudius needs a victory. A battle against the barbarian leader Caratacus could finally be the triumphant end that the Empire desperately need . . .

PRAETORIAN
AD 51, Rome

A shadowy republican movement threatens Rome and the Emperor Claudius. Treachery lurks within the Praetorian Guard and Cato and Macro begin to unravel more than one conspiracy against the Emperor . . .

The Return to Britannia

THE BLOOD CROWS
AD 51, Britannia

The Roman army's fight to hold Britannia continues almost a decade after invasion. A campaign to resist the relentless natives begins, and Macro and Cato return to the perilous British shores to aid it.

BROTHERS IN BLOOD
AD 51, Britannia

Prefect Cato and Centurion Macro are pursuing barbarian leader Caratacus through the mountains of Britannia. Defeating Caratacus seems within their grasp, but the plot against the two heroes threatens their lives . . .

BRITANNIA
AD 52, Britannia

The western tribes prepare to make a stand and Centurion Macro remains behind in charge of the fort as Prefect Cato leads an invasion deep into the hills. Cato's mission: to crush the Druid stronghold. But has the enemy been underestimated?

Hispania

INVICTUS
AD 54, Hispania

Cato and Macro have been recalled to Rome, but their time in the city is short. Soon they are travelling with the Praetorian Guard to Spain, where they battle for control in a land considered unconquerable . . .

The Return to Rome

DAY OF THE CAESARS
AD 54, Rome

When Cato catches the eye of rival factions who will stop at nothing to get him on side, he must play a cunning game and enlist the help of Macro. But as the conspiracy grows, it begins to look like a civil war could be on the horizon . . .

The Eastern Campaign

THE BLOOD OF ROME
AD 55, Armenia

The wily Parthian Empire has invaded Armenia, ousting ruthless King Rhadamistus. The Romans must restore him to power, as he is vital to Rome's strategic interests, while also preparing for war with the powerful Parthian Empire. And Cato and Macro must take the lead . . .

TRAITORS OF ROME
AD 56, Syria

Tribune Cato and Centurion Macro are garrisoned at the eastern border, aware that their movements are constantly monitored by spies from mysterious Parthia. But the enemy within could be the deadliest threat to the Legion . . . and the Empire.

THE EMPEROR'S EXILE
AD 57, Sardinia

Cato, isolated and unwelcome in Rome, is forced to escort Emperor Nero's volatile mistress to her exile in Sardinia. But on their arrival, Cato and his officers are faced with a violent insurgency . . . and a deadly plague.